TOP PRODUCER

A Novel of Suspense

LAURA WOLFE

For JP, for giving me the idea.

CITY OF CHICAGO POLICE DEPARTMENT

Case Report
CR No: 580000029-362
Written by: Harley, S.- Detective

On Tuesday, April 9th, at 1440hrs, construction foreman of LDR Renovations, David Harken, discovered unidentified human remains beneath a dirt subfloor while excavating the basement of a townhome located at 1934 N. Lincoln Avenue. Harken contacted police after digging into a blue tarp containing what appeared to be human bones.

Property owners, Phillip and Stephanie Mason, stated they purchased the townhome eight months ago and had no previous knowledge of the remains.

Forensics expert, M. Dully, was present at the scene and observed multiple fractures to the skull bone recovered from the property. Dully stated victim's cause of death is consistent with numerous blows to the head with a blunt instrument, such as a hammer.

Dental records are being processed for purposes of victim identification. Further supervised excavation of the basement is scheduled for tomorrow.

No further information at this time.

CHAPTER ONE

Three years earlier

This wasn't an interview for another dead-end office job. I wanted the position so badly I couldn't sit still. I scooted forward, trying to relax. Conversations and laughter bounced off the stone walls of Bistro Maria, magnifying the awkward silence between me and one of Chicago's top realtors, Jacqueline Hendersen. The competing aromas of sautéed vegetables and fried calamari drifted over from nearby tables as my stomach turned with nerves and hunger. I fumbled with the oversized lunch menu, unsure whether to balance it across the tiny table, tuck it behind my purse, or hide it in my lap.

Jacqueline tilted my resume, eyes flickering, and lips pinched.

The ice rattled in my glass as I raised it to my mouth, the bullet-pointed list of underwhelming work experience scrolling through my mind. My eyes connected with hers just as the menu slid off the table again. I set down the glass and snagged the enormous piece of cardstock with my other hand, pinning it under my appetizer plate.

Jacqueline leaned toward me. Her dirty-blonde hair was folded into a neat twist at the back of her head, her eyes unwavering.

"So, Mara. Why the sudden interest in real estate?"

I inhaled, retrieving my canned answer. "I've always had a

passion for real estate. I'm obsessed with the real estate shows on TV."

Jacqueline nodded but said nothing.

Sucking in my stomach and stretching up taller, I mimicked her perfect posture. A piece of my partially grown out bangs escaped from my bobby pin and fell over my eyes. I pushed my hair back into its clip and refocused. "I got my salespersons license about two months ago and hung it with a discount brokerage firm, and then I represented myself in the purchase of my condo."

Jacqueline's eyes glinted, her lips drawn together as she waited for me to continue.

"On the weekends, I like to wander through the neighborhood open houses for fun. I've gotten pretty familiar with pricing in different areas of the city. And there's something really appealing to me about being in control of how much money I make."

Jacqueline touched her chin and smiled. "That's true. We eat what we kill, so to speak." She pinched the corner of my resume with her manicured fingernails, then set it down again. "I see you were a consultant. Do you still work at Averly Consulting?"

"No. I recently quit." My hand balled into a fist as I glanced toward the windows. I'd been fired last week, although I'd dreamed of quitting. My boss had beaten me to it.

"That's good. I need a full-time assistant. You'll have to hang your license with Greystone Realty if you work for me." Her eyes darted toward my resume again. "I recognize your address."

I leaned in, my insides rippling with hope. "Yeah. I closed on my condo a little over a month ago. I'm not sure if you remember, but you were the listing agent. You showed it to me the first time. I worked with your assistant after that."

"Peter?"

"Yes."

Jacqueline made a face like she'd eaten a bad piece of fish. "He couldn't keep up."

I nodded. Her older assistant had been on the sulky side, but also helpful. He'd walked me through the forms after I'd submitted my offer.

Jacqueline strummed her fingers on the table. "I remember the condo, though. Great neighborhood. You got a good deal." She angled her gaze toward the ceiling as an L train clattered past the window behind her. "So, you bought a condo and then quit your job?"

My fingers pressed into my arm. She'd seen through my white lie. "The timing wasn't ideal, but I really wanted to throw myself head-first into real estate."

"Do you have a car?"

"Yes."

"Are you single?"

My hands dropped to the table, and I looked at the ragged stubs of my fingernails. I stretched them lower to hide them underneath the tablecloth. Her question was a little inappropriate for an interview. An image of Nate's face flashed through my mind. *I need to be with someone who acts like an adult.*

"Yes. I'm single." My skin bristled as I spoke the words.

Jacqueline gave a slight nod. "I'm asking because this is a demanding position. I'm extremely busy seven days a week. I'll need help with showings, listing appointments, and marketing, for starters. In this business, people don't always have time for relationships."

I blinked away the memory of Nate's face. "I'm a hard worker."

"I pay a twenty percent referral fee for everything you work on. On top of that, you'd be free to cultivate your own deals, as long as they don't interfere with the duties I've given you."

I sealed my lips together, stifling my smile. Jacqueline had sold $40 million in real estate last year. Even a half of one percent of that would add up to ten times more than what I'd earned by rotting away in my windowless cubicle at Averly Consulting. I could finally help Mom and Dad with Emma's medical bills.

"You came highly recommended by Tom."

I nodded, my jaw relaxing.

"How do you know him?"

"He works with my dad." The rogue strands of hair fell into my face again, and I silently cursed my decision to grow out my bangs.

Jacqueline's eyes traveled back to the paper. I hoped she wouldn't get hung up on my lack of relevant work experience or the short amount of time I'd survived at each of my previous employers.

"A marketing degree from Northern Illinois?"

I nodded. Her stone-faced expression gave nothing away, but I got the sinking feeling she was judging me. I'd done my research before we met, and her resume was impressive. She was a graduate of Duke University and Northwestern Law School; a former practicing real estate attorney; the Top Producer of Greystone Realty for the last two years; named as one of the top five realtors in the city by *Chicago Real Estate Monthly*; recognized as one of the Forty Under Forty by the Chicago Board of Realtors' *CBR Magazine*; and a recipient of the Chicago Board of Realtors' Good Neighbor Award three years in a row. The awards went on and on. As if that wasn't enough, she resembled a runway model.

The large-toothed waiter who'd brought us our drinks a few minutes earlier returned to our table. "Are you ready to order, ladies?" He hid his hands behind his back and raised his chin.

Jacqueline motioned toward me. "Go ahead."

I lifted the unruly menu, already having decided this morning to order the Pasta Arriabata. For weeks I'd been living off microwave popcorn, Reese's Pieces, and beer. Getting dumped by my boyfriend, buying a condo, and losing my job within a month had destroyed my resolve to stick to a healthy diet. The thought of a real meal had been a welcome distraction. One Yelp reviewer had described the bistro's famous Pasta Arriabata as "*the perfect combination of fresh tomatoes, garlic, and red chili peppers. Just spicy enough to dare you to take another bite.*"

"I'll have the Pasta Arriabata, please." The waiter reached for my menu, and I let out a breath of relief as I handed it to him, happy to get the sharp corners away from my face. He turned toward Jacqueline.

"I'll have the misto salad."

I glanced down, realizing a salad would have been the more appropriate thing to order on a lunch interview. No wonder

Jacqueline was so put-together. Meanwhile, I was wearing an outfit I'd piecemealed together from items I'd found in the back of my roommate, Grace's closet.

"What kind of marketing experience do you..." Jacqueline began to say.

A high-pitched scream tore through the restaurant followed by glass shattering across the floor. Jacqueline's fork fell from her hand, clanging against her plate. I turned toward the commotion. A warm mound scurried across the top of my shoe.

"AH!" I sprung from my chair. My heart slammed against my chest as a rat the size of a small raccoon wove between the table legs. It disappeared beneath a tablecloth, narrowly escaping a waiter who chased after it with a broom. People abandoned their tables. Grown men squealed and hid behind menus. The couple behind me lunged past me as they rushed out the door. A woman at the table next to us stood on her chair, shrieking, "Oh, my God! Oh, my God!" It took every ounce of my energy to not hop up on the table next to her. My stomach heaved, smothering all cravings for the Pasta Arriabata.

My leather tote rested against the legs of my chair, and I yanked it off the floor before any rats could contaminate it. I hugged the bag against my chest, feeling the weight of the blank notepads and unused ballpoints inside, everything I thought I might need for my interview. It was just my luck to lose my dream job to a runaway rat.

As people screamed and hyperventilated around us, Jacqueline placed her hands on the table and inhaled, composing herself. The tense muscles in her face softened, and her chest rose and fell in measured breaths. She leaned back in her chair and stared out the window as if she was calculating a math equation. I lowered myself back into my seat, trying to match her Zen.

"This place has been struggling." Her eyes scanned across the floor. "This is going to hurt their business even more." She pronounced it as a fact, not that she felt sorry about the rats damaging the bistro's business.

"Should we leave?" My stubby fingernails dug into the leather bag, and my knees bounced up and down beneath the table. Rats freaked me out, and I wished I could take off my shoe and wipe it down with Lysol, but I forced myself to stay focused on Jacqueline.

"No." She folded her napkin into a neat triangle, a sheen of sweat reflecting on her forehead. "Mara, here's the first rule of real estate: a problem for someone else is an opportunity for us."

A woman in the next room screamed as another rat scurried from under the kitchen door and raced across the red clay tiles, its long hairless tail dragging behind it like a dead, bony finger. A dish smashed against the floor. I shot upward, obeying my instinct to get away as the rat zigzagged past us.

"Sit down." Jacqueline's glare pierced through me, nailing me down in my chair. My feet hovered a few inches off the floor.

"This place is infested!" a guy in a suit shouted as he sprinted toward the door. I clung to the wooden slats of the chair, watching the restaurant clear out around us.

Next to the swinging door that led into the kitchen, a portly middle-aged couple yelled at each other in Italian. The woman wore a white apron around her thick midsection. She threw her hands in the air and sobbed. The man with the bushy black hair and matching mustache who had greeted us with smiles when we entered the bistro only twenty minutes earlier stopped shouting. He wrapped his arms around the woman and redirected his tirade toward a waiter.

We must have caught the man's eye because he wiped his palms on his pants and headed over to our table. We were the only people still sitting in the restaurant.

"Grazie. Thank you. Thank you for not leaving." His eyes watered, and he snapped his fingers at a busboy who trotted over to refill our water glasses. "There is no charge for food today. I hope you come again."

"I would eat here again, Mr. Sabatino." Jacqueline's voice was calm and even. "But you're going to lose business once word gets out about the rats."

Mr. Sabatino dropped his head, his eyelids sagging down in the corners. "I do not know how this happened. We have very clean kitchen."

"Let me help you." She pulled out a business card from a silver card holder and handed it to him. "I know a perfect spot for your restaurant in the West Loop. You'd make a fortune over there with the business lunch crowd."

The bistro's owner scrunched his eyebrows and studied her card before looking up. "We've been here for thirty years."

The man's gaze paused at a faux-stone wall dotted with antique frames. I tipped forward to get a better look at the pictures, black-and-white images of people cooking and fishing against rustic backgrounds. Relatives, maybe. Others were of celebrities and politicians who'd visited the restaurant over the years. Bistro Maria was the cozy kind of restaurant where Nate used to take me on dates. Minus the rats. Longing swirled next to the anxiety in my stomach.

The man turned his attention toward Jacqueline. "This place is like our home."

"I'm sure that's how you feel." Her brow furrowed. "Your food is the best, but there's a lot of new competition in Old Town. And now, with your rodent problem… Just think about what I said. I'll call you tomorrow after the dust settles."

"Yes. Okay. I think about it." He nodded and headed back toward his sobbing wife. A waiter with a broom jogged toward him.

As the restaurant workers disappeared beyond the kitchen doors, I stared at Jacqueline, unable to speak. Somehow, she'd turned the worst day of these people's lives into a listing appointment. She must have seen the shocked look on my face because she tipped her head toward me and whispered, "That's how you create your own business."

My mouth hung open as if I'd just witnessed a magic trick with no possible explanation.

"And by the way, Mara. You're hired."

CHAPTER TWO

"No, Astro!" I yanked the rubber sole from the dog's fangs, drool sliding down my hand and onto my area rug. Mutilated strips of leather littered the hardwood floor around his dog bed. The overgrown lab thumped his tail on the ground and then crouched down and barked. He thought this was all a game.

My first day of work at Greystone Realty started in thirty minutes, and, thanks to Grace's dog, I had no shoes to wear. I dug through the pile of dirty clothes on the bottom of my closet, desperate for another option. The beige flats were newer, but Grace's black pumps would blend in better with my dark pants. I shoved my feet into her shoes, discovering they were a half-size too big. As I bent to adjust my heel, Astro's tongue found the side of my face. Perfect. Now I'd been slimed, too.

I wiped my cheek as I stepped through my bedroom doorway and into my condo's open floorplan. Grace's belongings littered the couch. My shoulders tightened. Despite the mess—and the dog, I was grateful she had moved in. From the kitchen, the granite counters and stainless steel appliances gleamed in the morning light. The sustainable bamboo floor clicked under my feet, the floor-to-ceiling living room windows drawing me forward. I'd bought the condo on impulse. Dad said my decision had been reckless. But it was my first real estate investment, and I was going to make it work.

Over the last year, I'd become obsessed with real estate. I binge-watched reality shows featuring glamorous realtors and finicky clients. I signed up for a nighttime real estate course. I browsed local listings on Realtor.com, searching mostly from my computer at Averly Consulting to kill time in between phone calls to other mindless workers in other windowless cubicles across the country. Before long, I pushed aside the duties of my consulting job in exchange for the thrill of discovering new properties. Each condo, townhome, or single-family home held a different possibility, a fresh start for someone. My pulse quickened at the photos of Gold Coast penthouses with high-end finishes and rooftop decks. I giggled at the wildly overpriced generic boxes that the subpar developers tried to pass for "luxury city living." I practically drooled over the character-filled refurbished Victorian single-family homes in the city's most expensive neighborhoods. Hours would pass without me realizing it. My days at Averly Consulting had never passed so quickly.

Now, as I waited to leave for my first day as Jacqueline's assistant, the minutes passed slowly. My stomach bubbled with nerves, and my heels pressed into Grace's shoes. I checked my watch. There were still twenty minutes before I needed to leave. I peered down at the cars zooming past on the street below, thinking back to the first time I'd met Jacqueline. It was the day I'd discovered my condo. She'd been waiting outside a different listing on the other side of town, cloaked in a trim wool coat, tall leather boots, and a knit hat. A frigid January wind slid off the lake and cut into our faces. She waved me and my shivering lips in front of her into the shadowy interior of the garden level condo. The living room was narrow and cave-like, the kitchen smaller than represented online, and even dingier than my overpriced apartment. I sucked in a breath.

"Sorry. This one isn't for me."

Jacqueline had glanced over her shoulder, then refocused. "I understand." She leaned in close as if telling me a secret, her eyes shining. "I may have another listing that might be of interest. It's not hitting the MLS until Monday. You'd be the first to see it. 1630 N. Milwaukee Avenue."

My shoulders had straightened at the address. It was a prime location in the middle of Bucktown, one of the city's hippest neighborhoods located just north and west of downtown. I'd only recently passed my real estate salesperson class and had only scheduled the showings to get a feel for the market, but I recognized a good deal when I heard one.

Fifteen minutes later, we'd met in front of the converted loft building where I now lived, the lobby smelling of freshly cut flowers. We rode the elevator up to the fourth floor, my fingers still numb from the cold. I followed Jacqueline down the hallway to the corner unit. The burst of light streaming through the wall-to-wall windows almost knocked me backward as I stepped through the door. The condo was so much bigger and brighter than the seven other properties I'd seen that day.

"The owner is moving out of state for a new job," she'd told me. "He'll take $360,000 today, as long as there is a quick closing. Otherwise, he's going to list it at $389,000 next week. The price includes a garage parking space underneath the building."

I'd touched the granite counters, speechless. I'd imagined living in the condo with Nate, flipping pancakes in the kitchen on lazy Sunday mornings. I'd envisioned my sister, Emma, healthy and cancer-free, visiting from college on weekends, sitting with me in the living room watching bad horror movies. I'd inherited $35,000 from my grandma two years earlier and wondered out loud if it was enough for the down payment. Jacqueline handed me the card of a lender, who, she assured me with a wink, could work with my financial situation, whatever it was. After that, she'd passed me off to her assistant, Peter, a soft-spoken man in his late fifties with graying hair and a downturned mouth. He'd been patient with me as I worked my way through my first deal as both an agent and a buyer.

A siren blared in the distance. I turned away from the window, picking up Grace's discarded socks and tossing them toward her bedroom. Of course, things hadn't worked out the way I'd envisioned. My plan had gone sideways. Nate was supposed to have moved in with me to pay half the mortgage. We'd talked about it. I'd imagined the second bedroom as a home office and an engagement ring on my finger. It never occurred to me he didn't share the same vision.

I'd closed on the property three weeks after getting dumped by my boyfriend. Grace moved into the second bedroom, along with her semi-trained dog. I'd barely made my first mortgage payment when my boss, Leonard Hisson, called me into his office, his fingers resting on his desk in a temple formation. His weasel-like eyes peered at me as he cited my poor production numbers and previous warnings. He paused before clearing his throat for the knockout punch.

"I'm sorry, Mara, but Averly Consulting is letting you go."

Astro kicked at his ear, jingling the metal tags on his collar and pulling me from my memories. My mouth had gone dry, but I swallowed and smiled to myself. Losing my job at Averly Consulting had been for the best. Now, I had a chance at a career in real estate.

I gulped down the last of my coffee and checked myself in the full-length mirror. The deep blue color of my blouse offset my sandy-brown hair. With the top button undone, my neckline gaped. Unsure whether a hint of cleavage was appropriate for a real estate office, I fastened the button. I sighed and unhooked it again, repeating the process several times and wishing Grace was home so she could give me fashion advice. I secured my bangs in my fanciest bobby pin—the one with the silver rhinestones—and smoothed down my hair until it fell neatly past my shoulders. Astro panted next to me. I tossed him a treat before heading out the door with my top button undone and Grace's shoes slipping off my heels.

It was 9:45 a.m. when I parallel parked my Hyundai in an open spot a half-block from Greystone Realty. My new office sat in

Chicago's quaint Old Town neighborhood, an area just north of downtown that teemed with a mix of professionals, young families, old money socialites, and occasional thugs who'd wandered into the idyllic setting. Restaurants, bars, boutiques, and condos bordered the main drag, North Avenue. I exited my car, flattening the wrinkles out of my shirt and squinting against the late-March sun.

Across the street, a dogwalker led five dogs from a tree to a fire hydrant, somehow keeping the leashes from tangling. A woman with spandex pants and a neon pink shirt pushed a double-jogging stroller past me while her twins belted out the alphabet song. I smiled in her direction, my eyes pausing on the spire-tipped high rises poking into the sky in the distance. I stepped over a metal grate, holding my breath at the raw stench of sewage seeping from somewhere beneath the sidewalk. A homeless man bundled in rags eyed me as I hurried past him, my shoes wobbling with every other step. I averted my eyes, aware of the thumping in my chest.

"Hey, miss. You lost something. Lost something," the disheveled guy said, following me as I rounded the corner toward the office.

"Really?" I stopped and patted the bulk of my purse. It was snapped closed.

"The shine right off your shoes!" The man grinned at me through a gnarly beard and half-rotten teeth. He whipped out a shoe-shine rag and knelt in front of me, wiping specks of dirt off Grace's leather pumps.

I stepped back. "That's okay. Don't bother." My fingers scrambled across the bottom of my purse for coins but found none. The only money in my wallet was a twenty-dollar bill. I slid out the bill and handed it to him. If karma was real, now wasn't the time to mess with it.

"Hey, lady! Thanks, lady! Thanks!" He gave a wave. "My name's Tony."

"No problem, Tony," I said. Although, giving away twenty dollars when I had no income could definitely be a problem. Tony turned and limped away, mumbling and laughing.

My heart pounded faster as I reached for the metal bar on the glass door of Greystone Realty. My phone buzzed with an incoming text. Relieved to have an excuse to take a breath and calm myself down before entering the office, I stepped back onto the sidewalk and pulled my phone from my purse. I blinked against the reflection on my screen, surprised by the sender's name, Peter Zinsky. I hadn't heard from Jacqueline's former assistant since a routine follow-up a few days after my closing.

My eyes traveled over the words, sending a chill across my skin. I held the phone closer and reread the message.

Don't take the job!

CHAPTER THREE

I shoved my phone into my purse and peered over my shoulder, wondering if Peter was spying on me. My eyes drifted along the bustling street. There was no sign of him or the blue Prius I remembered him driving. He was probably angry about being replaced, especially by someone he knew. A tinge of guilt pulled at my insides as I remembered how helpful he'd been, but I wouldn't let Jacqueline's disgruntled former employee ruin my first day on the job.

Shaking away the unnerving feeling, I stepped inside Greystone Realty, wishing I hadn't opened the text. I tucked my hair behind my ear and refocused on my new career. A flood of natural light warmed my face as sweat prickled in my armpits. I scanned the double-story room, searching for Jacqueline amid the rows of sparkling, white desks.

The office had the bright and airy feel of an urban greenhouse. Towering windows overlooked vibrant North Avenue, not at all like the cramped cubicles at Averly Consulting where I'd languished under the florescent lights, my eyes drifting toward a blank space on the wall where a window should have been.

"Can I help you?" A middle-aged woman smiled from behind the front desk, her white blouse and turquoise jewelry popping against her dark skin and braided hair. The nameplate next to her said, "Valerie Johns."

"Yes. I'm Mara Butler. I'm looking for Jacqueline Hendersen."

"Just a minute." She picked up a phone and dialed some numbers. "Mara Butler is here to see you." The woman hung up the phone, her eyes twinkling at me. "She said for you to meet her in Maeve's office. Down the far aisle, third door on the left."

"Thanks." Realizing I'd stopped breathing, I pulled in another breath and headed down the hall, dragging Grace's gaping shoes along with my toes.

The door hung open, and Jacqueline stood up when she noticed me.

"Mara, nice to see you again." She pressed her crimson lips into a thin line. "This is the office manager, Maeve Wilkerson."

A round woman rose from her chair on the other side of the desk. She was short; her standing height not much different than when she'd been sitting. She looked me up and down, her coarse silver hair cut so short I could almost see her scalp.

"Nice to meet you," Maeve said, holding out her hand. Her voice carried the rough bellow of a smoker, and her jowls sagged as she smiled. Despite Maeve's limited stature, she didn't look like the type of person who would tolerate any nonsense. Her fingers felt cold against mine, and I wondered if she had any relation to my high school P.E. teacher. "I usually bring in the new agents, but no one argues with Jacqueline." Maeve winked at Jacqueline before sitting down and adjusting some reading glasses on the bridge of her nose. The office manager cleared her gravelly throat. "We need you to sign your independent contractor agreement with Greystone, and then you'll officially be a part of our team. Your Greystone training is scheduled for today at 2 p.m."

"She doesn't need that." Jacqueline crossed her arms and positioned herself toward Maeve. Their eyes locked in an unspoken challenge. "I'll train her myself."

Maeve glanced away and shrugged. I reached for the pen, anxious to make it official.

Maeve rubbed her hands together and offered me a half-smile.

15

"This is the standard agreement for all our salespeople. You start at a fifty percent split with Greystone and move up, depending on your sales."

"I'm at ninety percent," Jacqueline said. "You'll be there soon, too."

After signing the paperwork and thanking my new office manager, I shuffled behind Jacqueline toward her desk, doing my best to ignore the curious glances of nearby realtors.

"Your spot will be here. Next to me." She pointed to an empty desk located in the front corner of the office with a window view. "I ordered business cards for you. They should be here by the end of the week. Always carry them with you."

"Thanks." I looked around at the diverse assortment of people perched behind desks or gathered in small groups, talking and laughing. Before I could sit down, three women sporting brightly-colored power suits marched toward us.

"Hi, Jacqueline. Is this your new assistant?" the one with unnaturally red hair asked, flashing her ultra-white teeth.

"Yes. This is Mara. She's new to the business."

I raised my hand in a wave. "Hi."

"Welcome, Mara. I'm Lana." Lana motioned her diamond ring-encrusted fingers toward the two heavily made-up ladies standing next to her. "This is Rita and Missy. You're in for a wild ride." Lana winked.

"Okay, thanks." I slumped, suddenly feeling frumpy with my fake-rhinestone bobby pin and ill-fitting shoes.

"Good luck, sweetie," Lana said, raising her eyebrows at the other two.

The women giggled, then turned and sauntered away.

Jacqueline smirked. "Now, you've met the Real Housewives of Greystone."

"You're not joking. They seem nice, though."

Jacqueline fluttered her eyelids. "They're not. Don't trust anyone."

Unsure how to respond, I dug my teeth into my lower lip and glanced across the busy room.

The women outnumbered the men by two to one. People flipped through paperwork and checked voice mails. Some of the agents were much older, some were African American, Indian, Asian, and a few appeared to be fresh out of college like me. A cross-section of society. Smart. Jacqueline sat at her desk, ignoring passers-by as she scrolled through her emails.

"Okay, people, let's get started." Maeve's gruff voice boomed through the air from the front of the office. The laughter, chattering, and whispers faded.

"Let's start with announcements. First, we have a new member of our team who I'd like to introduce." She motioned for me to stand up. "Mara Butler."

My stomach lurched into my throat as I raised myself from my chair. Dozens of pairs of eyes stared back at me. I gave a quick wave to my new officemates and returned to my seat as fast as I could.

"Mara comes to us from a consulting background. She'll be working closely with Jacqueline."

An eerie stillness settled over the office, interrupted only by the metallic rattle of the homeless guy's jar of change outside. Two people whispered behind me. A man mumbled the name "Peter Zinsky." Someone else gasped. Peter's text flashed in my mind. *Don't take the job.* I pushed it away.

"So, welcome, Mara!"

The strained faces of Greystone's realtors smiled at me from around the silent room. They weren't exactly welcoming me with open arms. They probably viewed me as competition—one more realtor in a city full of real estate agents. Of course, they'd be jealous that Jacqueline had taken me under her wing. Who wouldn't want to work with the number one agent at Greystone? Or maybe they assumed I wouldn't last, that it wouldn't be worth the effort to get to know me before Jacqueline replaced me with someone else more qualified. I lifted my chin, determined to prove them wrong.

Maeve continued spouting off information about the week's new listings and the punishments for skipping floor time. I didn't know what "floor time" was, but I assumed it had something to do with answering phone calls and, also, that no one in the office wanted to do it. After another twenty minutes rolled by, my heart rate finally slowed.

"I'm texting out the list of properties on caravan today," Maeve said. "We have lots of new listings this week, so make sure you see all of them."

Groans echoed from around the room, but my pulse accelerated at the thought of viewing all the properties. This was the real-life experience I'd been craving. Everyone stood and discussed who would be riding in whose car. Jacqueline rolled her chair over to me and leaned in.

"We're not going on caravan. Leave that to people who have nothing better to do."

"Oh." My shoulders sunk.

"Caravans don't sell real estate." Her grey eyes latched onto mine, and the corners of her mouth turned up. "We have a listing appointment tomorrow at 1:00. At Bistro Maria. We need to prepare."

It took a second for me to process the information. Bistro Maria. The rats.

"Really?" My toes tapped under my new desk. I was preparing for a listing appointment on my first day? This was proof that good things happened when I followed my dreams.

"Jacqueline! I have someone who might be interested in your listing on Magnolia." A woman with fake eyelashes and over-inflated lips waved Jacqueline over to her desk on the far side of the office. Another Real Housewife.

Before I could pretend to be busy, a guy about my age, but a foot taller and half my weight, lurched over to me.

"Hi, I'm Oscar." He stuck out his bony hand, and I grasped it, feeling like I was shaking hands with a scarecrow. "I've been here a couple of years. Greystone is great. Let me know if you ever want to go to any seminars with me. There are some great ones downtown, but you have to know when they are. Last week, I went to the Seven S's of Sales. Have you heard of it? I learned so much."

"Okay, thanks." I had never heard anyone talk so fast. Oscar scurried away before I could ask what the seven S's of sales were.

"See ya," he yelled over his shoulder, a blur of knees and elbows disappearing into the next room.

Another man sidled up next to me, a cloud of flowery cologne and stale cigarette smoke announcing his arrival.

"Hi, Mara. I'm Kevin Lucas. Welcome aboard!" He shook my hand with calloused fingers and a firm grip, his eyes lingering a moment too long on my chest.

"Thank you." I cleared my throat, regretting my buttoning decision, and attempting to draw his gaze back to my face. Pressing my lips together, I tried not to inhale the overwhelming stench. He had the look of a used-car salesman with his thinning, slicked-back hair and rumpled suit. "Have you worked here long?" I asked.

"Only twelve years." He winked. "Always good to see fresh faces, though."

"It seems like a great office."

"Yeah, it is." He glanced at his phone, his lips drawing into a pucker. "So, how did you get in with Jacqueline?"

"She worked with a friend of my dad's a few years ago, and she sold me my condo."

Kevin stared at me like he was waiting for more information. "Well, good." He ran his hand over his shiny hair and lowered his voice. "Just watch your step with her."

My spine straightened. "What do you mean?"

"Let's just say, no one gets to be Greystone's Top Producer without screwing someone else over. Catch my drift?"

I held back my eye roll. "Okay. I'll keep that in mind."

Kevin nudged me with his elbow. "You need a ride for caravan?"

"No. Thanks. I'm preparing for my first listing appointment with Jacqueline."

"Wow! Big first day. Where's the property?"

My gut twisted. I searched the room for Jacqueline but couldn't find her. I wasn't sure if I was supposed to share the information, but it had already slipped out. Anyway, we all worked for Greystone.

"It's Bistro Maria."

"Oh, yeah. I heard about their rat problem. Too bad." He shook his head. "I know the owners. Best pasta arrabiata in the city."

"Yeah, that's what I heard." My stomach rumbled at the thought of eating a real meal.

"Well, good luck. Remember, never leave without a signature." He gave my arm a playful punch before dropping his eyes to my chest one more time and strutting back to his desk.

I turned toward the windows where Jacqueline glared at me from across the room. I swallowed against my parched throat, weaving in between the groups of realtors to make my way toward her.

Jacqueline dropped into her chair as I neared. "I see you met Kevin. Stay away from him. He's the kind of realtor that rifles through his clients' medicine cabinets to steal prescription drugs. The definition of a slime-ball."

"Yeah. I picked up on that."

I opened my desk drawers and cleared out some old papers left behind by Jacqueline's previous assistant. A business card with Peter Zinsky's name balanced in my hand. I wondered why the mild-mannered man had sent me that text. It was inappropriate, at the least. He and Jacqueline must have parted on bad terms. Someone with his experience could easily move to a larger company. My palm angled toward the floor, letting the card drop into the trash can. It was probably best not to mention him to Jacqueline, especially on my first day.

Color-coded stacks of folders lined the far side of Jacqueline's desk, the piles uniform and neat. Near the back sat a framed photo of her and an olive-skinned man with wispy black hair smiling on the beach.

I motioned toward the photo. "Who's that?"

Jacqueline looked up from her phone, her eyes darting toward the frame. "Oh. That's my boyfriend, Jeffery."

Scratching an imaginary itch on my arm, I remembered how Jacqueline had questioned my relationship status during the interview. I assumed she'd been single.

"He's in Africa for two years. The Peace Corps." She went back to scrolling through her phone messages. "He claims it's his life's calling."

A long-distance relationship made sense, given Jacqueline's demanding schedule. "Do you get to see him often?"

Jacqueline pinched her lips together. "No."

I shifted my gaze, deciding to change the subject. "What should I do to get ready for the listing appointment?"

"You're going to help me pull up comparable properties and put together the presentation folder." Her eyes traveled over me, stopping at my feet. "Those shoes aren't going to work. Take the afternoon off and buy a pair or two. Don't come back until you have some that fit you. Image is everything in this business."

My cheeks burned as I pushed my feet further under my desk. She'd noticed my too-big shoes. That was probably why the Real Housewives had been giggling at me. I wasn't even an hour into my first day, and I'd already screwed up. This was all Astro's fault.

"Meet me here at 9 a.m. tomorrow so we can go over some of my other properties before the meeting."

"Okay." I nodded, my head heavy.

"And, Mara, one more thing."

I trained my eyes on hers, letting her know I was eager to learn, that I wouldn't mess up again.

"Don't mention our appointment at Bistro Maria to anyone."

CHAPTER FOUR

I'd made the forty-five-minute drive to my parents' house in the northwest Chicago suburb of Hoffman Estates to see my sister, Emma, on her eighteenth birthday and share the details of my first day on the job. I pulled the kitchen chair toward my usual spot at the dining room table, the wooden legs scraping against the floor. The must of worn carpeting and dusty furniture was cut through with savory whiffs of roasting meat. Emma sat next to me. The red scarf tied around her head was a startling replacement for the auburn curls that used to fall to her shoulders.

As my weight sunk into the familiar seat, my thoughts traveled over my first day at Greystone. Despite a few rough spots, I'd survived, thankful that Jacqueline hadn't given me any real work yet. I wouldn't tell my parents, but I'd spent the afternoon browsing for shoes at DSW, Jacqueline's words still stinging me. *Image is everything in this business.*

My eyes refused to connect with the checkout woman as I handed her my credit card to pay for the new pair of shoes. Even with Grace paying me $1200 a month, my savings account would only cover one more month of my mortgage. My parents couldn't help either. Not that I'd ask. The silence on the phone when I'd told them I'd lost my consulting job had spoken loud enough.

Emma's expenses had stretched them to their limit, and I wouldn't be an added burden. I couldn't wear Grace's enormous shoes to listing appointments and showings, though. I'd look like an amateur. From now on, I'd store my shoes on the upper shelf of my closet, far away from Astro.

I scooted my chair closer to the table and smiled at Emma, who rested her chin in her hands and grinned back. Mom had gone all-out with her decorations again. A candy owl hung on the wall, and a dozen candles lined the middle of the table amid glitter and confetti. The homemade centerpiece flickered in the glow of the flames, the number "18" sculpted out of marshmallows and dotted with jellybeans.

Mom saw me staring and smiled. "I got the idea from Pinterest."

Emma was six years younger than me, but we shared a closeness only two people raised by the same quirky parents in the same overstuffed 1970's suburban split-level home could share. Like most little sisters, she'd annoyed me with her constant awareness of my location, my friends, and my activities. She'd only wanted me to include her, but I hadn't always been there. I'd been too consumed with my happiness to consider hers.

Now, Emma had Non-Hodgkin Lymphoma. Instead of enjoying her senior year of high school, she was undergoing endless diagnostic tests and chemotherapy. She was being poked and prodded by out-of-network doctors whose services were only fractionally covered by Dad's subpar health insurance policy. I lay awake at night plagued by guilt, wondering why Emma, the good one, the sweet, kind, athletic, straight-A student, was the one afflicted with cancer, while I, the screw-up, had skated by without a mark.

The four of us sat at the cluttered table, doing our best to pretend that everything was normal.

"How are you feeling, Em?" I asked. "Can you eat?"

"Kind of." She pressed her lips together and pushed the mashed potatoes around on her plate. "I'm taking medication for nausea, but I don't think it's working."

It had only been a month since I'd seen my sister, but I was caught off guard by the effects of the chemo. In addition to the hair loss, her tanned skin had faded to the sickly shade of sour milk. She'd lost weight before the diagnosis, but now she was even thinner, the sharp edges of her bones visible beneath her clothes. It was her eyes, though, that hurt me the most. The colorful glints of happiness were gone like someone had switched off the lights.

"Eat what you can, honey," Mom said. "Then you can go rest."

Emma nodded and turned a green bean over on her plate with the end of her fork.

"I'll watch a movie with you before I drive back to the city," I said.

"Oh, thanks." Emma looked down at her plate and then back at me. "I'm just…so tired. Sorry." Her gaunt face wavered in the candlelight.

I shifted in my seat, feeling useless. "It's okay. Mom's right. You should rest." Not wanting Emma to detect my fear, I focused my eyes on the marshmallow sculpture.

"How was your first day in the world of real estate?" Dad asked between bites of his pork chop.

"Great. I already have a listing appointment scheduled for tomorrow with Jacqueline. Remember the story I told you about the rats?"

"That was insane." Emma grinned. "What are the odds?" She reached for a glass of water. Blue veins bulged under her translucent skin.

"Yeah. I know. Anyway, Jacqueline says that a problem for someone else is an opportunity for us. She's going to convince the owners of Bistro Maria to sell the restaurant and find a new location. If they agree, they'll use her as their realtor, and I get twenty percent of everything." My voice had taken on a crazed tone. I'd never felt this much excitement while working at my mindless consulting job. Averly Consulting had been like a vise squeezing the soul out of my body. I didn't know which had been more depressing, my crappy paycheck, or working alongside a boatload of other desperate college grads who'd given up on their dreams.

"Well, I hope it works out for the long-term." Dad spit a piece of gristle into his hand. "You need to apply yourself more. Especially with that condo you went out and bought."

I lowered my fork and stared at my plate. Dad had warned me against buying the condo and made sure to bring it up every chance he got. My new career in real estate was different, though. It was finally something I cared about.

"Who knows where I'd be if I'd stayed with one company all these years." Dad's face drooped as if comprehending a lifetime of poorly planned lateral career moves. He wiped his mouth with his napkin. "And make sure you get good insurance coverage."

Mom widened her eyes and glanced at Emma. "I thought we weren't talking about that tonight. We're all together for Emma's birthday. That's what's important."

Emma peered at me. "Thanks for driving over."

"Of course." I fidgeted with my silverware, avoiding her empty eyes.

Dad cleared his throat. "Real estate's a risky business, Mara. You've got to be careful. Did you hear about that developer who shot himself in the head last month? He went from being a multi-millionaire to having nothing in the blink of an eye. Dad shook his head. "Pass the potatoes, please."

I closed my eyes and took a deep breath. "Dad, everyone knows that guy was super shady. He was connected to the mob or something. Besides, I'm not investing in anything."

Dad continued devouring his food. "At least you're learning from Jacqueline Hendersen and not jumping in headfirst like some idiot. Tom can't say enough good things about her. He was in a bad spot after his divorce."

"She's really good at what she does." I thought back to the day Jacqueline had shown me my condo. She'd impressed me with her knowledge, living up to her reputation as one of the city's top realtors. While the other sellers' agents had shown up late, fumbled for keys, stared blankly into space when asked about potential special assessments, Jacqueline had operated with confidence and efficiency. Information flowed from her lips in an effortless stream. She knew the history of the building, the background of the builder, the tax increases from the last three years, the ratings of the schools, the nearest grocery store, and the shortest route to the entrance ramp of I-94. I wanted to be as good as selling real estate as she was.

Dad stopped chewing, zeroing in on me. "Don't go quitting as soon as something doesn't go your way. We can't afford to make your condo payments."

It was clear that Dad and Nate held the same opinion of my work ethic. I straightened myself in my chair, hardening my voice. "Don't worry. I'm not going to do anything stupid."

Emma snorted. "Yeah, right."

Mom giggled, and Dad's frown morphed into a smile. I relaxed the grip on my fork and chuckled along with them. But as I reached for another roll, I couldn't bear to look at the untouched food on Emma's plate.

CHAPTER FIVE

Jacqueline zoomed her gleaming, black Mercedes sedan into an open spot in front of Bistro Maria. It was as if the space had been created just for her, as if she was a member of some secret city parking VIP list. The focused expression carved onto her face never faltered. She wasn't surprised by her luck. She expected it to be there.

"Always show up a few minutes early for appointments. It shows you're prepared." She held up her phone, tapping on the parking app to pay for the metered space.

Unbuckling my seat belt, I fought to contain the nervous energy surging through my veins. Jacqueline said I was only playing the role of a spectator today. My purpose was to watch and learn. Still, my knees bounced, and I caught myself chewing my thumbnail. My stomach growled, and I wasn't sure if it was from nerves or because I'd only had time to eat a granola bar for lunch.

"Let's do this." Jacqueline waved me toward her.

I bounded after her, my new shoes hugging the sides of my feet.

The Sabatinos burst through the swinging kitchen doors and welcomed us with hugs and kisses as if we were long-lost relatives. Jacqueline introduced me as her assistant. The couple smiled, nodded their heads, and insisted we call them Anthony and

Camilla. Camilla ushered us to a private table in the back corner of the restaurant. The luscious aroma of tomatoes, onions, and garlic wafted through the air. Diners occupied a couple of tables near the front windows, but most of the restaurant was empty. The news about the rats had taken its toll.

"Would you like some food?" Camilla asked as we pulled our chairs toward the table.

"No, thank you," Jacqueline said. "We're only here to discuss real estate today." She sat tall in her chair with hands folded in front of her.

"Our business is no good. You know, since the rats." Anthony looked at his hands and shook his head. "The city inspectors are coming tomorrow. They might force us to shut down for two weeks."

Jacqueline reached out and placed her hand on Camilla's arm. "I'm sorry to hear that. You need a new location to put this all behind you. We're here to help."

She slid a Greystone Realty brochure across the table to them. The quality was impressive, printed on thick blue card stock, and personalized for their location. She began to go over the contents with them, page by page.

"As you know, our office is only a couple of blocks away. We specialize in Old Town. I have several buyers on call who are always interested in anything for sale in this general area."

I smiled, pretending like I had buyers on call, too. I needed to stick with Jacqueline until I could build my portfolio. Her cell phone buzzed, and she reached down to silence it before continuing.

"This is a great time to sell. The market has rebounded, and prices have appreciated dramatically over the past two years."

Anthony and Camilla studied the first page.

"On the next page, you'll see a list of properties in this neighborhood that I've sold in the last five years."

Anthony flipped the page, revealing over fifty addresses. My mouth opened at the sheer length of the list. Remembering I was supposed to act like I knew what I was doing, I cleared my throat and sat up straighter in my chair.

"Wow!" The man looked at his wife. "You sell all these?"

"Yes, sir. I know the neighborhood very well."

I nodded along like I'd had something to do with the sales, too.

Jacqueline pointed to the corner of the brochure. "Starting on page five, you'll see the comparable properties that have sold in the area in the past year. As you can see, these buildings are averaging between $500 and $600 per square foot."

The couple flipped the pages, examining the addresses and photos as if reminiscing over old friends.

"Ah, yes. 1526 N. Wells. I remember when that sold. And Cafe Leone used to be in that spot. Much smaller space than ours. Very dark."

Jacqueline inserted herself into the conversation as soon as they reached the last property on the list. "Based on these recent sales, I'd suggest we list the property in the $4,900,000 to $5,000,000 range. We can always list it higher, but overpriced properties generally take much longer to sell."

Anthony's eyes stretched wide, and he faced his wife. Camilla covered her mouth with her hand, her eyes crinkling in the corners.

"This is good news. Yes?" Anthony squeezed Camilla's hands.

"The commission is five percent of the sale price." Jacqueline stated the commission as a fact. She had no conscience.

Anthony's smile sagged. He tilted his head toward the ceiling, appearing to do the calculations in his head.

"Two-and-a-half percent will go to the selling agent, and two-and-a-half percent will go to the listing agent, that's me, Mara, and Greystone," Jacqueline said, the confident tone of her voice leaving no room for haggling.

My stomach flipped at the mention of my name.

Jacqueline leaned closer. "All advertising costs are included in the commission."

Camilla cleared her throat. "You said you have a perfect restaurant for us in West Loop?"

"Yes. There are many options. Either leasing or buying." Jacqueline glanced around the empty restaurant. "At 1:00 p.m. in the West Loop, your restaurant will be packed with the business lunch crowd, and you'll get the local young professionals on the weekends."

She pushed a listing agreement toward them.

"My standard duration for a listing is six months to a year, but I think we can sell it much quicker than that." She handed them a pen. "All I need is your signature at the bottom, and I can list it in the MLS and all the commercial listing services. As I mentioned, I'd like to bring over a couple of buyers before inputting the listing."

Camilla started to pick up the pen, but her husband grabbed her hand.

"Uh, thank you, Jacqueline. Mara." He nodded to each of us. "Thank you so much for your time. I'd like one day to have our attorney look over the contract. This is big move for us. Then we will sign it. You have my word."

Jacqueline adjusted her position in her chair and forced a smile. "Yes, of course. There is no pressure." She began to stand, but then lowered herself back down. "Let's meet back here tomorrow at 10:00 a.m.? In the meantime, please call me with any questions."

"Yes. Okay, 10:00 a.m." They stood up from their chairs and shook our hands.

I buckled myself into the front seat of the Mercedes, amazed how Jacqueline had made everything look so easy.

"Sometimes they won't sign right away, especially if they have an attorney they trust to review contracts," she said without glancing at me. "But never pressure them. People don't like that."

"Yeah. No one likes a desperate salesperson." I tapped my toe, trying not to think of how desperate I would be if I didn't sell some real estate soon. "You specialize in Old Town?" I asked.

"I specialize in whatever neighborhood the property is located." She pulled out onto Wells Street. "And so do you." She smiled, her teeth as straight and white as polished marble.

My back sunk into the soft leather seat. "How many listings do you have right now?"

"Twenty-four, including some multi-unit buildings. Five are under contract." She turned right and circled back toward the office.

"Nice!" I straightened up, ignoring the way the seatbelt cut into me. "If you don't mind me asking, how did you get so many?"

"It's only the first few that are hard." Jacqueline shrugged and focused on the road. "When I started at Greystone, the lawyers at the firm where I used to work sent me tons of business. Then, people saw that I was successful, and they wanted to work with me. Right now, you need to remember three things."

My body leaned forward. "Location, Location, Location?"

She smirked. "No. Network, network, network. It sounds cheesy, but it's true. Tell everyone you meet that you're a realtor. *Everyone*. Give them your cards. Sometimes the most unlikely people will contact you. After that, success breeds more success."

Jacqueline stopped her car outside the front door of Greystone Realty.

"I'll see you in the morning. I'm taking a buyer on a tour of the West Loop."

"Okay." I unbuckled my seatbelt and opened the door.

"I emailed you a list of things to do before tomorrow. If you have any questions about the forms, ask Maeve."

"Okay."

"Meet me here at 9:00 a.m., and we'll go get that listing signed. If you do some work on it, I'll pay you twenty percent like we discussed."

"Great. Thanks!" A burst of triumph radiated through me, adding an extra bounce to my step. I waved goodbye to Jacqueline and strode toward the front door of Greystone, calculating my first commission in my head. Two and a half percent of $5,000,000 was around $125,000. My twenty percent cut of $125,000 was $25,000. After Greystone took its fifty percent from me, I'd still have over twelve-grand in my pocket for merely attending a meeting. And Jacqueline, she'd walk away with ninety percent of the remaining $100,000. Unbelievable! I breathed out and smiled. This commission would cover my living expenses for another three months, plus I could probably help with some of Emma's bills. I'd call my parents later and tell them the good news.

My fingers wrapped around my phone as I fought my instinct to text Nate and tell him he'd been wrong. I'd never be a realtor with a second job. I was already successful, and he should have believed in me. Releasing the phone, I pulled open Greystone's front door. *No.* I reminded myself, swallowing back the hint of acid that rose in my throat. I wouldn't give him the satisfaction of knowing I was thinking about him. He wasn't worth my time.

CHAPTER SIX

Jacqueline's email popped up on my computer screen. The subject line read "To Do." I slumped back in my chair as I scrolled down, scanning the fifty-three bullet-pointed items for me "to do" by tomorrow. There were properties to look up on the MLS, showings to schedule for her buyers, phone calls to return to agents confirming their showing requests of her listings, new listings to input into the MLS, follow-up phone calls to be made to inspectors, lenders, attorneys, and open house and ad forms to submit to Greystone's marketing department. My shoulders tightened as I checked the time. It was already close to 3:00 p.m. I could be here all night by the time I figured out how to do all of this. I leaned forward and dug in.

Three hours later, I'd completed everything on Jacqueline's list, or at least taken the first steps. I submitted most of the showing requests via the MLS. For others, I left messages. Now I waited to hear back on the showing confirmations. If the agents weren't available to show the properties, I'd have to scramble to find replacement properties to insert into Jacqueline's schedule. Agents in the city didn't use lockboxes. The listing agents attended all showings, which led to a lot of scheduling conflicts. After finishing my first round of phone calls, I'd asked Maeve for help submitting the new listings, having no idea what the abbreviations meant, or how to find the information on taxes and monthly assessments. The office manager pulled up a chair to my computer and skimmed over the information.

Maeve sighed and adjusted her glasses. "This is why we normally require our new agents to go through the training course on the first day. Jacqueline likes to do things her own way, though." She pointed to an abbreviation on the screen. "Anyway, 'POO,' stands for 'percent owner-occupied.' That one usually throws people for a loop."

"The POO in this building is a hundred percent," I said, and we both laughed.

I wouldn't forget that abbreviation again, but words continued to pour out of Maeve's mouth as she flipped back and forth through forms. My brain barely registered half of the instructions. After checking her watch for the third time, she stood.

"I need to get to a networking event tonight, but that should get you started."

"Okay, thanks." My feet fidgeted beneath the chair. I leaned my head back, overwhelmed by the information dump.

"It takes a few times. You'll get the hang of it." Maeve looped her bag over her shoulder and hurried toward the darkening windows at the front of the office.

I picked my way through the online MLS forms one abbreviation at a time, leaving some spaces blank and guessing which combinations of letters went in others. When I finally reached the Open House and Ad forms, I had no idea what to do. I searched my surroundings as if instructions would magically appear on the wall, but there was only one other person left in the office at 8 p.m.

Kevin shuffled papers at his desk in the back corner, humming a song to himself. I cursed Jacqueline under my breath. Why hadn't she given me more guidance? With no other options, I raised myself from my chair. The Berber carpeting felt more like wet cement as I approached his desk.

"Hey, Kevin." I held up my laptop, thankful, at least, that I'd selected a high-collared shirt today. "Would you mind helping me fill out these forms? I mean, if you're not too busy."

"Sure thing, darlin'." His mouth twisted to the side. "Didn't Jacqueline go over this stuff with you?"

I shook my head, clicking open the page on my screen.

"Well, you'll get the hang of it. I'm sure you'll do a better job than Peter." Kevin's eyebrows furrowed. "Poor bastard."

I straightened my shoulders. "What do you mean?"

Kevin leaned back in his chair, his eyes darting around the empty office. "That guy was off his rocker. He followed Jacqueline around like a puppy dog, barely muttering a word to anyone else. Then, a few weeks before Jacqueline canned him, something must have happened."

"What?"

Kevin threw his hands in the air. "Who knows? He started wearing the same clothes every day, skipping showings, and refusing to do Jacqueline's busywork. His eyes were red and swollen all the time. I tried to talk to the guy, you know, help him out, but he wouldn't even look at me." Kevin sighed, his chair creaking. "There's a rumor it was drugs. Rita heard he stole money from Greystone's escrow fund. The word on the street was that his marriage was on the rocks, too."

I tugged at my sleeve. "That's weird. Peter was so on top of things when he helped me with my condo."

Kevin chuckled. "Working with Jacqueline for so long probably drove the poor guy insane."

Peter's text scrolled through my mind. Maybe he had become unhinged. My muscles tightened as I cleared my throat. My instinct was to defend Jacqueline and tell Kevin I already had thousands of dollars coming my way *because of* Jacqueline, but it was pointless to argue.

"Where does Peter work now?"

"No clue. The guy didn't keep in touch with anyone." Kevin nudged me with his elbow. "Too bad Jacqueline's such an underhanded bitch because she sure is easy on the eyes." He raised his eyebrows.

The sickening sensation in my gut rose higher in my throat. "She has a boyfriend."

"Yeah. So I heard. The poor guy had to move to Africa to get away from her."

I crossed my arms in front of me. "He's in the Peace Corps."

Kevin waved my words away. "Yeah. Yeah. Whatever. Anyway, you have a good head on your shoulders, so I'm sure you'll come out on top. Just watch your step, like I said."

I nodded, my jaw clenching. Shifting my weight away from Kevin, I pointed toward my screen. "So, what about these forms?"

By the time I stepped into the lobby of my building, my eyelids drooped, and my stomach churned with hunger. A corner of an envelope poked through my mailbox, so I paused to unlock the box. On top of the junk mail lay a white envelope addressed to me from The West Gate Loft Condo Association. My condo board. I'd never attended any of the meetings, so the contents of the envelope were a mystery to me. I ripped it open, my eyes drawn to a giant red number glaring against the white paper: $3,895. I backed up and read more carefully.

As discussed in the last three meetings, the Board has approved a special assessment to replace faulty window caulking throughout the building. The amount owed by Unit 401 is $3,895, due within 120 days.

What? My back leaned into the wall. I remembered Peter mentioning something about discussions to replace the window caulking before my closing. But $3,895 for caulk? How was that even possible? I clenched the paper, envisioning my depleted bank account. Dad had warned me about the unexpected expenses of homeownership, but I'd ignored him. My breathing slowed with the memory of this morning's appointment at Bistro Maria. If we sold that property, this special assessment would be a non-issue. I folded the condo board letter and pressed the button for the elevator, confident everything was under control.

CHAPTER SEVEN

I cradled my steaming coffee mug, avoiding the pile of dirty dishes Grace had left on the counter the night before. Her hoop earrings and silver necklace lay in a heap dangerously close to the sink. Astro stood on two legs, his front paws resting on the counter. He skipped over the jewelry and sniffed the remains of her meal.

"Down!" I pushed Astro away. Grace was always leaving her things lying around. I'd have to talk to her about cleaning up after herself. And about training her dog. I'd had a rough night's sleep, my scattered thoughts bouncing from the surprise special assessment to Emma's frail condition, to competing feelings of longing and hatred for Nate.

On top of that, my second mortgage payment was due in a few days. I hadn't meant to, but I'd lied to my parents. My monthly payments were higher than my rent; eight-hundred dollars per month higher. I should have considered taxes and insurance and the possibility that Nate would leave me. Astro's tongue slid over the back of my hand, leaving a trail of drool. At least I had Grace.

My phone showed a missed call from Jacqueline. I gulped another mouthful of coffee and listened to the message.

"Mara, the listing for 1300 N. Astor was entered incorrectly.

Never leave the information blank if we have it. It makes it look like we're hiding something. Also, the photos you posted don't work. You have five photos of the bathroom and only one of the living room. The photo of the kitchen has a dirty dish in the sink. No one wants to envision themselves scrubbing dirty dishes in their new kitchen. You were supposed to choose the best photos, not use all of them!" She paused to take a breath. *"Next time, ask me if you don't know how to do something. Also, change your voicemail greeting to something more professional."*

My heels pressed into the floor. Jacqueline was demanding. She hadn't given me any instructions, so I didn't know how she could have expected anything different. Still, I felt like an idiot for the bathroom photos. The learning curve for my new career was steeper than I thought.

I lowered my phone, preparing myself for the day ahead and hoping my pink skirt with the white flowers was clean and unwrinkled. Once at Greystone, I'd make some adjustments to the MLS entries and redeem myself. Jacqueline could walk me through the things I'd had to guess at last night.

"Morning." Grace stumbled out of the second bedroom rubbing the sleep from her eyes. Even just out of bed, her shiny, black hair fell to her shoulders in smooth layers, her luminous skin glowing in the dim morning light. "I smell coffee."

"Help yourself." I waved toward the counter. My gourmet coffee maker had been a gift from Nate last Christmas, which had the unfortunate effect of making me think about him whenever I poured a cup.

Grace scratched Astro behind his ears and then pulled a mug from the cabinet. "Bummer, we keep missing each other. How's your new job going?"

My fingers squeezed the handle of my mug as Jacqueline's bitchy message echoed in my ears. "Okay. There's so much to learn."

"Any more rats run through restaurants?" Grace raised an eyebrow at me.

"No, but we're signing the listing with the restaurant owners today."

"Of course, you are." Grace chuckled as she poured herself some coffee. "You must have been Mother Theresa in a past life, the way the universe lines itself up for you."

Ever since Grace had first met Mom and Dad at parents' weekend six years earlier, she operated under the illusion that I lived a charmed life, despite overwhelming evidence to the contrary.

"My life's not that great, actually. Remember how my sister has cancer, and my boyfriend dumped me?"

Grace sipped her coffee, her eyelids lowering. "Emma is going to beat it, and I'm sure there's a male supermodel who's also the CEO of a Fortune 500 company preparing to move into the condo next door and sweep you off your feet." With a raise of her arm, Grace ambled back toward her bedroom, coffee cup in hand. "Good luck with the listing thing. Oh, hey. Can I have my shoes back?"

"I'm holding them ransom until you pay me your rent."

Grace grinned. "At least you've learned something useful at your new job."

Ignoring her, I headed toward my room to retrieve her shoes with Astro trotting behind me.

****

I arrived at the office ten minutes early, confident and put-together in my favorite silk skirt and tall boots. My hair was smoothed back into a low ponytail, the same way Jacqueline wore hers. She was on the phone and hadn't acknowledged me yet.

"You're a piece of shit, Kevin." Jacqueline spewed the words into her phone, glaring. "Your sorry ass can't find your own deals, so you have to steal them from me? Is that it?"

My teeth grated against each other as I perched on the edge of my office chair, unable to breathe. I was afraid to learn which deal he'd stolen. Mumbling echoed through her phone.

"Those were *my* clients. That was *my* listing." Jacqueline's eyes bulged, showing a circle of white all around her gray-blue irises. "If you don't think there's going to be payback for this, you're very wrong." Before Kevin could respond, she hit a button and killed the conversation.

"What's going on?" I rolled my chair back, my mouth turning dry.

She stared toward me, her eyes solidifying. "That son of a bitch set up a meeting with the Sabatinos yesterday afternoon."

My stomach dropped.

"He offered to list their building and only take a two percent commission for himself. They signed with him." She scribbled something on a piece of paper and shook her head.

I sucked in my breath and felt dizzy. I'd ignored my instincts and told Kevin about our listing appointment. How could I have been so stupid? He'd even warned me not to leave without a signature. I couldn't speak. I squeezed my eyelids closed and fell into my chair.

"I got a phone call from Anthony this morning," Jacqueline said. "He wanted to cancel our 10:00 a.m. appointment. I knew we'd gotten screwed by someone."

"You were right. Kevin is a slime-ball."

"Never tell him anything about our business. Do you understand?"

"Yeah." I twisted the beaded bracelet on my wrist, hoping Jacqueline couldn't detect the guilt flashing across my face. "Can't you complain to Maeve?"

Jacqueline huffed. "Maeve is useless. She'll slap him on the wrist and send him on his way." She narrowed her eyes and spun toward Kevin's empty desk. "That jackass! He's targeting me. I know it."

I followed Jacqueline's death stare toward Kevin's spot in the back corner of the office. "Why would he target you?"

She tapped her nails on her desk, her eyes drifting off into space. "Because, a while ago, he accused me of sabotaging one of my listings before the inspection. Kevin's buyer freaked out over a little mold in the basement. His buyer canceled the contract, and I ended up selling the property to one of my clients, instead. Kevin convinced himself that I somehow put the mold there before the inspection." She huffed and shook her head. "How would I even *do* that?"

"I don't know," I said. "That's crazy."

"Yes. It is."

My toes curled inside my boots. I hadn't been prepared for this much drama so early in the morning. I wondered how Kevin could have pretended to be a wise mentor to me last night while knowing the whole time he was screwing me over. Jacqueline was right. I couldn't trust anyone.

"What did Anthony Sabatino say to you?" I asked.

"He thought our commission was too high." Jacqueline slammed her hand down on the desk. "Those idiots! Don't they know they get what they pay for?"

I didn't answer. My cheeks burned, and I hoped my skin wasn't turning an embarrassing shade of red.

"Anthony said they want to work with us to find a new space, and he hoped I could still bring my buyer in." Jacqueline rolled her eyes.

"Can you?" I blurted out. "I mean, bring your buyer in?"

"I can, and I will." Her nostrils flared. "I'm not going to waste my time carting them around the West Loop. I'll leave that to you if you want to work with them."

"Okay." My heartbeat sped up at the chance to earn some money.

"Email them a Buyer's Rep agreement. Right now." She balled her manicured hand into a fist. "And don't do one minute of work until they sign it."

Jacqueline wouldn't give me a cut of the commission if she brought in her own buyer, but maybe I could still find the Sabatinos a new restaurant space. Even so, it would be months before I got paid. Thousands of dollars in commissions, gone. Just like that. The deadweight in my stomach multiplied, keeping me slumped in my chair. My mortgage payment loomed over me like a trap that would spring no matter which way I stepped. And now, I had my condo board's massive special assessment to pay on top of everything else.

Jacqueline returned from the wall of mailboxes flapping a shiny flier in front of me. "Looks like Kevin has all sorts of business." A colorful advertisement for Kevin Lucas' eight-unit development listing in University Village lay in front of me.

I cringed. "Who would list a development with a guy like Kevin?"

"It's amazing what people will do to save money." Jacqueline grabbed the flier back, wadded it into a ball, and tossed into the wastebasket under my desk. "An eight-unit development is a joke anyway. I like to aim higher."

My back pressed against my chair, waiting for her to continue.

"With a seventy-five or one-hundred-unit condo development, I could close ten or twenty deals at a time. Pre-sales are the way to go."

"Do you have any leads for something that big?"

"Working on it. But in the meantime, I picked up three new listings last week, all referrals from previous clients—a studio condo in Streeterville, a one-bedroom loft in Bucktown, and a three-bedroom townhome in River North." Jacqueline pulled folders from her bag and set them on my desk. "Enter these into the MLS as soon as possible."

"Okay. I'll cut back on the bathroom photos." I paused, hoping Jacqueline would find a little humor in my joke.

"Good." Without a laugh or even a hint of a smile, she stepped away, hesitated, then pivoted back toward me, her lips hovering inches from my ear. "Don't worry about Kevin, Mara. We'll find a way to even things up."

It took a couple of hours to enter the listings and return Jacqueline's phone calls for her. She'd left to meet a contractor at her townhome, which was undergoing major renovations to restore it to its former Victorian glory. I pulled out my laptop and emailed the Sabatinos, asking them to sign the attached Greystone Buyer's Representative agreement. Then, ignoring Jacqueline's instructions to not do any work for them, I logged into the MLS and searched for potential restaurant spaces in the West Loop.

The next time I glanced at the clock, forty-five minutes had passed, and my search had turned up twenty-five properties, none of which seemed that great. Of course, I didn't know what the hell I was doing, or which sites were better for an Italian restaurant, or how much the Sabatinos were willing to pay. I leaned back in my chair and sighed louder than intended. Maybe Nate had been right about me after all.

My palms turned clammy as I thought of my financial situation. With Grace's help, my bank account could supply my next mortgage payment. Maybe two, if I cut way back on everything else. After that, I'd be running on empty, especially with the special assessment to pay. I had less than sixty days to come up with a sizable commission.

"Hi, Mara." Out of nowhere, Oscar's tall, skeletal frame materialized in front of me. "How's business?"

I sucked in my gut, stretching taller in my chair. A section of hair had escaped from my slicked-back ponytail, and I tucked it behind my ear. "Pretty good."

"I'm going to a seminar at 1:00. It's supposed to be a game-changer. 'How to Triple your Real Estate Sales through Facebook.' I would have asked you to come with me, but I bought my ticket a month ago." The words rushed out of Oscar's mouth like a spilled jar of change.

"That's okay. Hope it's helpful." Despite his nervous energy, Oscar was nice enough. Still, I wondered how many seminars he went to and whether he had any actual clients.

He shifted his weight from one foot to the other and back again. "Look, I need someone to take over my floor time from 12:00 to 2:00 p.m. Can you help me out?"

I glanced at the clock. It was 11:55. I remembered everyone complaining about floor time at the office meeting and thought about making up an excuse, but couldn't think of one. Oscar must have noticed my hesitation.

"I got a $400,000 buyer from floor time last year. Lots of people get clients from floor time. All you have to do is answer the phone and give information about properties to people. If they don't have an agent, they can become your client."

I hadn't made any referral fees from helping Jacqueline yet, and I wasn't in a position to turn down potential leads. Anyway, it was only two hours of my time, and I could finish the busywork Jacqueline had given me between phone calls.

"Okay. I can do it."

"Thanks! I owe you." Oscar lumbered away. Before he reached the front door, he turned back to me. "I'll take notes for you!"

I gave him a thumbs-up. Just what I needed. Notes on how to triple my real estate sales through Facebook. Last time I checked, three times zero was still zero. I gathered my things and walked over to the floor time desk at the front of the office, reminding myself to keep a positive attitude. Every other realtor had started in this exact position, and most didn't have a mentor like Jacqueline. Anyone could call Greystone in the next two hours, even a million-dollar buyer without an agent. I had nothing to lose.

CHAPTER EIGHT

My legs lay strewn across the couch, Astro's head resting on the cushion of my thigh. A documentary about a college student who'd been wrongly accused of murdering his girlfriend played on TV. Grace had rushed out an hour earlier to attend a speed dating event, wearing a little black dress and glittery eyeshadow. I'd skipped out, too exhausted from my day to go with her and conveniently comforted by Jacqueline's approval of my single status.

The floor time I'd covered for Oscar this afternoon had paid off. A guy named Mike had called Greystone for more information on a two-bedroom condo at Belden and Cleveland. I pulled up the address, discovering the property was listed by one of the Real Housewives, Missy Lantosa.

"It's priced at $429,000," I told Mike.

"I'd like to see it," he said.

"Do you have an agent?"

"No."

My heart had thumped with the possibility of signing my first buyer as I made a mental note to pick up more floor time shifts. "Great. I can set that up for you. No problem."

I immediately emailed Missy with a showing request for 6:00 tomorrow night, receiving an automatic confirmation. I also arranged showings of two other similar properties in the area. Closing my eyes, I calculated what my final payout would be if Mike ended up buying the condo.

Three sharp knocks at my door pulled my eyes away from the TV. Astro perked his ears toward the knocking, a low growl rumbling in his throat. Visitors could only get past the lobby if they buzzed up first, but sometimes people slipped through the entryway behind someone entering or leaving. I raised myself off the couch and slunk toward the door, the back of my neck prickling at the unexpected intrusion. Astro prowled a step ahead. I peered through the peephole. A lanky, unkempt man hovered in the hallway. His angular body twisted away. Slowly, he turned toward me, his features registering. My breath lodged in my throat.

It was Peter Zinsky. He'd been thin a couple of months ago, but his face was gaunter than I'd remembered, his skin practically dripping from his bones. His graying hair, which had been neatly styled every time I'd encountered him, now strayed wildly in all directions. Squeezing my hands together, I stepped back, debating whether to open the door or pretend I wasn't home. Two more knocks cracked against the door. Astro barked.

"Mara? Are you in there? It's Peter Zinsky. I helped you with your closing."

My heart pounded so loudly in my chest; I worried it would give me away. Astro barked a series of warnings. My fingers grabbed the dog's collar as I pulled him back. I stepped lightly to prevent the floorboards from creaking.

"Mara. Please, open the door. Did you get my text? I need to tell you something." Peter's voice was strung tight, almost crazed.

I lowered myself, squatting on the rug and remembering the words of Peter's text. *Don't take the job.* I hugged my knees into my chest while Astro sniffed my face. Jacqueline had mentioned how Peter hadn't been able to keep up, but I didn't realize losing his job would take such a toll. He must have been devastated to lose his position with Jacqueline. I was ashamed I hadn't given him much thought.

"Mara. Can you hear me? Stay away from Jacqueline," Peter

shouted from the hallway. "She's bad news. She ruined my life. She'll ruin yours, too." His voice stretched with emotion, desperate.

Kevin had given me a similar warning. *Watch your step with Jacqueline*, he'd said. But Kevin was crooked and jealous. Maybe Peter was no different. He was probably angry at me for taking his spot, like one of those psycho ex-employees who felt he'd been slighted and returned to exact revenge. And based on his startling appearance, he was likely dealing with a drug problem. Kevin's comments about the drugs and stolen money and Peter's downward spiral looped through my mind. What if Peter had a gun hidden beneath his shirt? I shuddered, hoping Grace wouldn't arrive home until after the crazed man had left the building.

Two more thuds caused my muscles to tense. I pulled out my phone, ready to call 911 if Peter tried to bust through my door.

"Please. I'm begging you. Open the door."

Holding my breath, I stayed motionless on the floor, resting my hand on Astro's head as the dog's eyes ricocheted between me and the door, confused. Maybe Peter only wanted to talk, but it wasn't worth the risk. I was a single woman alone in my apartment, and I didn't trust Astro to protect me with anything other than a few ferocious licks. Besides, nothing good could come from listening to Peter badmouth Jacqueline. She'd given me the benefit of the doubt when she hired me. She'd looked past my spotty resume and lack of real estate experience. I'd lost her the listing for Bistro Maria with my naiveté and my big mouth. More than anything, though, I needed this job. I wouldn't leave Jacqueline based on the mutterings of her disgruntled former assistant.

The seconds dripped past as I waited, perched motionless on my rug until all signs of Peter disappeared. Hearing no noises from the hallway for almost five minutes, I tiptoed toward my peephole and peered through, relieved to find him gone.

CHAPTER NINE

My sweaty hands stuck to the steering wheel as I circled my battered Hyundai around the block near 2300 N. Cleveland searching for a parking space. My first potential buyer, Mike, was meeting me at a condo in Lincoln Park. I pulled up to a stop sign and let some pedestrians cross. I had the Buyer's Rep agreement tucked inside my folder, along with my business cards and the listing sheets. Nervous excitement hummed through me. I couldn't believe selling real estate could be this easy. Answer a phone call, meet a buyer, write a contract, collect thousands of dollars sixty days later. Now all I needed was a parking space.

Jacqueline always made this part look so easy, but as I crept around the block, time after time, I couldn't locate a spot, not even an illegal one. The minutes ticked by as I turned right and braked for a group of boys crossing Larrabee Street. The third time I drove past the property, my clock read 6:05. Missy hovered on the front step talking to a tall, dark-haired man. My buyer. A cold sweat coated my skin. Once again, there was no place to park on the narrow street. I turned the corner, searching for any sign of a car pulling out. Minutes passed as I circled again, hands clenching the wheel, and swearing at every person and car that got in my way. I was about to pass the address a fourth time when I saw Missy studying her diamond-studded watch. She turned and grasped the handle of the front door. My chest tightened. She was going to show my buyer the property without me!

I accelerated into an opening at the corner of the street, disregarding that the space was only big enough to fit half my car and located in front of a fire hydrant. It was my only option. I threw on the flashers and bounded toward the entrance of the property.

"Mara, there you are," Missy said. "We were about to get started without you."

I stuck out my hand to the man. "Sorry I'm late. Mara Butler."

"Mike," he said, giving my hand a quick shake and turning back toward Missy.

Mike followed the other realtor into the lobby of the three-story building and up a flight of stairs. I trailed behind them. She led us into the second-floor, two-bedroom unit, pointing out the details in the woodwork and the many upgrades installed by the owners: stainless steel appliances, one-and-a-quarter-inch granite countertops, refinished hardwood floors, professionally painted trim, and on and on. She explained how the owners had loved the place but were moving because of a job transfer.

"What are the assessments?" Mike asked her.

"$265 a month. That includes common area maintenance and trash removal."

My potential client took his time inspecting every room, asking about parking, storage, and laundry. Missy opened a slatted closet door in the hallway, revealing a stackable washer and dryer.

"There's a storage locker in the basement that comes with the unit. Would you like to see it?"

"Sure," he said, still only talking to Missy.

I'd ruined my chance at a positive first impression. Now, my limbs felt thick, my face warm, as I followed them. I didn't know what observations to make. I didn't know the answers to any of his questions. I racked my brain, trying to think of something of value to add to the conversation, but all I could envision was my car blocking the fire hydrant and sticking halfway into the street. The urge to run off and move it was overwhelming, but I continued a step behind them down the steps to the basement. I hugged my folder to my chest as Missy pointed out the storage locker, and Mike asked her about the dimensions.

"Do you think I could fit two bags of golf clubs in there along with a set of luggage and a fake Christmas tree?"

"You'd be surprised. It's bigger than it looks." She smiled at Mike. "Do you golf often?"

"Every chance I get. Just got back from Palm Desert. Beautiful courses out there."

"Yes! I was there last year. Where did you stay?"

Their conversation continued as if I wasn't in the room. I shifted my weight from foot to foot, thinking of a way to make myself relevant. I didn't golf. I'd never been to Palm Desert. I knew close to nothing about real estate. I needed the showing to be over so I could move my car.

"I hate to interrupt." I held up the folder. "But, Mike, I have two more showings scheduled for you. The next one is in two minutes."

Missy cocked her head, pressing her lips together.

Mike's hands dropped to his sides. "Okay, yeah."

As we left, Missy made a point of telling Mike her number was on the listing sheet if he had any questions. I shot her a look. "Or you can have your agent call me," she added.

I turned toward Mike as he trotted down the steps next to me. "The next property is at 2100 Lincoln Park West. Do you know where that is?" I asked.

"I know that building. I'll meet you there."

That first showing hadn't gone well, but it was because the parking situation had made me anxious. I'd get it together for the next one. I drew in a long breath and power-walked toward the corner. Coldness spread through my body. My feet stuck to the sidewalk. I blinked, hoping my eyes were playing tricks on me as they searched up and down the street. But they weren't. My car was gone.

I couldn't move. I shoved my hand into the side pocket of my purse and felt the sharp metal of my car keys. I exhaled. At least I had the keys. I didn't know how long I'd been standing there when Missy wandered out the front door and spotted me.

"Mara, what are you still doing here?" Her highlighted bangs skimmed the tops of her thick eyelashes.

I pointed to the empty space in front of the fire hydrant. "My car's gone."

"Oh, boy. Looks like the tow truck got you." She shook her head and clucked. "Do you need a ride back to the office?"

"No. Thanks."

My body weighed at least a thousand pounds as I crumpled into a pile on the cement steps. I texted Mike and told him to view the next property without me, knowing I'd never hear from him again. Nobody would choose to work with a realtor who showed up late and got her car towed. Part of me wanted to call Jacqueline and ask her what to do, but that would be a bad move. I couldn't let her find out how incompetent I was. I could handle all the busywork she threw at me, but trying to find my own clients was another story. At least this guy hadn't been her buyer. The word at the office was that she'd fired her other assistants for much less.

I told you so. Nate's pompous voice echoed in my head.

I called Grace. Fifteen minutes later, she pulled up next to me and lowered her window.

"Hey! Get in."

I fell into her passenger seat and closed my eyes, recounting the series of unfortunate events.

"That sucks." She looked over at me with wide eyes, her work clothes neatly pressed.

"Do you know where you're taking me?" I asked.

"Yeah. I drove a guy from work there once. It's underneath the city. Totally crazy, like driving into a Batman movie."

I rested my head on the seat, ignoring Grace's eagerness to drive to the underground tow lot. We entered the business loop, passing beneath a massive billboard sponsored by the Chicago Board of Realtors. *Congratulations to Chicago's Top Producer, Natalia Romanov!* it exclaimed. A petite dark-haired woman in a royal blue suit smiled down at me. I slunk down, assuming the posture of a failure. How had Natalia Romanov done it? How had she become so successful that she received a billboard in downtown Chicago, while I couldn't even complete a single showing? I tried to swallow, but my throat scratched like sandpaper. Grace exited on the ramp to Lower Wacker Drive and then took the exit marked "City Tow Lot." The ramp spiraled down further and further. Steam rose from below us, and I couldn't shake the feeling we were driving into hell. We plunged into the darkness. The yellow lights on the walls of the tunnel flitted by every couple of seconds.

"Doesn't this remind you of Gotham City?" She flashed a mischievous smile at me.

"I never knew this place was here. It's creepy."

Finally, a trailer appeared around a bend. Behind it, a chain-link fence encircled hundreds of cars. An overweight man in grease-stained jeans sat inside the open door of the trailer, smoking a cigarette. Grace parked. I got out and stepped toward him, overly aware of my wobbly heels and sweaty forehead.

"I'm here to get my car back."

The man blew a puff of smoke in my direction and asked for my license plate number. I gave it to him, and he typed it into his computer.

"Yep. We got it. That'll be five hundred."

"What?"

"Five hundred dollars. To get your car back." He spit at the ground, narrowly missing my new shoes.

He might as well have punched me in the stomach. *Five hundred dollars?* My body spun like water circling the drain. As if I had an extra five hundred dollars lying around. Yet, I needed my car back. There was no other choice. I reached into my purse and pulled out my wallet.

"Do you take credit cards?" I removed one, and my business card slid out alongside it.

The man's grubby fingers snatched the plastic out of my hand, knocking my business card to the ground. He reached down and picked it up, inspecting it.

"Real estate, eh?"

I formed my lips into a mechanical grin, remembering Jacqueline's refrain. *Network, network, network.* "If you ever need a realtor, give me a call."

The man smirked as he handed back my card. "If you ever need a cheap car, give *me* a call." He waved his arm back toward the fenced-in lot overflowing with unclaimed cars and coughed out a wet, raspy laugh.

A few minutes later, the man unlocked the gate. I drove through feeling sick, my heart racing at my growing debt. I'd totally messed up this time. I'd abandoned my first potential client, my car had gotten towed, and now I was out another five hundred dollars. The ticking bomb of my mortgage payment echoed in my head. Then there was the special assessment, not to mention Emma's medical bills. My window of time to make money was closing.

I didn't remember driving out of the dark tunnel. Somehow, I was now above ground and trailing behind Grace's car. She turned north on Clark Street, and I followed, thankful to have her leading the way, so I didn't have to think. A few blocks later, she pulled to a stop at a red light, and I slammed on the brakes, barely missing her bumper. A mass of pedestrians entered the walkway and trekked across the four-lane street.

Two stragglers holding hands at the back of the pack caught my eye. They stepped off the curb and into the street. The guy's back was to me. He tipped his head to the side and laughed before grasping the woman in a bear hug and kissing her on the lips. *Get a room.*

As he pulled away from her and reached for her hand again, I got a clear view; the messy brown hair, the crinkling eyes, the curve of his bicep muscle as he grasped her around the waist. My breath snagged in my throat, and I felt like I was careening off a tall building directly toward my death. It was Nate. He was wearing new clothes, but it was him. It hadn't even been two months, and he'd already found someone else.

The woman looked nothing like me. She had the lanky, muscular build of a volleyball player. Her short blonde hair reflected in the evening light. I wondered what was so great about her. Was it her looks? Or maybe it was because she acted like an adult and could hold a job? She probably didn't need to rely on her boyfriend to pay her mortgage. I couldn't shake the look on Nate's face. He beamed at her like she was some kind of treasure.

A horn blasted from the car behind me. The light had turned green, and Grace's car was no longer in sight. I wasn't sure how I made it back to my condo. My face burned as pressure built up behind my eyes. I'd felt this way that day in October when my parents informed me of Emma's cancer diagnosis. I hadn't been able to stop the tears then. And I remembered the time in high school when I received eight rejection letters from colleges and universities on the same day. Mom had hugged me and said, "Everyone chooses a different path." She'd probably meant to be reassuring, but I noticed the way her eyelids dropped ever-so-slightly. What she'd really wanted to say was, "Maybe you should have studied a little harder." I'd stomped up to my room, buried my head in my pillow, and cried. Now again, I couldn't stop the tears. I'd lost everything. My job, my boyfriend, my parents' trust, and maybe I'd lose my condo, too.

By the time I pulled into the parking space underneath my building, my surge of emotion had passed. I checked myself in the rearview mirror, finding my mascara smeared in streaks across my reddened cheeks. I wiped the leftover tears away, hoping to pull myself together before Grace saw me. Her car was parked in the space next to mine.

The elevator took me up to the fourth floor, where I limped down the hallway, taking a deep breath before opening the door to my condo. Grace stepped in front of me, hooking a leash onto Astro's collar. The dog's massive paws landed on my shoulders, his tongue dangling inches from my mouth.

"I'm taking Astro for a walk." Grace yanked on the leash, pulling her dog off me. "Want to go? I'm telling you, guys flock to him."

"No, thanks. I'm gonna take it easy for a while."

She paused, studying my face. "What happened? Are you okay?"

My mouth stammered, but no words came out. Then, I closed my eyes, but I couldn't stop the tears from flowing or the sobs from spilling out.

Grace looped her arm over my shoulders and ushered me inside to the couch while Astro tried to lick the saltiness from my cheeks. She grabbed two beers from the refrigerator while I described the woman I'd seen with Nate.

"He's a loser. You're better off without him." She elbowed me. "Besides, you have nothing but gold bars shoved up your ass. That male CEO supermodel we talked about is probably driving his moving truck toward you right now."

I chuckled through my tears. Grace was the best person to have on my side.

For the next hour, we drank beer, devoured nacho-flavored Doritos straight from the bag, and watched mindless reality TV, which was the quickest way to put the hellish day behind me. I told her about the weird visit from Peter the night before and the text he'd sent on my first day at Greystone. She'd listened with unblinking eyes, relieved I hadn't opened the door for him.

"You never know what will send someone off the deep end," she said. Then she told me funny stories about her awkward encounters with the guys at her speed dating event, making me doubly happy I hadn't tagged along with her. After her final tale of a pimply thirty-something who wouldn't make eye-contact with her, she paused and looked at me. "Our lives are turning out to be real shit shows, huh?"

We burst into a fit of sorry, self-indulgent laughter, the kind that only two friends who'd seen each other at their worst could understand. Astro jumped up onto the couch, tail wagging, and having no clue what was happening.

The final challenge of the cooking show ended. Grace brushed off her pants and gave me another hug, finally ready to take Astro out for his night walk. Just as she left, my phone buzzed. Another email. I sat up as Anthony Sabatino's name popped up on my phone. Maybe he'd signed the Buyer's Rep agreement I'd sent him. With everything else going on, I'd almost forgotten about the Sabatinos. I held my breath and opened the message.

"Mara, thank you for the email. We decided to use Kevin to help us find a new location for our restaurant. Anthony."

I buried my forehead in my hands, my neck unable to support the weight of my head for another second. My only lead had disappeared.

CHAPTER TEN

I pulled the covers over my head and hit snooze for the third time. A black cloud had attached itself to my life, and I couldn't escape it. I'd misjudged the time and effort it would take to start making money. Against everyone's advice, I'd jumped out the window of a tall building and hoped that a safety net would magically appear under me. Now I was hurtling toward the pavement below.

I pictured Emma with the scarf tied around her head, the vacant look in her eyes. I should have been the one with cancer, not her. Maybe if I'd spent more time with her, I would have noticed how severe the symptoms had gotten. I'd failed her. I'd failed myself.

Then there was Nate. If only I could talk to him. Work things out. He didn't know it, but I'd seen him last night, his eyes worshipping that other woman like she was the answer to his prayers, like he was so ecstatic that he'd ended up with her instead of me. He was probably with her right now. I forced my mind to stop there. I didn't want to imagine anything else. That wasn't even the part that hurt the most. The rusty nail through my heart was that Nate had been right all along. I was a loser who made bad decisions, a real estate agent with no clients. I couldn't find a parking space if my life depended on it. And now I couldn't pay my bills, much less Emma's. Although I'd gotten hooked up with Jacqueline, I had nothing to show for it. I'd given her hours of unpaid labor. I'd done her busy work for free. She'd duped me. She was closing deals left and right, but I wasn't involved in any of them.

My phone dinged with another incoming email, and I opened it. More to do lists from Jacqueline. No doubt, she'd already completed her morning run and was at the office scheduling dozens of closings for herself. She wanted me to come in and do her grunt work while she collected all the money. Forcing myself to get up and power through was the right thing to do, but my limbs hung with the weight of cement blocks. I dropped my phone on the nightstand and flipped on my side. Nothing sounded more welcoming than sleep. My eyelids closed, my head sinking into the pillow.

My buzzing phone jolted me upright in bed. The numbers on my clock glowed, 9:20. I'd fallen asleep again. Jacqueline's name flashed across my phone. She wanted to know why I wasn't at the office yet. She wanted updates and answers. The phone buzzed and buzzed like a chainsaw. I rolled over in bed and buried my face in the pillow.

Five minutes later, I heard more noises coming from my phone. This time cheerful beeps of incoming text messages. Why wouldn't she go away? *Leave me alone!* The beeps kept coming. Finally, I reached for my phone and read her last message.

Be here in ten minutes or you're fired.

By the time I parked near the office, it was almost 10:00 a.m. I moped down North Avenue, past the million-dollar townhomes, restaurants, and high-end storefronts. Tony, the homeless guy I'd met on my first day, stood at the corner, shaking his jar of change.

"Hey, Lady! Hey, Lady!" He grinned, flashing a checkerboard of teeth at me.

"Hi, Tony." I paused, digging into my purse for something to offer him.

"It's a beautiful day. Beautiful day. Isn't it?"

"I guess." It had been a terrible day, but talking to a homeless man who was happier than me forced things back into perspective. Two quarters, a dime and a nickel lay in my palm, and I tossed it into his jar. "Sorry, it's not more."

"I'm grateful. I'm grateful." He nodded. "Keep your chin up, lady. It's a beautiful day!"

"Thanks, Tony." I left him behind me as I pulled open the door to the office.

The door to Maeve's office was ajar, and I could hear her congratulating Jacqueline on a recent closing. I slid into my chair and tried to look like I cared. A property list lay on my desk with a sticky note attached, the words "Schedule these showings for tomorrow" scrawled in black marker. My reluctant fingers pressed the numbers. I stared out the window. A city bus lurched past Tony and pulled to a stop in front of the office. A woman in a pantsuit climbed aboard. If I didn't get some deals going soon, I'd be back to taking public transit to some nine-to-five job downtown, too. The thought made me feel like vomiting. Maybe Tony was on to something.

"You're late." My mentor appeared next to me. I straightened up in my chair and forced a smile.

"Sorry."

"I get up every morning at 5 a.m. and go for a five-mile run. Rain or shine. And you can't get to the office before 10 a.m.?"

Jacqueline glared at me, disgusted. I hunched forward, aware of the fold of flesh creeping over my waistband. Regular exercise had never been my thing.

"Pull that shit again, and you're fired." She shuffled papers on her desk.

I nodded.

The shuffling stopped, and she raised an eyebrow. "Something you want to tell me?"

"Yeah," I said, pausing to look at my hands. "I mean, I'm sorry about this morning. It won't happen again."

"Was there a problem?"

"Yeah. I mean, no," I said, stuttering. I didn't want to tell her that my car had gotten towed last night or that I'd seen my ex-boyfriend kissing another woman, so I went with the third option. "I'm getting kind of nervous about making money in time for my mortgage payment. I have the next couple payments, but after that . . ." My voice trailed off. "Anthony didn't sign the buyer's agreement. He said they're going to use Kevin."

"Don't let the Sabatinos get you down. It's a cutthroat business." Jacqueline put her hands on her hips. "Channel your anger into productivity."

I nodded again. Those mind tricks probably worked for someone like Greystone's top producer, but they wouldn't work for me.

"I'm going to Starbucks," she said. "Come with me. There's no privacy in this place."

With her bag slung over her shoulder, Jacqueline shoved through Greystone's front door as I scrambled a half-step behind. The sun seared my skin through a cloudless sky, and I realized Tony had been right. It was a beautiful day. I'd been too absorbed in self-pity to notice. A few feet away, Tony's coins clinked together in a metallic rhythm, and I raised my hand in a wave. Jacqueline turned toward me, her forehead creased.

"I wish the city would do something to get that bum away from our office. It's a disgrace." She huffed and trotted across four lanes of traffic to avoid walking past the homeless man.

I averted my eyes from Tony, stomach sinking, but forcing my feet to skitter after her. By the time we reached Starbuck's a few minutes later, I was breathless. Once inside, we approached the counter, the scent of the coffee beans, and the hiss of the steamer jolting me to full alertness.

"I'll have a grande soy latte." Jacqueline waved me forward.

"A tall Sumatra, please."

She paid, and we sat at a table near the front window.

I motioned toward her soy latte. "My mom is lactose intolerant, too."

"Oh, I'm not lactose intolerant. I don't like the way the dairy cows are treated." Her eyes turned glassy as if she was thinking about some faraway place. "Horrible." She shook her head before taking a sip of her dairy-free coffee.

"Really?" I didn't know what she was talking about, but I was surprised that Jacqueline, who lacked compassion for humans, was concerned about the treatment of cows.

"Anyway, let's talk about you." She leaned in. "I know I'm not the easiest person to work with. Some of my past assistants didn't stick around very long." She paused. "Not that it was my fault."

I looked down at my coffee. "Peter seemed pretty angry."

"What?" Jacqueline's mouth froze. "How would you know that?"

"I wasn't sure if I should mention anything. Peter sent me a text telling me not to take the job. Then he showed up at my condo two nights ago. I pretended I wasn't home."

Jacqueline's eyes hovered over me, her chin set.

"I think he knew I was inside, though. He was shouting through the door, telling me to stay away from you."

Jacqueline tipped her head back and closed her eyes. "I should have warned you. He's a very disturbed person. I suspect drugs might be involved."

"I didn't realize he'd be so upset about me taking his position."

She waved her hand in the air. "He's a jealous mess. That was one of the reasons I had to let him go. He didn't work well with others, and his behavior became more and more erratic. You were smart not to engage with him."

"Yeah. It was kind of unsettling."

"Let me know immediately if it happens again. We'll call the police. I'll take legal action. We can get a protective order, if necessary."

"Okay." I swallowed, remembering Jacqueline's legal background and hoping a protective order wouldn't be required. Either way, her support was reassuring.

She typed something into her phone and then shifted her chair closer to the window. "Let's not waste our energy on Peter right now. I want things to work out with you. You've got real potential,

Mara."

I smiled despite myself, hoping my cheeks weren't turning red.

"You said you're concerned about paying your mortgage?"

I nodded. "And I just got hit with a special assessment from my condo board. Almost $4000."

"You're kidding!" Jacqueline glanced over my shoulder. "I didn't remember anything about that in the meeting minutes."

"I know. They just voted on it. It came out of nowhere." I left out the part about not having attended any of the condo board meetings. "And my sister, Emma..." I paused, not sure if it was unprofessional to share my personal life with Jacqueline, but she nodded, encouraging me to continue. "She has cancer. Lymphoma. She's only eighteen."

"Oh, no. I'm so sorry."

"My parents are struggling to pay for her medical bills. It was stupid of me, but I thought I'd be able to help out."

"No, that's not stupid." Jacqueline strummed her nails on the table. She turned toward her bag, rustling through it before pulling out a stack of checks. "I'm going to pay you a draw." She ripped off the top check and held it out to me. "What do you need to take off some pressure? Three thousand? Five thousand?"

I observed her from across the table, unable to blink.

"Go ahead. Fill in the amount. Use it to pay your expenses until you get some deals coming in. You have six months to pay me back."

My eyes widened. She was serious. "Thanks. Five-thousand will be enough to get me through." I could almost feel five thousand pounds of weight lift off me. Now I'd owe Jacqueline too, but at least I'd have some breathing room with my other bills.

"Not many agents get draws. Don't mention it to anyone, or everyone in the office is going to want a check."

"I won't." The check was from her Greystone account. I filled in my name, date, and the amount and slid the check back to her to sign. She scrawled her messy signature across the bottom and passed it back to me.

"No one wants to work with a desperate realtor. People can

smell desperation."

I nodded.

"I have some potential leads I can give you, but you should be cultivating your own clients as well."

"Yeah, I'm trying," I said. "The problem is my friends are my age. You know, twenty-four, twenty-five. They don't have money to buy real estate."

"Lenders can be creative with financing options, as you know." She winked at me. "They can make things work for almost anyone with a steady job, especially with the relaxed regulations." She reached in her purse and pulled out a stack of cards. "Here are a few of Justin's cards. He gets deals done." She passed the cards over to me, the name on them already familiar because Jacqueline had given me the same card the day I'd first toured my condo. *Justin Blakely, Gold Coast Lending*. "Have some of your friends call him and see if they can get pre-approved. Once they know they qualify, they'll want to buy. Trust me." She tapped her temple with her index finger and smiled. "It's all psychological."

"Okay. Thanks." I tucked the cards into my pocket. It was a place to start. "I feel like I'm in a race against the clock to make my mortgage payment."

"Well, now you have some money." She nodded at the check. "And don't you have a roommate?"

"Yeah, but she only covers half." I thought about Grace's job. She was the executive assistant to the owner of one of the city's largest design firms. "She could probably pay more if I asked her. She's got a good job, but her dog's completely out of control." I glanced down at the new shoes I had to buy because of Astro. "If I'd known how destructive her dog was, I might not have let her move in." Astro's furry face leaped into my mind. In the previous weeks, Grace's dog had gnawed holes in two of my chairs, chewed through the drywall in my living room, shredded my bedspread, peed on my houseplant, and torn apart three pairs of socks, not to mention the shoes.

Jacqueline's eyebrows furrowed. "What kind of dog?"

"A crazy black lab."

"Maybe you can get the condo rules changed to prohibit dogs over a certain weight. Then she'll have to move out. And guess who she'll use as her realtor?" Jacqueline touched her blonde hair with her fingertips.

I leaned back in my chair. "Wow. You're good," I said, although something about it seemed slightly evil. "But then I'd be out a roommate."

"You can always find a new roommate."

She was right. My condo was a better option than the rundown apartments in the city that cost the same or more. Still, Grace had always been there for me. My stomach turned at the thought of pulling the rug out from under her.

"While you're working on getting your condo rules changed, I have a list of buildings you can call on." She slid a piece of paper across the table to me. "I have an investor who rehabs distressed buildings and then hires me to resell them after he makes repairs. You need to call the city building inspections department to report as many violations as you can. More than likely, the current owners won't be able to make the repairs and will be forced to sell. We'll watch the prices and tell my guy when to buy."

I stared at her gray eyes and her perfect mouth, talking in such a matter-of-fact tone. Her plan was brilliant. Slightly sketchy, but certainly nothing that broke the law. She was forcing people to follow the law if I really thought about it.

"Yeah. I'll do that. Thanks." I breathed out, relieved to have another potential lead, but my toes tapped under the table. "What kind of violations am I reporting?"

"Drive by the buildings. They all have major issues. Call up the inspector and pretend to be a tenant. They won't answer, so you'll have to leave a voice mail. You can complain about any exterior issues—the roof, the porches, the graffiti, the bricks falling off the side." She tapped the side of her latte with her finger. "That way, the inspectors won't need the owners' permission to enter the building. They're swamped. Your phone calls will push these buildings toward the top of the list."

I nodded as the information seeped into my brain. I'd learned more about the way real estate worked during one cup of coffee with Jacqueline than I had in my entire real estate course.

"I know this all might seem a little manufactured, but sometimes you have to make your own business. Think outside the box, as they say."

My eyes darted away. She'd said the same thing about making your own business after the rats had scurried through Bistro Maria. I couldn't help wondering if Jacqueline had been more than just a casual diner who happened to be eating at the restaurant at the exact time the rodents ran loose. She handed me a piece of paper, and I swallowed, reining in my imagination as I scanned the addresses.

Jacqueline cleared her throat. "But before you do that, follow up with the inquiries on my website. I don't want to lose any potential clients, and I'm way behind. I forwarded all the emails to you this morning."

"Okay."

Jacqueline took a long swig of her latte before she continued talking.

"When I was growing up, there was a guy in our neighborhood with a window repair business." She leaned in as if she was telling me a secret. "At one point, his business was so slow he almost had to close for good, but then he got an idea. He befriended the kids in the neighborhood. He gave us a bat and some baseballs and told us to play on the city sidewalks. 'Don't go into the street,' he'd always say. He didn't want anyone getting hurt. Without fail, one of us would hit the ball into a storefront window. Sometimes we hit car windows or townhome windows. It didn't matter. His shop was right there, and he always got the business. Everyone blamed the kids. Technically, he didn't do anything wrong." Jacqueline narrowed her eyes at me. "Do you understand what I'm saying?"

"I think so." I was still trying to figure out if the story she told was real or if it was some kind of metaphor for what she wanted me to do.

"Always be one step ahead of your client, Mara. Be creative."

"Okay."

It now seemed like maybe being "creative" included releasing rats in restaurants, but it was way too risky to ask her about that. Especially after everything she was doing to help me get started. Learning from her was the only way I'd succeed in this business. I shook off the ripple of unease her story had sent through me. Like she said, we weren't hurting anyone.

CHAPTER ELEVEN

A spring breeze blew through the open window of my car, sending an icy rush across my skin and lifting my hair by the roots. This was the freedom I craved, being on my own in the middle of the day while thousands of mindless workers rotted away in their windowless cubicles downtown. They might have security and steady paychecks and retirement funds and romantic partners, but I could do whatever I wanted today. I was in charge of myself. Something about Jacqueline's confidence, her refusal to accept defeat, had empowered me.

Minutes later, I unlocked the door to my condo, humming to myself as I entered my quiet sanctuary, preparing to get tons accomplished. Rays of light shone through my floor-to-ceiling windows and highlighted every dust particle and piece of dog hair floating in the air. Astro barked a short, happy bark and bounded toward me. I stepped forward just as I noticed the sour smell in the air. My heel slipped out from under me. My hands hit the slick floor before my body. Then a warm and awful sensation seeped through my pants. The intense, sour stench of urine burned through my nose. A yellow stain spread across the front of my favorite blouse. I lay in a heap in a puddle of dog pee, the acrid liquid clinging to my skin and eating away the lacquer of my sustainable bamboo floor.

"Astro!"

Astro bounced, he was so excited to see me. From my altered perspective on the floor, I could make out the damage he'd done to the legs of my coffee table. He'd gnawed every wooden spindle to the quick, like corn on the cob. My blood surged through my veins, but the dog's saucer eyes begged for forgiveness. Even sitting in a pool of pee, it was impossible to stay mad at him.

This was all Grace's fault. She must have skipped Astro's walk this morning. Did she think her dog would last all day without going out? Or maybe she assumed I would take care of him. Either way, she was wrong. This condo was my first real estate investment and, despite Grace's loyal emotional support, I wasn't going to let her dog destroy its value anymore.

Pushing with my palms, I boosted myself back onto my feet and removed my shoes. After mopping up the puddle with some paper towels, I peeled off my wet clothes and rushed into the shower. The streams of hot water blasted against my skin, washing away the sticky layer of dog pee as I weighed Jacqueline's scheme in my mind. Grace would always be my friend—even one of my best friends—but her dog was destroying my condo. It was time for them to leave. She'd told me about the money in her savings account, and her career was going well. She could afford her own place. Maybe one near a dog park. I'd suggest a dog-walker, too. And then there was the other thing. I needed a commission. Then I could find a new roommate, one without a dog. Everyone would be better off, even Astro.

Think creatively. Jacqueline's words stuck in my brain. She knew better than anyone how to be successful in real estate. I stepped out of the shower and toweled off, placing my soiled clothes into a paper bag to take to the dry cleaners. I'd take Astro for a walk around the block, and then I'd draw up the paperwork. I already had the letterhead from my condo board, thanks to the special assessment notice. I'd scan it into my computer to create a template. Then I'd write an official-looking fake letter stating that the building no longer allowed dogs over thirty pounds. There wasn't enough time to get actual approval from the board. That could take months. I had to be creative. Grace would be disappointed about the rule change, but with the letter from the condo board, she wouldn't question it.

The minutes dragged on forever as I waited for Grace to return from work, images of the forged condo board letter sending waves of nausea through me whenever I thought too long about my betrayal. I distracted myself by following up on the leads from Jacqueline's website. I left upbeat voicemail messages for people who didn't answer their phones. One call resulted in me scheduling a showing for an interested buyer at one of Jacqueline's many listings, but ninety-nine percent of real estate leads didn't go anywhere. Jacqueline was smart to push things along, make things happen. I swallowed, glancing at the gnawed-up legs of my coffee table. That was what I needed to do, too.

A reality show about naked people going on blind dates played on my TV screen as Grace burst through the door, shrugging off her baby-blue spring coat.

"Hey, girl." She nodded at me and headed toward the kitchen.

An ominous force tugged at my gut, warning me against what I was about to do. Astro bounded after his negligent owner.

"Hi, buddy! How's my good boy?" Grace patted the dog's head. The refrigerator door opened, followed by a rustling of packages. She appeared in the doorway, holding a bottle of coconut water. Drops of condensation streamed down the side of the bottle, where they clung before dripping to the floor.

"What a day." She shook her head, the strands of her metallic necklace clinking and her shiny black hair gliding into place. Then she flopped down on the couch next to me. "My boss is ridiculous! Talk about shit shows."

I didn't ask about her day, but only perched on the edge of the couch. Grace sipped her drink, laughing at the TV show.

My throat was thick and dry. Suddenly, I wanted to guzzle a bottle of coconut water myself. Or, better yet, a beer. Instead, I swallowed the one drop of saliva left in my mouth.

"Listen, Grace. I'm so sorry about this, but I have some bad news." I shuffled through the mail and held up the letter from the condo board. Only it wasn't really from the condo board.

"What?" Grace snatched the piece of paper from my hand and read it. "Are you serious? I just moved in!"

"I know. It sucks." My eyes refused to land on hers. Instead, I focused on the scratches on my floor from Astro's untrimmed nails. "Someone must have complained. They're going to start fining me if you and Astro don't leave."

Grace placed her water on the table and fell back against the cushions.

I turned toward her, shaking my head. "It's gotta be the old people upstairs. They have nothing better to do than sit around all day and make sure everyone is obeying the rules."

"What the hell? Where am I going to find a decent apartment that accepts big dogs?"

"You could buy a place." I shrugged as if I had just thought of the idea at that moment. "Most smaller condo buildings are dog-friendly."

"I don't think I can afford that." Grace dragged her pearly fingernails through Astro's fur and stared into space.

"I have the name of a lender who does creative financing. Sometimes you only need to put three percent down. That's what I did." *And look how well that turned out,* I thought to myself as I cleared my throat. "Depending on the price of the condo, a mortgage could be less than what you'd pay in rent." I handed her one of Justin Blakely's cards.

She took it and turned it over in her hand, inspecting it. "Yeah, yeah. Okay. I guess it wouldn't hurt to find out what I can afford." She turned to me. "Thanks."

"Sure."

"Hey. Could you pull up some properties for me, probably under $250,000? Just so I can see what's out there?"

I almost fell off the couch.

"Sure thing. I'll email them to you."

Maybe this was going to work.

CHAPTER TWELVE

My heel caught in a crack in the sidewalk, and I pulled it out, inspecting it for damage and brushing off the dirt. Thankfully, the scrape was easy to smooth out. Jacqueline strode several feet ahead.

We'd completed the final showing of several Lincoln Park condos with a couple of newlyweds who couldn't make up their minds about their preferred neighborhood. Jacqueline had instructed me to familiarize myself with their tastes so I could take over their future showings without her. They'd seemed interested in the last condo, especially after Jacqueline had pointed out that the extra bedroom was the perfect size for a nursery. The woman's eyes had gleamed as she surveyed the tiny bedroom, visualizing where she'd put the crib and the changing table.

"That went well," I said, jogging to catch up.

"They're going to make an offer on that last one." Jacqueline smirked. "People are so predictable."

"I think you're right," I said, although I had literally no previous experience. "Didn't we park that way." I pointed in the opposite direction of where we headed.

Jacqueline ignored me, her body gravitating toward some unknown destination, a glazed look in her eyes. I strode along beside her. A half-block later, she stopped on the Fullerton Avenue sidewalk, arms crossed in front of her chest as cars lurched and accelerated down the street. An enormous limestone single-family house loomed in front of us. The mansion was neatly tucked into a double city lot behind a manicured lawn and wrought-iron gate and surrounded by other similarly intimidating homes. Beyond the gate, massive flowerpots flanked the front door. Jacqueline gazed up at the blackened windows, pacing back and forth in front of the house.

I shifted my weight from foot to foot, gaping at the oversized house, its shadow dwarfing me. A woman brushed past and huffed about us taking up too much of the sidewalk. Jacqueline grasped one of the metal poles of the gate with her hand and peered through toward the back yard.

"Is this one of your listings?" I asked, still confused about what we were doing.

"No. I used to live here."

"Here?"

A car honked in the distance, and the weight of my bag pulled against my shoulder. She didn't respond. I looked from the ground to Jacqueline and back to the house. Had a light turned off upstairs? A blip of movement caught my eye in one of the second-story windows, and I froze. A chill ran through my limbs, the overwhelming sensation of being watched. I fixed my eyes on the opening, making out a shadowy figure behind the glass.

Jacqueline smoothed down her pants. "Just give me a second, please."

She punched in a code and pushed through the front gate, leaving me standing on the sidewalk. Marching up the steps she reached for the doorbell. No one answered. She pounded on the door with her fist.

"I know you're in there, Mother!"

My mouth fell open. Had Jacqueline had grown up in this mansion? She'd told me she'd been raised in the city, but she'd never said exactly where.

A moment later, the door creaked open, and a petite woman

stood in the opening.

"Can I help you?" The woman wore plain, dark clothes, and her voice held the hint of an accent.

"Yes. I'm Jacqueline. Martha's daughter." She stretched her shoulders back. "Please tell her I'm here to see her."

The woman, who I now realized was the housekeeper, looked her up and down and nodded. "Just a moment." She closed the door in her face, followed by the click of the deadbolt. Jacqueline stood, unwavering, like one of the garden statues.

A minute later, the door opened. "I'm sorry, miss. Martha does not wish to be disturbed."

Jacqueline flung her head back and sighed. "What about my father?"

"He also does not wish to be disturbed."

The woman closed the door and locked it.

I held my breath, not able to imagine anyone slamming a door in Jacqueline's face and getting away with it. I braced myself for more shouting and banging. Instead, Jacqueline turned and strode back toward me, her chin held high in the air and red splotches forming on her neck.

"My family is so fucked up."

I tried to imagine a scenario where my mom wouldn't come to the door for me but couldn't. My instinct was to offer her a hug, but an invisible forcefield surrounded her.

"Why won't she talk to you?" I asked.

"Because I'm a disappointment. I'm a lowly realtor instead of a partner in a big law firm. That's what my parents wanted."

I stepped back, dumbfounded. "But you're one of the most successful realtors in the city."

"Exactly. 'One of.' That's not good enough. I need to be the single most successful realtor, Top Producer of the entire City of Chicago. That's the only way they'll respect me. I'm going to prove them wrong. I'll make sure they see my face on the billboard every time they drive downtown. All their friends will see it too. They won't be able to ignore my success." Jacqueline's eyes remained trained ahead of her as she strode back toward our parking spot.

Hustling along beside her, I did my best to match her pace while avoiding cracks in the sidewalk. By the time we finally reached her Mercedes, my breath sputtered and heaved. Jacqueline wasn't winded at all. She clicked open the locks. I climbed inside, wondering if I should start going on early morning runs like her.

"Isn't Natalia Romanov the city's Top Producer?" I asked between gulps of air.

Jacqueline glared at me, her lips curled back like peeling paint. I glanced toward my hands, realizing I'd said the wrong thing.

"She *was* Top Producer last year. That's going to change." She started the car and swerved into the street. "This year, I'm going to claim the title. With your help."

I inhaled, a shiver of excitement rippling through my body at the prospect. At least Jacqueline considered me her teammate.

"Peter couldn't get the job done, but you're different."

My body glided along with her car, happy she'd recognized some potential in me.

"It's not just Natalia. There are a couple of other realtors in the running, too."

"Who?"

"Michelle Sentry. Marco Toranado."

A laugh slipped from my mouth. "The Tornado of Real Estate?" I'd seen his cheesy ads all over TV but didn't think anyone actually fell for them.

"It's hard to believe, but, yes. He's low-end, though. He'll need to do tons of volume to measure up to Natalia's level."

"What is Natalia's level?" I asked, leaning my weight into the leather passenger seat.

"$150 million."

"Wow." I gazed out the window, wondering how Jacqueline planned to increase her production by more than three times what she'd sold last year.

Jacqueline cleared her throat. "You're lucky you come from a good family. I'm not like my parents, you know."

I nodded, suddenly thankful for Mom and Dad, despite all their quirks.

Jacqueline tapped her fingers on the steering wheel as she pulled up to a red light.

"I was thinking about what you told me…about Emma."

"Yeah." My muscles tensed.

"I want to do a fundraiser for her. A charity run." She hesitated. "What do you think?"

"Wow. Really?"

Jacqueline blinked.

"That's so nice of you. I mean, that would be awesome."

"I know the weather's still a little sketchy, but what if we planned it two weeks from Sunday, along the lakeshore?"

"Yeah. That's great. I mean, are you sure?"

"Of course. It will combine something I love with a good cause. You know, I run every morning?"

"You mentioned that." My eyes scanned Jacqueline's lean body. She was built like a runner with legs that reached up past her waist.

"I take the same route every day, starting at my townhome on Lincoln Avenue and winding my way through the neighborhood before cutting down Fullerton through the Lincoln Park Zoo toward the lake."

"You run through the zoo?"

"It's the quickest way to the lakeshore path, and it gets my mind off real estate for a few minutes. Plus, I get to see Ellie every morning."

"Who's Ellie?"

Jacqueline cocked her head at me, a smile forming in the corners of lips. "The cow who lives in the Zoo."

I quieted my face, still dumbfounded by Jacqueline's soft spot for cows. "Oh, yeah. I know Ellie." Nate and I had strolled through the zoo hand-in-hand, a few times over the years. There had always been a crowd of children huddled around the makeshift pasture in the farm exhibit where the sleepy cow with the matted reddish-brown fur lived. I'd never thought of making the experience part of my exercise routine.

Jacqueline tipped back in her chair. "When I reach the lakeshore, I follow the trail along the water for a good three miles until it's time to cut back to my place. Five miles, every day. Rain or shine. Sleet or wind or snow. No excuses."

My hands moved to cover my gut. I was at peace with the curves of my body, but it was difficult not to feel frumpy next to Jacqueline's string bean physique. Despite my membership to 24 Hour Fitness, I only worked out a couple of times a month. Running wasn't one of my strengths. Hoping Jacqueline wouldn't notice my indifference toward physical activity, I swiveled toward her, a smile pulling at my lips.

"Thank you so much. I'll tell my parents. And I'll let my friends know."

"You're welcome." She braked at a crosswalk to let two joggers pass. "I'll get some flyers ordered, and I'll donate the first thousand dollars to get it started."

I gasped, my cheeks flushing with emotion. "Really?"

"Yes." She turned left in front of the office and unlocked the door for me to get out. "Now, get back to work."

"Okay, boss." I leaped out of the car and gave her a wave. Good things were happening.

CHAPTER THIRTEEN

The morning sun flooded my bedroom window, prickling against my cheeks and eyelids. Blinking away my sleepiness, I rolled out of bed, feeling lighter. Optimistic. It was 7:45 a.m., and I had tons to accomplish today. After coffee and a shower, I'd drive past the run-down buildings and make the calls to the city building inspector, per Jacqueline's instructions. Then I'd set up an online search for Grace and find some properties to show her. After that, I had to join Jacqueline on a condo tour in Lincoln Square.

I poured water into my coffee maker and tried not to think of Nate. Even the thought of him with his arms wrapped around his new girlfriend wasn't going to bring me down today. If anything, the joke would be on him. He'd soon realize he'd lost out on one wildly successful girlfriend, not to mention the top-of-the-line coffee maker was all mine.

A half-eaten bag of Reese's Pieces lay on the counter. I crumpled it up and heaved it into the trash can, promising myself to eat more vegetables today. I swallowed a bitter gulp of coffee, and my insides jolted to attention. My muscles loosened with every sip of caffeine as I envisioned the charity run Jacqueline was planning for Emma. I still couldn't believe she would offer up her time and money on behalf of my sister, who she'd never even met.

With the loan from Jacqueline, I finally had some breathing room. Peter and Kevin were wrong about her. She wouldn't have handed over a check for five-thousand dollars if she hadn't been sure I could pay it back. She believed in me. It was time I started believing in myself. Today was the day I was going to start making money in real estate.

"Let's do this!" I yelled and pumped my fist in the air. Astro jumped up from the couch and bounded over to me, assuming I was trying to play some sort of game with him. I patted him on the head and wondered if Grace had taken him out this morning.

An hour later, I weaved my way through traffic toward the first address on the list. It was only ten blocks west of my condo, but the neighborhood was rougher. Metal grates covered many of the windows. An occasional trendy-looking loft building dotted the landscape, but most of the buildings and houses needed repairs. The city building inspector's backlog was no surprise.

I parked in front of the property, a three-story building that looked like it had endured too many Chicago winters. It was divided into six units—a six-flat. I'd learned that lingo by listening to Jacqueline talk to her developer-clients on the phone. The building was beat-up, with missing shingles and a sagging roof. The rear balconies weren't visible, so I got out of my car and edged closer. As I neared the front, the cracks became more pronounced, crisscrossing some of the bricks.

I rounded the corner of the six-flat, halting as if someone had yanked back the collar of my shirt. Neon paint stretched across the side of the building, clashing with the faded bricks. An orange star reached out in six points with two purple pitchforks emerging from it. The purple and orange letters L and A, painted in an urban-calligraphy style, flanked the two sides of the star. In contrast to the rest of the tired building, which melted into the greyness of the cityscape, the paint sprung out bright and fresh. A warning rushed through me. My female intuition urged me to flee to the safety of my car, but I fought the impulse and stood my ground. I'd lived in the city long enough to recognize the elaborate design as a gang symbol. This building had been tagged. By which gang, I wasn't sure. My suburban upbringing hadn't schooled me in the differences between gang logos.

Snapping a quick photo of the graffiti with my phone, I ducked around to the back of the building where the wooden porches sagged. I took another photo. Then I hustled back to my car, hoping nobody had noticed me. I drove a few blocks east and parked before pulling to the curb and writing down my notes. Jacqueline wouldn't want her client to get involved in a dangerous situation.

The next two properties were on the northwest side, and I was thankful to escape the unnerving energy of the first location. A few minutes later, I exited my car, approaching the second building on foot. From the street, all the buildings looked the same—drab brick six-flats or eight-flats with deteriorating roofs, unstable porches, and cracked bricks. Whether it looked like it or not, these dilapidated buildings would be a jackpot for someone, assuming the price was right.

When I saw it again, I gasped out loud as if someone had punched me in the stomach. The same neon purple and orange gang symbol that covered the side of the first building popped out from this building too. The paint was just as fresh. Did this gang target run-down buildings? I didn't know what to think. I snapped another photo and moved on to the next property.

The third property was the biggest dump of all. It was vacant. At least, I hoped it was. Someone had smashed the windows, and a thick layer of moss crept over the roof. I inched around the building, half expecting to find another gang symbol, but there was none. Even so, I couldn't imagine anyone paying a dollar for this crumbling pile of bricks. I jotted down some notes and drove south on I-94 toward the Hyde Park property.

My GPS guided me along the highway for several miles, and then to an exit on 63rd. Dollar stores and pawnshops gave way to chain restaurants, tree-lined streets, and well-kept townhomes. "Welcome to Hyde Park," read a sign a couple of blocks later. I loosened my grip on the steering wheel, admiring the green parks and stately buildings of the University of Chicago's campus as I passed.

I pulled to the side when I reached the last address on my list. It was a freestanding house divided into three units. The location was ideal, just blocks from campus and one street over from a sprawling nature area. No obvious violations were visible from the street, so I left my car, stretching out my cramped legs. In contrast to the previous properties, the shiny bricks on the building aligned perfectly. The black roof was intact and sparkled in the sunlight. The buzz of power tools screeched through the air. I followed the alley around the side and almost ran into a workman on a ladder. He sprayed the bricks with an industrial-strength power washer. I sucked in my breath when I saw it again, the familiar orange points of a star and three purple spikes of a pitchfork stretched above the newly clean bricks. The worker switched off the motor and looked at me. His shirt read, "Chicago Graffiti Blasters."

"Watch out, miss! I don't want to get this stuff on you."

I stepped back, sweat prickling over my skin. "Is that a gang symbol?"

"Yeah. Owner called it in yesterday. These thugs have been tagging like crazy."

"Do you know which gang it is?" Not that I knew the difference between gangs, but I thought it would be helpful information to pass along to Jacqueline.

"Latin Angels." He pointed toward the graffiti that he hadn't washed away yet. "That's the 'L' and 'A' on the sides of the crown."

"Okay. Thanks." I snapped a photo and hurried back to my car, ignoring the confused look on the man's face.

My hands shook with something between excitement and fear as I started the ignition and headed east toward Lake Shore Drive. I swerved into the next lane, accelerating around a slow-moving car, but couldn't escape the sharp angles and ominous swirls of the gang markings painted in my mind.

CHAPTER FOURTEEN

Crouched behind my desk at Greystone, I clicked on my search results for 'Latin Angels gang tags.' The neon image on my screen was a perfect match to the designs I'd seen on the sides of the buildings. My chest burst with the anticipation of sharing my tantalizing and dangerous findings with Jacqueline. Hopefully, my discovery would be enough to impress her.

The buzz of my phone drew my attention away from my research. It was Grace.

"Hey, Mara."

A pang of guilt jolted my stomach, but I did my best to ignore it.

"Hey."

"I talked to the lender. Guess how much I'm pre-approved for?"

"I don't know. Five million?"

"Ha, ha. Close. $260,000."

I placed my hand on my desk and steadied myself. "Great."

"Can I get a decent place for that?"

"Yeah. Of course. I'll send you some options this afternoon." My body felt so light I worried I might float off my chair.

"Cool."

"What neighborhoods do you like?"

"I don't know. Bucktown. Or River North. Lincoln Park. Not the West Loop. Too much concrete."

"Okay. Maybe we can go look at some places tomorrow after work." My knees bounced beneath my desk as I spoke. Grace was officially my client. I'd help her become a homeowner just like me.

"Thanks, chica."

"Sure thing." I clicked on the MLS icon on my laptop, a new real estate search covering the images of gang symbols. My mouth stretched into a smile as I ended the call. Grace was pulling through for me. Before my euphoria had time to transform back into guilt, Jacqueline swooped in behind me and sat at her desk.

"Ahh. I hate it when buyers can't make a simple decision." She pounded on her keyboard and slammed her laptop shut. "What do you think of this flier for the charity run?"

She slid a glossy piece of paper toward me, featuring a stock photo of people in brightly-colored shirts running. *Help Emma Beat Cancer—5K Charity Run, April 30th. 8 a.m., North Avenue Beach.* A link to a website stretched across the bottom.

"I set up a temporary website for the event. It accepts payment for registration fees and allows people to leave additional donations."

"Wow. That looks great." I ran my fingers over the shiny images, wondering why I hadn't thought of a charity run for Emma. "Can I have some to give out?" I asked. I wanted to send it to Emma immediately, so she could see that I was doing something to help. I hadn't failed her yet.

"Sure. I'll email you the file. I'm going to print out two hundred. I'll leave some in all of the Greystone mailboxes, and you can have the extras." Jacqueline straightened the papers on her desk. "Have you accomplished anything today?"

"Yeah. I drove by the buildings. I'm going to call in the violations in a few minutes." I leaned toward her, my pulse quickening. My fingers clenched the edge of my desk as I envisioned the orange and purple crown and pitchforks on the brick walls. "Three of the buildings were tagged by a gang. The

Latin Angels."

She cocked her head at me.

"The graffiti blaster guy told me, and then I googled it. He was right. He was removing the paint from the Hyde Park building."

"Gang tags, huh?" Jacqueline strummed her fingers on her desk. "Well, this might be good news. Enough to scare an owner into selling, don't you think?" She smiled.

I steadied myself, confused by her reaction. "But does your buyer want to buy buildings in gang-infested neighborhoods?"

Jacqueline shrugged. "Gangs are everywhere. My buyer is a long-term thinker. He'll hold the building until it's worth enough to sell. If that takes five years, ten years, so be it."

I sat still and listened. I'd never thought of it like that, but of course, it made sense.

"Anyway, make the calls to the building inspector. We'll give it a few days for the violations to get back to the owners, and then I'll call them with my guy's offer."

I nodded and pulled out my notes, along with the phone number of the building inspector, as Jacqueline packed up her laptop.

"I have a few more things you can do for me," she said.

"Okay."

"First, I have a stack of listings for you to input ASAP." She picked up a pile of folders and set them on my desk. "Tomorrow at 1:00 p.m., I need you to meet a painter at my condo and open the door for him. The renovations never end!" she said.

I remembered her stories of the many updates she was having done to her townhome to get rid of the 90's décor and restore its Victorian character. She handed me a key attached to a silver key ring. A small, round pendant dangled from the ring and pictured a cartoon cow with the words, '*On the moo-ve!*' encircling the cow's head. Her address was written on the backside of the medallion— *1934 N. Lincoln.*

My eyes lingered on the keychain, and I fought to stifle a laugh. I hoped she'd tell me about her cow obsession, but she only cleared her throat.

"Also, tonight is the CBR charity dinner at Germania Place. I'm a speaker. I bought an extra ticket for you so that you can sit at my table. It's good to get out there and be seen. I'll pick you up at 6:15 at your condo. Wear a dress." She looked me up and down. "Something classy."

"Okay. Thanks." I squeezed my pen as I envisioned the five dresses hanging in my closet and wondered whether any of them were classy enough for Jacqueline. Ideally, I would have liked more notice, but I didn't have any plans. And free dinner and drinks at Germania Place sounded good.

"Tomorrow morning, we're going to drive over to a potential new listing in the South Loop. Be here by 9:00 at the latest."

"Okay," I said, entering the appointments into my phone while she talked.

"On Sunday, I'll need you to host an open house for me in Old Irving from 1:00 to 3:00, but meet me here by 12:30."

"No problem." I bit back my smile. There was a windfall of potential commissions coming my way.

"I also emailed you a list of things to do by tomorrow." She rested a bony hip against her desk as she watched the front door. "My friend, Haley, is coming by to pick me up for lunch, but I'll be back later."

"Okay. Are you going to the 'Best Practices' meeting at 2:00?"

Jacqueline tipped her head forward, letting out an exaggerated sigh. Then she stepped closer and leaned toward me.

"Oh, Mara. Don't waste your time with all these stupid Greystone meetings. 'Best practices' are for people who can't think for themselves. Common sense is the best practice." She waved her hand toward the back of the office. "None of these people have any, so they need to create pointless meetings to make themselves feel useful." Jacqueline's eyes tightened on me like screws turning. "We're not like them."

I looked from the pile of files on my desk into her steely eyes and nodded. She was right. No point wasting my time.

"Oh, there she is." Jacqueline raised her arm in a wave as another woman about her age, but with curly dark hair and cheerful eyes strode through the door. The woman smiled as she bounded toward us, giving Jacqueline a quick hug when she arrived at our desks.

"Haley, this is my new assistant, Mara. Mara, this is Haley, my only friend from law school." Both women chuckled as Haley shook my hand.

"So, you're Peter's replacement?" Haley asked.

"Yeah."

Haley closed her eyes and grimaced. "I'm so glad you got rid of that guy, Jackie. I don't think I could stand hearing any more of your complaints."

Jacqueline eyed me. "Mara is shaping up to be a much better assistant."

I stretched up a little taller and tried not to blush.

Jacqueline flashed a curious look at Haley. "So, what's the big news?"

"You'll never guess what happened." Haley fluttered her eyelids and shook her head. She leaned toward us and whispered, "I'm pregnant." Her eyes were round as saucers, and a smile revealed itself in the corners of her mouth.

"What?" Jacqueline slapped her hands down on the desk. "Oh, my God! That's great!"

"Congratulations," I said, feeling like a third-wheel.

"It wasn't planned," Haley said, still whispering. "I mean, I have no idea how it happened because I was on the pill. I swear I never forgot to take it. Thankfully, Rob is on board. We're going to move in together."

"In your studio?" Jacqueline's eyebrows lifted.

I peered toward the marketing room, devising a way to remove myself from the private conversation. They continued talking as if I wasn't there.

"No. Could you imagine all three of us in a studio?" Haley laughed. "That's kind of why I wanted to meet with you. I need you to list my condo and help me and Rob find a bigger place. Maybe a little farther north or west. Something with two bedrooms." Haley glanced at me and then back to Jacqueline. "Rob keeps talking about a friend of his who can find us a place, but I told him we're using you. You've always been there for me, Jackie."

"I'd love to work with you again. We shouldn't have any problem selling your condo. It's such a great location." Jacqueline's mouth curved downward. "I'm sorry you didn't get to stay there longer."

"Yeah, but things happen for a reason. It's time I move on with my life."

"I'm happy for you."

"I'd love to start looking at places as soon as possible. Even tonight, if you're available."

"I can't do it tonight. I'm speaking at a charity dinner at Germania Place."

Haley rolled her eyes. "Look at you, big shot."

"I can meet on Saturday afternoon to list your studio. I'll bring some comps, and I'll set you up on an automatic search for a new property."

"Sounds perfect." She elbowed Jacqueline. "Hey, there's a new guy at the office. He's really cute. And single."

"Not interested," Jacqueline said.

Haley narrowed her eyes. "Jackie, you can't pine after Jeffery forever. He's an ocean away. So what if you go out on a couple of dates with someone else?"

"Look, I appreciate what you're trying to do, but I don't have time for a new relationship right now. I'm one hundred percent focused on work."

"That's probably not healthy. You should take a break once in a while. Our weekly lunch meetings don't count."

"I have a shot at becoming Top Producer this year. Of the whole city. Right, Mara?" Jacqueline glanced toward me.

"That's the plan," I said.

Jacqueline crossed her arms. "That's worth more than any guy to me."

"And no doubt you'll succeed," Haley said. "Your perfectionism is frustrating."

"I need to beat out Natalia Romanov first."

Haley shook her head. "I drive by her billboard downtown every day. Isn't she trying to sell that building on Michigan Avenue? It's a few doors down from my office."

"Natalia has lots of buildings for sale," Jacqueline said, staring straight ahead as she spoke.

Haley picked a speck of lint off her sweater. "I heard she might be starring in a new reality show on HGTV or Bravo, or something like that. At least, that's what one of the receptionists in my office said."

My teeth clamped down on the inside of my cheek. There was no way Jacqueline could compete with a realtor who had her own TV show.

I could tell by the way Jacqueline's mouth froze that this was the first she'd heard of Natalia's reality show. She rolled back her shoulders, making herself taller. "I don't know about any TV show, but, supposedly, Natalia has connections to the Russian mob."

Haley's eyes popped wide open. "The mob? Jackie, you better be careful. That's not something to mess around with."

"Really?" My heart thumped against my ribcage. I hadn't heard of Natalia's mob connections before.

Jacqueline stuck out her chin. "Don't worry. I'm simply going to sell more real estate than her. There's nothing the mob can do about that."

Haley placed a hand on her hip. "Just be careful. There are lots of sketchy people out there."

"Gee. Thanks for the warning, ambulance-chasing attorney." Jacqueline made a face as she slung her bag over her shoulder. "See you later, Mara. Haley and I are headed out for lunch."

"Have fun."

The two women walked side-by-side past the front desk, Jacqueline striding ahead to hold the door open for her pregnant friend, and the tension in my shoulders inexplicably easing with each step she took away from me.

CHAPTER FIFTEEN

I'd never been inside Germania Place before. The historic building carved from massive red boulders looked impenetrable as if it was hiding government secrets. Arched windows resembled giant, watchful eyes and cut into the stone at evenly spaced intervals. The inside was even more impressive. Dark wooden beams crisscrossed the lofted ceiling and chandeliers dangled from sculpted plaster medallions. It was the kind of room that made me forget to breathe. The guests gave off an aura of confidence possessed by people who swam in money. They showed off their tailored clothes and sparkling jewelry, their chins held high and laughter bellowing from their lungs a little too forcefully.

I'd taken advantage of the free vodka and tonics during cocktail hour. Now, enjoying the hazy afterglow of top-shelf alcohol, I'd settled into my assigned seat at a white-clothed table listening to Jacqueline give a speech about real estate and helping people. She knew her stuff about both of those subjects. She'd gone above and beyond in helping me, even by inviting me to this dinner. And I still couldn't get over the charity run she was planning for Emma. After what I'd been through in the last month, it was about time luck landed on my side. If it weren't for Jacqueline, I'd be slumped on the couch watching bad TV while Astro destroyed another piece of my furniture. Instead, I was basking under the glow of chandeliers in the grand ballroom at Germania Place, and I'd soon be representing Grace in the purchase of her new condo.

I shifted in my chair as my lungs pulled in a strained breath. The Spanx I wore beneath my cocktail dress squeezed against my midsection. My hand reached for the crystal water glass in front of me, my eyes avoiding the others at the table. *Fake it 'til you make it.* I'd heard that somewhere once. I took a sip.

My bare shoulder raised to push the spaghetti strap of my dress higher, but it slid back down. I twisted to the side, discreetly positioning my strapless bra in a more stable location. It had been months since I'd worn a dress, and despite the minor wardrobe issues, I felt sophisticated.

Jacqueline's voice descended across the airy room like an eagle swooping off a skyscraper. Her silky dress skimmed the long lines of her body, and I would have bet the remaining money in my bank account that she wasn't wearing any Spanx. She'd been speaking for at least fifteen minutes already, her speech wrapping up. Her gaze wandered from face to face, as she made eye contact with the most important players. The mayor was on display at the front table, next to the president of the Chicago Board of Realtors. The city's most successful realtors, developers, and their significant others filled most of the other tables. Jacqueline's voice projected as she connected the dots between helping people and selling real estate for the tipsy audience.

"I help people every day," she said. "After a divorce, I help a distraught spouse pick up the pieces and start fresh. I've had the honor of helping a young couple find the perfect starter home to begin their lives together. And my dream is to one day assist people who sit homeless on the streets tonight in purchasing their first homes. This can happen with the 'set aside' programs instituted by the city and with many developers building affordable housing."

I swallowed and glanced toward the windows, remembering the way Jacqueline had rebuffed Tony for sitting outside the office the other day. Maybe I'd misunderstood her. Maybe she'd only wanted to help him get off the streets.

Jacqueline's voice continued to soar through the room. "With all of us working together, we *can* make the American dream a reality, one house at a time. Thank you."

She exited the podium to a chorus of thunderous applause. Jacqueline's heels clicked on the wooden floor and echoed across the ballroom until she arrived back to the seat next to mine. On her other side sat Roger Burton, the owner of Burton Development, one of Chicago's largest development companies. Roger's wife, Lydia, sat in the seat to Jacqueline's right, separating Jacqueline and her husband.

I smiled at Jacqueline. "Good job!"

"Well done, Jacqueline," said Lydia, dipping her chin with approval.

Roger scowled and looked away, his cropped, dark hair mismatched with his salt-and-pepper goatee.

The MC announced there would be a break in the speeches until after dinner, when the headliners, Natalia Romanov, and the mayor, would take the podium. Jacqueline's face hardened at the mention of Natalia's name.

"I can never get over the exquisite architecture of this building." Lydia waved her hand toward one of the oversized arched windows that lined the room.

Jacqueline slid her napkin to the side. "This building has such an interesting history."

"It was built by German immigrants, wasn't it?" asked Lydia.

"A German singing society in 1888. The acoustics are better than in any modern concert hall."

"So much history in this city. Have you ever taken the architectural cruise down the Chicago River? Roger and I did that last summer. So fascinating."

Lydia and Jacqueline slipped into easy conversation after discovering their shared interest in Chicago's architecture. They discussed their favorite buildings and reminded each other of the stories behind them while I sat with a dumb smile.

Still, I was lucky to be by Jacqueline's side. I'd learned so much just by watching her. I never knew building inspectors existed, much less that violations could reduce a building's perceived value. Jacqueline made it look so easy—locate potential buildings, report the violations, wait a few days for the owners to receive news of the violations, and then contact the owners and tell them we have an interested buyer. There was no need for them to correct the defects. The buyer would take the problems off their hands. My head buzzed, light and fuzzy, just thinking about the simple brilliance of it.

Jacqueline reached inside her purse and huffed. She leaned toward me, the vanilla and citrus notes of her perfume sweetening the air.

"Mara, can you run out to my car and get my card holder for me? It's in the front seat console." She handed me the valet ticket.

"Yeah. Of course." I took the ticket out of her hand and slipped away from the table, grabbing my cardigan and trying not to twist my ankles in the three-inch heels I'd borrowed from Grace.

Down the hall, a red-vested valet leaned against a mahogany wall near the front door.

"I'm not leaving," I said, handing him the ticket. "I just need to get something out of the car."

"It's parked right out front." The valet passed me the keys and pointed down the street where the shadowy outline of the Mercedes reflected under the light of the streetlamps. It was parked between an Audi and a Tesla about halfway down the block.

"Thanks." Keys in hand, I wrapped my cardigan around me and entered the crisp night air. I placed my feet carefully as I descended the steps, then checked my surroundings before continuing down the sidewalk. My fingers fidgeted with the key fob as I approached the back of Jacqueline's car. With one last twirl around my index finger, the keys slipped from my grip. I snatched them from the mid-air, but fumbled, my senses dulled from too much alcohol. With a second effort, I saved the keys before they hit the ground but accidentally hit the bottom button on the key fob in the process.

A dull hiss of air escaped from the trunk of Jacqueline's car as it popped open. An object caught my eye through the sliver of an opening, a twinge of familiarity searing through me. It was a flash of neon orange I would have ignored, except I'd seen the exact same color this morning—three times on the sides of the buildings. Stepping forward, I swung the trunk door up higher, and a thousand pin picks rippled over my body. Under the spotlight of the streetlamp, an open cardboard box lay in plain sight with two cans of spray paint inside it. Orange and purple.

My mind spun, the lightness in my head snuffed out by the shadowy items lying before me. Was it a coincidence? Maybe Jacqueline was using the paint for some sort of project. It was ordinary spray paint anyone could buy at Home Depot. Hundreds, or even thousands, of people probably owned those identical colors for one reason or another. My mind struggled to explain it away, but my nausea swirled in a circle, rising higher. The odds of her having the same colors of paint in her car were too small to be a coincidence. The neon orange matched the shade of the six-pointed stars, and the bright purple matched the pitchforks. Drops of paint dripped down the sides of the white cans. They'd been used.

I thought back to my first meeting with Jacqueline, and the rats that had run through Bistro Maria. *Sometimes you have to make your own business.* That's what she'd said. Is this what she'd meant? A folding in my gut knew Jacqueline was behind the gang tags. And maybe the rats. I couldn't imagine her getting her hands dirty, though. She must have paid someone else to do it. Still, I couldn't accuse her of anything, especially after all she'd done for me: the leads, the draw, the charity run. I wouldn't betray her like that. She'd never said I could look in the trunk anyway. Her cards were in the front seat. I slammed the trunk closed.

My hand shook as I unlocked the door and opened the console. The silver cardholder lay exactly where she said it would be, and my fingers tightened around it.

I stumbled back toward the entrance to Germania Place, clutching the cardholder in my sweaty palm. What an idiot I'd been. So naive. Jacqueline had been right when she'd told me I still had so much to learn. Yet, I didn't know the whole story. I didn't have the facts. This was probably one of Jacqueline's "thinking outside the box" strategies. So maybe she took it a little too far. Things were going my way, and I wasn't going to mess it up over some stupid paint on the side of a few buildings. Dad had warned me not to quit another job. He'd instructed me to power through the roadblocks, even when things weren't going my way. I needed to stick with it. Otherwise, I'd lose my condo.

Without making eye contact, I handed the keys back to the valet. Then I made a beeline to the ladies' room, where I inhaled several times through my nose, blotted a damp towel on my forehead, reapplied my lipstick, and yanked up my strapless bra. Waiters and waitresses balancing plates of steak and roasted vegetables on enormous trays surrounded me as I left the safety of the bathroom and maneuvered back toward the table.

Jacqueline was deep in conversation with Lydia, but she glanced at me as I neared.

"Here you go." I set the cardholder above her silverware, suddenly thankful for the pressure of my Spanx against my seizing gut. We all had secrets. Jacqueline's was safe with me.

CHAPTER SIXTEEN

My eyelids weighed against my swollen eyes, my body suffering from a lack of sleep and coffee as I arrived at the office at 8:30. Jacqueline paced back and forth behind her desk listening to a stream of voice mails

"Ready to go?" she asked as soon as she saw me.

Her nervous energy pierced through my fog of exhaustion. I adjusted the strap of my bag on my shoulder, thankful I hadn't had anything more to drink at the charity dinner last night.

"Sure." My arms dropped to my sides. I wanted to sit for a minute, to drink a second cup of coffee, and get some showings scheduled for Grace, but I'd have to get to that later.

Jacqueline drove, as usual. She darted her Mercedes in and out of traffic, zooming through yellow lights, and narrowly avoiding pedestrians, while I tried not to envision the cans of spray paint rolling around in her trunk. Hopefully, she'd gotten rid of them.

We wound our way south, past downtown and under the massive billboard sponsored by the Chicago Board of Realtors. It loomed over I-94 at the entrance to the business loop. Natalia's gigantic airbrushed face smiled down on us from the sign, the writing below proclaiming, "Congratulations, Natalia Romonav, Chicago's Top Producer!" CBR swapped out the picture on the billboard every year, depending on who won the Top Producer Award. Natalia's face had been plastered on the sign for the last three years. It was the best advertising a realtor could have.

I studied Natalia's image as we drove past, calculating the number of people who saw that billboard every day. "Can you imagine how much business you'd get if your face was up there?"

Jacqueline glared at me, her grey eyes flecked with yellow. "My face *will* be up there."

My shoulders slunk back against the leather seat.

Jacqueline accelerated down the highway, while I kept my eyes trained out the window. She exited at the south end of the Loop and wound her way several blocks farther south. At last, she parked outside a brick three-flat. Converted loft buildings on either side dwarfed the three-story structure. Just beyond the loft buildings, traffic from I-94 whirred past.

"This is it." Her voice had returned to a conversational tone. "Here's the deal. I sold the first-floor unit to my client, Julia, about two years ago. Her boyfriend used to live here with her, but they broke up so now she's alone. It's a two-bedroom with a parking space out in back. Julia thinks there's a lot of crime in this neighborhood. She doesn't feel safe and is considering moving north, or to a bigger building with a doorman."

"Are we meeting her now?" My stomach squeezed into a knot. I was completely unprepared.

"No. She's not home, but she said we could look around to preview the place before we list it." Jacqueline fumbled through her purse. "Here are the keys. You can head inside. I need to return a phone call."

"Okay." I took the keys and opened the car door.

"Wait. One more thing," Jacqueline said. "There's a white metal box in the top drawer of her dresser. Bring that out to me when you come back. That's where she keeps her condo documents and extra keys. She told me to take it."

"Her top dresser drawer?" I asked, dread trickling through me at the thought of rummaging through the drawer of a stranger.

"Yep." Jacqueline pressed a button on her phone and looked

away, already on to the next event.

"Okay." I angled my reluctant face away from her. After following the walkway past a wrought-iron fence toward the front door, I jiggled the bigger key around in the door until it opened. A musty smell filled my mouth inside the cramped foyer. Another door marked "Unit 1" stood to my left. The smaller key fit the lock, and I turned the handle. The door creaked open.

"Hello?" I yelled, just in case the owner had decided to stay home. My skin tingled with nervous electricity. There was no answer.

I inched through the doorway where the living room opened up, surprisingly bright compared to the gloomy foyer. But a second later, the sour stench of old garbage smacked me in the face. My throat gagged as I shielded my nose with my hand and surveyed the condo. A pile of laundry lay heaped in the middle of the hardwood floor. Beyond the living room, a tall counter and three pendant lights separated the kitchen. I flipped on the lights above the countertop.

Despite the filth, the condo had the potential to show well with stainless steel appliances and granite counters. A stack of dirty dishes filled the sink. Trash spilled out of a plastic bag that sagged on the floor next to a garbage can. My own condo wasn't spotless by any stretch of the imagination, but Julia could have cleaned up a little before inviting us over.

Breathing in shallow breaths, I wandered down a narrow hallway, the heels of my shoes clacking against the wood floor. I poked my head into a home office. The over-sized desk, chair, and shelving unit filled every inch of the small space. Halfway down the hall, a slatted closet door sat open, revealing a stackable washer and dryer. The door next to the closet led to the master bedroom. The room was trashed. Covers were twisted in a heap on the bed. Clothes were pulled inside-out and strewn across the floor. I wove around the debris to check out the bathroom. Through the layer of towels and beauty products, I could barely make out a white counter featuring double-bowl sinks. Drops of water clung to the glass shower door.

It was a little too personal, and I turned on my heel to get out of there but paused, remembering the box. I stumbled back across the bedroom and around the bed to the dresser, pulling open the top drawer and trying to touch as little as possible. A pile of satin and lace panties stared up at me from inside the drawer. Even with permission, this was creepy—serial killer creepy. It was weird to sift through someone else's lingerie. My chest clenched, my annoyance with Jacqueline growing. She should have been the one doing this, not me. My hands rummaged through until they hit something hard and cold. My fingers latched around it, and I pulled it to the surface. It was a white metal box with a lock. I plunged my hand into the drawer again, sifting through underwear and bras for a key, but came up empty. If Jacqueline wanted the key, she'd have to come back for it herself. I pushed the drawer closed and bolted out of there, turning off the lights behind me.

Jacqueline watched from the car as I carried the box outside. I pulled open the car door and slid back into the safety of my passenger-side seat. I handed it over to her.

"You didn't tell me it was in her underwear drawer."

She shrugged.

"The box is locked," I said.

"That's okay. Julia gave me the key last time I met with her." Jacqueline dropped the box into her bag. "I'm going to run in and take a quick look. Stay here. I'll be right back."

I bit my lip and stared out the car window, irritated that she couldn't have come inside with me five minutes earlier. "The place is a mess, just to warn you."

Jacqueline laughed. "Not surprising, knowing Julia."

She drifted toward the front door and disappeared inside. A spindly tree sprouted up through a grate in the sidewalk next to me, drooping and out of place. Something about the sapling growing in the middle of a concrete jungle made my heart sink. The task of sucking in all the city air pollution would be too much for the plant's capabilities. I wondered if the tree would die, or if it would beat the odds and flourish. Maybe one day, years from now, I'd walk down this sidewalk and see the tree transformed into a massive oak, shading the sidewalk, shaking its leaves at all the doubters. I closed my eyes, craving sleep.

The door swung open, jarring me from my thoughts.

"All set. Let's go back to the office, and you can pull up some comps. I'll have to talk to Julia about cleaning up the place." Jacqueline shook her head in disgust.

"Do you think she's a hoarder?" I asked, only half-joking.

"I've seen worse." Jacqueline put her car in gear and peeled out into the street before stopping at a red light. She turned toward me. "You want to come over and hang out tonight? I was thinking of ordering pizza. We can drink some wine and talk shop."

My jaw froze. I was supposed to go to a networking event with Grace. Her boss was making her attend, and she'd insisted it would be a perfect place for me to find new clients. I hadn't committed yet, though. My fingers fidgeted against the seatbelt buckle.

"You can come over at seven. Just for an hour or so," Jacqueline said.

The light turned green, and she accelerated into the intersection. My hands slid to my sides.

"Sure. That sounds great."

"Good." Jacqueline's red lips curved upward. "1934 N. Lincoln. Don't be late."

CHAPTER SEVENTEEN

I winced, my ankle twisting as I climbed up the cement steps to 1934 N. Lincoln Ave. I caught myself, nearly dropping the bottle of Chardonnay pinned under my arm. The eighteen-dollar price tag was more than I'd normally spend on a bottle, but Jacqueline had good taste, and the guy at Binny's insisted it paired well with pizza, although by the flash of amusement in his eyes he might have been messing with me.

Jacqueline's mammoth front door loomed above me. Rotating my foot, I worked out the strain in my ankle and pressed the doorbell. A half-second later, the door swung open, and Jacqueline appeared wearing jeans and a grey sweatshirt that said Northwestern Law in purple lettering across the front. I'd never seen her so casual before, and I forced my lips into a smile to hide my surprise. I hadn't gotten the "jeans" memo and was still wearing my tight-waisted work pants and heeled sandals that caused my ankles to collapse without warning.

"Hi, Mara. Come on in."

I held out the bottle. "This is for you."

"Thank you." She took the bottle, eyeing the label, and waving me forward. I stepped into the foyer where hardwood floors gleamed beneath an oriental rug. Pale walls stretched up above our heads, only stopping when they reached a skylight a story above.

Jacqueline's socked feet shuffled in front of me, bypassing a narrow hallway to the right and wandering through a wide opening that led to a spacious and airy living room. The solid crown-molding, wrought iron light fixtures, and wide-planked floors accentuated the Victorian character of the home. An expensive-looking piece of modern artwork hung in a thick frame above her fireplace, the swirl of colors pulling together the grey and white colors of the room, along with pops of bright blue accents. It looked as if a home stager had positioned every piece of furniture and accessory.

Afraid to touch anything, I followed behind Jacqueline as she passed the living room and continued into an open-concept kitchen where the yeasty aroma of freshly-baked pizza surrounded us. She placed my wine on the counter next to the double-door refrigerator, its white-paneled front matching dozens of nearby cabinets. A massive kitchen island featured Carrara marble and a waterfall edge. An orange pizza box and a Greek salad lay on the island.

"Wow. Your house is beautiful."

"Thanks. It's a work-in-progress like I said."

"How long have you lived here?"

"Over two years. The previous owners destroyed its charm, so I've been restoring it. I couldn't pass up the location. I'm close to the lake and only a few blocks from the office. My architect redesigned the kitchen and living room into an open concept, and upstairs we reconfigured the master suite to add a walk-in closet and gutted the master bathroom. My designer, Anastasia, helped me chose finishes."

"Sounds like a project."

Jacqueline rubbed her temples and sighed. "You have no idea. During the renovations, my contractor discovered outdated plumbing. They had to dig out the basement floor. After living through that mess, it would have been stupid not to finish the lower level. That's how renovations always go, one project leading to another. I'll give you a tour after we eat."

"Great."

She shifted toward the food on the counter. "I already ordered the pizza. It's vegan cheese. I hope you don't mind."

I gritted my teeth and smiled. "Oh. Sure. It's fine."

"How about a glass of wine?" she asked. "Red or white?"

"White, please."

From a wine fridge built into the side of the island, she removed a bottle of Sauvignon Blanc with a French label glittering in gold words I couldn't pronounce. Uncorking it, she poured a tiny bit into her glass, swirled it, angled the golden liquid under her high-end light fixtures, then lowered the glass beneath her nose and inhaled. Finally, she took a sip.

"Mmm. That's good." She pursed her lips and poured wine into two glasses and pushed one toward me, raising the other one in a toast. "To the good life."

"To the good life," I repeated, before taking a sip. The smooth wine glided down my throat as my stomach sunk with the suspicion that her bottle cost way more than eighteen-dollars.

"Let's eat." Jacqueline pulled two plates from one of her cabinets and set them on the island before opening the pizza box and placing a slice on each plate. We spooned out the salad, Jacqueline drizzling a tiny stream of vinaigrette across a couple of her leaves of lettuce.

She slid out a stool for me, and we sat at the island, nibbling our pizza and crunching the salad.

"I've never tried vegan cheese before. It's pretty good," I said.

She rolled her eyes. "It's Jeffery's fault."

My muscles stiffened, remembering the photo on her desk.

"He was always trying to save the world." She took another bite of lettuce and swallowed. "He still is, I guess."

"He's in the Peace Corps?"

"Yep. He wanted to spend his life helping a bunch of malnourished kids on another continent, instead of staying here with me."

"I'm sure he's helping a lot of people."

"Yes. Sorry." She tucked a piece of hair behind her ear and set down her fork. "I get bitter sometimes. He's been gone almost a year now. I threw a big going away party for him. Right here." She motioned toward the living room. "It was an African safari theme. So much work." Jacqueline shook her head. "I had to hire a whole cleaning crew to clean up the construction dust, not to mention a caterer and a bartender. A part of me thought once he saw how much trouble I went to, he'd change his mind and stay, but he was so driven to help others."

"I've heard long-distance relationships are tough, but I'm sure he won't stay there forever."

Jacqueline flicked her hand in the air. "Who knows? Anyway, he's the one who made me watch the documentary about dairy cows. I've never been the same."

"Oh." I bit into the slice of crust, not wanting to hear anymore.

"The screams of the mother cows as their babies are taken away from them..." Jacqueline closed her eyes and pressed her fingertips into her temples. "It's just horrible. I'll never be able to erase it from my mind."

I stopped chewing and shifted in my seat. "I had no idea."

"The funny thing is that my mother wouldn't have cared if someone had stolen me from her, not the way those cows did. She probably would have been relieved to have been saved from hundreds of thousands of dollars on private schools and nannies, saved from a lifetime of disappointments."

I lowered my fork, remembering how Jacqueline's mom had refused to come to the door of their Lincoln Park mansion for her. Suddenly, Jacqueline's soy lattes, vegan pizzas, whimsical keychains, and daily runs past Ellie made sense. She envied the love of the mother cows for their babies.

I sipped my wine, not sure what to say. "Moms can be difficult."

Jacqueline grunted. "So fucked up."

"Do you have any plans to see Jeffery soon?"

Her eyes flickered as if I'd knocked her from her daydream. "I'm thinking of flying to Africa after the new year to surprise him."

"That's a great idea."

She tapped a fingernail against her wine glass. "Maybe. Maybe not. It might be for the best if we go our separate ways. For good. Our relationship interfered with my work. I need to stay focused, especially if I want to outsell Natalia this year."

"Yeah. I just broke up with my boyfriend." I sat back, the words escaping my mouth before I realized I'd spoken them.

Jacqueline raised an eyebrow at me.

"It happened right before I started working for you. It's probably for the best, like you said." My eyes focused on a Greek olive, hoping Jacqueline couldn't detect my wavering emotions when it came to Nate. I hated that my heartbeat sped up whenever I thought of him, which was frequently.

A smile stretched across Jacqueline's face. "Who needs them? To strong, successful women!" She raised her glass, and I clinked mine against it.

"I'll drink to that."

We continued the meal perched on our bar stools and discussing Jacqueline's new listings.

"Real estate is an emotional business, Mara. Your friends and neighbors will screw you over without a second thought, but you have to be strong."

Nothing like that had happened to me, but I nodded anyway.

Jacqueline's eyes swirled with a strange combination of joy and rage. "Nothing kills a realtor more than losing out on a listing in her own building."

She was right. A few days earlier, I'd received a postcard advertising a condo for sale in my building listed by another realtor. The announcement felt like a punch in the stomach.

"Last year, my next-door neighbor listed his townhome with another company." Jacqueline shook her head. "This was after I'd watered his plants for him for three weeks while he vacationed in the Bahamas. Can you believe the nerve?"

"That's crazy."

"Don't worry. I got the listing in the end. The other realtor couldn't overcome the dog problem."

"What's the dog problem?"

Jacqueline smiled. "Whenever I saw anyone showing the property, I pointed my speakers at our common wall and blasted a recording of barking dogs. No one wants to live next door to barking dogs. His place sat on the market for three months."

"Oh." I swallowed back the lump in my throat. "Wasn't your neighbor mad?"

"He didn't know it was me. He was never home during the showings. Besides, I don't even have any dogs." She raised her palms in the air and shrugged. "When he finally listed with me, I sold his place in five days for over asking. He recommended me to everyone he knew."

"Wow." I pushed my plate a few inches away, realizing I was full.

Jacqueline hopped down from her stool.

"Be right back. Then I'll give you the complete tour. You have to see the renovations to the lower level," she said. "My architect added a bar and extra sitting area for parties."

My eyes darted sideways as I wondered how many parties Jacqueline hosted. She didn't have many friends outside of Haley, who she occasionally met for lunch.

"Sounds like you're almost finished with the renovations."

"That's what I thought, too, but I realized a few days ago that I should have added a bathroom on the lower level. I've been kicking myself for ignoring my architect's suggestion. A bathroom on each floor is the most practical design. And it will increase the resale value when the time comes. Not that I'm planning on selling anytime soon."

"Yeah. I'm sure you'll want to stay there for a while after all the work you've put in."

"You got that right. I'll be back in a second." She turned down the hall toward the powder room.

"Okay." I stood to clear the plates, noticing pizza sauce and crumbs splattered on the counter in front of where I'd been sitting. In contrast, the countertop in front of Jacqueline's seat gleamed as if it had just been polished. A roll of paper towel rested on the far side of the kitchen next to Jacqueline's Gucci purse, and I headed toward it, anxious to clean up my mess before she returned. As I reached to rip off a couple of squares, my elbow bumped her bag, tipping it toward the edge of the counter. The contents spilled across the floor.

I swung my head over my shoulder, heat prickling through me, and my heart racing. It was just like me to make a bad situation worse. Crouching down, I gathered up two tubes of lipstick, three quarters, the all-too-recognizable key fob to Jacqueline's car, and a bottle of natural herbs. *St. John's Wort.* The name was familiar because I'd taken the same herb to treat my anxiety and depression during my freshman year of college. Maybe Jacqueline's rocky relationships with Jeffery and her mom were taking a bigger toll on her than she let on. My heart seized for her. The herb had helped me back then, and I hoped it would give Jacqueline a boost, too.

A toilet flushed from the down the hall, and I rolled my shoulders back, remembering what I'd been doing. I scooped the recovered items back into the purse then ripped off the paper towel. The pizza weighed in my stomach as I gathered a pile of crumbs. Jacqueline appeared behind me, hands on her hips.

"Looks like you made a mess."

CHAPTER EIGHTEEN

It had been almost two weeks since I'd reported the damage to the rundown buildings to the building inspector. Jacqueline said enough time had passed to contact the slumlord owners. The violations should have made their way back to them by now.

"There's a script to follow for this type of call," Jacqueline said, speaking in a low whisper so the agents walking past our desks couldn't hear. "Listen and learn."

I pulled my chair over to her, twisting the beaded bracelet around my wrist. She pressed the numbers on her phone and waited.

"Hello, Mr. Bakersfield. This is Jacqueline Hendersen from Greystone Realty. I understand you're the owner of the building on the corner of Schubert and Ridgeway. I have a buyer who is interested in purchasing your building for cash."

Muffled mumbling sputtered from Jacqueline's phone, but I couldn't make out what the man was saying.

"The property appears to need quite a bit of work. The porch is sagging, and most of the bricks are cracked. And we noticed gang tags on the side of the building a few weeks ago." Jacqueline made a horrified face.

Images of the gang tags and the matching cans of spray paint in

Jacqueline's trunk hovered before me. My insides wobbled like an unstable building, but I pressed my lips together, determined not to let it show.

"If you're interested in having my buyer take the building off your hands, he's willing to offer $700,000."

More mumbling.

"Well, let me know after you think about it. I'll get it in writing and send it over to you for your consideration."

The next three calls went about the same. No one committed on the phone. Jacqueline said that it was normal, that people wanted to get the offer in writing and run it by their attorneys. She positioned herself in front of me, a silver necklace adorned with a diamond-encrusted key dangling into the V of her neckline.

"Once we email the contract to them, it's like waving bloody flesh in front of a swarm of sharks. There's always a few bites."

"Will you get both sides of the commission?" I asked.

Jacqueline raised an eyebrow. "I don't see any other realtors here, do you?"

My fingers clutched the edge of my chair. "Just me."

"You'll get your twenty percent," Jacqueline said, her eyes glinting.

I wheeled my chair back to my desk, not bothering to hide the stupid grin plastered to my face.

I helped Jacqueline fill out the contracts. She showed me which clauses to cross out and which boxes to check. She filled in her name in both the Seller's Agent and Buyer's Agent spaces on all four contracts and attached the Dual Representation Rider to ensure she'd receive the full five percent commission on each deal. Jacqueline clicked the button on her pen.

"My cash buyer, Don Garrett, is stopping by the office at 6:30 tonight to sign the contracts. Then I'll email the written offers to the owners."

The next morning, I sat in the same spot at my desk as Jacqueline informed me that two of the four building owners took the bait, eager to get their violation-ridden, gang-tagged buildings off their hands.

"The other two owners told me to go screw myself." Jacqueline shook her head and chuckled. "Two outta four ain't bad."

I coughed out a laugh and leaned into my chair. "Do you know how much money you're going to make off of this?"

"Yes." Jacqueline twisted her lips to the side and stared at the ceiling. "Approximately $88,000 after the house takes their cut."

My mouth fell open.

"I guess it will be less after I pay you twenty percent. You'll clear about $10,000."

I tipped my head back, letting my ponytail reach down my back. "Yes!" I'd be able to pay back the draw and make my next mortgage payment with money left over.

"You didn't think I was going to screw you over, did you?" Jacqueline stared at me, wide-eyed. "You're the one who drove by the buildings and called in the violations."

"This is so amazingly awesome."

"Of course, we should never count our commissions before they hatch." A shadow passed over her face, and I turned away.

A few minutes later, Jacqueline wheeled her chair over to my desk. "Let me tell you about Don." A hint of a smile crept onto her mouth. "He's one of my top investors. I met him at a networking event a few months after I started at Greystone. We even dated for a while, but it didn't last. Outside of real estate, the guy was dumber than a two-by-four."

"Ha."

"Anyway, one night over martinis, he asked me this question. He said, 'Do you know the fastest way to increase the value of a residential building?'"

I shook my head at her. "How?"

"'Add a unit. Or two,' he said. Then he smiled his crooked, yellow teeth at me."

"You can't just decide to add units. Don't you need permits?" I crossed my arms in front of me but wanted to learn more.

"That's what I thought, too. Don reminded me that the Chicago Water Department holds the oldest records on every property in the city. All you need is for them to change the number of units in the building."

I leaned forward, intrigued.

Jacqueline narrowed her eyes at me. "Guess who has a connection in the water department?"

My back pressed into the cushiony chair, my lips parting in awe. "Don?"

Jacqueline's pupils flickered. "After that, I brought him a steady stream of "undesirable" buildings, to which he promptly added a minimum of two residential units and resold for enormous profits. I collected the commissions on both ends and didn't ask too many questions. His trick was simple and brilliant. I wasn't doing anything wrong by selling the buildings for him, and his use of city connections wasn't hurting anyone. Besides, whatever Don did on his own time was none of my business."

I ran my fingers through my ponytail as a warning bristled down my spine. My intuition told me Don's actions were illegal. Then again, I didn't want to ruin my opportunity to earn a $10,000 referral fee. He wasn't hurting anyone. And like Jacqueline said, whatever Don did on his own time was none of our business.

An hour later, my stomach turned over with hunger. Jacqueline had left to follow up with a potential client, so I decided to make a run back to my condo for a quick lunch. After I collected the $10,000 windfall, I'd be able to eat out more often, but for now, I'd salvage whatever I could from my fridge at home. Packing up my things, I wandered toward the front door, waving to the receptionist, Valerie, on the way out. A layer of clouds hung low in the sky, making it feel like dusk, rather than early afternoon. Traffic zoomed and lurched down North Avenue as a jogger narrowly collided with me on the sidewalk. The corner where Tony usually hung out sat quiet and vacant, the cement sidewalk littered with cigarette butts and a tattered fast-food wrapper. I wondered where he'd set up shop today. I turned left down the neighborhood street where I'd parked.

As I approached my car, a shadow slipped behind a tree beside me. My gut trembled, the cold sweat erupting across my forehead causing me to stop short. Something wasn't right. I glanced back towards Tony's spot, but of course, he wasn't there. Before I could turn around, a towering figure lunged in front of me, a bony hand tightening around my arm. Peter blocked my path, his sunken eyeballs bulging and crazed.

"Mara, please. Listen."

I yanked my arm away, searching the tree-lined street for someone to help me. I debated shoving past him and making a run for my driver's side door. I could lock him out and speed away. Before I had a chance, he grabbed my other arm, his grip pinning me in place. With his free hand, he pulled something out of his pocket and flicked it open. The metallic blade of a jackknife hovered inches from my stomach. He stepped closer, his wrinkled shirt pressing against my new blouse.

"I'm sorry to do this, but I need you to listen. Jacqueline will ruin your life, just like she ruined mine."

Peter's voice was gravelly and desperate, and I wondered when he'd last had a drink of water, much less a meal. His unwashed hair stuck in thinning clumps to his head. I froze, terrified to be at the mercy of a drug addict whose actions could be violent and unpredictable. For a second, I felt sorry for him, but then his fingers squeezed tighter, and my eyes caught a glint of the blade. Fear vibrated through me.

Peter's mouth pushed close to my ear. "She's evil."

I'd come to realize Jacqueline wasn't perfect. Visions of spray-painted gang symbols, altered water records, and maybe even strategically released rats scurried through my mind. Maybe she bent the rules to help further her business, but what successful businessperson didn't push the boundaries of the law? To label Jacqueline as evil was a stretch, especially after everything she'd taught me.

Peter's mouth quivered. "No one else will hire me."

I swallowed, every muscle in my body ready to run. "I'm sorry, Peter. Take my purse. Please. Let me go."

"I don't want your purse. I need you to listen to me." Peter's breath was sour against my face. "Promise me you'll stay away from Jacqueline. She's not who you think she is. She'll make you do bad things."

I strained against him. "You're wrong."

"Think about it, Mara. The reasons people sell their properties. It's because bad things happened to them. Divorces, job losses, unexpected illnesses, death." His eyeball bulged. "She's behind it all."

"People move for good reasons, too," I said, my voice barely above a whisper.

He grimaced and shook his head, the blade edging closer to my abdomen. A garbage truck lurched past. There might have been a shred of truth in Peter's words, but he was taking his accusations way too far. He'd gone off the deep end. I fought the urge to scream for help. It was too risky.

"She's not going to give you your job back," I said.

Peter let out a clipped laugh. "I don't want my job back. That job was the worst thing that ever happened to me. I'm trying to save you. From her."

All at once, I realized that he only wanted me to agree with him. That was the quickest and safest way out of the situation. Then I could run back to the office and call Jacqueline and the police. I nodded. "Alright. I'll leave. I'm sure I can find another position."

"Promise me. Do it today."

"I promise."

Peter's jaw tightened. "And don't tell her you talked to me. Not a single mention of my name."

"I won't."

The grip on my arm loosened, and Peter stepped back, his features relaxing. Looking over his shoulder, he closed the jackknife and shoved it into his pocket, gave me a nod, and jogged away. I exhaled, shocked that he'd required nothing more than my word. As soon as he was out of sight, I bolted back to Greystone, where I tumbled through the front door and burst into tears, recounting my life-threatening experience to Valerie between sobs. Valerie draped her arm around me and called 911. As we waited for the police to arrive, I finally caught my breath and drank a glass of water. Then I called Jacqueline and told her everything.

CHAPTER NINETEEN

Two uniformed police officers arrived at Greystone within twenty minutes of Valerie's 911 call, but Jacqueline had beat them there, her presence calming and reassuring. First, she helped me fill out the police report and answer questions about Peter.

A few hours later, the police located Peter at his home and arrested him for assault and battery. Jacqueline hovered over my desk when we'd heard the news, a grim look on her face.

"Don't let your guard down," she said. "Our legal system is screwed up. They'll release him in a day or two."

My pulse accelerated, my stomach tightening at the memory of Peter's knife hovering millimeters from my skin.

Jacqueline patted my shoulder. "Don't worry. I'm going to call in a favor to a friend at my former law firm. He's in the criminal law division. I'll have him file a protective order for workplace harassment. It will keep Peter away from us, whether or not he's in jail."

"Okay. That's a good idea." I inhaled, wiping my palms against my thighs. "What do I need to do?"

"Nothing, right now. You might have to sign a statement in a day or two, but I'll handle the rest." Jacqueline strode back toward her desk, her tall shadow passing over me.

"Thanks for your help." I planted my feet into the floor, feeling more secure already.

****

The morning of Emma's charity run arrived two days later. I adjusted the elastic waistband of my new running pants and vowed to only focus on positive thoughts. A run along the lake to help my sister would be the perfect remedy for my shaken nerves.

It was 7:45 a.m., and the spring chill in the air caused the waiting runners to jump and bounce in place as they pulled their new T-shirts over their running gear. Jacqueline stood behind the table, checking the names of pre-registered runners off her list and handing out shirts.

She waved me over and handed me a shirt. "Good morning, Mara!"

My teeth clenched as I read the white lettering across the royal blue background: *First Annual 5K Charity Run—JACQUELINE HENDERSEN—The Realtor Chicago Trusts!—www.JacquelineHendersen.com.* I stared at it, taking it in. I'd expected the T-shirt to be more like the temporary website Jacqueline had set up for the event, with Emma's name appearing somewhere, or the mention of Non-Hodgkin's Lymphoma, or the fact that this was a fundraiser and not an advertisement for Jacqueline's real estate services. I envisioned the shirts being in more of a cancer-fighting color, like pink, instead of Greystone's blue and white.

"What do you think? Perfect, right?" Jacqueline flashed a broad smile as I studied the shirt.

"Oh, yeah. It's great," I said, biting my lip but remembering the $10,000 already raised from the entry fees and donations.

Jacqueline held up a blue water bottle with her website printed in capital letters across the front. "And everyone who finishes gets a free water bottle."

"Okay." I looked down to mask the disappointment in my eyes.

"One-hundred and sixty-two people have registered. About half have checked in so far." She waved me off. "I'll do this. You go mingle."

Mingle? I wondered at her choice of words.

Grace approached from behind a cluster of people, her glossy ponytail fluttering in the wind, and Astro pulling her toward the beach.

"Thanks for doing this," I said as I reached down to pat Astro on the head. He sniffed my hand, followed by a slimy lick.

"Of course. Running is the worst, but Astro can pull me when I get tired." Grace jiggled the leash and smiled.

I snaked through a crowd of people to where my parents and Emma sat on folding chairs. They'd come to watch the event and show their appreciation. Emma had undergone another round of chemo since I'd last seen her, and I decided it was better not to mention the ordeal with Peter to my family. They didn't need to worry about anything else.

Emma's body was collapsing in upon itself. She wore a pink knitted hat pulled down over her ears. Her heavy clothing couldn't conceal the thin arms she crossed in front of her chest. I walked up next to her and squeezed her shoulder, feeling the points of her bones through the coat.

"Looks like a good turnout. We're expecting over one hundred and sixty runners." I surveyed the crowd, which continued to grow. Some of Emma's friends had made the trek from the suburbs and were picking up their T-shirts from the registration table. Others, who I didn't recognize, gathered in small groups talking and stretching. Many of Greystone's realtors were milling around, including a few of the Real Housewives. Even Kevin Lucas was there. They all wore the blue T-shirts, at least, everyone except Kevin, who balled the shirt in his hand.

Emma turned to me and smiled. "Thanks, Mara. This is amazing."

"It was Jacqueline's idea."

"She seems nice. I'm glad you're working for someone cool."

"Next year, you'll be running in this." My hand squeezed Emma's bony shoulder. "To help someone else."

"Yeah," Emma said, but her voice was thin as if she didn't really believe it. Looking at her twig of a body, I wasn't sure if I believed it either. The chemo looked like it was doing more damage to her than cancer ever did.

"This will be a big help," Mom said. "Tell Jacqueline again how much we appreciate it."

"Yep. I will."

Dad tapped me on the shoulder and motioned for me to step away with him. I followed him to an open area behind a cluster of trees. He cleared his throat and leaned in close. "How much do you think you'll raise?"

"I don't know the exact amount. Jacqueline said we've raised close to $10,000." I noticed the wrinkles on his forehead. "How much do you need?"

Silence loomed for several seconds as I registered Dad's concern. He'd never been one to share his financial problems with me.

"We're in over forty K now." Dad inhaled. "Not sure what our next step is…"

"Forty thousand?" I asked, wondering if I'd heard the number right. "Even with the Go Fund Me account?"

"Yes."

My legs felt as if they might give out. I stared out at the lake, comprehending the situation. My Dad's subpar insurance policy wasn't getting it done. My parents desperately needed the ten thousand dollars from this event. Jacqueline's self-promotion was tacky—at best—but I wouldn't complain about any of it.

"What about the equity line?" I asked.

"We've gone through it. We had to draw on it a few times over the years when I was in between jobs. And now, with all the bills. We might have to sell the house…" Dad's voice dissolved, his eyes darting toward the lake.

"What? No!" A jolt of panic turned my stomach. I pictured our dated, split-level home with its brick and vinyl exterior. It had looked pretty much the same for as far back as I could remember, nondescript to someone just passing by, but filled with a lifetime of memories for Emma and me and my parents. We couldn't lose it. "That doesn't make any sense. You guys need someplace to live."

The horn sounded, and everyone turned toward the registration table. I touched Dad on the arm.

"We'll figure it out."

His eyelids sagged, but he nodded. I followed him back to where Mom and Emma sat several yards away.

Jacqueline held a megaphone up to her mouth. "Thank you, everyone, for coming out this morning. The run will begin in five minutes, but first, I'd like to tell you how much we appreciate you being here for Emma Butler, who is my assistant, Mara Butler's sister." Jacqueline pointed toward us. "Emma is going to win her battle with cancer, thanks to all of you!"

Cheers, applause, and whistles rang out from all around.

Emma held up her hand and waved at the crowd. "Thank you," she said, although I could barely hear her.

"We'll meet you back here at the end of the run, where you can pick up your free water bottle! Good luck!"

People lined up. I said goodbye to my family and made my way over to Jacqueline, who stood on one leg while stretching her other leg behind her.

"Ready?" she asked me.

"Yeah," I said, despite being unprepared for the run. I held my foot behind me, copying Jacqueline's stretch. My balance dissolved, and I toppled sideways. Finding my feet, I closed my eyes and inhaled the cold, damp lakeside air. It was only a 5K, but I hadn't trained for it at all, not like Jacqueline, who ran twice as far every single morning. I lined up next to her, tugging the too-large T-shirt over my head.

A horn blared behind us, and everyone took off, some faster than others. Grace jogged to the right of me, struggling against Astro's leash as the dog barreled toward a stray seagull. Jacqueline ran on my left in an even, steady stride. As Grace lapsed behind, Jacqueline and I fell into step with each other.

She ran like a practiced professional. Her blonde ponytail swayed rhythmically in the wind, and her eyes stayed trained ahead. I bobbled along, powering through my breathlessness while she sprung higher in the air with each step.

"You can go on ahead," I told her about five minutes into the run when a cramp stabbed at my side.

"No way. We're in this together. We're a team." She wasn't out of breath at all. She slowed her pace to match mine. We continued along the route, Jacqueline easily finding her stride while I pretended the searing pain in my abdomen wasn't bothering me. I focused on putting one foot in front of the other as we dodged the Sunday morning bikers and runners traveling toward us. Once in a while, we'd pass people we knew.

"Hi, Missy. Hi, Rita," Jacqueline said as we jogged around a couple of the Real Housewives who were now power walking.

"Thanks for coming," I managed to spit out in between breaths.

I wished Jacqueline would separate from me, so I could walk for a minute and catch my breath, so I could shake away the image of the 'For Sale' sign in front of my childhood home. But Jacqueline stuck by my side, oblivious to my agony.

At last, we reached the halfway mark and turned back toward our starting point. Maybe it was because the wind was at my back, but my muscles loosened, and the run felt easier. I picked up the pace. Jacqueline nodded at me and matched my speed. As I found my stride, I started to enjoy the experience—the spring breeze brushing against my skin, the soothing rhythm of the waves crashing against the shoreline, the fresh smell of the water. Lake Michigan seemed to stretch on forever. I focused on my breathing. The route was a temporary escape from the claustrophobia of the city. Suddenly, I understood the appeal of Jacqueline's morning runs.

As we passed a stretch of beach, a memory of a different beach many miles away and several years earlier played in my head. It had been spring break. I was fifteen, Emma seven. We took a rare family vacation to Florida where Mom and Dad had rented a tired, one-bedroom condo a block from the ocean.

On the first morning, Emma's squeals and laughter had woken me up as she ripped open the dusty curtains in the living room of the condo. The weather report was perfect—82 degrees and sunny. We filled oversized beach bags with snacks, sunscreen, and toys and headed to the public beach, Dad dragging a cooler of lunches and drinks behind him and Emma skipping ahead in her rainbow bathing suit unable to contain her excitement. We arrived ahead of the crowd and staked out a spot on a prime section of sand, not too far from the water.

Emma and I raced toward the ocean, dipping our toes into the freezing surf. I pretended to push her into the water, and she shrieked before running back to the safety of land. Then, camped out on my towel, the sun warmed my back like a blanket.

"Let's build a sandcastle," Emma said a few minutes later, jumping up and down.

I was too old to build sandcastles, but I did it anyway, happy to use Emma as an excuse. Over and over, my sister raced between the ocean and our sand mountain, her bucket brimming with ocean water before she dumped it into the mote. The water sat for a second before disappearing into the ground.

"Better get more water." Piling the sand higher and higher, I smirked and wondered when she'd realize the water wouldn't stay. Emma never gave up. She was the opposite of me, a ball of positive energy. She kept running back and forth, filling the mote, determined.

"Maybe one more," she said, breathless. Mom looked up from her novel and chuckled.

Jacqueline coughed, and my head jerked toward her. I did a doubletake at the North Avenue beach, which sat in the distance, the downtown high rises poking into the sky on the other side of Lake Shore Drive. The second half of the run had gone by fast. Emma, my parents, and a small crowd of onlookers waited beyond a red and white "Finish Line" banner. Cheers rang out as we approached. A few runners who had already completed the race loitered nearby drinking Dixie cups of water. I glanced at Jacqueline, envisioning us crossing the finish line together, a team.

When we were a few hundred feet from the finish, Jacqueline pushed out her chest, focused straight ahead, and bolted ahead of me in a burst of unexpected speed.

"Go, Jacqueline!" someone yelled. The crowd cheered.

I stretched my feet out farther to match her stride, but it was too late. She raised her arms in the air like an Olympic gold medalist and crossed the finish line without me. With my side aching and my sense of accomplishment deflated, my pace slowed to something between a walk and a jog.

"Yeah, Mara!" A woman yelled. The banner rippled in the wind.

The applause continued. My breath ripped through my lungs. I pushed through the shock and agony and stumbled across the finish line a few seconds behind Jacqueline.

She stood with a hand on her hip and shoved a Dixie cup filled with water toward me. "You did it."

I stared at my feet. My shoulders heaved as hunched forward, resting my hands on my knees. "I thought we were going to cross the finish line together."

She shrugged. "Sorry. I guess I got carried away."

Emma and my parents pressed toward us through the crowd.

I raised my shoulders, drawing strength from the cheering voices nearby. "At least the run was a success," I said between labored breaths.

Jacqueline grinned. "Definitely." She scanned the beach and then leaned toward me. "I don't see Natalia Romanov hosting any charity runs. Do you?"

CHAPTER TWENTY

My toes curled inside my heeled shoes, and my knees jiggled under the closing table in the windowless conference room at Title One. Grace sat next to me, signing page after page of documents. She looked like a celebrity in her trendy horn-rimmed glasses, and a pink scarf looped around her neck. Between each signature, she pressed the tips of her fingers into her forehead.

"This is a workout." She seemed to be only half-joking as she glanced from me to the attorney.

I needed her to sign everything, to work her way to the bottom of that pile. Make it official. My first commission check waited on the printer.

I'd only shown Grace four condos. It took one hour. She loved all of them, but she ended up putting in an offer on the one across from the dog park in River North.

"Astro will love this," she said as we stood on the balcony watching the dogs sniff each other and race after muddy tennis balls. "I bet this is a great place to meet guys, too."

"There's a doggy daycare right down the street." I handed her the coupons I'd snagged from the front counter.

Grace was painfully predictable. I probably should have insisted that she look at some more places, but I knew her too well. I didn't want to mess up the deal. *Never argue with a yes.* That's what Jacqueline always said.

It had been forty-two days since I presented Grace with the fake letter from my condo board. The sour taste of guilt occasionally rose in my throat over the method I'd chosen to push out my roommate, Peter's warnings edging their way into my head from time to time. *She'll make you do bad things.*

I shook his words away. No one had made me do anything. Besides, everyone would be better off this way. Even Astro. Despite her painstakingly slow signatures at the closing table, Grace was excited to become a property owner.

My commission wouldn't be much after Greystone took its fifty percent cut, but it could supply my next mortgage payment and pay down my credit card. I wanted to pay back some of the draw from Jacqueline and my building's ridiculous special assessment, but that would have to come from another deal. Today was the first drop in the bucket. Losing my job at Averly Consulting was the best thing that had ever happened to me. I was right, and Nate was wrong. I was going to be successful in real estate.

There were a few other deals in the works, too. Grace had already referred one of her co-workers to me. The others were referral fees from Jacqueline, but they would be good-size checks. As long as I stuck with her, deals were finding me. I was already on track to make more in my first six months at Greystone than my entire salary last year.

"And here we have a check for Greystone Realty." The portly woman handed me the check at last.

After pinning the check inside my folder, I passed Grace two sets of keys to her new condo.

"Thanks, Mara." She stood, grinning.

"You're welcome and congratulations."

I extended my hand to shake hers. Instead, she wrapped her arms around me in a hug so tight I couldn't breathe.

****

Jacqueline strode down North Avenue, yelling into her phone at an attorney. I shuffled after her, enjoying the heat of the sun on my face. I'd just turned in my first commission check to the accounting department, and Jacqueline insisted on treating me to a coffee at Starbuck's.

I appreciated everything she was doing for me, but she made a better mentor than a friend. She could be moody, for one. Some of her methods were questionable. But this was big-city real estate. And it wasn't like she was hurting anyone. It was annoying that she'd commercialized Emma's charity run, but the event had raised some much-needed funds. The fake gang symbols were more troubling, but the graffiti blasters removed everything within days, or hours even. Her investor would have bought those buildings anyway. She wasn't evil like Kevin and Peter had wanted me to believe. She was only pushing things along a little faster, making things happen. Kind of like I'd done with Grace. And that guy from her story who owned a window repair business.

Tony threw his hand in the air as we rounded the corner toward Starbucks.

"Hey, Mara. Beautiful day. Beautiful day."

"Hi, Tony." I dug into my purse and pulled out a five-dollar bill.

"Thank you. Thank you." Tony nodded at me as he slipped the bill in his pocket.

Jacqueline disappeared behind the glass door before it slammed in my face.

I pulled the door open, and it took a second for my eyes to adjust to Starbuck's dim interior.

"You shouldn't give money to those people," she said under her breath. "He's just going to spend it on alcohol."

I tilted my head, remembering her "helping people" speech at Germania Place. I shrugged, not wanting to argue with her. Tony seemed like a decent human being whose life had gone off track. Giving the guy a few bucks a couple of times a week was the least I could do. The way he repeated everything twice made me smile.

Jacqueline ordered her soy latte and pushed me toward the counter. I ordered a chai, and we drifted toward a tall, round table near the window.

"Congrats!" She raised her coffee cup, and I tapped it with mine. "To your first deal!"

I gulped more of the tea than I meant to, scalding my throat. "Thanks," I said.

Jacqueline glanced over my shoulder. "You haven't had any more problems with Peter, have you?"

Just as Jacqueline had predicted, Peter was released from jail less than two days after they arrested him and slapped with nothing more than a warning and fifty hours of community service.

"No," I said, remembering the forms for the Protective Order Jacqueline had me sign several days earlier. "The Protective Order must be working."

"Good." She tapped her fingernails against the cardboard cup. "I thought that would do the trick."

"Did you get in your run this morning?" I asked.

"I always get in my run, Mara." She pressed her lips together into a thin line. "There were more people than usual out today. The warmer weather does that."

"I wouldn't know. There's always a swarm of people at my crappy gym." My eyes traveled away from her, hoping she didn't pick up on the fact that I didn't "always" go to the gym. It was a good month if I dragged myself onto the stair climber once or twice.

"With all the deals coming your way, you'll be able to join any gym you want." She leaned in and locked eyes with me. "You've already lasted longer than most of my other assistants. You have what it takes, Mara." The light streaming in through the window reflected off the mirrored surface of Jacqueline's eyes. "I want to share something with you. Something I don't usually tell people."

My heart stopped beating, and I forgot to breathe. "Okay." Was she going to tell me about the spray paint? That she'd been the one behind it? Or, something about the rats?

"I'm going to be Top Producer." The corners of her mouth turned up into a smile. "It's going to happen *this* year."

I exhaled, relieved she had not shared anything more sinister. "I thought you already were Greystone's Top Producer."

"Yes, but not just at Greystone. I'm going to be the top-producing realtor in the entire City of Chicago." Her eyes gleamed with joy as if she had already won the award. "And I want you to help me."

I slid my cup toward me, not having realized that Jacqueline was within reach of the title. "Of course. Whatever you need."

"I checked the sales numbers this morning. Michelle Sentry and The Tornado of Real Estate are both way behind me. I only have one real competitor—Natalia Romanov."

The image of Natalia's face leering down at me from the CBR billboard flashed through my mind. I wondered how Jacqueline would appear on the billboard. Would she be smiling? Or would she go for the "I'll kick your ass" expression I'd seen so much of lately?

"What about Natalia's mob connections?" I asked.

Jacqueline tossed back her chin and laughed, her teeth sparkling white, despite all the coffee.

"It's probably only a rumor." Her eyes darted toward the wall, and she cleared her throat. "Anyway, I need you to monitor Natalia's listings for me. Let me know whenever she takes a new listing or closes a deal. I looked up her sales numbers on the MLS. $65 million so far. I'm not far behind."

I stopped scribbling my notes and looked up. "$65 million?" I asked. It was only the end of May.

Jacqueline ignored my question and kept talking. "I'm going to need you at my disposal to keep up with everything. Showings, searches, inspections, closings, open houses, networking events. Don't even think about wasting your time by going on caravan or doing floor time."

I nodded.

"You'll be compensated. Twenty percent, as we discussed."

A lightness floated up from the soles of my feet and spread throughout my body. Good things were happening.

CHAPTER TWENTY-ONE

The glowing numbers on my clock floated through the blackened room—11:32 p.m. I pulled my sheets over me and squeezed my eyes closed. It had been a twelve-hour workday, and I should have been exhausted, but I was wide awake. It wasn't the huge commission coming my way, or that I'd tricked Grace into moving out of my place that was keeping me awake. It wasn't even Emma's cancer and the stacks of unpaid bills for her treatment, or the thought of my parents losing their house. It was Nate. I missed everything about him: the salty smell of his skin, his warm, solid body pressed next to me in bed, the way a crease formed down the middle of his forehead when he was worried. A hollow ache pulsed through my body. How had he moved onto someone else so quickly? Maybe that other woman was just a fling, a rebound, to make himself feel better. We'd shared so much. He had to be missing me, too.

The morning after the break-up, I'd called him and tried to convince him to change his mind. After that, we hadn't texted or spoken. There was no grey area. He'd told me not to contact him again. "It's better that way," he'd said.

Still, I hadn't put up enough fight. I realized that now. If anyone was worth fighting for, it was Nate. He wasn't like other guys. My parents had loved him. We read the same books and laughed at the same jokes. We'd been one of those annoying couples who finished each other sentences and held hands on our way to the grocery store. Maybe he'd see things differently now that a few months had passed, and my career was taking off. I'd put him in a tough spot when I'd lost my job and pressured him to pay my mortgage. I'd asked him to place too much faith in the unknown.

I sat up in bed and raised my phone off the nightstand, scrolling down to his name and typing the message I'd stopped myself from sending so many times before.

I miss you. Real estate business is going great. Can we talk sometime?

My sweaty hands shook. My finger hovered over the send button. I let out a breath as I pressed it, then closed my eyes. There was no backing out this time. The message was delivered.

Minutes passed. The more time went by, the more the bile churned in my stomach. I began to sweat like I might throw up. What had I done? Maybe he was already asleep and didn't get it. Maybe that other woman was with him, and they were reading my text together and laughing at me. I stumbled out of bed and paced back and forth across my bamboo floor. Twelve minutes after I'd sent the message, I'd given up all hope.

Ding!

It was my phone. My hand shook as I fumbled to pick it up, my eyes scanning over the words. I couldn't breathe.

Glad real estate is working out for you but there's nothing more to say. Sorry

My mouth turned dry. Blood surged through my veins. *Fuck!* How could I have been so stupid? I dropped my phone and doubled over. I was done with Nate. For good. I floundered into the kitchen where I pulled over a chair and climbed up on it, grabbing a bag of Reese's Pieces from my secret stash in the cupboard above the refrigerator and not bothering to wipe away the tears that rolled down my cheeks.

****

Two days later, my "Natalia Romanov" search returned five

new results. The first four listings were too small to worry about. According to Jacqueline, anything under $2 million was "too small." Too small for what, I wasn't entirely sure. I stood up from my chair when I saw Natalia's fifth and newest listing. A development site bordering the hospital district, 2.3 acres, all formerly warehouse space, now empty and zoned for development. Asking price: $24 million.

I printed the listing and placed it on Jacqueline's desk, interrupting her price negotiations with another realtor. Her eyes bulged when she saw the asking price.

"I'll call you when I hear back from my seller," she told the other realtor, before clicking off her phone.

"Well, well. What do we have here?" Her voice carried the same tone as an evil queen in a Disney movie. "Natalia thinks she's going to close a $24 million deal this year." Jacqueline pulled a commercial contract out of her desk drawer. "Not so fast."

"What are you going to do?" I asked, even though I could see she was filling out a purchase contract for the address on the listing sheet. She ignored my question and continued writing. "Are you going to buy that property?"

"Don is going to get this property under contract." She pressed her lips together and smirked. "No one is going to buy this property."

I crossed my arms and stared at the scene unfolding before me, still confused. "Doesn't he have to buy it? I mean, if they sign the contract?"

She stopped writing and gave me a hard look. "Do you have any idea how screwed up our legal system is?"

I didn't respond. A shiver bristled down my spine as I thought of Peter and how he walked the streets as a free man despite being a drug addict who had threatened me with a knife.

Jacqueline sighed and fluttered her eyelids, pained by my stupidity.

"Let me spell it out for you, Mara. I submit this contract from my straw buyer. Natalia's seller accepts it. We'll have at least sixty days for due diligence. Then we may need extra time for site reviews and zoning appeals, not to mention environmental reports. We'll make sure it takes months to get past all the contingencies. No way will we close before the end of the year. Once we're past the contingency period, we record the contract at City Hall. Nothing else needs to be done. We've clouded the title. No one else can buy it. I just decreased Natalia's sales production by $24 million. They can sue for performance, but we can countersue for them to sell us the property. These legal battles take years. Eventually, Don can sell the contract to someone else for a profit. Or, he might have enough money to actually close on it in a few years."

I nodded, the pieces of the puzzle moving into place. Only the completed picture wasn't as pretty as I'd envisioned.

"Don will go along with it as long as I cover the out-of-pocket expenses."

"Isn't that illegal?" A coldness seeped through me. I didn't remember reading about this scenario in the ethics section of my real estate course.

She shot me another hard look. "This is real estate, Mara. Not Sunday school. It's kill or be killed." She continued filling in the blanks on the contract and then paused. "Do you have a problem with that?" Her eyes transformed into those of a wolf challenging a pack member.

"No. It's fine." I shrugged, ignoring the pit in my stomach. "I just didn't know how it all worked."

The next afternoon, I lay on my couch as a low-budget commercial droned across my TV. *I'm Marco Toranado, The Tornado of Real Estate! I blow the competition away! Call my 1-800 number now for your free property analysis.* I snorted at the extreme cheesiness of the guy. Who would list their house with a man dressed up like a tornado? It blew my mind that Marco Toranado would have any clients, much less be one of the top producers in the city. I flipped the channel.

My cell phone buzzed, jolting me upright. My condo had been so much quieter since Grace and Astro moved out, and I found myself dozing off in front of the TV at weird times. I didn't recognize the number, so I sat up and cleared my throat.

"Mara Butler."

"Yes. Hi, Mara," said a fragile voice. "This is Betty Lewis. I don't know if you remember me, but we spoke a few weeks ago about listing my house in Old Town, and I told you I'd decided on another realtor."

I tipped my head back. *Betty Lewis*, the name sounded familiar. She was one of the leads I'd followed up on from Jacqueline's website. I'd left her a message several weeks earlier, but she hadn't responded.

"Yes, Betty. How are you?"

"Well, I'm fine. The realtor I was going to use didn't work out, so I was hoping I could meet with you and get your opinion on the price. Are you available?"

"Me?"

"You are a realtor with Greystone, right?"

"Yes. Absolutely." A chill traveled through my body. What was I doing? Technically, Betty was Jacqueline's client. The lead was from Jacqueline's website. But Betty said she wanted to meet with me, not Jacqueline. And Jacqueline was way too swamped to check inquiries on her website. She'd pawned off that duty to me the minute I'd arrived at Greystone. She would never know how I got the lead. This could be my first real listing.

I pulled at my ponytail. "What's the address?"

"1907 N. Mohawk. It's a big house." Betty breathed heavily. "I'm moving to my condo in Florida. No more Chicago winters."

"I'm jealous."

Betty laughed.

I scrolled through my schedule. "Are you available on Tuesday at 1:00?"

"Well, yes. That works just fine."

I ended the call and pulled out my laptop, typing the address into the MLS. 1907 N. Mohawk was a high-end single-family Victorian on a full city lot in a prime location. It could easily sell for over $2 million. My stomach flipped at the thought of my potential commission. I could make a dent in Emma's medical bills. My parents wouldn't have to move. Maybe I could finally trade in my crappy Hyundai for something more impressive—a Lexus or a Mercedes, like Jacqueline. And *my* name would be on the sign out in front, not Jacqueline's. I was due for a break like this.

I envisioned Nate jogging by the property on a Saturday morning, seeing the FOR SALE sign on the lawn of a $2 million property with my name on it. He'd stop running—mid-stride—and stare. Then he'd know for sure that he'd been wrong about me. He'd made a mistake by leaving. Not that I cared.

With my shiny new lead, I headed to the office to put together a listing presentation for Betty. If Jacqueline asked how I'd gotten the listing, I'd tell her it was a referral from a family friend. Jacqueline had more business than she could handle. I needed this commission more than her. She'd said it herself—this was real estate, not Sunday school.

CHAPTER TWENTY-TWO

I hunched over my desk, analyzing the comparable properties for one of Jacqueline's properties. Kevin marched passed, leaving a trail of his cheap cologne behind him. Two of the Real Housewives sauntered in the other direction, arguing too loudly about where to order the best sushi in Lincoln Park. Jacqueline appeared out of nowhere and slapped down a contract in front of me, causing me to jump.

"I have an offer on Mohawk."

"Wow. Already?" Betty's house had only been on the market for two days. Not surprisingly, Jacqueline had been the first agent to bring a buyer through my exclusive new listing.

"It showed well. My buyer has been looking for a house like that for months."

I flipped to the second page, scanning through the major points. My eyes paused on the amount of the offer—$1,950,000—only $50,000 below asking.

"Thanks. I'll call the seller and let her know."

Jacqueline rested her hand on her hip. "It's a solid offer. Don't try to haggle too much on the price."

I ignored her and kept reading the contract, searching for the catch, but the offer was clean.

She pulled her chair over and sat down next to me. "How did you get that listing, anyway?"

My jaw tightened, but I kept my eyes glued to the contract. Something besides blind curiosity tinged at the edge of Jacqueline's voice. Drops of sweat formed in my armpits. "I already told you. A family friend referred it to me."

She laughed and stretched her shoulders back. "Nice family friend."

My stomach folded. Jacqueline couldn't know I'd stolen the lead, could she? I'd deleted the inquiry from her inbox immediately after Betty's unexpected phone call. I looked up from the contract, my fingers pinching the edges of the paper. "I think she'll accept this," I said, not only because I was desperate to change the subject, but also because it was true.

Jacqueline rolled her eyes at me. "You're not supposed to tell me that."

"I know, I just…" My toes tapped against the floor under the desk. "This is exciting."

"Yes. Call your client and get back to me." She strode off toward the marketing room.

I immediately called Betty, who accepted the terms. No haggling required. Jacqueline's client's offer was more than fair. It would close in thirty days. Jacqueline and I would split the nearly $100,000 commission, minus Greystone's cut. Like Jacqueline always said, everybody won.

****

The morning light speared through Greystone's front windows. I perched at my desk, scrolling through my calendar. Outside of the limited time I'd spent working on the sale of the Mohawk property, Jacqueline filled my days and nights with her real estate busywork. I now covered the showings at over half of her properties and hosted the weekend open houses she couldn't attend. She praised me for my instincts and for being a quick learner, but also reminded me to keep my eye on the prize—helping her beat out Natalia Romanov for Top Producer. There were six months left in the year. According to Jacqueline, that was plenty of time to close enough deals to make it happen.

My first ten minutes at the office were taken up by Jacqueline describing how she'd shown one of her multi-million dollar "premier" properties to Natalia and her client last night. Unfortunately, the townhome hadn't impressed them, and the sting of the rejection was lacquered all over Jacqueline's face. She slammed a folder closed and huffed. Her sudden plunges into foul moods were becoming more and more common. I closed my calendar and scrolled through emails, deflecting her negative energy.

She rolled back her chair and sidled up to my desk. "Mara, I have a mission for you."

"I've already got a bunch of showings today," I said, my chest squeezing with my ever-growing to-do list.

"You can do this in between the showings." She narrowed her eyes and lowered her voice. "Do you remember what Natalia Romanov looks like?"

"Yeah, of course. Everyone knows what she looks like. Her face is on the billboard…" Jacqueline's scowl hooked into me. I glanced toward the windows, my voice fading.

Jacqueline held up her hand, her mouth pulling back with irritation. "Do you know what Natalia's car looks like?"

"No." I leaned back in my chair. "Why?"

"She drives a silver Jaguar. The license plate says 'Top Producer,' except with no vowels." Jacqueline rolled her eyes, then looked over my shoulder to make sure no one was within earshot. "It's usually parked in front of her office at Blue Shore Group. I want you to follow her. Today. Tomorrow. All week if you have to."

"What? Why?"

"I want to know what she's doing. Find out where her listing appointments are." Her eyes gleamed as if she'd revealed the door to a secret room.

"Isn't that a little creepy, though?" I twirled a pen in my hand, a weight forming in my gut.

"She won't know that you're following her."

I lay the pen down. "I know. That's what makes it creepy."

Jacqueline sighed and removed a stack of glossy fliers from her desk drawer. "Mara, look. It's time to get creative."

The fliers displayed her new tagline: 'Jacqueline Hendersen— the Realtor Chicago Trusts!'.

She leaned toward me. "After Natalia leaves a property if you think she was giving a listing presentation, place one of these in the door." She shoved a flier at me, forcing me to take it. "Write down the address and look up the owner's name. I'll call them, swoop in, and steal the listing."

"How am I supposed to know if she's there for a listing presentation?"

Jacqueline took a deep breath and squared her jaw. "If she goes in by herself and comes out twenty or thirty minutes later by herself, then it's probably a listing presentation. It's common sense!"

She was struggling to hold it together, and I decided not to test her. Things were beginning to take off for me just like I'd imagined they would when I'd been rotting away in my cubicle at Averly Consulting. I'd already sold a condo to Grace, and now I had my first listing under contract. On top of that, all the referral fees from Jacqueline's deals were adding up. Emma's face illuminated in my mind.

I held up my hands. "Whatever you say, boss."

"And, Mara," she said.

"What?"

"Make sure Natalia doesn't see you."

CHAPTER TWENTY-THREE

"To Mara selling her first listing," Grace shouted as we raised our beers in the air, music thumping in the background. She was back at my condo, this time temporarily and without Astro. She'd brought our friend, Chloe, who we knew from our college days, three guys she worked with, and a couple of loud women who lived across the hall from her new condo.

The deal on Mohawk had closed this morning. My split with Greystone had already increased to sixty percent. After they took their cut, I'd walk away with almost $30,000. There'd never been a better excuse to throw a party.

My body tingled as I gulped down a mouthful of ice-cold beer, the tension in my shoulders easing with my plans for the payout. First, I'd pay back the rest of the draw from Jacqueline, and then I'd take care of my condo's special assessment. After that, I'd pre-pay my next month's mortgage. I'd already splurged on some new work clothes now that I couldn't raid Grace's closet. Whatever was left would be used to pay down Emma's medical expenses. We'd keep chipping away at the bills, bit by bit, just like she was doing with the cancer.

Someone banged on my front door, and I went to open it, hoping it wasn't an angry neighbor.

"Hey, Mara!" Marcus, my former co-worker at Averly and his girlfriend, stood in the doorway, holding a six-pack. "Nice pad! You remember Lilly," he said, pointing to the petite, red-haired woman next to him.

"Thanks. Yes, of course." I smiled and waved them inside. "Come on in."

Marcus and Lilly made their way into the living room and immediately cracked open two beers.

"Congrats for getting out of the rat race." A jealous haze fogged over his eyes. "How's real estate treating you?"

"Great. I work with Jacqueline Hendersen. She's the best." I glanced at the floor, leaving out the details. I'd spent the majority of the last two weeks following Natalia Romanov around the city, staying two or three car-lengths behind her, my eyes barely peering over the steering wheel. I now knew where she lived, ate lunch, did her banking, worked out, and got her hair cut. I spent almost as much time spying on Natalia's assistant, a wiry guy who wore skinny jeans and button-down shirts in a variety of pastel colors. The first day, he carried an expensive-looking camera and followed her to a walk-up building in Logan Square. Other days, he met her outside their office to exchange folders and keys. I wondered if Natalia forced him to do crazy stuff, too. From what I'd observed so far, it didn't seem like it.

There'd been a couple of close calls with my new mission. Natalia had made eye contact with me the second time I'd parked outside her office. My entire body had tensed, my breath strangling my throat before I glanced away. I casually exited my car, keeping my shoulders loose as if I was lost or had just randomly parked in that spot. Then I strolled in the opposite direction to avoid suspicion. The next day, as she pranced down the steps of her multi-million-dollar Lincoln Park single-family home, her head swung toward me again, like she somehow sensed I was watching her. Before our eyes meet, I ducked down, out of sight, and waited. By the time I found the courage to straighten up in my seat, she was gone.

For the city's number one realtor, Natalia spent a surprisingly little amount of time in her office. As crazy as Jacqueline's orders had sounded, I'd discovered some inside information on Natalia's potential listings. Last week, I'd followed her through the pouring rain to a single-family in Wrigleyville. Just as Jacqueline had predicted, Natalia had hurried up the steps shielded by her umbrella, and with a Blue Shore Group folder tucked inside her arm. No buyers in sight. Twenty minutes later, she left, ducking back into her car and out of the rain. My nerves prickled at the realization. She must have been there for a listing presentation. Like Jacqueline said, it was common sense.

As the Jaguar zoomed away, I grabbed one of Jacqueline's fliers and emerged from the car. Tossing aside my umbrella when it only opened on one side, I slunk down, scanning the area to see if anyone was watching. The rain pelted around me as I darted up the steps, struggling not to slip or twist my ankle, and stuffed the brochure into the mailbox next to the front door. Then I hurried back to the safety of my car, my heart pounding as if I were robbing a bank. I wrote down the address and delivered it to Jacqueline as soon as I returned to Greystone. Somehow, she'd known what to do with the information. The next day the owner listed the property with her instead of Natalia.

"Great work, Mara," Jacqueline said. "You'll get your twenty percent."

"Well, you aren't missing anything at Averly, that's for sure." Marcus' voice brought me back to my party, to the cold beer in my hand.

I laughed, remembering those depressing cubicles, the flickering fluorescent lights, and the giant sticker in the shape of a window affixed to the side of Marcus' wall. "Yeah. I'm sure."

The party continued late into the night with conversation and music and pizza and numerous rounds of beer pong.

"Your condo's awesome." Chloe had abandoned the loud conversation in the kitchen and gazed out at the city lights through the floor-to-ceiling windows in the living room. Her platinum blonde hair was parted in the middle and braided into matching twists on either side of her head. A wrap skirt hugged her narrow waist. Glittery fringe hung off the sleeves of her shirt and glistened next to her bronzed skin.

I stumbled next to her, feeling slightly frumpy in my jeans and black T-shirt. The alcohol made my arms and legs feel as if they were floating.

"I've been looking for a place like this," she said.

"You're looking for a condo?" I stopped breathing. Even through the haze of too many beers, my realtor alarm bell rang clearly. I reached into my pocket, fumbling for a card. "I can set up a search for you."

Chloe shook her head. "Oh, no. I'm already working with someone else. She's from my networking group."

"What? Who?" The blood drained from my face, sliding through my body like wet paint, my hands and feet suddenly heavy.

"Her name's Katie Walsh. She's with Keller Williams. She's really on top of the market." Chloe took a swig of her beer as if she hadn't just stabbed me in the heart.

"Never heard of her," I said, biting back my anger.

"What's up, ladies?" Grace leaped over the couch, a lock of her dark hair falling into her face.

I nodded toward the traitor. "Chloe's buying a condo. She's using some lady from her networking group as her realtor." I crossed my arms in front of me, my heart pounding louder with each beat.

"Seriously! What?" Grace threw her head back and then elbowed me. "Why not use Mara? She found my place for me. She was great!"

Chloe squared her shoulders. "I'm already working with someone."

Grace stared down Chloe, her green eyes brewing with diabolicf. "You can switch."

"I don't want to switch."

"Why not?" Grace shook her head, the smile on her face fading. "Why not help a friend out?"

Chloe sneered at me, her fingernails brushing at the stupid

fringe dangling from her shirt. "I'd rather use someone more experienced. I mean, Mara just got fired from her consulting job and decided she was going to be a realtor. Come on."

I bit my lip hard, the tinny taste of blood dripping near my tongue. Chloe was talking about me like I wasn't even standing there. Like she hadn't betrayed me. Like she wasn't a guest at *my* party at *my* condo.

Chloe chuckled. "She doesn't even drive a nice car."

A pulse of heat surged from my feet and collected in my face, my skin burning. This bitch didn't know anything about me, about what I'd been through. She didn't know what it had taken for me to get where I was. She was wrong. I knew plenty about real estate. I was learning from the best. I didn't drive a nice car because I was donating every extra penny I earned to pay for my sister's cancer treatment. My hand squeezed the glass bottle so hard I thought it might crack. I set my beer on the windowsill, steadying myself.

Chloe smirked. "I can't believe you're Hyundai is still running. Do you drive people around in that?"

The alcohol blurred my mind, but my body was clear. Blood raced through my veins, and my muscles tensed. Something inside me snapped.

"Get out of my house!" I grabbed the beer bottle and lunged toward Chloe, the lukewarm liquid splashing across her spiral braids and smug face and streaming down the front of her designer shirt. Arms shaking, I slammed the bottle down on the stone ledge behind me, the glass shattering and a shard cutting into my hand.

Someone screamed. Chloe's shocked eyes peered through her fingers at me, her jaw hanging open. Liquid dripped from the tip of her nose. I gripped the broken bottle inside my hand, and blood oozed from a cut on my finger. By the time I realized what I'd done, Chloe was lunging toward me, the whites of her eyes showing. Grace stepped in front of her, blocking her path. Others ran toward us.

"Are you crazy?" Chloe yelled. A splatter of beer covered her head and face, smearing her mascara under her eyes like war paint.

"Leave," I said, my breath jagged and blood leaking from my

hand.

Marcus stepped between us, holding out his arms. "What the hell happened?"

"You need to leave." Grace squared her shoulders and corralled Chloe toward the door.

Lilly jogged after Chloe with a wad of paper towels. Someone else turned off the music.

Chloe reached the hallway, hatred burning in her eyes. "Screw y...," she started to say, but Grace slammed the door.

My guests stood in the living room, raising eyebrows and opening mouths at each other. Pain throbbed from my finger. A soup of alcohol, pizza, and bile swirled in my stomach. I'd released the broken bottle from my grip but couldn't unclench my fist.

"What was her deal?" someone whispered.

"You should sit down." Grace rushed over, pointing at my hand and holding out a napkin. She cleared her throat, a smile creeping onto her face. "Just so everyone knows... *that's* what happens if you don't use Mara as your realtor."

Nervous laughter rippled through the room. My body sank into the couch, my good hand pressing a wad of napkins against the cut as I closed my eyes, simultaneously ashamed and proud of myself. I'd overreacted, but I'd had no choice but to defend myself. Chloe had backed me into a corner and insulted me.

Grace knelt, collecting pieces of glass from the floor.

Marcus teetered nearby, raising his arm in a wave. "We're taking off." Lilly hovered next to him, her face pale.

"Thanks for coming."

Lilly's eyes swerved away from me. They hurried toward the door with the rest of Grace's friends following close behind.

The party was over.

CHAPTER TWENTY-FOUR

"What happened to your hand?" Jacqueline eyed the bandage wrapped around my finger, her lips pulling back. We stood in front of a red brick single-family home on Addison, two blocks from Wrigley Field. It was Jacqueline's new listing, the one I'd helped steal from Natalia.

"Oh." I hid my arms behind my back. My stomach lurched, a result of too much beer the night before. "Just a cooking injury. My knife slipped. It's no big deal."

Jacqueline strummed her fingers on her thigh, considering my story. "Hopefully, you can still open a door. I'm going to add this listing to the properties you're in charge of showing."

My body sunk, as any hope of taking a day or two off over the upcoming Fourth of July weekend vanished. Before I could protest about my increasing workload, she added, "You'll be compensated."

I shifted my weight from one foot to the other, grateful for the comfortable flat shoes I'd decided on this morning and the bottle of Gatorade I'd downed on the way over. "Yeah. I can handle it."

"Good. I'll give you a tour." I followed her up the front steps, gawking at the way her pressed linen pants hung perfectly over her fat-free hips. I yanked down at my shirt, making sure it wasn't stained.

Jacqueline turned toward me and whispered. "Here's the deal. After you gave me the address, I looked up the tax records and called the owner, Bill Miles. Thanks to your detective work, I knew Natalia had already been to see him and had given him her sales pitch. She's good, so I half-expected Bill to tell me he'd already signed with her. Instead, he said Natalia tried to undervalue his property. He hadn't signed anything." Jacqueline stopped talking and grinned at me, her metallic eyes gleaming.

"I met him here yesterday morning before he left for work, property analysis and listing agreement in hand. The place is a real shithole. Of course, Bill thinks it's worth as much the new construction a block over. I explained how overpriced listings run the risk of sitting on the market and devaluing themselves. He said he didn't mind if it sat." Jacqueline shrugged. "So, we're going to humor him. We're listing at $1,900,000. In a couple of months, when it doesn't sell, we'll lower the price."

"What's the right price?"

"Something closer to $1,200,000." Jacqueline unlocked the door. "But at least Natalia won't get the sale."

We entered the foyer. The lighting was dark. The hodgepodge of '80s and '90s finishes were outdated and tired with beige Formica counters in the kitchen, mismatched appliances, and carpeting so dingy and stained I couldn't even guess at the original color. Bill's belongings cluttered the hallways. The property would be a tough sell until it was priced right. I hoped it wouldn't suck up too much of my time.

After completing the underwhelming tour, Jacqueline turned toward me. "Hey. Do you still have the key to my townhome?"

"Yeah."

"Great. I need you to let my designer, Anastasia, into my place tomorrow. I'm going to be out with a buyer all day. I'll get back to you with the time."

"Okay."

"I've got to go meet Haley now."

I thought of Jacqueline's friend from law school and how

stressful it must have been for her to learn she was pregnant and then to have to sell her one-room condo because of it.

"How's she doing?"

Jacqueline fluttered her eyelashes and sighed. "A little high-maintenance, to be honest. You'd think she was the first person to ever deal with a surprise pregnancy. Everyone knows the pill isn't a hundred percent effective."

"I guess," I said, although I remembered my doctor telling me the pill was nearly a hundred percent effective as long as it was taken daily.

Perspiration prickled on my forehead. I stepped back, Haley's remarks from a few weeks earlier replaying in my ears. *I have no idea how it happened because I was on the pill. I swear I never forgot to take it.* All at once, another vision emerged from the dark corners of my mind, the bottle of St. John's Wort spilling from Jacqueline's purse the night she'd invited me over for pizza. I remembered the reason I'd stopped taking the herb. The decision had come at the advice of my doctor after she'd learned I used the pill for contraception. St. John's Wort was known to interfere with birth control pills, rendering them virtually ineffective. Leaning back, I steadied myself against the wall. Now it was Peter's harrowing words that echoed through me. The more I tried to silence them, the louder they spoke. *Think about it, Mara. The reasons people sell their properties. It's because bad things happened to them...She's behind it all.* I sucked in a breath, a horrible thought leeching into my brain.

How low would Jacqueline stoop to get a listing? She met Haley every week for lunch. What if she'd slipped the St. John's Wort into her friend's food or drink? Haley would never have known her birth control pills were useless.

"See you at the office." Jacqueline's chipper voice yanked me away from my spiraling thoughts and back to Bill's foyer. She placed the keys to the overpriced listing in my uninjured hand and headed toward her car. I watched her leave, reining in my imagination. I'd been hearing too many news stories about men slipping drugs into women's drinks, and now I was projecting their actions onto Jacqueline. There was no proof she had done anything to her friend. Jacqueline had probably bought the herb to manage the anxiety caused by her stressful career. Haley had most likely forgotten to take her pills once or twice without realizing it. My back pressed against the brick wall as I exhaled. Still, I couldn't ignore the rock turning over in my gut.

****

A woman with papery skin and a bouffant hairstyle straight out of the 1950s meandered toward the steps of Jacqueline's townhome, a leather tote pinned under one arm. Her clashing purple pants and yellow-and-grey plaid shirt seemed to have been paired together on purpose. She paused in front of the steps, lowering her tortoise-shell glasses at me.

"Mara?"

"Yes. Are you Anastasia?"

"That's me." She made her way up the steps. "Thanks for letting me in. I know Jacqueline is extremely busy."

"Sure." I unlocked her door and waved the designer in front of me. Ever since Jacqueline had decided to move forward with her plan to add another bathroom to her lower level, I'd gotten used to my post on the front step, letting construction crews and handymen into her townhome. "Jacqueline said you can turn the bottom lock when you leave."

"Oh. Actually, I might need your help with something." She waited, so I stepped behind her into the air-conditioned foyer, unable to imagine how I could help. "There are some paint color samples in here somewhere. Jacqueline thought they might be in the kitchen or the office. Can you be a dear and help me look? I'll take the kitchen. You take the office." She pointed down a hallway with French doors at the end.

My eyes scanned down the hallway to the open floorplan beyond Anastasia's tall hairdo. In typical Jacqueline fashion, nothing was out of place. Not a box, a book, a grocery bag, or even a crumb.

"Sure. I'll look in the office." I followed the gleaming

hardwood floors toward the cut-glass doors at the end of the hall. I'd only poked my head into Jacqueline's home office when I'd come over for pizza several weeks earlier. Now I gaped as I passed through the double doors, the perfectly restored interior reminding me of the kind of old-fashioned library only seen in movies based on Jane Austen novels. An oversized mahogany desk faced me, complimented by matching wood-paneled walls. Behind the desk, slivers of daylight peeked through wooden blinds. Built-in shelves filled with antique books lined the far wall. A framed photograph of a younger-looking Jacqueline tilted toward me. She sat astride a gleaming chestnut horse, a proud smile on her face, and a blue ribbon pinned to the horse's bridle. I swallowed, my eyes traveling to the framed diplomas and awards symmetrically arranged along the panel next to me, including the Greystone Top Producer Award from the last two years.

A stack of financial statements rested in a neat pile on the corner of the desk. I averted my eyes from the numbers, not wanting to invade her privacy any more than necessary. The top desk drawer slid open easily, revealing five pens arranged in a row, a pair of scissors, a packet of note cards, a cup of paperclips, a stapler, and a roll of tape. I laughed out loud, never having seen such a sparse and organized drawer in my entire life. I closed it and opened the next one, which held files arranged in alphabetical order. The bottom drawer stuck at first. With a second yank, it creaked toward me.

The clinking of metal drew my eyes even before I saw the mountain of keys, all labeled with street numbers. The familiar strings of numbers leered back at me. They were the addresses of Jacqueline's recent listings, ones that had already closed. My bandaged fingers hovered over the pile as my mind struggled to make sense of the contents. Realtors were required to turn keys over to the new owners at closing, but Jacqueline had saved these.

"I found it!" Anastasia's voice jolted me upright. My pulse racing, I slammed the drawer closed and hurried toward Jacqueline's kitchen. The designer held up a strip of paint samples in a variety of shades of grey. "They were in the drawer over here."

"Sounds good." I raised my hand to her and turned toward the door, anxious to leave.

Anastasia's mouth curved downward. "Oh, dear. What happened to your hand?"

I hesitated, spinning back toward her. "Cooking accident."

"Ouch. Nothing too serious, I hope?"

"Just a cut. It'll be fine."

My body tensed, yearning to escape outside into the warm air, but my feet refused to move, the all-too-familiar feeling of unease rippling through me. Anastasia smiled at me, but I couldn't smile back. A splinter of terror formed deep within me, a prick of truth that needled through my chest and pinned me to the floor. Troubling thoughts and worries bombarded me in random order. *Spray paint, rats, fake contracts, unplanned pregnancy, spying, water records, Peter's warnings.* And now a new question whose answer I didn't want to know: What was Jacqueline doing with all those keys?

CHAPTER TWENTY-FIVE

Nikes tightly laced, I bounded down the steps of the East Coast Club, my skin clammy with sweat. The late August humidity wasn't helping my complexion, especially after the hour I'd spent with my personal trainer, a piece of eastern European eye-candy named Cyrek. It had been almost two months since I'd discovered the secret drawer of keys. I'd debated asking Jacqueline about my findings, but she quashed my moral dilemma the day after my discovery when she handed me three checks totaling ten thousand dollars. Two days later, there were more checks. The referral fees and commissions rolled in, one after another. Besides, whatever reason Jacqueline had for saving those keys was none of my business.

Now, standing on the steaming asphalt, I swallowed, throat prickly. As soon as my finger had healed, I'd joined the East Coast Club, where I worked out three afternoons a week, the green energy smoothie at the juice bar replacing my daily chocolate craving. Jacqueline had been right; joining East Coast was key to making business connections. The club was a cross between a country club, a Wall Street office, and an Olympic workout facility. There were other perks, too. I admired the slope of my newly defined biceps, feeling empowered.

My fingertip eased against the button, unlocking the door to my new Five Series BMW. Silver like I'd always wanted. I smirked, remembering the night I'd splashed my beer in Chloe's face. *Who drove a crappy car now?*

A suffocating wave of heat surrounded me as I slid into the leather upholstery. Pushing the keyless ignition, a blast of arctic air rushed through the air-conditioned seats, my sweat evaporating in an instant. This car was unbelievable; sunroof, GPS, zero to sixty in a nanosecond. I made a point of lowering the window and driving past Nate's apartment at least once a week, hoping he'd see me. He hadn't yet. At least as far as I knew, but it was only a matter of time. I bet Nate didn't have a membership to East Coast. I bet his girlfriend didn't drive a car like this. The ball of my foot pressed against the pedal as I eased out of the secured parking lot.

The car had been a splurge, but I hadn't been irresponsible. The last few months had sped by like a movie played on fast-forward. Ever since I'd sold Betty's property on Mohawk, my business had gone viral. Jacqueline had been annoyed at my luck in landing the Mohawk listing, but she'd never accused me of doing anything shady. She'd gotten the buyer's side of the commission, anyway.

Things were going better in my personal life, too. Emma had completed her last round of chemo, and my financial contributions were making a big dent in the medical bills. She had called two weeks ago, her voice cracking.

"Good news, Mara. We got the test results. The cancer is gone!"

I'd tightened my jaw, afraid I might have misheard her.

"Mara? Did you hear me? I'm all better."

"Yeah," I said softly at first, followed by a surge of joy. "YEAH! EMMA! YOU DID IT!" I jumped up and down in my living room, my eyes welling with tears. The nightmare was over. Emma and I laughed uncontrollably at her news, at my outburst— just like we used to do when we were kids. We'd dodged the bullet. My little sister had done it. She'd been stronger than all of us and conquered cancer. She could continue with her plans to move into her freshman dorm at Illinois, just like any other healthy eighteen-year-old. Now, I leaned back in the leather seat and smiled at the thought.

A call from an unidentified number rang through the speakers of my car, and I sent it to voicemail. While we'd broken through one roadblock with Emma, another still loomed in front of me. Jacqueline's mission to become Chicago's next Top Producer was all-consuming. I did my best to keep up.

A battered SUV swerved in front of me and darted through the light. I hit the brakes, my car sliding to a stop just as a new email beeped on my phone. It was another forwarded message from Jacqueline.

Her demands were relentless. She pushed the neediest clients on me. When deals fell through, it was my fault every time. There was always something I should have done or said differently. When Natalia listed a new property, it was because I hadn't followed her closely enough, or because I'd lost my focus. Still, I was learning more about real estate than I ever imagined. And the commission checks and referral fees kept flowing in, my bank account growing. I'd made over $90,000 in the last three months. There was no need to find another roommate to replace Grace. I easily afforded my mortgage payments, new car, East Coast Club membership fees, and pretty much anything else I wanted.

A call rang through my speakers from an unfamiliar number. I picked up, expecting it to be someone calling on one of Jacqueline's listings.

"This is Mara."

"Hi, Mara. This is Patricia Abramson, the editor of the *Chicago Board of Realtors' Magazine*."

I stopped breathing for a second. "Hi, Patricia. How are you?"

"Just fine, thanks. And you?"

"Good."

"Great. I'm calling with some good news. Our feature article for next month's issue will name 'Thirty Under Thirty.' That's thirty Chicago Realtors under the age of thirty who are ones to watch in the industry. Rising stars," she said in a bubbly voice. "We'd like to spotlight you as one of the realtors."

I pulled into a nearby parking lot and stopped my car, heart pounding. "Really?"

"Yes. Do we have your permission?"

"What? Yes. Of course." I wiped the sweat from my forehead, wondering what Jacqueline would think.

"Great. I'll email you a questionnaire to fill out. After you send that back to me, we'll schedule a time for your photoshoot."

"Photoshoot?"

The woman chuckled. "Yes. It's no big deal. It shouldn't take more than thirty minutes."

"Okay. Yeah. That sounds great." I envisioned a full-page spread of myself wearing my new sleeveless cocktail dress with the blush-colored sandals. I wondered if the photographer would place a fan just off-camera to give me that wild, wind-blown look, and whether I should offer a warm smile, or one of those sly, half-grins I'd seen Jacqueline flash so many times.

"Okay, then. Look for my email and let me know if you have any questions."

"I will, thanks."

The light turned green and pulled back onto the road, smiling. Jacqueline was right. Success breeds more success. I accelerated toward the exit ramp to I-94. What I wouldn't give to see the shock, the remorse, on Nate's face when he saw the article. I imagined one of his friends reading it and passing it along to him. His eyes would stretch wide, his mouth gaping open, the color draining from his face as he realized that breaking up with me was the biggest mistake he'd ever made. I turned up the volume on a rap song that pounded through my speakers, nodding my head along with the angry words. My foot pressed the gas pedal, and my car flew onto the highway, speeding ahead of traffic and merging into the far-left lane. Things were going my way.

****

My BMW hummed to a halt in a space outside the Title One office in River North. I tucked my hair behind my ear, thankful my bangs had finally grown long enough not to fall back into my face. Jacqueline's client, Julia, was closing on a two-bedroom condo in Lakeview, strategically located on the fourth floor in a building with a doorman. Other than the initial visit to Julia's condo the morning I'd dug through her underwear drawer, I hadn't been involved in the deal until today. Jacqueline needed time to get ready for her tour of penthouse condos with her multi-million-dollar buyers. She instructed me to meet Julia at the title company. I agreed, lured by Jacqueline's promise of a twenty percent referral fee for merely attending the closing.

"Don't mention anything about her old condo," Jacqueline had said, her plucked eyebrows crunching together. "So many bad things happened to her there. It makes her uncomfortable to talk about it."

There wasn't much for a buyer's agent to do at closing, other than holding the buyer's hand and making sure all documents were signed, keys delivered, and commission checks collected. This would be the easiest referral fee I'd ever earned. I perched in the chair across from Julia and watched her sign page after page of papers. Her loopy and flowery signature didn't match her tiny frame, soft-spoken voice, or the messy condo she'd inhabited. She glanced up at me from beneath her auburn bangs every once in a while and smiled. I'd gotten an all-too intimate glimpse into her life the morning I'd rummaged through her lingerie.

"Are you excited about your new place?" I asked her, careful to avoid mention of the old place.

"Yes. It will be a good move for me. I didn't really feel safe in my other neighborhood." She smiled at me again.

"Oh, yeah." My toes tapped under the table. "Jacqueline told me about your car. And the mugging. That's horrible." I shook my head, remembering all the times I'd felt vulnerable walking alone at night down the city streets, not to mention the time Peter had leaped out from behind the tree and held a knife to me. A shudder swelled through me, but I shook it off, relieved he'd been obeying the Protective Order, and hadn't tried to approach me again. I was about to change the subject to the restaurant scene in Lakeview, but Julia spoke first.

"It was the break-in that really got to me." She stopped signing and drew in a long breath. "I thought I was so clever hiding my valuables in my underwear drawer, but I guess that's the first place they look." She rolled her eyes.

My heels dug into the floor, my spine pressing against the chair back. My teeth clenched so forcefully I thought they might splinter as my brain registered the information. Valuables in her underwear drawer? That's where I'd found the box I'd removed months earlier, but I'd only been following Jacqueline's instructions. What had been inside that locked box?

My thoughts traveled back to that day. There was a horrible mess in the condo. Maybe it was messy because Julia didn't know we were coming over. Wouldn't she have tidied up if she'd been expecting us? It all seemed so obvious now. My cheeks burned, but my fingers turned colder than icicles. I remembered Jacqueline going back into the condo while I waited in the car. What had she done?

I existed in an alternate reality for several minutes, staring at my manicured fingernails as the closing proceeded around me. Questions were asked. Jokes were made. People laughed. Jacqueline had tricked me into stealing from Julia, violating her privacy, making an innocent woman think she'd been robbed so that Jacqueline could increase her sales record. I'd done some shady things too—lying to Grace, helping myself to Jacqueline's listing on Mohawk—but this was different. This crossed the line.

Peter's gaunt face flashed before me. *She'll make you do bad things.*

"And here we have a check for Greystone Realty." The same smiley woman who oversaw many of my Title One closings handed me the check.

Not knowing what to do or say without implicating myself in the robbery, I grasped the payout. Everyone else stood and gathered their belongings.

"Thanks for your help, Mara." Julia held out her slender hand.

"Anytime." I swallowed against my parched throat, gently squeezing her warm fingers as if to offer an apology. In my left hand, I pinched the commission check behind my back.

****

"What was in the box? The one I took from Julia's dresser?" My voice was breathless as if I'd just sprinted to the phone instead of sitting slumped in the front seat of my car.

"It's better if you don't know."

My hand gripped the steering wheel of my parked car. "What are you talking about? I never agreed to steal anything from anybody, Jacqueline!"

She huffed. "Get over it. It's all for the best. Better for Julia to believe someone robbed her than for her to actually get robbed by a real thug. It was only a matter of time before it happened."

I squeezed my eyes closed. "Your creative thinking is going too far. This is messed up!"

"Okay, then." She paused. "You're fired."

My chest strained against my seatbelt. "Seriously? You trick me into stealing and then fire me? Are you kidding me?"

"You don't like the way I do business?" she asked. "Fine. Go work for someone else."

The line went dead. Jacqueline had hung up on me. I swallowed and tipped my head back. She'd cemented me into a corner. As angry as I was, I couldn't walk away from the stream of referral fees I made off her. Without Jacqueline, my business would decline. I was good at selling real estate, but I needed more time to establish my own clients. I needed to set myself up for success, to prove people like Nate and Chloe wrong. I'd promised Dad I wouldn't quit as soon as something didn't go my way, but the number of things not going my way were piling up.

I couldn't stop Peter's hollow, desperate face from flashing before me. What if he'd been right? Maybe Jacqueline was evil. She'd probably tricked him into doing some of her dirty work, too. Maybe that was why he'd been warning me. But Peter's business had completely dissolved once he'd left Jacqueline's side. He'd become nothing but a drug addict who'd threatened me with a knife. I hugged my arms across my chest, wondering if I'd be able to avoid a similar fate if I left.

Slumping into the leather seats, I watched the people moving outside my window. A woman in polyester pants and an oversized T-shirt jogged toward a bus stop just as the bus sputtered away. She waved her hands and screamed, "Wait!" The bus lurched and spewed diesel, driving off without her as she kicked the ground, shoulders drooping. My stomach dropped. I remembered being in that woman's place a little too vividly. My fingers brushed the leather trim of my seat, and I inhaled the chemically-clean new car scent, thankful to be sitting inside my shiny BMW with the satellite radio and air conditioning. I didn't want to go back to riding the bus. My eyes found the woman again. She slumped a bench reading a book. If I wasn't waist-deep in Jacqueline's bullshit, I might have offered her a ride.

With a long breath, I pressed Jacqueline's number. The phone rang twice, followed by Jacqueline's recorded message instructing callers to dial my number to schedule all showings. Pulling in more breaths and squeezing my eyelids shut, I waited. This is what I had to do. Two minutes passed, and I tried again.

"Yes," Jacqueline said, her voice hard and cold.

I let out my breath. "Hi. Maybe I overreacted, but I don't want to be kept in the dark. Can we put it behind us?"

"Agreed," she said. "We're on the same team, Mara. Things between us will be an open book from now on."

I turned over the silver bracelet on my wrist. "Okay. Sorry I flipped out."

"Apology accepted."

Jacqueline's words made the fine hairs on my neck bristle. She should have been the one apologizing to me. I dropped my phone into my purse, focusing on my breathing, and coming to terms with swallowing my pride. The situation was under control. No need to waste any more energy thinking about it. I pulled my BMW into traffic, stealing a final glimpse of the woman hunched on the bench, before turning toward the office.

CHAPTER TWENTY-SIX

It was a few minutes before 8 a.m., and a line of caffeine-addicted professionals extended out the door of Starbuck's. I slid my chair closer and glanced at Jacqueline. She placed her cardboard cup on the tiny black table between us, the corner of her mouth twisting upward.

"I have good news."

"Me too," I said.

"You go first."

"*CBR Magazine* is naming me as one of the Thirty under Thirty in next month's issue." I kept my face still, not sure how Jacqueline would respond to me being in the spotlight.

"No kidding." She smiled and shook her head. "Nice to see hard work paying off. Congrats."

I exhaled. "Thanks. What's your news?"

"I sold a four-million-dollar penthouse unit to my elderly clients last night. A 4,200 square-foot condo that occupies the entire top level of the building at 800 N. Michigan Avenue."

"Wow." I pulled my cup toward me, my stomach sinking. Jacqueline had kept the deal to herself. No referral fee.

"When this deal closes, my numbers will be right on par with Natalia's, especially since Don finally agreed to help me tie up her

$24 million listing."

I nodded, remembering Jacqueline's scheme from a few months earlier to take Natalia's listing off the market with her fake buyer. The coffee cup scorched my hand, so I laced my fingers together and shifted my chair.

"You should have seen Natalia's face when I presented her with the contract so quickly. I could practically see the dollar signs flickering in her eyes. It's been two months of delays, but she hasn't figured out yet that Don won't fulfill any of the contract terms. No increase in earnest money. No closing. I can already envision the angry phone calls and threatening letters from attorneys, but no one will be able to do anything about it. They'd have to go to court to sue for performance, and that could take years. She won't be able to pin it on me. If anything, I'll pretend to be on Natalia's side. My buyer is the problem. My shady, no-good buyer who lied to me and over whom I had no control." Jacqueline crinkled her nose and laughed. "Don't you love real estate?"

"Yeah," I said, although it was becoming obvious Jacqueline and I didn't love it for the same reasons.

Jacqueline tapped her nails on the table and stared past my shoulder. "Our sales numbers are too close, though. I don't know what other deals Natalia has in her pocket for the rest of the year. I need more inside information."

"I'm already following her."

"I'm thinking of something bigger. We need to get into the CCC."

"The Chicago Construction Club?"

"That's right."

"But only men can join the CCC."

Jacqueline scowled. "It's such backward bullshit. The CCC is a cesspool of real estate leads, though. Natalia has her sources there. Everyone knows she got divorced because she had an affair with Howard Aldrich." She leaned forward, lowering her voice. "He's the slumlord who owns Chicago Rentals, the largest apartment rental company in Chicago. He gave Natalia the lead on her new $24 million listing. I'm sure of it. He must have heard about the deal from his cronies at the CCC. I need access."

My gut looped into a knot as I imagined what Jacqueline would do to get through the door of the all-male club. I braced myself for her to suggest I get a sex change operation.

"I've been making friends with Lydia Burton. Her husband, Roger, is one of the founders of the CCC."

I remembered Lydia as the older woman sitting next to Jacqueline at Germania Place the night I discovered the spray paint in the trunk. Lydia's husband, Roger, seemed like an asshole.

Jacqueline checked her watch, then smoothed down her shirt. "Anyway, I'm hoping Lydia will change Roger's negative opinion of me. I took her out for lunch last week, and we've already made plans to visit the Institute of Art next Tuesday. I was waiting for the perfect opportunity to slant our conversations toward real estate, toward me listing Roger's developments, but it's taking too much time."

"So, what are you thinking?"

"No one will let me into the CCC. They know me too well, but you could slip under the radar and go to one of their events, then report back to me."

"How?" My hand bumped against my cup, splattering drips of coffee across the table. I searched for a napkin but had forgotten to take one.

Jacqueline's eyes fluttered toward the mess, then refocused on me. "Let me think about it. We'll revisit this idea in a day or two."

I dropped my chin and pulled in a deep breath through my nose, hoping Jacqueline would get distracted with something else and forget about the CCC.

A few minutes later, I'd mopped up my spilled coffee, and we headed down North Avenue back to the office. Twenty feet ahead, Tony slumped against the side of the building with a Styrofoam cup of change in front of him. I began to dig through my purse for some spare coins. Jacqueline stepped toward me with an angry look, but her toe caught on something, and she tumbled forward and fell to the sidewalk.

"Ah!" She lay on the ground, wincing and clutching her ankle next to a gaping crack in the uneven cement.

"Are you okay?" I leaned over her, retrieving the high-heeled shoe that had slipped off her foot.

Deep, bellowing laughter erupted from Tony's mouth, slowly transforming into raspy, wet coughing. It was the kind of cough that made me glad I never took up smoking. Tony wore too many layers of clothes for such a hot morning. Maybe to balance out his overabundance of clothing, he wore no shoes, and his yellowish toenails twitched dangerously close to Jacqueline's eyes. His face was dirty and unshaven. Specks of white food or possibly garbage clung to his hair and beard. He looked toward me and pointed at Jacqueline, the violent coughing shaking his entire body and jingling the change inside his cup.

Jacqueline sneered at him. "What are you looking at?"

Tony laughed harder, choking on his saliva.

She pushed herself up off the ground, then yanked the shoe from my hand and shoved her foot into it. "Why do people like him have to exist?" She placed her foot down and yelped before raising it again.

My eyes found Tony, who had now stopped coughing. His still face waited for my response. "Sorry," I said to him but held my arm out for Jacqueline to lean on. I teetered between them, not sure what to do next.

Jacqueline's fingers dug into my arm, squeezing tighter. I tried to guide her past Tony, but she resisted. Her leg reached back, then swung forward with a burst of force.

"No!" I shouted, backing away from Jacqueline just as she kicked Tony's cup of change.

The cup flew into the air and rained down in a metallic shower. Coins scattered across the sidewalk, bouncing and rolling into the street as the tires of passing cars crunched over the man's life savings.

The breath left my lungs.

Tony threw his arms in the air, his eyes bulging toward Jacqueline. "Hey! Why'd you do that? Why'd you do that?" He scrounged on his hands and knees, mumbling to himself and scraping the scattered coins into a pile.

My muscles twitched, my stomach seizing. What kind of sick person would kick a homeless man's jar of change? The speech Jacqueline had given at Germania Place about helping homeless people replayed through my mind. My stomach folded, confirming what I already knew. She was a fraud.

Jacqueline smirked and continued limping toward the office.

"You crazy bitch! Crazy bitch!" Tony yelled after her.

My feet wouldn't budge, my limbs weighed down with disgust as I watched Jacqueline hobble away. Tony's soiled fingernails searched frantically through the cracks.

"Let me help you." I crouched down, shoulder-to-shoulder with him, my fingers shaking as they scraped against the hot cement to retrieve the man's coins.

CHAPTER TWENTY-SEVEN

Despite being 11 a.m. and sunny, I'd turned on all the lights in Bill's house. He'd taken Jacqueline's advice and gotten rid of the books, boxes, and clothing that had previously lined the hallways. He'd vacuumed, too. The place didn't look half-bad. I pulled the tray of deep-dish pizza from the oven, its doughy aroma competing with the flowery scent of the Febreeze Bill must have spritzed throughout the house before I arrived. I placed the pre-cut slices next to the tossed salad on the counter. The Broker's Open House started in two minutes, and there'd soon be a crowd of hungry realtors showing up for free lunch, regardless of whether or not they had a potential buyer.

As I arranged the food, I struggled to set aside yesterday's drama. After spending fifteen minutes helping Tony gather his spilled change, I'd returned to the office where Jacqueline sat with her leg propped up, a bag of ice resting on her ankle, and half a dozen realtors gathered around her asking if she was okay.

"I tripped on that horrible sidewalk," she'd said with no mention of Tony or what she'd done to him. "The city is lucky I'm so busy. Otherwise, I'd sue them."

Missy Lantosa clicked her tongue. "They should really do something about those uneven sidewalks. I almost twisted my

162

ankle the other day."

I'd shuffled papers as loudly as I could while Jacqueline pretended not to notice me. When the crowd around her had finally dwindled, my conscience had strengthened in protest, taking a grip of my throat and refusing to let the difference between right and wrong go unnoticed for a second longer. Jacqueline needed to hear it.

I stepped in front of her desk, forcing her to look at me. "Why did you do that?"

Jacqueline cocked her head. "Do what?"

"Kick Tony's cup? That's all he has. Can't you give the guy a break?"

"He brought it on himself, Mara. He acted like a child, so I treated him like a child."

My jaw clenched.

"And my ankle will be fine, by the way. Thanks for asking."

With my tongue thick in my mouth, I'd gathered my things, turned my back on my mentor, and headed out to my next showing.

Now I surveyed Bill's kitchen, thankful to have some space from Jacqueline, at least for a couple of hours. It was easier to focus on selling real estate than to dwell on how to deal with her misguided behavior. I'd only had a handful of showing requests at Bill's property. Jacqueline had insisted on a Broker's Open House as a way for us to gather agent feedback on the price point. If enough people told Bill his property was overpriced, maybe he'd consider lowering it.

The front door opened, and two guys about my age walked in. One had slicked-back hair and wore a T-shirt and jeans. The other was tall and skinny and wore a suit. They looked around, admiring the front room as they made their way back to the kitchen.

"Cool place," said the one with the gelled hair, placing his card on the counter. The skinny guy did the same. They were with City View Properties.

"Do you mind?" The first guy pointed to the pizza.

"Go for it," I told him.

The slickster grabbed a paper plate and slid two slices of pizza onto it. His friend went for the salad first. They devoured the food as if they hadn't eaten in days. I was guessing neither of them had a viable buyer for the property.

"After you eat, take a look upstairs and let me know what you think of the price." I pretended to check my phone as they ate. They seemed desperate. A pit formed in my stomach as I realized how easily I could have found myself in their place, trolling broker's open houses for free food. As much as Jacqueline's recent behavior bothered me, I'd probably be standing where they were if it hadn't been for her taking me under her wing.

"Sure thing," said the slickster. They grabbed cans of Coke off the counter and headed upstairs.

A minute later, three women about my mom's age wandered through the door, talking loudly about the cost of parking permits. The one with her bangs cut too short approached me and insisted she might have a buyer.

"This is exactly what he's looking for," she said. "I'll take one of your brochures with me." The women wandered around for a few minutes and then approached the kitchen island to ask if they could have some pizza and salad.

"Help yourself." I flashed my most realtor-like smile. "That's what it's there for."

The guys from City View sauntered past, telling me the price was too high. The women in the kitchen agreed and followed them out the door, thanking me for the food.

I sat around for another fifteen minutes admiring the silky fabric of my new floral sundress and waiting for more realtors to show up. Sometimes agents with legitimate buyers brought them along to the open houses. Maybe someone would do that today. The door opened. I rearranged the pizza and salad on the counter.

Footsteps clicked against the floor, and I looked up. A pair of dark and familiar eyes shot through me like bullets, causing me to stumble backward. Natalia Romanov stood in front of me. Alone. She wore high heels and a sleeveless black dress. Her brunette hair was cropped to chin-length and cut at an angle like the models in

Milan.

"So, you ended up with this listing?" She spoke with a slight Russian accent.

"Yeah. Well, no." My heart hammered in my chest as I struggled to spit out the words. "It's Jacqueline Hendersen's listing. I'm her assistant."

"I've seen you before." Natalia's black eyes were cast from iron. "You've been following me."

"No. I don't think so." I looked down, hoping she couldn't detect the beads of sweat collecting on my forehead.

"Yes. I think so."

Shit! She'd seen me. What if the rumors were true? What if Natalia was involved in the Russian mob. She could put a hit on me. Why had Jacqueline put me in this situation? It had been reckless.

The Russian leaned toward me, speaking in barely more than a whisper. "You tell Jacqueline that whatever game she is playing, I do not like it. I am watching her very closely."

I nodded. "Okay. I'll tell her. But there aren't any games."

She glared at me. "I saw you outside my house a couple of weeks ago. I do not forget faces!"

Every muscle in my body tensed. It took all my strength to stand upright, instead of hiding inside a nearby cabinet or racing out the back door. I inhaled, trying to think of what to say next. "I'll tell her."

Natalia's stare bore into me, her eyes unwavering. Finally, she turned away and strode toward the front entrance. Just before exiting, she flipped around, twisting her thin lips to the side. "You'll never sell the property at this price. It is way too high."

CHAPTER TWENTY-EIGHT

I shoved through Greystone's front door and staggered toward Jacqueline, pushing my hair from my sweaty face. My heart still pounded from my encounter with Natalia. Jacqueline perched on the chair behind her desk.

"She knows." I leaned over her, my voice barely above a whisper. "Natalia. She saw me following her."

"What?" Jacqueline shook her head. "No way."

"Natalia stopped by the broker's open to confront me." My eyes grasped onto Jacqueline's. "She figured it out."

Jacqueline stared out Greystone's front windows and shifted her legs. Her ankle was wrapped in an ace bandage, which she'd tried to hide under her pant leg. "Why did you follow her so closely? You should have been more careful!"

My face burned. I cleared my throat, ignoring her comment. "Natalia said to tell you that she doesn't know what kind of games you're playing, but she's watching you closely."

A sheen of perspiration formed on Jacqueline's skin, her complexion fading to the color of ceiling paint. She tapped her nails on her desk and took a deep breath.

"Don't worry." Her eyes flickered. "There's nothing she can do. She has no proof."

I tipped my chin back and inhaled. "I don't want to follow her anymore."

"Fine. It hasn't been that productive anyway. We'll move on to something else."

I shuffled toward my desk and took my seat, relieved that Jacqueline had let me off the hook and that my risky spy mission was officially over.

Maeve had rescheduled this week's office meeting for this afternoon, and Greystone's realtors swarmed around me. Even the ones who hadn't done a deal in a good six months, like empty nester, Ellen Barkley, and stay-at-home mom, Stacey Goldman, pretended to review contracts on their desks and ask others about their new listings. I knew they didn't have any business because Jacqueline had ordered me to track everyone's sales in the office. I knew the agents who produced deals and the ones who hung around their desk merely to socialize.

Before I had a chance to give Jacqueline feedback from the open house, Maeve clapped her hands and waved to catch everyone's attention.

"Let's get started, people." A ripple of silence spread over the room. "Announcements first." Maeve stood near the far wall and cleared her throat. She proceeded to read the new listings for the previous week, the majority of which were Jacqueline's.

When Maeve called my name after one of the properties, Jacqueline pinched her lips together and raised her eyebrows at me. I hadn't told her about my new listing in Logan Square. My side business was gaining momentum. So far, the increase in my workload hadn't been an issue. I'd been able to keep up with everything she'd thrown at me

"And now, a special announcement." Maeve tipped her chin down. "I've been told that one of our realtors is going to be named by *CBR Magazine* as one of the 'Thirty Under Thirty' in Chicago real estate." She paused to build suspense, then smiled like a proud grandma. "Congratulations, Mara!" She clapped her hands in the air, and a smattering of applause echoed throughout the office, followed by quiet mumbling.

I sat up straight, my heart beating double time. I offered a sheepish smile and an obligatory thank you wave to the others in the room as I felt my cheeks reddening. Jacqueline caught my eye and winked at me, nodding in approval.

"And next, a quick reminder about our yearly in-house competition for Greystone's Top Producer Award. Jacqueline Hendersen is currently in first place for the THIRD year in a row, but there are still four months left in the year." She pumped her fist in the air. "Let's get those deals signed and give Jacqueline a run for her money!" Despite Maeve's energetic appeal, the response was subdued. No one cheered. A couple of people chuckled. Jacqueline scowled. I exhaled, thankful the focus was no longer on me.

Maeve introduced the guest speaker, a lender with mousy, shoulder-length hair wearing a red power suit. As the woman droned on about the differences between pre-qualification and pre-approval, Jacqueline rolled her chair closer to my desk. I eyed the bandage on her ankle and tried not to think about Tony.

"How's your ankle?"

"Fine. No big deal." She tucked her legs under her chair and lowered her voice to a whisper. "Listen, I need you to do something for me today."

I swallowed and looked at my hands.

"Go on caravan with Kevin. Try to make friends."

My head jolted upright. "Why?"

"Kevin is in the CCC. He likes you. He might take you with him—as a guest. It's the best way for us to get new leads on developments."

"But I'm a woman."

"They have special events. Holiday parties and crap like that. Women are allowed at those."

"Why don't *you* go, then?"

Jacqueline narrowed her eyes at me. "I told you already. They don't like me. They know the developers would rather sign with me than them. Someone like you isn't a threat. You can fly under the radar."

I fiddled with the pen in my hand, fingers tightening around it at Jacqueline's backhanded compliment. I pictured Natalia's eyes burning into me, and Jacqueline's foot kicking Tony's jar of change into the street. Now she wanted me to start hanging out with Kevin? I wanted to tell her to fuck off. Kevin was a slimeball. He'd probably use it as an excuse to try to get in my pants.

When I didn't respond, Jacqueline leaned in even closer. "Before your head gets too big, the 'Thirty Under Thirty' award? That was all me."

I scratched an itch on my elbow, confused.

"I made it happen for you." Her grey eyes surrounded me like prison bars. "You never would have been nominated if I hadn't made a phone call on your behalf to Patricia Abramson. She owed me a favor."

My phone call with *CBR Magazine* spun through my head. Patricia Abramson was the same person who'd selected Jacqueline as one of the 'Forty under Forty' the year before. Jacqueline had mentioned Patricia's name in passing every time we found a new issue of *CBR Magazine* in our mailboxes. Maybe I hadn't earned the honor on my own after all.

"Now, you do this for me." She paused before stating the obvious. "Don't tell Kevin anything about any of our deals."

I slumped over my desk, my previous resolve to stand up to Jacqueline's demands crumbling like a decaying house. "Okay."

CHAPTER TWENTY-NINE

"Do you mind if I catch a ride with you for caravan?" I teetered in front of Kevin's desk, tugging the skirt of my sundress down to increase its coverage of my bare legs. People milled around me, jingling car keys and arguing over who would ride shotgun. Even from a couple of feet away, I couldn't escape the noxious fog of his cologne.

He stopped his busywork and pressed his lips into a smile. "I thought you didn't go on caravan."

"I decided I should go once in a while." I shifted my weight from my left foot to my right foot. "You know, just to see what's out there."

"I'm kidding, Mara. Relax. You can ride with me." Kevin threw his man bag over his shoulder and headed toward the front of the office. "Let's go. Don't want to be late."

I shot a look at Jacqueline as I followed Kevin out the front door. She glanced up and watched me leave, stone-faced.

"Thanks for the ride." I slid into the passenger seat of Kevin's Lexus.

"Sure thing. Let's see where we're going." He scanned the property list on his phone. "A single-family in Old Irving." He pulled onto North Avenue and headed toward the expressway.

"Congrats on being one of the 'Thirty Under Thirty.'"

"Thanks." I kept my eyes focused out the window, hoping no one would find out it was all a scam. "I wasn't expecting it."

"It's a big fucking deal. You'll get a lot of business from that."

"You think?"

"I don't think. I know." His eyes flicked from the road to my exposed knees while he talked. "So, how's it working with Jacqueline?"

Buildings flitted by outside, and I wished I was locked safely inside one of them. "It's good. I've learned a ton from her." I left out the parts about her making me a target of the Russian mob, kicking a jar of change out of homeless guy's hand, tricking me into stealing family heirlooms from an innocent woman's condo, and the handful of other illegal things she'd done.

"She hasn't slit your throat and left you on the side of the road yet, so that's good." He chuckled. "You should probably separate yourself from her, now that you've got your footing. Her ethics are questionable if you know what I mean."

I wondered if Kevin saw the irony in the situation. A guy with hair slicked back, doused in cheap cologne, wearing a gold chain around his neck, and engaging in borderline sexual harassment giving advice on ethics.

"Oh, no. Jacqueline is fine. She's never screwed me on a commission or anything." I straightened my shoulders, inexplicably feeling the urge to defend her. Part of me wanted to confess that *I* was the one who screwed her out of the listing on Mohawk, but I'd never mention it. My hands encircled my purse, sliding it forward onto my knees as my fingernails gouged into the leather.

Despite Jacqueline's missteps, it was uncomfortable talking about her behind her back after she'd done so much to help me. She'd kept me in business with the draw she'd given me. She'd held a fundraiser for Emma. She'd paid for the legal work to get the protective order against Peter. Besides, Kevin was the one who'd duped me, not Jacqueline. He'd stolen the Sabatinos' listing from under our noses.

"You find the Sabatinos a restaurant space yet?" I held my breath. It was a sore subject, but I wanted to remind Kevin what he'd done.

"No. Those people." He shook his head in disgust. "I've found them the perfect space about ten times now. They find something wrong with every one of them. So high maintenance."

I smiled to myself, thankful I wasn't dealing with them right now. With everything I had on my plate, I barely had time to work out, much less hang out with my friends, or go on a date. Kevin veered off at the Irving Park exit and headed west before stopping at a red light.

"Why does everyone think Jacqueline is so unethical?"

Kevin threw his head back and laughed. "Are you serious?"

I shrugged, not saying anything. I knew why *I* thought she was shady—spray-painting gang tags on buildings, staging a robbery, sabotaging Natalia's business, forcing me to go on caravan with Kevin to weasel my way into the CCC. But, as far as I knew, no one else knew about these things.

"No one gets as far as she has in Chicago real estate without screwing people over." He studied my face as if gauging my level of understanding. "She'd kill her own mother to get both sides of a commission."

The light turned green, and we drove on in silence.

"Has she ever mentioned anything about the property on Byron Street?" He gripped the steering wheel so tight I could see the whites of his knuckles.

"I'm not sure."

"I brought in a buyer there last year. Solid offer, only contingent on the inspection. Long story short, black mold and water suddenly appear in the basement the morning of the inspection. I swear it hadn't been there when we toured the property five days earlier." He paused, looking over at me. "My buyer walked. A few days later, guess who brings in her own buyer?" Kevin poked his finger through his crispy hair and scratched his scalp, his eyes searching me. "See what I mean?"

"Yeah. She did mention that. She said the mold had been there all along."

"No fucking way. It wasn't there."

"It sounds a little sketchy, but you have no proof."

"There's never any proof, Mara. That's the problem."

I thought about Natalia's threat to expose us and hoped that Kevin was right.

Kevin turned on his flashers and parked in an illegal spot in front of a white Colonial-style single-family where baskets of geraniums lined the porch.

Deal-less Ellen Barkley emerged from the car behind us carrying a spiral notebook, a pen tucked behind her ear. "What wonderful curb appeal!" she said, craning her neck toward the upstairs windows and removing the pen to write something on her pad.

I was beginning to understand why Jacqueline didn't do well on caravan.

It was a long tour—eight properties scattered across the west and north side of the city. After the seventh condo, a studio in Edgewater, Kevin studied the list on his phone.

"What do you say we bail on the last property and grab something to eat?"

My teeth clamped down on the inside of my cheek, a tightening in my gut telling me to avoid any more one-on-one time with Kevin. But I hadn't found a good time to bring up the CCC yet. And I was curious to hear more of his stories about Jacqueline. On top of that, I'd only eaten half of a piece of pizza at the broker's open. My stomach rumbled.

I pointed toward the lake. "There's a good sushi place a couple of blocks over."

"Can't. I'm allergic to shellfish. My EpiPen is in my bag, in case you ever see me blowing up like a balloon." He pretended to jab an object into his leg and laughed. "Do you like Indian food?"

A few minutes later, we were seated across from each other at a miniature table at The Jewel of India restaurant. I tore off a piece of naan and bit into it.

"So, what do you do for fun? You know, in all your spare

time?" Kevin chuckled as he chewed.

"I don't know—I workout at East Coast. Hang out with my friends once in a while. That's about it." I looked down, trying not to think about how lame my life sounded.

"I'm recruiting volunteers to join our Habitat group. Thought you might be interested."

"Habitat group?"

"Habitat for Humanity. We build houses for deserving families. It's only one day a month. Gets you outside. Helps people. All that. No skills required."

Kevin built houses for needy people in his spare time? I nodded, hoping my face didn't betray my shock. "Cool. Yeah. As long as it fits with my schedule, I'll be there."

"Great. I'll shoot you an email later." He continued chewing. "How's your sister doing, anyway?"

"Oh. Emma's good." I picked up my fork and then set it down. "She finished her last round of chemo, and the doctor says she's cancer-free. She's starting at Illinois in a few weeks."

Kevin tipped back in his chair. "Wow! That's great news. I've been pulling for her."

The slackened look of relief on his face told me his feelings were genuine. I remembered how he'd participated in the charity run while refusing to wear Jacqueline's self-promoting T-shirt, and I couldn't help smiling.

"Thanks." I tore off another piece of bread and took a deep breath. Kevin had disarmed me with his thoughtfulness, but I needed to stay focused on Jacqueline's mission. I cleared my throat and leaned forward. "So, I heard you're in the CCC. It's like a secret society, right?"

"Not really. I own a few rental buildings. Two in Edgewater, one in North Center." Kevin gulped his iced tea. "You have to own or develop commercial real estate in the city to be a member."

"And not be a woman," I said, my voice slipping out sharper than I'd planned.

Kevin tipped his head back and made a face. "Yeah. Yeah. That, too. A guy I know invited me to a meeting once. I guess I schmoozed my way in."

"What's it like?" I diverted my eyes toward a mural on the wall, hoping to hide my false intentions.

"Honestly, it's the shit. Lots of big players. It's good to know who the heavy hitters are, you know?"

"Yeah. That sounds great."

"These guys have so much money it's sick." He smirked, shaking his head. "We can bring guests to some of the events." He winked. "Men or women. You should come with me sometime. Those developers would love to have one of the 'Thirty Under Thirty' show up at their party."

"Thanks." I exhaled, amazed it had been so easy, but also feeling slightly nauseous. I hoped he was inviting me as a colleague and not as his date.

He lowered his eyes at me. "As long as you don't steal any leads for Jacqueline."

My stomach sunk with unexpected weight. "No. I'd never do that."

Kevin chuckled. "I'm only messing with you, Mara. You need to loosen up a little bit."

I nodded, smiling. Kevin was only trying to be nice. It didn't feel right to take advantage. Yet he hadn't hesitated to take advantage of me on the Bistro Maria listing. According to Jacqueline, we were merely evening the playing field.

CHAPTER THIRTY

"Sweet car!" Emma leaned through the front door of my parents' house as I stepped out of my BMW. Despite the ninety-degree temperature, she wore the same pink knit hat that she'd worn at the charity run four months earlier. I did a doubletake at her appearance, which had deteriorated even further since I'd seen her five weeks ago.

"Yeah. I'm pretty cool." I hugged Emma, her body like a sack of twigs in my arms.

She covered her mouth and turned away, coughing.

"How are you feeling?" I asked.

"Good." She cleared her throat. "I'm done with chemo!" She hopped off the ground as she said the words.

"That's awesome. I knew you'd beat it."

I stepped inside where Mom and Dad appeared in the shadowy hallway.

"We kicked that thing, didn't we, Em?" Dad patted Emma on the back. My sister nodded. It had only been a few weeks, but Dad looked older somehow, his hair a lighter shade of gray. Or was he thinner? I couldn't put my finger on it.

Mom peered around me toward my new car. "Well, isn't that sharp?"

"That's my new ride." My smile froze when I saw Dad's expression.

His forehead creased with wrinkles. "A BMW? Isn't that a little excessive?"

I'd kept my luxury car a secret from my family for as long as possible. With my extravagant purchase exposed, I felt slightly ridiculous. Dad had been busting his butt in the marketing world for years, and he still drove a Ford. The city was a different world, though.

"Everyone expects realtors in the city to drive nice cars," I said. "Clients want to work with successful agents. Success breeds more success. That's what Jacqueline says."

My cell phone buzzed with incoming texts. I scanned the messages. No emergencies.

Dad frowned. "Just be careful. Real estate is cyclical. You need to save up your money for a rainy day."

"I am, Dad." I rubbed the edge of the paper folded inside my pocket and smiled to myself.

Mom waved us through the kitchen. "I just put some appetizers out on the patio. The heat's not too bad in the shade." She opened the sliding glass door. "Does everyone want some lemonade?"

"Sure." I followed Dad and Emma outside.

We found our seats on the patio, and Mom joined us a minute later carrying a glass pitcher sweating with condensation and filled with ice cubes and lemonade. She poured four glasses and then thrust a bowl of pretzels in my face. I took one, although my late lunch at Jewel of India sat like a brick in my stomach.

"Dig in." She leaned forward, smiling. "It's so good to have you home."

I breathed in, my body feeling lighter than it had in the city. The four of us were together. I made a conscious effort to appreciate the time with my family. Emma's disease reminded me that it could all be taken away so quickly. The fenced-in back yard beyond the patio was small by suburban standards, but enormous compared to city lots I'd been spending so much time in lately. Everything about the yard was familiar and welcoming—the rose bushes in the corner, the towering maple tree, the wooden privacy fence. My parents installed the fence when I was seven. I stared at a brown spot on the grass where I'd once shown a toddler-aged Emma how to run through the sprinkler, encouraging her to lean into the cold water and get her face wet. She'd been wearing a red bathing suit that looked like a ladybug. That day had been hot like today and smelled the same, too. Images of birthday parties, picnics, and family soccer games flickered through my mind. Suddenly, I wished I could get those days back, that I'd known enough to appreciate them. At least Emma's treatment would soon be paid off, and my parents wouldn't have to sell the house.

I refocused my attention on the pretzels in front of me. "Anything exciting been going on here?"

"I got an email from my roommate," Emma said. "Her name is McKenzie. She's really nice. I warned her about my hair." Emma pointed to her head. "She said she'd shave her head, too, and grow her hair out with me, but I told her she didn't need to do that."

"She sounds great. Will you be able to start classes on time?" I didn't want to make a big deal about my sister's sickly appearance, but she didn't look strong enough to handle the stress of starting college.

"If my doctor gives me the green light, I can move into the dorm in a couple of weeks. The same as everyone else." Emma coughed again. "I'll just have to drive back for checkups."

"She's been registering for classes, haven't you, Em?" Mom smiled.

I nodded, happy that my sister's life hadn't been disrupted too badly.

My phone buzzed in my pocket. I pulled it out and saw that an inspector was returning my call. I sent it to voicemail.

"How's the real estate business?"

"Great." I set down my glass and leaned in. "I was just named one of 'Thirty Under Thirty' by *CBR Magazine*."

Dad raised his eyebrows at me and nodded. "That's great, Mara."

"Cool." Emma yawned and laid her head back in her chair. I

looked from Mom to Dad to see if they seemed concerned, but their faces showed no emotion. Emma hunched forward and sipped some of her lemonade. "Sorry."

"It's okay." I shifted toward her. "Want to watch a movie later? I brought a classic—*I know What You Did Last Summer*," I said, using my creepiest voice.

"Yeah. I love that one." She rubbed her eyes and yawned again. "I might go lie down for a few minutes. I'm so tired all of a sudden."

I nodded. Despite the oppressive heat, a coldness trickled through me. Five minutes sitting on the porch had made Emma tired? My parents had been telling me how much progress Emma had been making, how she'd completed chemo, and was cancer-free, but she seemed worse than the last time I'd seen her. Were they in denial? The sliding door closed behind Emma, and she hobbled toward her bedroom.

"Are you sure she's better?" I said when I was sure Emma was out of earshot.

"Well, yes," Mom said. "The test results confirmed it."

"I know. It's just that…" I pressed my lips together and forced the heat away from my face. "She looks worse than she did five weeks ago." I lowered my voice. "How is she going to handle starting college?"

"The nurse at the clinic said treatment is harder on some people than others. I think Emma's body is especially sensitive to the medicine. Now that it's over, she should bounce back quickly." Dad clutched his lemonade in his hand but didn't drink it. "Anyway, she's going in for another follow-up test next week. Just to confirm everything is good before she leaves."

I stared at the wooden slats of the fence.

"Mara, honey." Mom stood next to me now and placed her hand on top of mine. "It's going to be fine."

I nodded, hoping she was right. "How are the bills coming?"

Dad swirled the ice in his glass. "We've made a big dent in them. The charity run helped a lot. We're down to twelve grand. I should be able to pay it off over the next year or two if my business stays steady."

I reached into my pocket and pulled out the blank check and a pen. "You can pay it off now." I set the check on the table in front of me and made it out for twelve-thousand dollars. Then I handed it to Dad. He stared at it and blinked back the moisture in his eyes.

"Are you sure you can afford this?"

"Yeah. Business is going well."

"Thank you." He bit his lip and handed the check to Mom.

"We're proud of you, Mara." Mom stood up and kissed me on the head.

I straightened myself up in my chair. "I finally found something I'm good at."

Dad chuckled. "You sure did."

"I've learned so much from Jacqueline." I stared at the shiny straps of my sandals, envisioning the starving realtors who'd inhaled the food at the broker's open this morning. Only my association with Jacqueline separated myself from them. Some of her methods were reprehensible—yes—but she'd also shown me what it took to rise above the crowd. My phone buzzed in my pocket with another incoming call. I reached down and silenced it.

"Well, it's good you're tied in with her," Dad said. "She was very impressive. Tom still raves about her. She helped him out of a big mess."

"What happened with Tom anyway?" I leaned in, realizing I'd never heard the whole story.

Dad shook his head. "Helluva thing. So, Tom gets a call in the middle day from the gas company. They tell him there's some kind of problem with the gas line in his townhome, possibly a leak. It's an emergency, you know? So, he rushes home from work to open the door and, lo and behold, he walks in on his wife and another guy messing around right there in the living room " Dad coughed out a laugh. "Nearly destroyed the poor guy. And here's the kicker—there was no gas leak."

I uncrossed my legs, my hands dropping to my sides. "And Jacqueline helped him?"

"Apparently, he and Bonnie, his ex-wife, had met her at a

charity dinner a few weeks earlier. They'd hit it off. So, when he discovered the, uh, indiscretion, he'd called Jacqueline to list their townhome. He said using Jacqueline as their realtor was the only thing he and Bonnie could agree on." Dad laughed, and Mom chuckled, too. "It was a beautiful house in River North. A shame." Dad shook his head. "Tom lives in Evanston now. Only a five-minute commute to the office. Can't beat that."

"Jacqueline knows her stuff," I said, although I couldn't ignore the unease that spread through my stomach.

Think about it, Mara. The reasons people sell their properties...Divorces, job losses, unexpected illnesses, death...She's behind it all. I blinked away Peter's face, wondering about Jacqueline's role in Tom's divorce. If she could orchestrate a fake break-in, what else could she have done? I gulped my lemonade.

"Have you heard from Nate?" Mom asked, passing a platter of chips and salsa toward me.

"No." My face burned at the mention of his name.

"There are lots of fish in the sea, Mara." Dad winked at me. "You should move on."

"I know. It's just probably better if I'm not in a relationship right now. My job is demanding."

The sad truth was the more I tried to forget about Nate, the more he seemed irreplaceable. No one compared to him. Not that I would take him back. I wouldn't. How could I be with someone who didn't believe in me? He'd already moved on anyway.

My phone buzzed again. This time I pulled it out to see who was calling. Bill. I'd already left him a voicemail with feedback from the broker's open. My parents stared at me, waiting to see what I'd do. I silenced the call and slid the phone back into my pocket.

We continued talking, my parents sharing the mundane details of their suburban life between disruptions from my phone.

Dad sighed. "Can you turn that thing off?"

"Sorry." I shrugged. "It's the business."

A minute later, a text message beeped through from Jacqueline.

How'd it go with Kevin? I flipped my phone upside down. Another message beeped through. Then another. I glanced at the screen. Jacqueline's most recent text alerted me to a new condo she'd listed. I started typing a message back but decided it could wait.

More texts from Jacqueline appeared a few seconds later. She told me to meet her at a condo in uptown tomorrow—an additional listing that I'd be responsible for showing. I hadn't even responded to her first message yet. I grumbled about the interruptions, the familiar tension in my shoulders returning. She knew I was taking the night off to visit Emma, but I guess she didn't care.

CHAPTER THIRTY-ONE

The bitter scent of brewing espresso beans swirled with the sweet aroma of vanilla scones as I pressed my back against the metal slats of the bistro chair. A beam of sunlight shot through the window of Starbuck's and directly into my eyes.

"How'd it go with Kevin? Why didn't you answer my texts?" Jacqueline's voice was stretched thin. She clutched a soy latte in her hands.

I shrugged. "It went well. He didn't suspect anything. At least as far as I could tell." I lifted my phone and scrolled through my emails to avoid eye contact.

"Did you bring up the CCC?"

"Yeah." My eyes squinted through the blinding light to meet hers. "I'm in. Kevin invited me to the next party."

"Yes!" She slapped her hand on the table, the sudden noise causing me to jump. "What else? Did you learn anything about his deals?"

"No. Not really. Except the Sabatinos are turning out to be difficult buyers."

"When's the CCC party?"

"Next Wednesday night at seven o'clock."

"What else? What else? Tell me everything."

I shifted my chair toward Jacqueline, noticing the way her back faced the sun. "We went out to lunch together. Indian food. He's deathly allergic to shellfish. EpiPen's in his bag if you ever see him blowing up like a balloon." I looked at the ceiling.

"Anything that has to do with real estate? Your lack of detail is killing me. Did he say anything about me?"

"Um, yeah. Kevin thinks you're unethical."

Jacqueline laughed. "*I'm* unethical? He's the one who slithered in to steal our listing." She leaned in closer. "Why does he think that?"

"The deal on Byron Street. Mold appeared before the inspection, and then you brought in your own buyer."

Jacqueline crossed her arms in front of her and sighed. "That sorry piece of shit. If that's all he has on me, he's not going to get very far."

My eyes traveled to the floor. *If that's all he has on me...* Her statement clawed at my insides. Not exactly a denial.

"Mara. Let's talk about what you're going to do when you're at the CCC. Pay attention to everything everyone says, especially the developers."

I nodded, lips pinched.

"Try to separate yourself from me, like you're going to be doing your own thing soon. These guys are a bunch of self-important pricks. They take every opportunity to brag about new business. Take down every address you hear, the person who mentioned it, and what it is."

I processed her instructions before looking up. "Won't they think it's weird if I'm taking notes?"

Jacqueline tipped her head back and massaged her temples with her fingers as if she were talking to the dumbest person in the world. She lowered her hands and leaned toward me again. "Be discreet. Be creative. Don't drink too much. You need to be a step ahead of these guys. Pretend you're a spy."

I smiled. "Okay. Yeah, cool."

"Any questions?"

My toes tapped against the floor as I remembered the way

Kevin had ogled my chest and my bare legs. "What if Kevin makes a move on me?"

Jacqueline smirked. "He probably won't do that until the end of the night. Pretend you need to take a call and get the hell out."

****

It was Wednesday night, and I'd already changed my outfit three times. I stepped into the living room wearing modest heels and my most business-like little black dress, the one that showed off my toned arms and stomach but had a conservative neckline and a hem that fell at an angle past my knees. Underneath, my Spanx hugged against my skin like a security blanket.

I glanced out the window, checking for Kevin's car. He'd insisted on picking me up. The CCC reserved a parking spot for him behind the building, and he thought it would be a waste for us not to take advantage of it. I twisted the bracelet on my wrist, worried I'd put myself in an awkward situation. Hopefully, Kevin understood this was a networking event and not a date. My plan was to cut out early to avoid riding home with him.

The clock in the kitchen said 7:05—ten more minutes until Kevin would be here. I paced back into the living room, smoothing my hair down and double-checking my clutch for keys, driver's license, phone, lipstick, credit card, business cards, and a pen. As I rested my shoulder against the gas fireplace I'd never used, a fuzzy layer of dust on top of the mantel caught my eye. Housekeeping had never been one of my strengths, but I had even less time to clean and dust with all the work Jacqueline had been throwing at me. Maybe it was time to hire a cleaning service.

Discoloration on the surface of the mantel caused me to bend forward and take a closer look. A thick line had been dragged through the dust, leaving a fresh trail of lacquered wood peeking through the hazy layer of filth. My eye followed the path to a framed photo of my family that I kept displayed above the fireplace. I hadn't touched the photo in weeks, or possibly months, but someone else had. My fingers shook as I lifted the frame. It had been moved, pulled forward, and then set back in almost the same spot on the mantel where I usually kept it, except the pattern in the dust showed it now sat slightly further to the left.

I sucked in my breath, trying to recall anyone who'd been inside my condo in the last few days but couldn't remember having any visitors. Maybe I'd bumped the photo without realizing it, although I couldn't remember anything like that happening, either. Peter's desperate face flashed in my mind, as a sickening dread rose inside me, my heartbeat accelerating. I'd promised him I'd stay away from Jacqueline, and then I hadn't kept my word. What if Peter had violated the protective order and returned? He'd handled my closing. He could have copied the key to my condo and saved it, just like I'd discovered Jacqueline had been doing. Or maybe Jacqueline had saved my key along with all the others in her drawer? But why? I couldn't think of any possible motive.

I shuddered, realizing I had more than one enemy. Natalia's smoldering eyes hovered before me. What if she'd reversed the chase and begun following me? What if she'd sent one of her mobsters to teach me a lesson? My stomach seized. Now they knew what my family looked like, too. My life—and my family's—was in danger.

My eyes darted around the room in search of anything else missing or out of place. Everything appeared to be just as I'd left it. I'd rifled through my jewelry box minutes earlier, and my earrings, bracelets, and necklaces had been in their usual spots.

I flattened my back against the wall, my mind grasping for a more logical explanation. Of course. The electrician. I inhaled, feeling the blood return to my face. He'd been in my condo last Tuesday to fix my bathroom fan. I'd been home to let him in but had trusted him to let himself out after he'd completed the work. He must have gotten curious and had a look around before leaving. It was creepy and unprofessional, but much more likely than Peter, or Jacqueline, or Natalia's henchman breaking in only to move a photo and leave. My shoulders relaxed, as I realized how tightly strung I'd become since working with Jacqueline. Not everything was a crooked conspiracy.

A text beeped through on my phone, and I checked the message.

It was Kevin. *I'm parked out front. Come down when you're ready.*

CHAPTER THIRTY-TWO

The sun sunk lower in the September sky, casting long shadows behind the buildings and street signs of Lincoln Park. Just as I'd feared, Kevin's insistence on driving, coupled with his eyes skimming the curves of my body as I approached his car, made the outing feel like an awkward date. He turned into an alley off Armitage Avenue and pulled his car into a narrow spot with a "Reserved" sign posted above it.

"Parking for CCC members only." He turned toward me, smiling.

"Nice." I unbuckled and concentrated on my breathing, trying to calm myself. Instead, I inhaled Kevin's nauseating cologne. My nerves were getting out of control. I needed to calm down.

"Don't be nervous," he said. "These guys are just regular people. Regular people with millions and millions of dollars." He laughed at his own joke and pointed his key fob at his Lexus, locking the doors.

There was no turning back now. I followed behind as he walked to the front of the brick building and pushed the buzzer.

"Yep," said a deep voice crackling through the speaker.

"It's Kevin Lucas." He glanced up toward a camera mounted above the door and gave a half-hearted wave.

The door vibrated, and Kevin pulled it open, ushering me through in front of him.

"Up the stairs," he said.

The air tasted like wet cement as I forced my legs to climb the narrow staircase. I could practically feel Kevin's eyes groping my ass as he followed a step behind. How had I agreed to this in the first place? I didn't feel prepared to be surrounded by the top guns of Chicago real estate. As if that wasn't enough pressure, I'd have to spy for Jacqueline, too. My hands shook, and I steadied them on the railing. I was in over my head. Music and laughter drifted out from behind the double-door in front of me. I stopped and turned back to look at my companion, hoping he would offer to go first.

"What are you waiting for?" Kevin reached past me and pulled open the door, revealing a spacious room with lofted ceilings. The solid wood walls reminded me of a royal parlor and increased my curiosity about the exclusive club. A dozen or so men stood in clusters, drinks in hand, talking and laughing with one another. A couple of women wearing cocktail dresses and sparkling jewelry leaned close together and nibbled on appetizers. No one noticed our entry. I was probably making too big a deal out of this whole thing. My shoulders relaxed. Kevin jabbed my arm with his elbow.

"Let's get a drink," he said.

I walked next to him toward the far side of the room. His stubby fingers brushed against the small of my back, and I flinched. I stepped away from his hand and closer to the mirrored shelves of the bar in front of us. A tall guy about my age wore a formal bartender uniform and poured a drink behind the counter. He pushed the glass toward an overweight man in a business suit.

"What can I get you?" the bartender turned toward us. His longish, dirty-blonde hair fell past his ears, his turquoise eyes disarming me. I glanced toward Kevin.

"Black Label on the rocks," Kevin said.

The bartender's eyes connected with mine, holding on a beat longer than necessary and causing me to forget how to speak.

"Vodka and tonic." I smiled and tightened my abs.

He nodded and grabbed a bottle of Kettle One, giving a

generous pour into a glass.

Jacqueline had instructed me not to drink too much, but I needed at least one to take the edge off. Besides, I couldn't pass up free top-shelf alcohol. The gorgeous man slid the drinks across the counter toward us.

"Thanks," Kevin said.

I flashed a demure smile toward the bartender. "Thank you."

A broad-shouldered man who looked like he'd once been the quarterback of his college football team stormed up behind us and patted Kevin on the back.

"Kevin, nice to see you!"

"Howard! How's business?"

"Well, you know. Not too bad." The men laughed as if sharing a private joke. Howard glanced over at me.

"This is Mara Butler." Kevin pushed me forward. "She's a realtor at Greystone. *CBR Magazine* just named her one of 'Thirty Under Thirty' in Chicago real estate."

"Ah, a big shot!" Howard held out his hand, and I shook it with a firm grip. "Howard Aldrich. Nice to meet you."

"You too." I tried to think of something charming to say but drew a blank.

"Well, I'm due for another drink. I'll see you around." Howard stepped toward the bar as Kevin pulled me toward the appetizer table.

Kevin leaned in close. "You know who Howard Aldrich is, right?"

"It sounds familiar," I said, remembering what Jacqueline had told me about Natalia's affair with the man.

"He owns Chicago Rentals, the biggest apartment rental company in the city. The guy owns more square feet of the city than any other person here."

Then I remembered more. Chicago Rentals owned one of the dilapidated buildings Jacqueline had me report to the building inspector. One of the buildings she'd tagged with spray paint. Howard wasn't one of the owners who'd sold out. After hanging up with him, she'd called him a slumlord. If he was a slumlord, he was good at it.

As we inched closer to the spread of food, I surveyed the guests. It was an older crowd, lots of gray and thinning hair offset by thick midsections. I was one of only a handful of women who'd been invited to the party. Thankfully, Natalia was nowhere in sight. Other than the hot guy behind the bar, I was by far the youngest person around. Every couple of minutes, a thunder of bellowing laughter would erupt and rumble through the room like an earthquake. I recognized a few familiar faces—Jay Benito, the owner of City First Realty, Pete Lousa, a swarthy lender I'd met at the charity dinner, and Roger Burton, one of the city's most successful developers. Roger was the main reason Jacqueline had sent me here tonight.

I balanced the small glass plate on my hand and used my other hand to pluck some cocktail shrimp with the tongs. The selection was impressive—shrimp, cheeses, pâté, and even caviar.

Kevin wandered away from the table, absorbed into a group of boisterous men laughing about commissions. I occupied myself by piling my plate with an assortment of food and hoping my loner status wasn't too noticeable.

Two men behind me discussed a deal on south State Street. I couldn't make out an address, and it sounded like the deal had already happened. The task Jacqueline had given me was unrealistic. No one was going to give up confidential information to some realtor they'd met only minutes before. My teeth slid through the creamy Gruyere cheese before crunching into the crispy rice cracker. As long as I was here, I'd enjoy the food and not stress about Jacqueline's expectations.

"You going to beat out Jacqueline for Top Producer this year?"

A lump of food lodged itself in my throat. I spun around. Kevin stood behind me with Roger Burton by his side.

"I'm trying." Kevin looked at the floor and shook his head. "She's way ahead of me right now."

I breathed again, realizing the question was directed at Kevin, not me.

Roger touched his silver goatee, the side of his mouth curving into a lopsided smile. "I might be able to help you out."

Both men glanced at me.

"Roger, this is Mara Butler. She's a realtor at Greystone. She made *CBR Magazine's* 'Thirty Under Thirty' list this year."

Roger eyed me, showing no recollection of having already met me at the CBR charity dinner. "Congratulations. Nice to meet you. Hope you don't mind if I steal Kevin for a while." Without waiting for an answer, Roger motioned for Kevin to follow him, and I was once again left standing alone.

I set down my plate. What was he telling Kevin? It was something they didn't want me to hear. I hovered close to the food table, watching the two men stop in the far corner of the room. Roger acted animated, leaning toward Kevin and waving his hand while he spoke. I couldn't hear their conversation without following them. That would be too obvious.

A finger tapped me on the shoulder, and I jumped.

"Hi. I'm Pete Lousa, Corcoran Brothers Lending."

"Yeah, hi." I straightened my shoulders, regaining my composure. "I think we met at Germania Place a few months back."

Pete and I engaged in small talk for several minutes, eventually exchanging cards even though I still had several of his cards from our last encounter. Pete didn't need to know I'd never recommend him over my guy, Justin Blakely from Gold Coast Lending, although Maeve constantly reminded us we were supposed to give buyers at least three options when it came to lenders and inspectors. Like Jacqueline said, Justin got deals done. Sometimes only one referral was needed.

I made my way toward the restroom, planning to hit the bar for another drink on my way out. Kevin and Roger remained stationed at the far corner of the room, engaged in some sort of private meeting.

"I heard you're funding Roger's newest condo project?" Some guy behind me was speaking to another man. I didn't recognize either of them, but I froze when I heard Roger's name, my senses hyper-alert.

"Sure am. It's a big one. Eighty units," said the other man. "On Orchard, near Arlington Place."

"Great location. How'd Roger get his hands on that building?"

"Don't know. You'll have to ask him."

"Who's doing the brokerage?"

"He mentioned someone from Greystone. Kevin something or another."

"Oh. Kevin Lucas. Good for him."

My heart pounded. Beads of sweat formed on my forehead. The room buzzed around me. Roger was going to announce a new condo development in Lincoln Park. Eighty units. On Orchard, near Arlington. And Kevin was going to list them all. A curtain of cigar smoke obscured the far corner of the room. Through the haze, I could make out Kevin, holding a cigar in one hand, a drink in the other, and grinning like he'd won the lottery.

I rushed into the empty women's bathroom and locked the door behind me. On the back of Pete Lousa's business card, I scrawled, *Roger Burton, 80-unit condo development on Orchard near Arlington.* Jacqueline was going to freak, but at least I'd obtained some confidential information for her. Mission accomplished.

I took a few deep breaths and reapplied my lipstick, waiting for my heart rate to return to normal. Then, I slipped back into the room and approached the bar, craving another drink. The bartender noticed me and smiled. His blue eyes were the color of the sea. They pulled me toward him like the tide. The square set of his jaw paralyzed me. I struggled to say hello, but the word got caught in my throat.

"Would you like another?" he asked, his voice deep and strong.

"Yes. Please," were the only words I could form. An unfamiliar giddiness fluttered in my stomach as I watched him pour me another vodka and tonic. He'd remembered what I'd ordered. That had to be a good sign. Of course, he was probably trained to remember the drinks people ordered. I wanted to know more about him. Where was he from? What was his name? Did he have a girlfriend? Women probably threw themselves at him all the time.

Kevin materialized through the smoke and let his hand linger on my arm. The bartender's eyes followed mine toward the unwanted touch.

"Sorry to leave you alone for so long," Kevin said. "Having a good time?"

My skin crawled as I pulled my arm away from Kevin. "Yeah. It's been great." I couldn't look at him. "How about you?"

"Yeah, you know. Same ol', same ol'." Kevin crossed his arms and cleared his throat.

I waited. Part of me thought Kevin would share the big news with me, that he trusted me. But he didn't say a word, just puffed on his cigar and scanned the room for more important people. A minute later, he drifted off into another conversation. I glanced toward the bartender again, but he'd already moved on. Further down the counter, he chatted with two older women while he rattled a martini shaker in his hand.

I drank fast, appreciating each gulp of the smooth vodka as it slid down my throat. A banker and an owner of a construction company sidled up to me, congratulating me on my "Thirty Under Thirty" title. After making my way around the room one last time, I said my goodbyes and my thank yous. It was getting late, and I had a meeting scheduled with Jacqueline at the crack of dawn.

Kevin looped his arm around my shoulders, his breath saturated with cigars and scotch. "I can drive you home, you know."

My muscles constricted. "That's okay. I'm taking off now. I already called an Uber."

He stepped back and squeezed my arm. "Maybe another time, then."

I raised my hand in a wave. "Thanks for inviting me. It was fun." Before Kevin could make any more inappropriate comments, I turned and strode toward the bar. The bartender's eyes connected with mine. He smiled.

An unexpected surge of confidence rushed through me, and I wasn't sure if it stemmed from the alcohol, or my determination to get over Nate, or that I knew I looked good in my little black dress. I pulled out my card and handed it to him. "I'm Mara."

"Hi, Mara. I'm Damon." He stopped wiping down the counter.

His gaze hung onto me, boring straight through to my soul. The electricity between us was tangible.

He tipped his head in Kevin's direction. "Is that your boyfriend?"

I made a face. "No. Not even close."

"Good." He smiled again, a stray piece of his blonde hair skimming the side of his unshaven face. "Can I take you out to dinner sometime?"

"Yeah," I said, feeling as if I couldn't breathe. "That would be great."

He lifted my card. "Now, I've got your number."

"Well, I've got to get going."

"Have a good night, Mara."

"You, too."

I scrambled out the door and down the stairs, desperate to leave before I did something embarrassing to cause Damon to change his mind.

Have a good night, Mara. I loved the way he'd said my name, how the word balanced on his tongue, and flowed smoothly from his lips. Cars whizzed past as I strolled down Armitage, my feet bouncing with each step. Damon's face floated in front of me, the stubble on his skin, and those eyes like the ocean. I chuckled under my breath, awestruck by our chance encounter. When I reached the corner, I took in my surroundings and remembered where I was. Much too far from home to walk. I'd forgotten to call an Uber. I raised my hand, and a cab pulled next to the curb. My body landed heavily in the back seat as I climbed in and gave the driver my address. I lowered the window, enjoying the sensation of the wind in my hair. I imagined I was perched on the spire of the Hancock Building, flying high above the city.

****

I arrived at Starbuck's five minutes late and found Jacqueline sitting at a table near the front windows, a scowl on her face. I slipped into the chair across from her, my body still levitating from my encounter with Damon. Before I could report back to her on

195

the CCC meeting, she shoved the newest issue of *CBR Magazine* toward me. I grabbed it, dying to see my profile. But Jacqueline had opened the magazine to a different page. An article entitled, 'Chicago's Top Producer Balances Work and Family,' accompanied by a full-spread photo of Natalia Romanov, her two kids, their three nannies, and a Labradoodle filled the page. Natalia's assistant hadn't made it into the picture.

"Three nannies for two kids?" I asked. "That must be how she balances work and family."

"What bullshit." Jacqueline shook her head in disgust. "This article confirms all the rumors I've been hearing about her lately."

"You mean about the Russian mob?"

"No. Not those rumors," she said, a sharp edge to her voice. "Natalia's going to be starring in some stupid reality show on HGTV. What a joke."

"Oh, man." I could tell by the faraway look in Jacqueline's eyes that she was jealous. "Natalia might need to hire a couple more nannies," I said, trying to lighten the mood.

Jacqueline didn't laugh. Before I could flip the page over to the 'Thirty Under Thirty' article, she snatched the magazine back and stuffed it in her bag.

"What did you learn at the CCC meeting?"

I leaned toward her, my fingertips gripping the edge of the table. "Roger Burton is announcing a new development in Lincoln Park, on Orchard near Arlington. Eighty units."

Her eyes grew wide. "Good work!"

"There's one more thing," I paused and looked down at the floor. "Kevin is listing the development."

She cocked her head, eyes simmering. Her fists slammed against the table, nearly toppling my fresh cup of coffee. "Roger's listing eighty units with Kevin?" Her forehead scrunched into creases. "Fuck!"

A woman sitting behind us glared over her shoulder. A pudgy toddler gnawed on a cake pop beside her. Jacqueline stared beyond them, taking no notice.

"It won't affect you this year," I said. "Those condos won't be ready to close for six months, at least."

Jacqueline clutched her coffee and shook her head. "I don't care. It affects next year. That development should have been mine."

"There will be other developments," I said, keeping my voice upbeat. "Besides, you already have so much business. It doesn't really matter."

Her steely eyes liquefied, surrounding me. "Every deal matters, Mara."

I slunk back in my chair, my face stinging as if she'd slapped me. The image of Betty's Victorian on Mohawk flashed in my head, and I suddenly wished I hadn't stolen the listing for myself.

"Did you get any other leads?"

I looked at my hands. "No." The only other lead I'd gotten was for a potential date with Damon, but I wasn't about to tell Jacqueline about that. I'd never seen her in such a foul mood.

"Fucking Kevin," she said. "Why do good things happen to horrible people?"

I shrugged, knowing better than to tell her that Kevin was a decent guy in some ways. A little slimy, maybe, but not the purely evil villain she made him out to be.

The woman with the toddler huffed. She scraped her chair backward, pulling her sticky child out the door while throwing a disapproving glance in our direction.

Jacqueline sighed and stared out the window like she was on another planet.

After a minute of awkward silence, I scooted my chair out, eager to get away from her. "I got the showing schedule you emailed me for today. All twelve of them. And I'll cover the inspection at 1:00."

She nodded, but her eyes were glazed and unfocused. I slung my bag over my shoulder and scurried out the door, leaving her sitting alone, staring off into space.

CHAPTER THIRTY-THREE

Lydia Burton sat across from Jacqueline and me, sipping butternut squash soup off her spoon. The older woman's makeup was overdone, and her hair perfectly molded into two large curls at her shoulders. Jacqueline had forced me to come along to the lunch meeting at Cafe Nordstrom, telling me it was time to talk real estate with Lydia and that Roger's new development on Orchard should have been hers. She was a thousand times more qualified than Kevin to handle such a large project. Lydia was her only chance to get in on the deal.

I broke apart a steaming roll, my fingertips holding on gingerly. The quiver of excitement rippling through my body was interfering with my usual appetite. Damon had called me last night and asked me to go out for sushi with him on Friday night. After I'd happily accepted, we talked for another fifteen minutes about the CCC, my career in real estate, and his part-time job as a bartender while he completed his second year of law school. The conversation had been easy like we already knew each other and had simply forgotten the details of each other's lives. We hadn't even gone on a date yet, and he already blew Nate out of the water.

The clang of Lydia's spoon against the edge of her bowl brought me back to the table. "The depth of flavor in this soup is exquisite," she said, pursing her bright-red lips.

"I heard Roger has a new condo development in Lincoln Park." Jacqueline's voice was light and bubbly as if she didn't have a care in the world.

"Oh, yes, Jacqueline." Lydia stirred her soup before sipping another spoonful. "He's always got some development or another in the works."

"Did you know he's planning on using a realtor from Greystone to list the units?" Jacqueline paused. "Kevin Lucas."

Lydia stared at her soup. "No, we don't usually discuss those things."

Jacqueline leaned closer to Lydia, lowering her voice. "I don't like to talk badly about other realtors, especially ones from my own office, but Kevin is known to be a crooked character."

"Oh, dear." Lydia shook her head. "Well, it's not surprising, I guess, given the nature of the business." She stirred her soup and glanced from me to Jacqueline. "If it were up to me, I'd have you list the building. You are very impressive."

Jacqueline squinted and offered a bashful smile. "You're too nice, Lydia." She straightened up her shoulders. "I do have a lot of experience selling large volumes of condos. And I specialize in Lincoln Park. Your husband wouldn't be disappointed with my service."

"I'm sure he wouldn't." She gazed at Jacqueline like a proud mother. Then, as if it were her idea, she said, "Tell you what, I'll recommend you to Roger. In fact, I'll insist he hire you."

"Oh! Really? Thank you." Jacqueline reached across the table, feigning surprise. "That's very kind."

Lydia held up her hand, signaling Jacqueline to slow down. "Roger's a man of his word, though. He's not likely to change his mind about the Lincoln Park project if he already promised the listing to this Kevin character."

"I understand." Jacqueline nodded. "A man who keeps his word. That's admirable."

The three of us chuckled at Jacqueline's jab at the male species. Then, as if Lydia could see Jacqueline's mind wandering back to the man in her life who hadn't kept his word, she patted Jacqueline's hand.

"Don't you worry, honey. There's a good man out there for you somewhere. You just haven't found him yet."

"Well, I have Jeffery." Jacqueline swallowed, her eyes darting in every direction. "He's in Africa right now."

"Yes, dear. I forgot. Of course, you do.

****

Two days later, Roger Burton loomed over a massive black table in a conference room at the office of Burton Development. The company's in-house attorney, a balding man with pasty skin and a charcoal suit, sat next to Roger, flipping through a stack of papers. Jacqueline paused before entering the room, pointing to a spot in the hallway outside where she wanted me to wait. I hovered awkwardly near the doorway and hoped Kevin couldn't see me. Jacqueline strode into the conference room, leaving the door cracked open for my benefit.

My feet ached, and I wished she hadn't insisted I come with her. A receptionist from Burton Development wandered past, so I pretended to look at my phone, trying not to make it obvious that I was eavesdropping. Jacqueline claimed an open seat across from Roger and his attorney. From where I stood, I could only see the back of Jacqueline's head. Her hair was pulled into a French twist, and a tailored suit jacket skimmed her shoulders. Kevin slouched into a leather chair two seats to her right. I hoped he didn't suspect me of telling Jacqueline about his new development listing.

Roger cleared his throat. "As I mentioned on the phone, we're meeting here today because Burton Development would like the two of you to list our newest development in Lincoln Park, Arlington on the Park. You will be co-listers and split all sales fifty-fifty."

Jacqueline nodded. "Thank you, Roger."

Kevin grunted and shook his head.

Roger shifted toward Kevin. "Kevin, I know you think you can handle this development on your own, but I disagree. Eighty units is a lot for one person to sell, even with some junior agents assisting you. Jacqueline will be a valuable asset."

"This isn't the deal we agreed on, Roger." Kevin rolled his chair back from the table.

"We never put it in writing, Kevin. The deal we're signing today is the deal we agree on. If you don't like it, I can always list with another company."

A tense silence hung in the air. Even the attorney stopped shuffling papers.

"That won't be necessary," Jacqueline said.

"Are you ready to move forward, Kevin?" Roger asked.

"Yes." Kevin angled his shoulders toward Roger, refusing to acknowledge Jacqueline's presence.

Lydia had pulled through for Jacqueline, and I had to give the woman credit. She must have given her husband an earful. Jacqueline had wanted the development all to herself, but fifty percent was better than nothing.

I tried not to zone out completely as the attorney reviewed every word of the thirty-page contract. The terms designated Kevin and Jacqueline as the exclusive listing agents for a period of twelve months, renewable by the agreement of both parties. They'd receive a two percent commission on each sale, minus their cut to Greystone. They'd split all commissions fifty-fifty regardless of which one of them showed the unit or wrote the contract. They'd be paid at closing. They'd operate out of a sales center that Burton Development had recently finished constructing on the site, which contained a model unit. The contract required them to hold open houses at the sales center every Sunday from 1:00 p.m. to 4:00 p.m. No exceptions. Failure to do so was grounds for termination.

This development sounded like a time suck, and I got a sinking feeling that Jacqueline planned to pawn the open houses off on me.

After everyone signed the paperwork, shook hands, and made small talk about the state of the Chicago real estate market, Jacqueline gathered her things to leave. She raised her eyebrows at me as she strode into the hallway. I jogged to keep up with her through the front door of the building.

Jacqueline's eyes beamed at me as I caught up to her. "Did you hear all that?" she asked.

"Yeah. I can't believe Lyd…"

Before I could finish my sentence, footsteps pounded behind me, the fine hairs on my arm standing on end as I gagged on a stale mixture of cologne and sweat. Kevin pushed past me and thrust his body toward Jacqueline, trapping her between himself and the brick wall of the building. He glared at her, nostrils flaring.

"How did you get your claws into this deal, Jacqueline? This was my development." His eyes bounced toward me but landed back on her.

I kept my face still as my chest flooded with guilt. Kevin had offered to take me to the CCC after I'd shown an interest in it. Maybe his motives hadn't been completely pure, but I'd still betrayed him.

"I guess someone put in a good word for me." Jacqueline shrugged.

"You're an underhanded bitch. You know that? Don't expect me to make things easy for you."

"Right back at you." Jacqueline smiled at him. Then she shoved his arm out of her path and marched down the sidewalk.

Kevin turned toward me, a bewildered expression on his face. "You're too good for her, Mara. Get out while you still can."

I gulped and turned away, unable to ignore the tremor that crawled down my spine.

CHAPTER THIRTY-FOUR

Jacqueline's desk sat empty amid the afternoon hum of the real estate office. I took the rare opportunity to scan through my potential leads, the ones not connected to her. Kevin's warning had been turning over in my head since our encounter outside Burton Development yesterday. *Get out while you still can.*

Maybe he was right. Maybe it was time to separate myself from Jacqueline before I lost grasp of all my moral bearings. Her troubling behavior had been easier to shake off when her schemes didn't involve me. But, now she'd tricked me into taking the driver's seat, had pushed me into betraying unsuspecting people one too many times. My actions didn't sit right, no matter what the payoff.

My body weighed with worry as I studied the document on my laptop. My list of independent clients was shorter than I'd hoped— only two potential buyers and one two-bedroom listing in Lincoln Square.

Dad's name flashed on my phone.

"Hi."

"Mara, we've got some bad news," I could barely hear Dad's voice against the background noise of chatting realtors. He paused and cleared his throat. "Are you sitting down?"

I clenched my phone with one hand and braced myself against my desk with the other. "Yeah."

"The results of Emma's follow-up tests came back. Her cancer has returned."

"What?" I clutched my phone tighter, not wanting to believe the words.

"It's recurring Lymphoma." Dad sighed. "The doctor said it's common for cancer to come back shortly after treatment. Mom's upstairs with Emma now. It's been…upsetting."

I couldn't shake the memory of Emma's starchy complexion, her hollow eyes. I swallowed, trying to control the anger that rose inside of me. *I'd known.* As soon as I'd heard her quivering voice and watched her frail body collapse in the chair, I'd known. Now we'd lost another week.

"What are we going to do?" I couldn't breathe.

"She'll have to go through chemo again. Then, depending on her blood cell counts, she might need a transfusion."

"NO!" I slammed my fist on my desk, not letting him finish his sentence. Valerie turned from her post at the front desk, tossing a curious glance my way.

Dad cleared his throat. "She's going to beat it, Mara."

Pressure built up behind my eyes, and I blinked to hold back the tears. I was beginning to understand what Emma had probably already realized. She wouldn't be moving into the dorm. Not even a late arrival was possible now. She'd watch all her friends pack up and head to college while she stayed home with our parents in the suburbs fighting for her life. I closed my eyes.

"Maybe she needs a better doctor," I said. "A second opinion."

Dad sighed again. "Normally, I'd agree, but her oncologist is one of the best in the country. He says recurrence is common."

"What about college?"

"We have to put that on hold." He gasped, then made a choking sound. It took a second for me to realize he was crying.

"Dad… it's going to be okay." I said the words as much to reassure myself as to comfort him. "I'll help with the bills."

Dad exhaled. "Well, I've been thinking about it. We can still sell the house if we have to."

It felt like he'd yanked my chair out from underneath me. My heart hammered in my chest at the thought of my parents selling my childhood home, the years of memories erased, and their life savings spent. "It won't come to that. We'll find another way."

We ended the phone call and I stared out the window, still rattled by the conversation. I stood from my desk and paced in circles, unsure what to do with myself. A text buzzed through on my phone. Jacqueline again. *Follow up with seller re: Argyle property.* I wouldn't be able to part ways with her yet. I needed to keep her happy, to work even harder to keep my cut of her commissions rolling in. But I needed to expand my personal client list at the same time. My expenses were adding up, and now there'd be more bills from Emma's doctors. Jacqueline had used the information I'd given her from the CCC meeting to work her way into Kevin's new development listing. The referral fees I'd earn from those sales would be huge, but those units wouldn't close until next year.

I pulled up the calendar on my phone to see where I needed to be today. Damon's name caught my eye, my tumbling heart replacing the gut-punch I'd just received. Our first date was tomorrow night. I dropped my head down, not feeling in any way prepared to impress a potential new boyfriend. Still, I wouldn't cancel. The possibility of getting to know Damon was the only bright spot in my life. I'd never needed to claim something for myself more. My shoulders fell backward into my chair. I pressed my fingers over my eyes, holding in the tears while trying to envision which outfit to wear.

CHAPTER THIRTY-FIVE

"When do you think the first units will be delivered?" Oscar cornered me next to a display of granite samples inside the sales center.

"Early next year." I'd never seen him dressed in anything nicer than a button-down shirt, and he didn't look half-bad in his suit and tie. I glanced over his angular shoulder and forced a smile at other Greystone realtors who'd recently arrived. The grand opening party for Arlington on the Park was underway, the over-the-top gala attracting hundreds of realtors and potential buyers. While the majority of guests were only here for the free cocktails and appetizers, Jacqueline promised there'd be some potential buyers, too.

Oscar grasped his sharp elbows with opposite hands, strumming his fingers against them. "You ever go to any seminars? There's one next week with a marketing guru from New York. It's supposed to be really good if you want to go with me." He talked so fast that I could barely register the words rushing from his mouth. I wanted to tell him not to waste his time on seminars, but I stopped myself, realizing I'd sound exactly like Jacqueline.

"Oh, thanks, but I don't have time," I said, waving my hand at the sales center.

"Yeah. I guess you're busy. Let me know if you change your mind." Oscar raised his lanky arm in a wave and wandered toward the refreshments.

People stammered in various directions, admiring the black-and-white renderings of the completed project, or commenting on the limitless finishes for the kitchens and bathrooms while weaving their way toward the bar. Jacqueline mingled with a few realtors from other companies, glancing in my direction every couple of minutes to ensure I was making the rounds. Kevin was there, too, but I noticed he and Jacqueline had positioned themselves on opposite sides of the crowded room.

I wished I could ditch the party and hang out with Damon instead. His disarming smile and messy hair had been painted in my mind since our date three nights ago. My heart jolted at the thought of him. He'd arrived at the door of my condo looking even more handsome than I remembered in his dark jeans and a button-down shirt, holding a bundle of wildflowers out to me.

"They're not roses," he'd said. "I don't like clichés."

"Me neither." We both giggled as I grasped the bundle of stems, trying to hide the tremor in my hand. My finger brushed against his. "Thank you. They're beautiful."

"You look great." His gaze flitted toward the deep neckline of my black sleeveless top, before bouncing back to my eyes.

"So do you."

When we'd arrived at Sushi Zan, Damon strode in front of me as we neared the solid red door, reaching forward to hold it open. Over dinner, he described the details of his life as a second-year law student. He was planning to specialize in environmental law so he could fight against big corporations that recklessly polluted our air and water in the name of profits. His idealism enthralled me. He was a breath of fresh air after spending so much time with Jacqueline.

Damon told me funny stories from the bartending jobs he picked up once in a while to help pay the bills. He asked me about my career, so I told him about real estate and Jacqueline and how much I'd hated my old consulting job. He wanted to know about my family. I told him about Emma because her relapse had been weighing on me. He reached across the table and squeezed my hand, his skin rough and warm against mine. He said how sorry he was and asked if he could meet her sometime. I said that he could. I imagined they'd get along well.

After dinner, we strolled hand-in-hand along Chestnut Street, catching glimpses of people dining and drinking through the illuminated windows of bars and restaurants, his presence next to me as natural as if we'd known each other for years, or maybe in a past life. We wandered to the edge of a park where he pulled me under an oak tree, the energy between us tangible and magnetic. He kissed me, his lips firm and gentle as they pressed against mine, his tongue welcome in my mouth. When we finally pulled apart, breathless and smiling, his arms remained wrapped around me, solid and strong, the heat from our bodies melding. I could have stayed with him forever.

"Mara! Why aren't you talking to anyone?" Jacqueline's voice ripped me from my daydream.

I pushed the spaghetti strap of my dress back up on my shoulder, where it immediately slid back down my arm.

Jacqueline nodded toward the entryway. "Go chat up some of The Real Housewives."

I followed her gaze. Sure enough, The Real Housewives of Greystone had arrived. Missy tossed back her vibrant hair and laughed loudly at something one of the others had said. Lana posed with her hand on her hip, displaying the designer dress she was wearing.

I swallowed, not having the energy to approach them yet. "How are sales going?"

Jacqueline rolled her shoulders back, the jewels on her necklace glittering under the lights. "We've got ten units under contract."

"Already?"

"These units practically sell themselves. People want to live here."

I stared through the wide entryway beyond the sales center and into the high-end model unit featuring lofty ceilings, massive windows, radiant floor heating, solid oak doors, walk-in closets, and a chef's kitchen. Burton Development had spared no expense in the construction. The finishes were luxurious, but tasteful, appealing equally to young professionals and aging socialites. Greystone had begun marketing the development two days earlier as the premier upscale residence for the savvy Lincoln Park buyer. Apparently, the strategy was working.

"Sounds like we're going to make a lot of money." I wondered what twenty percent of Jacqueline's fifty percent of the sale of eighty units would look like. I hadn't done the math, but I hoped it would be enough to cut through Emma's upcoming medical bills

Jacqueline squared her shoulders, her grey eyes sliding over to mine. "There is no 'we.' Arlington on the Park is my development."

My body froze as the room dissolved around me. The cold glare in her eyes told me she was serious. My stomach heaved, feeling as if I'd had the wind knocked out of me. I realized what she was trying to do. My jaw tightened as I stepped closer to her.

"I was the one who told you about this development." I spoke in a loud whisper, glancing over my shoulder to make sure Kevin wasn't nearby. "You wouldn't have known about it if I hadn't gone to the CCC meeting and reported back to you."

Jacqueline straightened her shoulders, her lithe frame towering over me. "Wrong. I got this development on my own through my friendship with Lydia Burton. She told me about it."

My fingers balled into fists. "I was at that lunch. Lydia didn't mention it. You brought it up because I'd told you about it!"

"It was much more than just one lunch. I've been wining and dining that woman for months."

"This is bullshit!"

Jacqueline's eyes flicked sideways. "Keep your voice down. I earned this development. Kevin is already taking half. I can't give away any more of my commission."

A waiter pushed past me, and I almost toppled over. What was I doing at this party if Jacqueline wasn't going to pay me for my work?

"Keep your chin up, Mara. We have plenty of other deals in the works."

"Emma's cancer is back." The words slipped out of my dry throat.

Jacqueline stared at me, her lips parting slightly. "I'm sorry, but that has no bearing on our commission agreement."

A waiter paused next to us, holding a tray of champagne. Jacqueline lifted a glass and turned to join a group of middle-aged men in suits. My face burned, my pulse racing. Kevin stood near the far window with his back to me, glimpses of his scalp showing beneath his thinning hair. I resisted the urge to approach him and apologize, to tell him I should have listened. Instead, I grasped a flute off the tray and took a long swig, the champagne bubbles exploding in my mouth as I strode through the crowded room toward the exit. Jacqueline had tricked me once again.

****

It was Sunday afternoon, two weeks since the grand opening of Arlington on the Park, and Jacqueline was busier than ever. Meanwhile, I'd wasted four hours hosting open houses at two of Jacqueline's stagnant listings. With my body drooped over my desk, I scanned through recent emails organizing my Monday's to-do list—nine showings at Jacqueline's properties, an inspection at 1 p.m., and three new listings to input into the MLS. She'd been dumping increasing loads of work on me now that the new development sucked up more of her time. Between the showings, inspections, marketing duties, buyer tours, and evening networking events she required me to attend, I was working way more hours than I ever did at my consulting job. My days dragged on longer than ever, my hopes and ambitions weighed down by Jacqueline's betrayal and the news of Emma's cancer relapse.

Thankfully, Damon was a welcome distraction. We'd gone out almost every night since our first date. On our third date, he came over to my place, and we watched a cheesy romantic comedy on Netflix. While we pretended to follow the movie, our hands wandered over each other. My fingers followed the contours of his muscles. Soon, we were ripping off clothes as we stumbled into the bedroom, breathless. Nate breaking up with me was the best thing that had ever happened.

Jacqueline huffed and slammed down her phone. My shoulders tightened as I glanced toward her. She leered toward Kevin's empty desk.

"He's such a waste of space. I'm doing all the work, and somehow he gets fifty percent of the commissions."

I bit my tongue, stopping myself from pointing out that I was getting nothing.

Jacqueline narrowed her eyes. "That person called to view a unit at Arlington yesterday and was told to call back today. Kevin's pushing buyers onto my days. I know it. He's setting it up so I'll have to do all the work."

"Wow," I said, my voice flat.

She and Kevin had arranged a rotating schedule to handle the showings and Sunday open houses at Arlington on the Park, with Jacqueline complaining loudly and often that she'd gotten another seven units under contract, while Kevin had only sold one.

Jacqueline's phone buzzed. "This is Jacqueline." She leaned forward in her chair. "So, you're at the sales center now?" The color drained from Jacqueline's already pale face as she rested her forehead in her hand. "Kevin should be there…The door is locked, and there's nobody there? Okay, I'll be right over." Her fingers squeezed the phone before she dropped it on her desk.

I planted my feet on the floor, bracing myself for Jacqueline's outburst. She shoveled her things into her bag.

"That asshole," she said under her breath. "He didn't show up to the open house."

An hour-and-a-half later, I was still at the office. I searched comparable properties for a potential new listing one of Damon's friends had sent to me. Jacqueline stormed through the front door and marched inside.

Hand on her hip, she hovered over me. "How would you like to get that twenty percent on Arlington on the Park?"

I looked up, confused. "Yeah. Of course."

"Let's make a phone call." Jacqueline nodded toward a conference room.

I stood, and Jacqueline ushered me inside a brightly lit conference room with a large table.

"Who are we calling?"

"I think Roger Burton needs to know that Kevin didn't show up to the open house today. Don't you? Once he's kicked off the listing, I'll bring you in to take his place. You'll get twenty percent. I'll get eighty percent. Everyone wins."

My jaw clenched. *How about fifty-fifty?* I wanted to say but held my tongue. Even twenty percent of the massive development would be a windfall. Still, something turned in my gut and warned me not to get involved. I'd already betrayed Kevin once, and I didn't want to do it again, especially after he'd tried to help me. Whatever issues Jacqueline had with him weren't my problem. Before I could respond, Jacqueline pushed a button, and a phone rang through the speaker on the table.

"Yep." Roger's gruff voice grunted on the other end.

"Hi, Roger. It's Jacqueline."

"Sell any units today?"

"Yes, I did. That's actually why I'm calling. It seems I've been selling almost all of the units, and Kevin has only sold a couple." She paused, but Roger did not speak. "Today was Kevin's day to host the open house, and he didn't show up."

"No one hosted the open house? Goddammit!" A bang echoed through the speaker. "That was your number one responsibility!"

"I drove to the sales center as soon as I realized Kevin neglected his duties. I sold another unit, too. My point is, Kevin is dead weight. He's not reliable."

"You've got to be kidding me. Jesus Christ!"

The line went dead. Jacqueline's mouth hung open.

"Should you call him back?" I asked.

She tilted her head back and closed her eyes. "No. He won't pick up. He's probably calling Kevin right now. No doubt Kevin will make up some lie to make me look bad."

Jacqueline tapped her nails on the table, staring off into space. Then she ranted about every mistake Kevin had made since they'd begun selling the development. I wanted to leave and get back to my price analysis. The phone rang through the speaker as I stood.

Jacqueline motioned for me to sit down. I did as she instructed, my forehead resting on my fingertips.

"This is Jacqueline."

"Sounds like you've been causing problems." It was Maeve.

"Not really. Kevin is the one who hasn't been fulfilling his duties. I thought the owner should know."

"Well, now he knows, and he's not very happy. You need to come to me with these issues, not bother Roger."

"Okay." Jacqueline rolled her eyes. "What are we going to do about Kevin?"

"I just spoke to him. He said you were scheduled to host the open house today. You were the one who forgot."

I sucked in a breath and looked up.

Jacqueline's face tightened. "No. That's not right. You can check the schedule." She slid out her laptop, fingers pounding against the keys as she logged into the shared schedule. Her eyes remained glued in one spot, their color darkening. "That son of a bitch."

"I'm looking at it," Maeve said. "Kevin was right. It was your day to host."

Jacqueline's lips puckered, her face eyes constricting. I could almost see the steam coming from her ears.

"Kevin offered to switch weeks with you if you'd like."

"No. The schedule is wrong. Kevin changed it without notifying me." Jacqueline's hands rested on the table, her fists clenched so tightly that her fingers had turned white.

CHAPTER THIRTY-SIX

Damon wrapped his arms around my waist and pulled me into his chest. His skin was rough against my cheek and carried the scent of exotic spices. He peered at me, his eyes sparkling like the ocean. The night blackened the windows behind him. The corners of his mouth curved into a smile. I kissed him. He squeezed my hand before turning back toward my shiny 60" flat-screen TV.

"Does that look centered?" he asked, sliding it a couple of inches to the right, the curve of his pec muscles visible through his T-shirt.

I stepped back. "That's good." My eyes were drawn from my new TV to my new boyfriend, who'd come straight from his four-hour study session to help set up my entertainment center. Even with his wrinkled shirt and messy hair, I wouldn't change a thing.

Damon plugged a bundle of cords into the back of the TV, then pulled the cable box toward him, eyebrows furrowed as he inspected the back panel. "Do you have a screwdriver?"

I admired the thin, weightless remote with one hand while waving toward the stack of narrow drawers at the edge of my kitchen with the other. "I think there's one in the drawer over there."

Damon wandered toward the drawers and began rifling through

the top one.

"Did I tell you I talked to Emma yesterday?" I said.

"No. How did she sound?"

"Okay. I mean, considering. I don't know how she does it." In truth, the deadened tone in my sister's voice had sent a worrying chill through me. She'd given me some details from her multiple visits to the oncologist. They'd taken her blood, performed biopsies, and conducted another MRI. Yet, I couldn't help wondering if it was all for nothing, if the disease would grow more resilient than my sister in the end. The more I learned about medicine, the more I realized the doctors had no more control than I did. "I'm hoping Jacqueline will give me a day off soon, so I can spend some time with Emma. Maybe drive her to an appointment or something."

Damon stopped rummaging and stared at me. "She's lucky she has you."

I lowered my hand, looking away. "I guess."

While I hadn't always been there for Emma, not in all the ways that a big sister should have been, I hoped it wasn't too late to make it up to her. Paying for her medical treatment was a good start. Dad had been forwarding me copies of Emma's bills, per my request. The bill for the most recent diagnostic tests arrived yesterday. $23,000. The amount didn't include the chemo or the medications to counteract the effects of the chemo, which would make the first bill seem like a drop in the bucket. Suddenly, buying that BMW didn't seem like the smartest decision. Maybe Dad was right. I should have gone with something more sensible, like a used Honda or a Ford.

"Are these real?" Damon crouched over the lowest drawer, which was pulled open with a heap of dishtowels spilling over the side. A sparkling strand of blood-red rubies dangled from his fingers. His other hand scraped against the bottom of the drawer before his fist opened to reveal a matching set of earrings.

I stepped closer, never having seen the jewelry before. I lifted the necklace from his hand, feeling its solid weight. The angled cuts in the earrings glinted in the lights of the passing traffic from the street below. "They're beautiful."

"Aren't they yours?"

"No."

"They were under the dishtowels in here." Damon pointed toward the open drawer, the one I was pretty sure I hadn't opened in weeks.

Fear surged through me at the sight of the unfamiliar items, but the memory of my former roommate extinguished the panic. Grace had always sprinkled her truckload of belongings throughout my condo, like glitter. Her clothes, shoes, books, makeup, and electronic devices had infiltrated every cupboard and countertop. Yesterday I'd discovered her forgotten Fitbit under the cushion of my living room chair.

"They're probably Grace's. She loved her jewelry, and she was always putting her stuff where it didn't belong."

"I bet she'll be happy to get these back." Damon placed the earrings into my palm. "They look like the real deal."

"Yeah. I'll tell her that you found them." I placed the jewelry on the counter next to last month's copy of *CBR Magazine*.

Damon lifted the magazine and flipped to the earmarked page where my airbrushed face smiled back from a glossy half-page spread. I was happy with the way the photo turned out, a flattering image of me wearing a blue cashmere sweater and black pants with the heels. The two-paragraph bio underneath my photo portrayed me as a wholesome, go-getter who'd busted onto the Chicago real estate scene without any warning.

"I can't believe I'm dating a famous realtor." He looped his arms around me as I chuckled.

I smiled. Although I was far from famous, new business had been finding me. Since the article, a surge in clients helped make up for Jacqueline screwing me out of my cut of Arlington on the Park. I'd gotten two new listings and four new buyers, all telling me they heard I was one of the "Thirty Under Thirty." *Success breeds more success.*

No one had to know I only made the list because Jacqueline had called in a favor. It wasn't like I hadn't put in the time. I'd been working twenty-four/seven for months. I hadn't reached Top Producer status, but I'd make well into the six figures this year. Not bad for someone who, just a few months ago, was barely making ends meet at her dead-end consulting job. With all of Jacqueline's showings and appointments and closings, plus my personal clients, I could barely keep my head above water. Someday, I'd have to hire my own assistant. I almost chuckled at the thought, but the image of Natalia, her two kids, and three nannies flickered in my mind. My blood turned cold at the memory of her eyes boring into mine at the broker's open house.

Damon's hands found the buttons on my shirt. He'd given up on finding the screwdriver. I tried to focus on his touch and push away thoughts of Natalia's threats. I'd been steering clear of the Russian realtor since the afternoon she'd confronted me. She hadn't sent any hitmen after me. At least, not yet. Her problem seemed to be more with Jacqueline.

Damon kissed my neck, but my mind refused to switch gears, traveling back to the listing that Jacqueline had stolen from Natalia. Bill's property lingered on the market, overpriced by a half-million dollars, and not a buyer in sight. Maybe Natalia would get the last laugh.

Damon pulled away, breath heavy. "What's wrong?"

My eyes focused on his. I exhaled, banishing all thoughts of Natalia. My face pressed against him, the stubble of his unshaven face prickling my skin as I led him into the bedroom. "Nothing."

****

"This is Mara." I held my cell phone to my ear as I hurried down State Street toward the garage where I'd parked my car. I'd left one of Jacqueline's closings and was heading back to the office to put together some comps for a listing presentation. The past week had been a blur of meetings, showings, phone calls, closings, and inspections.

"Hi. I'm calling about the studio for sale at 35 East Delaware."

The address was one of Jacqueline's listings, the studio belonging to her suspiciously pregnant friend, Haley. Jacqueline had sloughed off the scheduling of appointments and the handling of showings on me like she did with all her low-end listings. Meanwhile, she kept the big deals, like Arlington on the Park, for herself.

"I left you a message on your office number, but no one returned my call."

"Sorry, I'm a little behind." My chest tightened as I thought about all the calls I needed to catch up on today. "Are you working with a realtor?" I asked.

"No, I don't have an agent yet. I'm in town for the day, and I need to buy something soon before I start my new job. Can I see it today?"

I inhaled. A few months ago, I would have been ecstatic to get this phone call. Now it was one more thing on my to-do list. But Haley's listing was my responsibility, and this woman didn't have an agent. If she ended up buying the condo, I'd get the buyer's side of the commission, too, even if it was only a studio.

"Yeah. I can meet you over there." I pushed my way past a crowd of office workers blocking the sidewalk on their lunch break, recognizing the deadened look in their eyes from my time at Averly Consulting. "How about two o'clock?"

"Perfect."

I wrote down the woman's name and phone number and called Haley to let her know about the showing, apologizing for the short notice.

Two hours later, I paced across the lobby of 35 E. Delaware, waiting to meet the potential buyer. Out-of-town buyers were almost always late, not realizing how impossible it was to find an affordable parking space downtown. I swung the keyring around my finger and gazed through the massive lobby windows. Pedestrians of all shapes and sizes, races and ethnicities, rushed past on the sidewalk outside, everyone hurrying to someplace important, some urgent meeting to attend. The frantic vibe of downtown energized me. It was contagious.

A woman entered, and I smiled at her. She strode past me and scanned her entry card, unlocking the glass lobby door to the elevator bank. Not my buyer. I nodded at the doorman who scowled down his nose at me. *Another big shot Realtor*, he was probably thinking. I shifted my weight from foot to foot and checked my phone. It was ten after two. This lady had five more minutes. Then I was bailing.

The glass door into the elevator bank swung open behind me, and I turned. My foot stepped backward. The impeccably dressed tall blonde was Jacqueline.

"Hey," I said.

Jacqueline jerked sideways, doing a doubletake. "Oh. Hi, Mara." She smoothed her pants down with her hands.

"What are you doing here?" I asked. "I thought I was handling Haley's showings."

"Oh." She paused and looked back toward the elevators as if I'd asked her a difficult question. "Just checking on a carpet stain in the studio. Haley wanted to know if she should install hardwood floors." Jacqueline shook her head, her face shiny with perspiration. "There's no need. No. I mean…I'll call her." Her words were jumbled.

I motioned toward the elevators. "I got a last-minute showing request. No agent."

Jacqueline looked at me, not saying anything. Her face was paler than usual.

"She might be a no-show," I continued. "I'll give her five more minutes."

Jacqueline nodded. "I'm late for a meeting." She brushed past me and barged through the tall glass doors, disappearing into a stream of people on the sidewalk.

I'd never seen her flustered before, not that she'd been flustered by normal people's standards, but she wasn't her usual self. Maybe Kevin's efforts to get under her skin were working. Or maybe she was coming down with something—the flu or a fever? Leave it to Jacqueline to try to work through it.

Two minutes later, a petite brunette wearing black leggings and an oversized sweatshirt burst through the front door. The woman was out of breath and looking around, confused.

"Kelly?" I asked.

"Yes." She smiled and shook my hand. "I'm sorry for being late. I couldn't find anywhere to park."

CHAPTER THIRTY-SEVEN

I kicked my sweaty gym shoes off my feet, closing the door to my condo behind me. My quads and triceps already felt sore thanks to my recent workout with Cyrek. Admittedly, the four pounds I'd lost were more likely due to the euphoric haze of new love. Who needed food, anyway? The late-night pizza slices and stolen handfuls of Reese's Pieces that used to comfort me were silly indulgences compared to the security of Damon's arms. My phone buzzed from my gym bag, and I pulled it out. Jacqueline.

"Hi."

"It's been a long week already. Get a drink with me." Jacqueline spoke in a forceful voice. She must have been feeling better since I'd spotted her in the lobby of Haley's building this afternoon.

My throat tightened. "I'm going to hang out with my boyfriend tonight." I laced my fingers together, the word "boyfriend" feeling weird on my tongue.

"Boyfriend?" she asked, emphasizing the word. "Sounds serious."

My cheeks flushed. Damon and I finally had the girlfriend-boyfriend conversation a few days earlier. I still couldn't believe he wanted to be with me exclusively. Remembering Jacqueline's disdain for relationships, I backtracked. "We started dating a couple of weeks ago."

"Ha! I thought your face had an especially rosy glow lately."

I swallowed, not sure how to respond.

Jacqueline sighed dramatically. "Mara. It's only a drink. Don't make me drink alone. Meet me at Drumbar at eight o'clock. You can meet up with your boyfriend later."

"Okay." My lungs deflated as I said the word. It was easier to agree with her. As much as her behavior bothered me, I also felt sorry for her. Her boyfriend had moved an ocean away, and she only had a couple of friends. Not to mention parents who'd disowned her. Besides, maybe I could finally convince her to cut me in on Arlington on the Park, even with Kevin still in the picture.

Two hours later, I exited the cramped elevator and walked through the mahogany-walled entrance of the Streeterville lounge. Bottles of alcohol lined the metallic shelves behind the bar, and a bartender mixed drinks for a crowd of young professionals still wearing their work clothes. A few of them resembled my former co-workers at Averly. I scanned the room for any familiar faces but came up empty. Then I searched for Jacqueline but didn't see her either. The beat of techno music pounded from outside, so I made my way to the rooftop. Jacqueline lounged on a cushioned chair across from an outdoor fireplace and sipped a drink.

"Mara," she said, giving me a half-wave. She pointed to the cushion of the chair across from her, and I sunk into it.

A gazelle-like waitress wove her way toward us, her tall, thin frame gracefully avoiding drunken patrons.

"Can I get a drink for you?" she asked.

"Have one of these," Jacqueline insisted, pointing to her drink. "It's whiskey and ginger and some other things mixed in. So good."

I shrugged. "Okay. I'll have the same thing."

The waitress smiled and nodded before gliding back through the

222

crowd.

"Tough day, huh?" I asked.

"Not really. It's just that working all the time gets to me after a while."

"Yeah." I nodded.

"Did the woman ever show up this afternoon for Haley's place?" She swirled the ice around in her glass.

"Yeah. I think she liked it. She wants to see a few more condos before making a decision."

"Good. Let's get that place sold."

"I didn't see any carpet stain."

"I know." She looked out at the skyline and took a long sip of her drink. "That's what I told Haley."

The waitress reappeared and handed me a drink. "Here you go. Anything else?"

"Not right now, thank you," Jacqueline answered for me.

Two guys in ripped jeans and T-shirts strode over and claimed the chairs next to ours. Although they were about my age, they didn't fit with the young-professional crowd from the lounge. Sleeves of tattoos covered the arms of a darker-haired guy, accentuating his muscles. He sat across from me, dangerously close to Jacqueline. His eyes were the most unusual shade of green, and I couldn't help but wonder if he was a model. He looked at me and smiled before turning back to his friend.

My heart skipped a beat at the unexpected attention, although he wasn't my type. And I had a boyfriend.

The guy pulled out a cigarette and leaned back, legs casually splayed open.

"Do you have a light?" he asked me.

"No. Sorry," I said.

"Lovely," Jacqueline said under her breath.

I wasn't sure if she was referring to the cigarette or the tattoos or the fact that two hot men chose to sit right next to us. Probably all three.

Jacqueline cleared her throat and redirected our conversation back to real estate. We picked apart Natalia's sales numbers and discussed how Jacqueline could continue to surge ahead in the next few weeks.

"I can't wait to replace her picture on that CBR billboard with mine." Jacqueline closed her eyes and smiled as if she was picturing the new billboard in her mind. "Don't worry, Mara. When I win Top Producer, it will ignite *both* of our careers."

I nodded, knowing it was true. Emma's bills wouldn't be an issue.

"Will my picture be on the billboard, too?" I asked her with a laugh.

Jacqueline smiled but didn't respond.

I gulped too much of my whiskey drink and started coughing. The weight of someone's eyes hovered over me. When I looked up, the male model was staring at me. He smiled again, and I looked away. I didn't want to give him the wrong impression. Maybe before I met Damon, I would have played this game, but not now.

The drinks disappeared quickly. Jacqueline ordered another round.

"I heard HGTV is going to start filming Natalia's reality show next week. It's called, *SOLD*," I said.

Jacqueline rolled her eyes and took a swig of her drink.

"What a dumb name," I added.

"You know what, Mara? Let Natalia have her reality show. I think it will hurt her sales numbers."

"Really?"

"Yes. Most high-end buyers don't want to be on TV. They want to keep their wealth private. Natalia's show will win her some Euro-trash and new-money clients. Everyone else will come to me."

"You're probably right." I hadn't thought about it like that before, but it made sense.

When I looked up, the dark-haired guy with the exotic eyes was honed-in on me again, his muscles flexing under his tattoos. He looked like someone who knew what he was doing. I stared into the flickering flames of the fire.

"Mara. Earth to Mara." Jacqueline jolted me back to our conversation.

"Oh, sorry. I wasn't paying attention."

"Obviously."

The drinks had gone right through me. "I'm going to run to the bathroom. Be right back." I got up and dug my way through the crowd, techno music pounding in my ears. When I emerged from the ladies' room a minute later, the male model was standing in front of me. He reached out and squeezed my arm.

"Hey. Want to dance?"

"Oh, thanks, but not really." I stepped to the side, trying to get past him, but he touched me again. He smiled and leaned closer.

"Come on. I love this song." His sex-filled eyes held onto me, pleading.

"I have a boyfriend."

The guy shrugged. "He's not here. Is he?"

I pressed my lips together and looked away.

"Come on. It's just one dance. Then you can go back to your friend."

My feet shifted, as my eyes traveled to the people laughing and bouncing on the dance floor. It was only one song. There was no harm in enjoying some attention for a few minutes. I nodded.

"I'm Juan."

"Mara." Guilt tugged at my gut. I was flirting with an attractive man while Damon was in a library studying somewhere.

Juan grabbed my hand and led me to the rooftop where the DJ was spinning. He turned toward me and pulsated his hips to the beat of the music. There was nothing I could do now without being rude. Besides, the attention was flattering, and it wasn't like Damon and I were married.

After a couple of long minutes, the song came to an end. Juan circled his arms around me and leaned all his weight against my body, almost knocking me off balance. I clutched his shoulders to keep from falling, both of us chuckling at our clumsiness. Another song pounded through the speakers, people around us jumping up and down to the beat. I stepped backward, eager to get back to my seat. Juan stepped in front of me and set his jaw, his eyes locking onto mine. And then he kissed me. Right on the lips. He even slid in his tongue. It took me a second to realize what was happening and why I had to stop it. Damon's face flashed through my mind again. My back stiffened, and I pushed the stranger away. I scanned the rooftop as my face burned. Jacqueline hovered a few feet away, mouth open. She'd seen the whole thing.

I scurried toward her, my heart pounding. "Let's go."

"I already paid." She walked toward the elevator, and I followed close behind, the DJ's next song pounding in my ears.

As soon as the elevator doors slid open, I dove inside, banging the button for the lobby with my fist. The doors couldn't close fast enough. I needed to get out of there, back to Damon. Jacqueline stared straight ahead, expressionless.

"Lucky your boyfriend didn't see that."

As the elevator lurched downward, I inhaled deep breaths of stale air and pressed my back against the wall. I didn't risk opening my mouth to speak for fear of getting sick. Jacqueline sighed.

My stomach turned with the downward fall of the elevator, my own betrayal burning inside me. But something else had fueled the sickening feeling in my gut. As we plummeted toward the ground floor, Jacqueline's lips twitched, almost as if she was trying to suppress a smile.

****

The chaotic buzz of the office before the weekly meeting was calmer today, like someone had dimmed the lights and turned down the volume a few notches. I scribbled a list of people to call as soon as the meeting ended. Damon hadn't wanted me to come over last night. He had class early this morning, and I'd gotten back from the bar too late, so we'd only talked for a few minutes. I decided not to mention my encounter with the guy at the bar. Telling him would only cause issues, and I didn't have time to deal with that. My head throbbed, and I wished I hadn't agreed to meet Jacqueline the night before. I hadn't even had a chance to bring up Arlington on the Park.

I studied the list of people I needed to call. First, there was an attorney who was threatening to kill one of my deals over a couple of minor inspection issues. On another deal, my client's lender was dragging his feet on the appraisal. We needed to get that today. Hopefully, Kevin wasn't expecting me to ride on caravan with him again. I didn't have time. People talked in hushed whispers around me.

"Okay, everyone. Quiet, please." Maeve said, calling the meeting to order. I cocked my head, her normally powerful voice sounding shaky and delicate. "Some of you may have heard. I have some very sad news to share. One of our long-time agents, Kevin Lucas, has passed away."

My stomach dropped to the floor. I planted my hands on the desk in front of me, holding myself up. Maybe I'd misheard Maeve. I turned and looked back toward Kevin's desk, half expecting to see him there. It sat empty. A stack of folders lay neatly piled next to his office phone like a snapshot of his last day at work. A wave of gasps and shaking heads rippled through the office. Jacqueline sat next to me, wide-eyed. Her mouth gaped open.

Maeve coughed, then cleared her throat. "Kevin suffered from a very severe shellfish allergy. He had an extreme reaction to something he ate."

More hushed whispers and a few sobs sounded from around the office.

"Oh my God!" squealed one of the Real Housewives, fanning herself with a flier.

"They found his body in his condo yesterday after he didn't show up to several appointments." Maeve shook her head and looked at the floor. "I don't know anything about the funeral or memorial service at this time, but I will let you all know as soon as I receive that information. In light of everything that's happened, we are canceling this week's meeting and caravan. Feel free to go home if you feel you're not able to work today. I know some of you were close with Kevin." Maeve shuffled back to her office. A few people packed their bags to leave. Jacqueline sat rigid with her hands clasped in front of her.

"Oh, my God," I said under my breath, shaking my head. It wasn't as if I was great friends with Kevin, but he'd been nice enough to me in the past few weeks. He'd welcomed me on caravan. He'd invited to join his Habitat for Humanity group. He'd taken me under his wing to the CCC meeting. He'd even participated in the charity run for Emma. Black spots danced in front of my eyes. I'd been using him the whole time. I'd never see him again. I'd never get to apologize or explain myself.

"I'm sorry, Mara." Oscar stood in front of my desk, wringing his bony hands. "I know you and Kevin were friends. Man, I can't believe it." Without waiting for me to respond, Oscar moped out the front door, staring at the ground.

Jacqueline looked at me with her eyebrows furrowed. "It's a shocker. You okay?"

"Yeah." My stomach turned over.

She clucked. "Karma finally caught up with the guy, I guess."

My skin bristled at the insensitivity of Jacqueline's comment. I shifted away from her, pretending to look at something while I struggled to push down the emotions rising inside me. Outside, people walked past the window in a hurry to get to wherever they were going. The randomness of death weighed on me. I thought of Emma lying in bed, the cancer cells multiplying inside of her. *Would she be next?* I hated myself for having the thought.

Poor Kevin. He hadn't had any warning. My watery eyes watched the people outside as the office cleared out. Jacqueline resumed her work.

"I've got so much to do today." She sighed. "Can you input these two listings for me?" She handed me two folders. "I'll email the photos to you."

She had recovered quickly from the shock of Kevin's death. Back to business as usual. I knew she hated the guy, but still, she could show a little compassion.

"Okay." I spit out the word, but my mind was reeling. I needed to go home. I needed to talk to Damon and hear his voice. "I'm going to work from home today."

She shot me a sideways glance. "We've got a lot to do, Mara."

"I know. I'll get it done, but I can't be here right now." I shuffled my papers into a pile and stuffed everything into my bag.

Jacqueline shrugged. "Fine. You still need to take that buyer out at 6:00 tonight. Remember?"

"Yeah," I said, even though I'd forgotten. "I'll do it."

She was already on the phone with somebody else.

CHAPTER THIRTY-EIGHT

I flipped on the TV and slumped onto my couch. Kevin was gone. He was really dead. Other than my grandma and grandpa passing away, I didn't have much experience with death. At least they'd lived long lives. We had time to say our goodbyes and hug and cry. An image of the grim reaper formed in my mind, his face hidden by a dark hood, his skeleton-like hands reaching out toward my sister. With Emma, we had some warning. We had time to raise an army and to fight, to delay the inevitable, strangling grip of death. Kevin's loss was so unexpected. I kept reminding myself that we weren't even friends.

I picked up my phone to call Damon, to tell him everything but remembered he'd be in class. My laptop rested on the couch next to me. Jacqueline needed me to take out her buyers tonight, and I hadn't scheduled any of the showings yet. I opened the MLS home page and set up a search for three-bedroom condos and townhomes between $400,000 and $600,000 in Lincoln Park, Lakeview, and Wrigleyville. I typed in some additional criteria to narrow down the results. Her clients were two attorneys, no kids. They would probably want garage parking for two cars. Based on what little I knew about them, they'd require a laundry room and formal dining room.

"A local realtor was found dead in his condo yesterday . . ." The face of the female newscaster stretched across the enormous screen of my new flat-screen TV. She recited the words evenly as if it were just another headline. My fingers froze on the keyboard. The reporter stood on a sidewalk outside of a familiar building. I leaned back and pieced together the images on the screen, the gray brick and tinted glass doors. Haley's building towered behind the newscaster.

"Kevin Lucas, a long-time realtor with Greystone Realty, died of an apparent shellfish allergy inside his high-rise condo at 35 East Delaware."

I forced myself to breathe, and the hair on my neck stiffened. I'd known Kevin lived downtown, but I'd never asked him his exact address.

"An EpiPen was found in his condo, but police say he was unable to reach it in time. Approximately twelve million people suffer from food allergies, and about 150 people die from these allergies each year."

The reporter's voice faded to the background as she discussed food safety protocols. I planted my feet firmly on the floor, afraid my spinning mind might carry me away. Kevin lived at 35 E. Delaware? I'd been at his building yesterday, just hours before he died. I'd seen Jacqueline there, leaving in a hurry. She'd been acting strangely, nervously even. Then she'd insisted on meeting me for a drink last night. She'd made a point of telling me where she'd been all afternoon. Had she done something to him? Had she figured out a way to let herself into his condo and contaminate his food? Had she moved his EpiPen somewhere he wouldn't find it? She'd been so angry at Kevin after he'd changed the open house schedule. How far was she willing to go to win Top Producer?

Her "outside the box" thinking was spiraling out of control. I thought back to the rats running through Bistro Maria, the bottles of spray paint hidden in the trunk of her car, the box she'd tricked me into stealing from Julia's condo, the fake contract she'd submitted on Natalia's twenty-four-million-dollar listing, her friend's unplanned pregnancy, and the jingling drawer of keys.

Half the things she did to gain business were illegal and immoral, but I'd never seen her physically hurt anyone. And I wasn't even sure she was behind the rats or the pregnancy. I'd done a few dishonest things, too, but nothing like this. No. Not even close.

I inhaled deeply and braced myself against the wall. *No*, I scolded myself, shaking my head. This was crazy. I couldn't let my imagination run away with me, creating a wild story without any proof.

An unexpected wave of nausea overtook me. I staggered to the bathroom, and dry heaved into the toilet. As I hunched over the bowl, slivers of memories that once seemed irrelevant began to surface. I was the one who had told Jacqueline that Kevin suffered from a severe shellfish allergy. After caravan that day, she'd asked me for real estate information. I'd shared information about his allergy instead. I'd even told her where he kept his EpiPen.

Peter's warning echoed through my head. *She'll make you do bad things.*

I swallowed, remembering the office meeting this morning. Jacqueline recovered way too quickly when Maeve announced Kevin's death. Everyone at Greystone was sobbing and crying and leaving work early, but she continued making phone calls, almost expressionless as if nothing had happened. And her motive was clear. She'd wanted Kevin kicked off the Arlington on the Park listing, especially after he'd made her look bad in front of Roger Burton.

I pulled myself up from the bathroom floor, my muscles weak, my stomach hollow and shaky. My gut knew the truth. Jacqueline had murdered Kevin.

My phone peeked out of my pocket. I pulled it out, but then I froze. I couldn't think of who to call or what to say. I wrung my hands in my lap as I ran through my options. Confronting Jacqueline would be reckless. Dangerous, even. Besides, she'd deny the accusation and then fire me. Plus, I didn't have any proof.

I could call the police and tell them my suspicions, but what if I was wrong? Jacqueline would fire me. My accusations would ruin her career. Possibly her life.

Confiding in Maeve seemed like the worst idea of all. She wouldn't believe me, and then she'd get everyone involved.

I tugged at the collar of my shirt, which was damp from the cold water I'd splashed on my face. The shag carpet rug in the doorway caught my eye, and I sat up straighter. There was a way to find out if she was telling the truth about her reason for being in Kevin's building yesterday. I hadn't seen any carpet stain when I'd shown Haley's condo to my buyer, but maybe I wasn't looking in the right place.

My phone weighed like a brick in my hand as I scrolled through my contacts and finally pressed Haley's name. She picked up on the second ring. I made a conscious effort to breathe.

"Hi, Mara." Her voice sounded light and hopeful.

"Hi, Haley."

"Any leads on my condo?"

"Uh, not really. I mean, there is one woman who seemed to like it." My voice trailed off, and I took a deep breath, reminding myself to sound casual. "Um, I was just calling about the stain on your carpet."

"What stain?"

My stomach folded over itself, the phone shaking in my hand. "The one you asked Jacqueline to look at the other day."

"I'm sorry, Mara. She must have been talking about a different condo. I never talked to Jackie about a carpet stain."

"Okay. My mistake. Sorry to bother you." My insides squeezed, and I thought I might hurl again.

"Oh, Mara," Haley said before I could hang up. "I'm sorry to hear about the real estate agent who died. He was from your office, right?"

My forehead erupted with beads of sweat. "Yeah. Kevin."

"I guess he lived a few floors above me. There were reporters everywhere this morning."

"Yeah. I saw it on the news. Kevin was a good guy."

"Not to be callous or anything, but . . ." Haley paused. "You don't think this will hurt my chances of selling, do you?"

I caught my breath, my voice switching back to realtor mode.

"Oh, no. People die in these buildings all the time." Then before I could stop myself, "It's not like he was murdered or anything."

"Good point. Okay, gotta run."

My phone dropped to the floor, and I rested my forehead in my hands. The facts hovered over me, pinning me down. I couldn't get away from them. There was no stain on Haley's carpet. Jacqueline had been in the building to murder Kevin. Why else would she lie? Now I knew the truth, and as much as I wanted to, I couldn't unknow it.

I fought the urge to call Damon. It was more important to shield him from Jacqueline. If I told Damon my suspicions, he'd feel some lawyerly obligation to report Jacqueline to the police. He had a childlike tendency to see things in black and white. "People who break the law are bad. Bad people go to jail," he'd told me once. I loved his sincerity, but it was better if he didn't know about Jacqueline's methods or my participation. I'd deal with this myself.

Although calling the police was probably the moral thing to do, I couldn't do that either. Jacqueline would never let me off the hook. She'd find a way to implicate me, if not in Kevin's murder, then in something else. I'd worked too hard the past several months building my real estate business to have Jacqueline flush everything down the toilet. I wouldn't put Emma at risk. I was the only one who could pay for her treatment.

My phone buzzed, flashing with Damon's name. I took a few deep breaths and cleared my throat.

"Hey."

"Hi."

I pulled down on the ends of my hair. "It's so good to hear your voice. I thought you'd be in class."

"I was. I've got a few minutes before the next one starts."

My chest swelled with emotion. I was lucky to have such a caring, smart, and loyal boyfriend. My voice caught in my throat as I remembered how I'd betrayed him the night before. I should never have agreed to dance with that guy.

"Is everything okay?" he asked.

"Yeah. I'm just really busy with work." I stared out the window at the goliath concrete building being erected across the street. "And remember Kevin, the realtor in my office who brought me to the CCC the night we met?"

"Yeah."

"He died yesterday."

"Holy, crap! Are you Serious?"

I breathed in and out several times, composing myself.

"What happened?" Damon asked.

"He was allergic to shellfish. Couldn't get to his EpiPen in time, I guess." My eyes inspected an imperfection in my hardwood flooring. I was reciting Jacqueline's version of events to my boyfriend. There was no going back now.

"That's crazy." He paused. "I'm sorry. Is there anything I can do?"

"No. Thanks. It's not like we were that close, but he was a decent guy. I mean, for the most part." I shuffled over to my couch and sat down, debating how much of the truth to tell him. "He lived at 35 East Delaware. The same building where I've been doing all the showings for Jacqueline's studio listing."

"That's crazy," Damon said again.

We sat in silence for a couple of seconds.

"Speaking of Jacqueline, I got an email from her this morning. That's why I called you. She must have sent it before she found out about Kevin."

Every hair on my body stood on end. I struggled to speak but couldn't force my voice out of my constricted throat.

"Jacqueline said we should all get together sometime. She mentioned she might be able to help me find an internship this summer. And there was something about funny photos of you that she'd have to send me some time."

"What?" That was all I could muster. My legs gave out, and I fell onto my couch.

"Yeah. So, tell her that sounds great. Maybe she can help me get a job at that firm she used to work for."

"Yeah. Okay."

"What are the funny photos?"

I swallowed against my scratchy throat. "I have no idea."

"That's weird."

"Yeah."

"Okay. Well, I've got to go to class. I'm sorry about Kevin."

"Thanks."

"Love you."

"Love you, too." I ended the call. Dread weighed down my body. What was Jacqueline doing? How had she gotten Damon's email address? I cradled my head in my hands, struggling to figure out her angle. Ten minutes later, my phone buzzed with the answer to my question.

CHAPTER THIRTY-NINE

Heard you talked to Haley. Just in case you're thinking of doing anything irresponsible...

Below the text from Jacqueline was a photo of two people groping each other and making out in a dimly lit bar. I had the same skirt as the woman in the photo. It took a second to sink in—the woman was me, and the man was the tattooed slimeball who'd forced himself on me at Drumbar. The blood drained from my body, replaced with poisonous anger that surged through my veins. Jacqueline had snapped a photo of me with the guy at the bar. I remembered the empty chairs next to us and the convenient arrival of the male supermodel who'd gone out of his way to ask me for light and follow me to the bathroom. She'd set me up.

I imagined Damon looking at that photo. No gray area there. He'd leave me for sure. *Shit!* I threw my phone and watched it skid across my hardwood floor before colliding with the wall. I straightened up, my body aching with the memory of the lonely nights before I'd met Damon. Not this time. This was where I drew the line. Jacqueline might be a step ahead of most people, but she wasn't smarter than me. I wasn't going to let her control me any longer.

I pulled in a deep breath, picked up my phone, and called her.

237

She answered on the first ring.

"Mara. I trust you got my message?"

"What are you doing? Stay the hell away from my boyfriend!" I dug my fingernails into the drywall.

"Calm down. I needed a little insurance policy in case you get any crazy ideas."

"Crazy ideas about what?" I wanted to hear her say it. Admit that she murdered Kevin.

"I don't know," she responded. "You tell me why you called Haley, and then I'll decide what to do with this photo."

I hesitated, not being as accomplished a liar as Jacqueline. "Just wanted to make sure the carpet stain issue was squared away."

"And is it? Squared away?"

I clenched my fingers into a fist, barely able to force myself to say the word. "Yes."

"Great. Then there's no need for the photo." She paused. "Let's move past this and get back to business. Now that Kevin isn't around to help with Arlington on the Park, I can probably find a spot for you. That's what you wanted, right?"

I couldn't speak.

Jacqueline sighed. "Your motive was the same as mine. Don't forget it."

My eyes squeezed closed.

Jacqueline's voice lightened. "It will be our normal referral fee arrangement. You'll get twenty percent of all sold units."

My hand shook as I held the phone to my ear. I would never have wanted a spot on the development if I'd known the cost. She was twisting everything around, trying to make it seem like I was just as guilty as her.

"Okay," I said, not really believing that she was going to get away with murdering Kevin, that I was going to let her get away with it. Then again, turning her into the police would be too high of a price to pay. I couldn't risk Damon seeing that photo. I couldn't lose my income. I had Emma to think about, not to mention my mortgage and car payments. And twenty percent of an 80-unit development wasn't something I could afford to turn down.

She sighed. "I thought you'd be a little more excited. The units practically sell themselves. Do you have any idea how much money you'll make on this?"

"I'm still in shock about Kevin."

"Get over it. Focus on work. Let's grab coffee tomorrow at 8:00 a.m. We can review the details of the development and then head over to the sales center. You'll be handling most of the showings over there. I still need to talk to Roger just to make sure he's okay with bringing you on board."

"Okay."

"Don't forget to take my buyers out tonight."

My back slid down the wall. "Yeah. I know."

"I need you to cover a couple of showings at the Ravenswood house for me this afternoon, too. I'm swamped. I'll email you the schedule."

I stared at the ceiling and closed my eyes. Jacqueline owned me.

"Okay," I said, no longer trying to hide the disgust in my voice.

So that was Jacqueline's plan. Kill Kevin and bring me on board to do all the work while she sat back and collected eighty percent of the commissions, instead of the fifty percent she would have earned with Kevin. Only I didn't know which I found more disturbing, Jacqueline's criminal scheme, or that I might be willing to let her get away with it. I clenched my jaw, keeping my disgust locked inside.

For the rest of the day, I kept myself busy, trying to outrun the troubling reality that shadowed me. Telling the truth wasn't an option. There was too much to lose. I needed a better plan, a way to protect myself. I survived minute-by-minute, breath-by-breath, scheduling showings for Jacqueline's buyers, inputting Jacqueline's new listings, checking stats on our websites, opening the doors for potential buyers at Jacqueline's properties while she did who-knew-what.

I'd deleted the text with the damaging photo of me immediately after opening it, but Jacqueline still had a copy. The photo haunted me. Maybe Damon would understand if I explained everything. Or maybe he'd be angry for a while and eventually forgive me. Then again, maybe he wouldn't. Damon was the bright spot in my life. I couldn't risk losing him.

At 6:00 p.m., I met Jacqueline's buyers at the first property, leading them around for two hours while they found things to dislike at every location.

"This parking space will be hard to back out of in the winter. . . I don't care for the choice of granite. . . I prefer carpet in the bedrooms, not hardwood. . . Why aren't there light switches for the closets?" And on and on and on.

I forced myself to smile, assuring them we'd find the perfect home.

"Why couldn't Jacqueline meet us tonight?" asked the balding, pot-bellied husband as we toured the fourth property.

She's too busy murdering her competition, I wanted to say. Instead, I cracked my knuckles and stared at a vase of fake flowers strategically positioned on the dining room table.

"She had another commitment and couldn't reschedule," I said, which may or may not have been true. She was blackmailing me. I was doing all her work, and she was only paying me twenty percent. The gratefulness I'd felt at the beginning of our relationship had transformed into resentment.

CHAPTER FORTY

At 8:05 a.m. Jacqueline sat across from me at a private table in the corner of Starbuck's, barking orders into her phone.

"Hi, Don. We have an offer coming in on Sawyer. Call me back."

"Is that the Sawyer building I called the violations in on?" I asked.

"Yep." She hugged her cardboard cup between her hands and smiled. "Don added two units already. I'm going to make a killing on this flip."

"You mean *we're* going to make a killing."

"No, Mara. I paid you twenty percent on the initial sale. This second sale is all mine. That was our agreement. Don't pull this bullshit with me."

It could have been the horrible lighting inside Starbuck's, or maybe it was because I knew she was a murderer, but her eyes were a darker shade of gray today.

"Are the Mattisons going to write an offer?" she asked, changing the subject.

"They didn't seem crazy about anything I showed them last night."

"Well, get them to write something. Then you'll get twenty

percent of that."

"Oh, gee, thanks," I said, my voice thick with sarcasm.

Jacqueline's eyes bulged, and she leaned in close. "You ungrateful little bitch. Do you know how many realtors in this city would chop off their right arms for twenty percent of my deals? Do you realize you've only gotten as far as you have because of me?"

She was expecting me to back off and apologize as I'd done so many times before, but something inside me had bolstered and tightened. I'd lain awake for half the night mulling over the situation in my head, and I'd come up with a good play. I'd lie, telling her I'd decided to come clean, that I'd already told Damon all about the guy at Drumbar. Damon had been angry, naturally, but we were going to work it out. Then Jacqueline wouldn't have any power over me. Instead, I'd be the one with all the power because I knew she was a murderer. Next, I'd demand fifty percent of the Arlington on the Park commissions to keep her secret safe. Twenty percent wouldn't cut it with the hundreds of thousands of dollars of Emma's medical bills I'd soon have to pay. I leaned in even closer to her face, feeling her soy latte breath on my skin.

"I know what you did," I whispered.

Something flinched within her metallic eyes. "You don't know anything."

I refused to look away. "There was no carpet stain in Haley's studio."

Jacqueline glanced down, shaking her head and laughing. "Oh, Mara. I thought we were past this."

"You just happened to be in Kevin's building hours before he dies of a shellfish allergy? An allergy I know you knew about. What did you do? Poison his food and hide his EpiPen? And then you lie about being in the building to check on a carpet stain that doesn't exist. Was that really the best you could come up with?"

She reached across the table and grabbed my wrist. "If you even *think* about sharing your little theory with anyone, I will destroy you. That's a promise."

"I already told Damon about the guy at the bar," I said, reciting the lie I'd rehearsed. "You've got nothing on me."

"Oh, really? How did you get the listing at 1907 N. Mohawk?" She crossed her arms in front of her and leaned back in her chair.

My stomach rolled backward. I glanced down at my feet. "A family friend referred it to me. I told you that."

"Or did you get that lead through my website?" The corners of her mouth bent into a curve.

"What? No!" Beads of sweat formed on my forehead.

"The owner of 1907 N. Mohawk tried to contact me through my website, Mara. I went back and reviewed my old online inquiries. Betty Lewis. That was her name, right? You expect me to believe it was just a coincidence that you listed the very same property?"

"What do you care?" I asked, inching forward. "You brought in the buyer anyway."

"So, let me get this straight...I organized a charity run to benefit your sister, and you repay me by stealing a listing from my website?" Jacqueline shook her head.

My hands balled into fists as I remembered the T-shirts and water bottles promoting Jacqueline's website. "You turned the charity run into a giant ad for yourself. And don't try to compare stealing a listing with committing murder!"

"Keep your voice down!" Jacqueline looked over her shoulder, but only an empty table sat behind us. She swiveled back toward me, the muscles in her jaw pulsing. "So, Grace is one of your good friends, huh?"

I stared at her, not sure what she was getting at.

"How do you think Grace would feel if she found out her best friend lied to her about the condo rules? She'd probably be devastated to realize you tricked her into moving out just to get a sale."

My stomach plummeted to the floor. "That was your idea."

"I told you to get the rules changed. You took a shortcut and changed them yourself. That's even worse. Isn't it?"

My fingers clutched the edges of my chair as I tried to steady myself.

Grace could never know I'd lied to her, especially after she'd been such a loyal friend. She'd saved me from losing my condo after Nate dumped me. She never thought twice about lending me her clothes, including me in her nights out, or driving me to that horrible underground tow lot.

"Grace will forgive me. I'll explain everything." I gulped, hoping Jacqueline didn't detect the quiver in my voice.

"I don't think that's true, but let's say you're right. Maybe what you did to Grace wasn't so bad." She looked up and grimaced. "Robbery's pretty bad, though. You could get jail time for that." She scrolled through her phone and slid it across the table toward me.

A rush of panic surged through me. I had no idea what she wanted to show me, but I sensed it wouldn't be good. My finger shook as if I were about to detonate a bomb. I forced myself to push the arrow to play the video on the screen.

The camera panned across the outside of a familiar red brick building, dwarfed by two taller loft buildings on either side. I recognized the building as Julia's former condo near the South Loop. I struggled to breathe, but all the oxygen had disappeared from my lungs. I knew what was coming next. Sure enough, the camera's slow pan stopped cold as the front door of the condo building flung open. I watched myself barge through the door, the early-summer sun illuminating me as I walked toward the camera. Something bright and shiny and white stood out against the cement-colored background. In my hands, I clutched the white metal box filled with Julia's grandmother's jewelry.

The movie stopped abruptly, blurring to a halt as my former self approached the car.

My fingernails dug into the edge of the table. The memory of the ruby earrings and necklace dangling from Damon's hand flashed in my mind, causing me to double-over. The truth behind his discovery was obvious now, the fresh trail through the layer of dust on my mantel suddenly making sense. It wasn't Natalia or Peter or the electrician who'd moved my family photo. Grace hadn't left the jewelry behind. Jacqueline had been inside my condo. She'd recorded me stealing Julia's box, and then broken into my home to plant evidence. It would have been impossible for her to leave without inspecting the framed photo of my smiling family, as desperate as she was for attention from her own parents. She'd planned this all along, holding on to her fake evidence until she needed to use it against me.

"You might want to think twice about voicing your suspicions." Jacqueline stared me square in the eyes and smiled. "And you will continue working for me until I win the Top Producer Award at the end of the year. Non-negotiable." She took a long, slow sip from her cup.

"Non-negotiable?" I slammed my hand on the table. "This isn't a dictatorship. I'm not your slave."

A hint of a smile crept over Jacqueline's face. "You're right. You're not a slave. You're getting paid way too much for that."

My face burned, my heart hammering. The damn broke, a tirade of profanities spewing from my mouth as I told Jacqueline what I thought of her. When my stream of insults trickled out, I crossed my arms, my throat constricting with hatred.

Jacqueline rolled her eyes. "Calm down, Mara. January first, when my face is on the billboard, we can go our separate ways. All sins forgiven. This is the deal—we keep each other's secrets, or you go down with me."

Hot liquid rolled over my thumb, and I pulled my hand away from my coffee cup, realizing I'd crushed it.

Jacqueline pushed a napkin toward me. Nothing fazed her. She was ten moves ahead of me. I had no hard evidence against her, only my suspicions. She, on the other hand, could destroy my entire life with that video. Returning the jewelry to Julia was an option, but Damon had already discovered the earrings and necklace hidden in my condo. What would he think if he saw the recording?

Even if Damon believed me, he'd never get over me kissing the guy at Drumbar. I'd been set up, but I'd also betrayed his trust. Jacqueline could undermine my friendship with Grace, too. All she'd have to do is pull up my condo board's rules and show Grace they'd never been changed, that dogs over thirty pounds were perfectly fine to live in my building. Jacqueline could end my career by filing a complaint about 1907 N. Mohawk with Greystone or the Board of Realtors. Even if I could explain what really happened at Julia's condo, or at Drumbar, who would believe my version of events over hers? There was no way to defend myself as far as Mohawk went. She was right. I *had* stolen the lead from her website.

We walked back to the office to fill out the paperwork, choosing opposite sides of the street. Tony slumped on the edge of the sidewalk near the stone wall of a building. His face was sunburned and peeling, and he'd collected two more layers of coats since the last time I'd seen him.

"Hey, Mara. Hey, Mara. Trouble in paradise?" He nodded toward Jacqueline, laughter coughing from his lungs.

"Hi, Tony." I pulled out my wallet and dropped a five-dollar bill into his cup, ignoring his comment.

"She's a bitch. A bitch," he repeated.

Jacqueline strutted down the south side of North Avenue as if she owned the city. I hugged my bag to my chest, lowering myself next to Tony on the dirty, cement sidewalk.

"You're right, Tony. She is."

A large banner hung in front of a restaurant across the street and rippled in the wind. *Spooktacular Halloween Bash! Live Music! Half off pitchers!* I'd completely forgotten that Halloween was only a few days away. It didn't seem like Halloween. It didn't seem like any season or any holiday. My life had become nothing more than a bottomless, shifting sinkhole trying to swallow me.

If only I could go back in time. Regret flooded my chest as I wished I could return to my childhood home in Hoffman Estates, where another Halloween ten years earlier reeled through my mind. I'd been fourteen, so Emma must have been six. Three of my friends had met up in our living room before heading out for trick-or-treating. We'd dressed in the kind of lame costumes that fourteen-year-old girls who knew they were too old for trick-or-treating dressed in—jeans and simple headbands with cat ears propped on our heads. We carried white pillowcases for our candy.

Emma jumped up and down next to us, dressed as a butterfly.

Her wings flapped, and her sparkly antennas bounced each time she leaped into the air. She gripped an orange plastic bucket shaped like a jack-o-lantern in her hand.

"Can I go with you guys, Mara?" she asked, her pudgy fingers tugging at my shirt.

"No, Em," I said. "You won't be able to keep up."

"Come on! Please!" She jumped higher now.

"Just let her go around the block with you, Mara," Mom said, poking her head into the room. "She won't hurt anything."

"Mom!" I said, my voice ripe with teenage angst. "I just want to be with my friends."

"I'll take you, Em." Dad stepped toward Emma and lifted her off the ground.

"But why can't we all go together?" Emma's lower lip stuck out, a signal that she was about to cry.

"Because!" I turned to my friends. "Come on, guys. Let's go!" We rushed out the door yelling and laughing, leaving Emma sobbing in Dad's arms.

What an ass I'd been. What kind of person ruins Halloween for her six-year-old sister? I'd done that to Emma. I'd caused her that pain. If only I could go back in time and let her come with us. I'd let her glittery butterfly wings lead the pack. Then I'd give her all my candy, even the Reese's. But I couldn't go back in time. I could only face reality. I was slumped next to a homeless guy on the side of North Avenue. Emma was battling cancer that had been diagnosed months too late. And now I had to fight off Jacqueline, too. She was like a disease on my life, infecting everything she touched. I lifted myself off the sidewalk, unable to shake the memory of Emma crying in her butterfly costume.

"See you around, Tony."

"Bye, Mara. Bye."

I wouldn't let a narcissistic, power-hungry realtor destroy my life, and I wouldn't let Emma down again. I'd pay for her treatment, even if it meant keeping Jacqueline's secrets.

****

I balanced on the edge of my chair while Jacqueline called Roger and explained how she wanted to bring me in on Arlington on the Park as her assistant.

"There's no need to hire anyone to replace Kevin. I can handle the sales, especially with Mara helping me." I could hear some grumbling through the phone. "Mara was a friend of Kevin's." More mumbling. "Yes. She was named one of the 'Thirty Under Thirty.' A real rising star." There was a pause followed by muffled talking. "Great, Roger. I'll have Mara send you the sales report at the end of the week." She gave me a thumbs-up as if she hadn't threatened to destroy my life minutes earlier.

Next, we hovered in Maeve's office, where Jacqueline handed the revised Arlington on the Park contract over to her. In a hushed voice, Jacqueline requested Maeve to sign off on our new commission agreement. The office manager lowered her eyes through the bifocals resting on the tip of her nose. She scrawled her name across the bottom of the page. I couldn't tell if Maeve suspected foul play on Jacqueline's part, but she didn't say anything. Like the rest of us, she had no proof. And from what I knew of Maeve, she wouldn't do anything to mess with the success of her cash cow.

CHAPTER FORTY-ONE

I cracked open the driver's side window, gulping in the crisp October air to fuel my sleep-deprived body. I hunched down, relieved to have found a parking spot on the crowded residential street but too nervous to move from the cover of my car. My fingers gripped the copied page of the Protective Order Jacqueline had filed on my behalf against Peter Zinsky five months earlier. I scanned over the address again, confirming I was parked directly outside Peter's last-known address on Cornelia. A desolate vibe radiated from the stark, red brick three-flat that loomed on the other side of the sidewalk. The building lacked the pumpkins, political signs, and Cubs paraphernalia decorating the surrounding homes.

Closing my eyes, I counted to ten and gathered my courage. The last time I'd seen Peter, he'd held a knife to my stomach, and I wondered if seeking him out was proof I'd gone crazy. My eyelids weighed heavily from my sleepless night. Jacqueline's threats had left me anxious and scared. She'd backed me into a corner. I'd lain awake until early morning, thankful that Damon hadn't been with me. His upcoming exams had limited his overnight stays. As I tossed and turned, my mind kept wandering back to the erratic behavior of Jacqueline's previous assistant.

Peter had been so patient and helpful with my closing,

explaining contract terms, and providing the riders I'd been missing with my offer. Now that I understood what Jacqueline was capable of, it seemed unlikely Peter had suddenly transformed from a soft-spoken professional into a violent, paranoid, drug addict. She must have set him up, too.

Promise me you'll stay away from her! She's not who you think she is! His warnings had been screaming through my mind all night. I'd witnessed the way his eyes had stretched with fear, his lip quivering in desperation. I'd been so blinded by the promise of working with one of Chicago's top realtors that I hadn't bothered to listen to him. Hopefully, Peter would forgive me for not keeping my word, for ratting him out to Jacqueline and calling the police, instead of finding a new position as I'd promised. I hoped I could still convince him to tell me what he knew. We needed to join forces and share whatever dirt we had on Jacqueline with each other. Two victims were more believable than one.

With another deep breath, I emerged from my car and smoothed down my pants. I crept up the cement steps looking over my shoulder to make sure Jacqueline hadn't tailed me. The street lay quiet behind me. My finger pressed the buzzer for unit 2.

"Who is it?" A woman's tight voice crackled through the speaker.

"Hi. I'm looking for Peter Zinsky." I crossed my arms in front of me, shifting my weight. "Is he home?"

The static of the speaker cut out, replaced by silence. I was about to push the doorbell again when the door creaked open.

A woman with shoulder-length white hair and washed out features poked her head through the opening. Her baggy eyes narrowed at me. "Can I help you?"

"Hi. Yes. I'm a friend of Peter's. He helped me buy my condo a while back. I was hoping to talk to him"

The woman pulled her chin into her chest, her eyes drooping in the corners.

I swallowed and stepped to the side. "I can come back later if this isn't a good time."

She shook her head as she bit her lip and blinked. "I'm sorry to have to tell you this. Peter passed away a few months ago."

I lurched backward, feeling like she'd whacked me in the gut with a sledgehammer. The woman reached toward me, placing a steady hand on my arm.

"Are you sure?" I asked, struggling to keep my balance.

"I'm afraid so," she said, her voice splintering. "I'm Denise. Peter's wife."

I shuffled my feet to the side, glancing toward the street to hide my despair. "I'm so sorry. Was he sick?"

She swallowed and stared up at the sky. "No. I'm afraid he took his own life."

"What?" The cement steps spun beneath me.

"He became very depressed after losing his job. I still can't believe it."

My hand grasped for the door frame. Peter had committed suicide? Had it been my fault for blowing him off? For not listening to him? Jacqueline's sinister grin flashed in my mind.

"I'm so sorry," I said again. "This is such a shock."

"It still is for me, too."

"Do you mind if I ask…" I swallowed against my parched throat, not sure how to dig for the information I needed. "Did he say why?"

The woman shook her head, lips quivering. "There was no note. Only the gun in his hand."

"Gun?"

"I know. It doesn't make sense." Her eyes dropped to the floor. "He always hated guns. We both did. But I guess when depression takes hold of someone, they just want the pain to end. That's what my therapist has been telling me, anyway."

"You said he was depressed about not working at Greystone anymore?"

Peter's wife stepped further into the entryway, the door creaking shut behind her. "Well, yes. The woman he worked for was extremely demanding. She blamed him for everything that went wrong." She blinked several times, a sheen of liquid pooling in the corners of her eyes. "Looking back, that's when Peter's downward spiral began. After Jacqueline fired him, no other real estate office in the city would return his calls. It was almost as if she'd sabotaged him."

I nodded, a pool of unease rising inside me.

Peter's wife continued. "He got into some legal trouble. It was so unlike him, but he promised me that would be the end of it." She rubbed her arm with her opposite hand, eyes drifting into space.

Bile rose in my throat. She must have been referring to the assault and battery against me.

"It will never make sense to me." The woman shook her head. "I don't know where he got the gun. They couldn't find any records."

I laced my fingers together in front of me, my knuckles turning white as I kept my eyes focused on the row of metal mailboxes in the entryway. "I'm sorry."

The woman pressed her colorless lips together. "I don't understand why he didn't talk to me."

Because he was protecting you, I wanted to scream as a sickening dread tunneled through me. My knees weakened, a thousand questions spiraling through my mind. What had Jacqueline been holding over him? Why hadn't anyone at Greystone heard about Peter's death? He'd been a loner, but someone must have notified Jacqueline. A lawyer at her former law firm had filed the paperwork for the protective order. Wouldn't they have a duty to inform her that Peter had died?

A dark space expanded in my gut as a new understanding formed. Maybe Jacqueline had never filed a protective order. I'd given a written statement to Jacqueline after the altercation with Peter. But I'd never been required to appear before a judge. The document in my car was unstamped. The protective order was probably a forgery she'd printed for my benefit. She hadn't needed to file it because she'd already killed him. And why hadn't Peter left a note? Surely, he would have wanted to explain his last drastic action to his wife. Would a guy who hated guns use a gun to end his own life? It was more likely that Jacqueline had let herself into

Peter's condo and shot him, staging the scene to make it appear like a suicide, just like she'd made Kevin's death look like an allergic reaction. A chill traveled through my body, causing my teeth to click. She'd let herself into my condo, too.

The woman stepped toward me, her brow furrowing in concern. "What did you say your name was again?"

The muscles in my jaw twitched, my body wavering on the top step. "M-Megan. I'm sorry. I'm sorry for your loss. Your husband was a good man. I've got to get going." Turning on my heel, I jogged down the steps feeling as if I was running for my life.

****

Outside, gathering clouds had turned the sky murky and gray as a light rain gathered force and pelted against my living room window. I'd driven directly home from my visit with Peter's wife as my fingers gripped around the steering wheel, and my heart thumped wildly inside my chest. Now, my unclenched fingers stumbled across the keyboard, hitting the wrong letters then backing up to retype again.

At last, I formulated a search—*Peter Zinsky obituary Chicago*. I held my breath as a screenful of results appeared. I clicked on the top result from the *Tribune*, opening a black-and-white thumbnail of Peter's face along with a two-paragraph obituary. I lowered my face next to the screen, my eyes flying over the words.

Peter Kyle Zinsky, loving husband, father, and son, born December 3rd...died at his home in Chicago on May 20th at the age of 61...survived by his wife, Denise, son, Matthew, and sister, Jeanine. He is predeceased by his mother, Anne, and his father, John.

Peter lived his life quietly and compassionately, frequently volunteering at the New Hope Soup Kitchen and as an English tutor for recent immigrants...graduated with a degree in communications from Marquette University...worked most of his adult life in marketing and real estate sales.

I skimmed over the details of the memorial service, snagging to a halt on the last line.

In lieu of flowers, the family requests donations in Peter's memory be sent to the National Suicide Prevention Lifeline.

My toes curled down into the floor, my breath jagged and dry at the idea of Peter's family believing he'd committed suicide. Peter had died on May 20th. That was over five months ago, just a couple of weeks after he'd confronted me with the knife. What had I been doing on that day? Had Jacqueline been with me? I couldn't remember.

I clicked back to the search results, not finding anything related to Peter. I entered another search—*suicide Chicago gun May*, leading to another Tribune article dated May 21st—*Local Man Found Dead in Garage; Suicide Suspected.*

Chicago Police responded to a call on Chicago's north side on Wednesday night, discovering the remains of a man who was believed to have shot himself in the head. The victim, who will remain unnamed until all family is notified, was discovered by his wife in a detached garage behind the home. She immediately called 911.

"All early indications point to suicide," said police officer Bill McCaffery. "A revolver was found in the victim's right hand. The door to the garage was locked with no sign of forced entry. We have not located a note, but the victim's wife said her husband had recently been struggling with depression after losing his job."

Over 38,000 Americans die by suicide each year, with men being almost four times more likely to take their own lives than women...

My phone buzzed, pulling my eyes toward it. Jacqueline. I swallowed back the nausea spreading through me, my hand quivering as I answered the call. Before I could utter a word, Jacqueline barked at me.

"Mara. I need you to input yesterday's sales at Arlington on the Park into the MLS. Units 501 and 304 are still coming up as active."

"Okay."

"Why aren't you in the office?"

I stood up and paced toward the window. "Did you know that

Peter Zinsky died?"

"What?"

"Peter Zinsky. The man who was your assistant before me. He committed suicide on May 20th."

"Really?" Jacqueline's breath rushed in and out a few times. "Oh, my gosh. No. I had no idea." Her voice rang hollow.

I gripped the hem of my shirt in my fist and squeezed.

Jacqueline cleared her throat. "I guess it shouldn't be a surprise. He was so unstable." She clucked. "At least he won't be bothering you anymore."

My face burned. I wanted to scream, to tell Jacqueline that she wasn't going to get away with this, but a dark warning pulsated through me. I couldn't let her know I knew the truth. It would be reckless. I'd be putting my own life at risk. My fingers released the crumpled lining of my shirt.

"Yeah," I said, my throat tightening as I forced out the word.

"So, get that MLS information corrected ASAP."

"Yeah," I said again because I couldn't come up with any other words. I ended the call.

Below me, red brake lights cut through the haze of rain as a line of cars formed behind the traffic light on Milwaukee Avenue. A man jogged across the intersection, his umbrella catching in the wind and flipping inside out. Another woman pulled her jacket over her head for shelter as she scurried up the sidewalk. Even caught in a storm, soaking wet in the freezing rain, I envied their freedom.

My phone buzzed again, my muscles tensing as I half-expected to see Jacqueline's name on the screen again. It was Damon.

"Hey, beautiful."

"Hi."

"How's your day?"

My lips moved, but no words came out. A hot tingling sensation forced its way up my throat, through my nose, behind my eyes. "Okay," I finally managed, but my voice cracked, and my nose sniffled.

"What's wrong?"

I stepped over to my computer, resting my palm on my desk. Peter's face smiled up at me from his obituary. "Remember the guy I told you about who used to work for Jacqueline? Peter Zinsky?"

"The one who pulled a knife on you?"

"Yeah."

"Did that piece of shit do something else?"

"He committed suicide."

Damon exhaled. "What? Are you serious?"

"Yeah. He shot himself. Back in May. I just found out about it today."

"Man. He must have been even more screwed up than you realized."

"I know." I bit my tongue, fighting the urge to tell Damon everything I suspected, everything I *knew*. But telling him wasn't worth the risk. He'd go to the authorities, just as he would have done if I'd told him the truth about Kevin's death, and who knew what Jacqueline would do for revenge? I needed the commissions from Arlington on the Park. I needed to keep my part in Jacqueline's schemes hidden, to make sure the damaging evidence she held over my head never saw daylight.

"Do you want me to come over? I don't have any more classes today."

"Sorry. I can't. I have to do some stuff for Jacqueline. Maybe tomorrow, though."

I didn't trust myself not to tell him more. I massaged my temple, silently convincing myself that lying by omission wasn't as bad as telling an outright lie. Still, I'd repeated Jacqueline's false versions of reality so many times that the line between reality and fiction was blurring. It was getting harder to keep track of all the lies.

CHAPTER FORTY-TWO

I double-parked in front of Damon's apartment building as Friday traffic lurched past. A layer of November snow glazed the sidewalks and grass with gray blotches of cement bleeding through to the surface. The white covering turned brown at the edges as melting water dripped off rooftops. I stepped onto the curb, avoiding a murky puddle of slush, and tried not to destroy my suede boots. I waved to Damon and ducked back into my car, anxious to escape the damp air.

He unloaded his bag into the trunk and leaned near my open window "Do you want me to drive?"

"I'm good," I said.

An agonizing month had passed since I'd learned both Kevin and Peter had died under suspicious circumstances. I'd kept my lips sealed, Jacqueline's threats following me everywhere, my eyes popping open throughout the night, my muscles jumping at every loud noise. I'd had the locks to my condo changed and a security system installed, but Jacqueline was capable of anything. Despite my best efforts to disguise my fear, it lived inside me. One wrong move and I'd be her next victim. Even if she didn't murder me, she could destroy my life with her lies.

I'd been working on overdrive trying to keep her happy at the

Arlington on the Park sales center by hosting the Sunday open houses, returning phone calls, filing the correct paperwork, and recording the sold units on the master plat. Jacqueline only stopped by once a week to make sure I was completing my assigned duties. Our relationship had grown more toxic than black mold, but we managed to continue our business as usual. We were like a married couple that each knew the other was sleeping with someone else. Divorce was inevitable, but we agreed to stay together for the kids. She needed to win Top Producer to earn back the love of her parents—or at least one-up them—by having her face plastered to the billboard on I-94. And I needed to preserve my life, not to mention Emma's. Jacqueline and I put on a convincing front for co-workers and clients. I doubted anyone suspected we wanted to push each other down the elevator shaft of a tall building.

In a few weeks, Jacqueline's reign as Chicago's Top Producer would begin, and I could finally break free, just as Kevin and Peter had urged me to do. Her sales numbers exceeded Natalia's by over ten million dollars. She'd been right about Natalia's reality show. For every one client who wanted his business aired on TV, there were three more who did not. Natalia was losing clients almost as fast as Jacqueline was gaining them. Jacqueline had nine closings already scheduled for December and one for early January that she was angling to push up to the end of December. On top of her regular sales, Arlington on the Park was doing well in pre-sales. In the first eight weeks since the sales center opened, we'd pre-sold forty-eight units. She'd have a head start on Natalia for next year, too.

Unbelievably, I'd make over $200,000 in my first year as a realtor. It was more money than I'd ever dreamed of yet, if not for Emma, it wouldn't have been worth everything Jacqueline had put me through.

Damon climbed into the passenger seat, his cold hand squeezing mine and a tentative smile on his face. A dark shadow hovered over me as I forced a smile and kissed him. I'd been keeping so many secrets from him, not willing to risk sharing my suspicions about Jacqueline's murderous tendencies and other illegal schemes. He'd grown frustrated with me the last few weeks, sensing that I was hiding something. Sometimes I blamed my distant stares on Emma or work. Most times, I assured him it was nothing. Still, an invisible wall had formed between us, our nights together less frequent and even less passionate.

The weekend getaway to my friend, Brianna's wedding in Michigan, was meant to be the perfect remedy. I pictured the lacey new lingerie folded at the bottom of my suitcase and tapped my freshly manicured fingernails on the steering wheel. The two-and-a-half-hour drive to the lakeside town of South Haven would be a welcome escape from the city, from Jacqueline. Plus, as much as I hated to admit it, a part of me was eager to show off my new success to my college friends, to watch their mouths drop open as I got out of my BMW with a handsome law student by my side. I merged onto 94-East, ready to leave the stress of my day-to-day life behind, at least for a weekend.

We crept along the expressway in bumper-to-bumper traffic. My phone buzzed steadily with incoming phone calls and emails. Damon stared at me.

"Turn it off. We can't even have a conversation."

I nodded and hit the power button. This weekend would be all about Damon and me. Work could wait. As I drove, he told funny stories about his law school classmates—a woman who sat in the front row and asked dumb questions just as class was about to end, a guy who reeked of garlic and always sat next to him, and another guy who copied his notes and was a useless member of his study group.

The landscape outside our windows changed as we made our way south of the city. Rundown, treeless subdivisions bordered the highway on either side. Roofs sagged. Windows boarded and barred. Just when we thought the surroundings couldn't get more depressing, we passed a trailer park bordered by a landfill on one side and the highway on the other.

"Can you imagine if you lived there?" he asked, his mouth curving into a frown.

"That would suck." I wanted to engage more, to have a deeper conversation about how some people left their circumstances up to chance, but I was too distracted. Not just by all the calls and emails I was ignoring, but also by everything going on with Jacqueline. She was vindictive. She'd agreed to give me a two-day "vacation" for the wedding, but I worried she'd want payback for my time off. In the last six months, I hadn't enjoyed a single day without phone calls, showings, and emails. Still, she'd glared at me and shook her head when I told her I was going to Michigan for the weekend. A sour feeling settled at the bottom of my stomach as I wondered what she'd do for revenge. The image of me with the guy at Drumbar kept popping into my mind, a constant reminder my life could implode at any minute. All Jacqueline had to do was email that photo to Damon, and she could destroy our relationship. She could knock me down from my trendy Bucktown condo to the trailer park by the landfill. It would only take one email. Or one video.

As Damon rambled on about one of his friends who repeatedly bailed out on their basketball games, I considered telling him about the meaningless kiss. If I came clean and explained what had happened, then Jacqueline wouldn't have that power over me. I glanced over at my boyfriend's smiling lips, his kind eyes, and strong arms. As soon as I had the thought, I trashed it as a horrible idea. There was too much to lose. My confession would ruin our weekend, and he might not be as forgiving as I imagined.

I tried to get my mind off my dilemma by switching radio stations and listening to Damon sing off-key. There were only six more weeks to survive with Jacqueline. Then I'd be free to work for myself. She'd promised as long as I helped her win Top Producer, she'd set me free. I could do it, but I wasn't going to let her mess up my business with my own clients. Those clients would be mine after we went our separate ways, and I couldn't lose them. I sucked in a sharp breath as I envisioned all the negative reviews that had been posted about me recently on the internet. Admittedly, I'd had to reschedule with my buyers a few times, and I missed a showing at one of my listings because of Jacqueline's demands. Still, I didn't think my actions warranted being called "irresponsible" and "disorganized." My gut needled with the suspicion that Jacqueline had been sabotaging me. She preferred I spend my time and energy working on her deals. Everything else I did took away from her bottom-line.

We passed over the skyway through Gary, Indiana. The nasty, chemical smell of air pollution spewed from the steel factories and seeped into my car.

"How is this legal?" I asked, pointing to an industrial chimney churning out black smoke.

Damon stopped singing and covered his nose. He punched the button on my dashboard to recirculate the car's interior air. "This might be worse than that trailer park next to the landfill."

I glanced at my phone and nodded. "I guess things can always be worse."

****

It was easier to forget about work and about Jacqueline once we arrived at the Inn in South Haven. The sky had darkened by the time we checked in, but the air somehow felt lighter. For the first time in months, I could breathe.

We checked into our Victorian-themed room, giggling at the creepy antique doll resting on a wooden cabinet in the corner of the wallpapered room. Famished, we dropped our bags on the floor and headed to a waterside bar where we ate greasy fish and chips and downed some draft beer. By the first sip of my second beer, I'd completely transformed, my body relaxed, my attention focused only on Damon. I'd been under Jacqueline's thumb for so long I'd forgotten what it felt like to be free. We ordered another beer. And another. The walls around the tiny booth felt safe and secure. I never wanted to leave.

By the time we stumbled back to the inn, Damon had to prop me up, my legs sagging under my weight.

"Maybe you shouldn't have had that last one," he said as he helped me to bed, pulling my shoes from my feet.

I woke in the morning, my fancy lingerie still tucked into the bottom of my suitcase, my stomach sour, and my head splitting in pain. Damon brought me water, and I apologized for over-drinking. After my shower, Damon returned from the hotel lobby with an assortment of muffins and fruit. I nibbled what I could and told him I felt better, although my head pulsed. We wandered down to the pier, cradling cups of coffee in our hands. I couldn't drink mine because of the smell.

We strolled down the beach bundled up in our coats as a frigid November wind whipped off Lake Michigan. Later, we browsed the shops in town, buying small mementos like candles and blueberry jam. By lunchtime, my head had cleared, and my stomach gnawed with hunger. We met up with my friend, Beth, and her boyfriend, Matt, at an old bank that had been converted into a restaurant. Damon chatted with my friends as if he'd known them for years. I leaned back in the vinyl booth, awed by my perfect boyfriend, and basking in the change of pace from my usual Saturdays. The others sipped their micro-brews, while I stuck to water.

Damon nodded toward me. "She was overserved last night." He gave me a wink to let me know he wasn't mad.

The others chuckled at my state of recovery, as the waitress placed a stack of enormous battered onion rings in front of us. Beth and I caught up on mutual friends. I filled her in on Grace's new condo and told her how Chloe had screwed me by not using me as her realtor, leaving out the part about dumping my beer in her face.

All the while, the voicemails, emails, and texts piled up on my phone. I scanned them when Damon wasn't looking, just to make sure there were no emergencies, no fires to put out. Most of the calls were showing requests for Arlington on the Park, which I forwarded to Jacqueline. I turned off my phone and hid it in my pocket.

Later that afternoon, we changed into our formal clothes. I wore a floral dress with long sleeves and a plunging neckline. Damon whistled at me as I emerged from the bathroom, my legs feeling long and lean in my three-inch heels. I whistled right back at him because he looked like a million bucks in his suit and tie.

Damon and I held hands as we sat next to Matt and Beth at the old stone church and watched Brianna profess her love to the man she was marrying. I'd never met him, but by the tears in his eyes, as he recited his vows, I could tell she made him happy. As Damon squeezed my palm in his, I couldn't help wondering if we'd be standing in their spots one day and whether Damon was wondering the same thing.

The reception took place in the airy ballroom of our hotel, featuring an impressive selection of appetizers and drinks, and a quartet of violinists playing classical music in the background. The aroma of fresh flowers and mini quiches swirled around us, and I was thankful my hangover had passed. I looped my arm inside Damon's, envisioning the look on his face when he'd see me later wearing the lacey number I'd picked up from a boutique on Chestnut Street.

We stepped toward the windows, the blue-gray waves crashing against the shoreline.

Damon squeezed my hand. "Look at that view. It's so cool."

"Yeah." I took a sip of my wine, awed by the way Lake Michigan stretched on forever and thankful that Jacqueline was somewhere on the other side.

Brianna's older brother stepped next to us, and I introduced Damon to him. My cell phone buzzed from inside my purse. At first, I ignored it, annoyed at the intrusion during my weekend off. I promised Damon there'd be no real estate. No Jacqueline. But the unanswered call nagged at me. *Who was it?* After a couple of minutes of small talk, the mystery voicemail became an itch I needed to scratch. I pulled my phone from my clutch and checked my messages. Justin Cotwell. He was a buyer I'd been working with for the last few weeks. He'd been looking to buy a townhome in the River North area, and I'd shown him just about every property on the market. Justin would have to wait. This weekend was about Damon and me.

I refocused on the conversation in front of me. Damon and Brianna's brother talked about all the resort towns on Michigan's west coast. My phone dinged with a text. I tipped my head back and sighed, reaching into my clutch again.

The text was from Justin. *Want to write an offer on 30 S. Canal*

ASAP. Call me back.

My heart sunk as I squeezed Damon's shoulder, interrupting his conversation. I pointed toward the door. "I need to go make a phone call."

He cocked his head at me but nodded.

The noise from the party was quieter in the hallway. I pressed Justin's number on my phone and waited.

"Mara!" he said after one ring. "I found the perfect property. I walked through the open house today. I don't want to miss out on this one. Can you meet up with me right now, so I can write up an offer?"

I cringed at the horrible timing. "Actually, I'm in Michigan at a wedding. But I can meet you tomorrow afternoon as soon as I get back."

"Oh, man! Is there another realtor at your office I could meet with tonight? Maybe that Jacqueline woman? I really want this townhome. I'm going to offer full price."

My chest tightened at the thought of losing the deal. Or, even worse, having to give Jacqueline a cut. Although his timing was awful, I needed to keep Justin happy. In six weeks, I'd separate myself from Jacqueline, and I'd need all the referrals I could get.

Holding the air in my lungs, I silently debated my options. "Tell you what, I can cut my weekend short and come back first thing tomorrow morning. I'll meet you at 9:00 a.m. at my office. I'll call the listing agent and let them know you'll be submitting an offer in the morning and not to accept anything else before then."

He sighed on the other end. "I guess that would work. As long as you call the listing agent right now."

"Don't worry. I'm on it."

"Great. I'll see you at 9:00."

I pulled Damon into a corner, crouching low in an attempt to appear small and meek as I broke the news to him.

"That was a client. I'm so sorry, but we need to be on the road by 6:30 a.m. tomorrow, at the latest." I squeezed his hands in mine.

He laughed at first, but when I didn't laugh too, his face froze, and his mouth pulled back.

"I need to get back to Chicago as soon as possible, or I'm going to lose this deal," I said.

Damon's back straightened, his lip twitching with anger. "What about brunch? And our plans to drive up the coast and explore all the towns?"

"I'm sorry. I don't have a choice."

"Of course you do. Tell him you'll meet him later."

"I can't."

We were the first to leave the reception. My sudden change in plans had ruined the night as far as Damon was concerned. Back in our room, I left a message for the listing agent and pulled up some comps to prepare for my meeting with Justin in the morning. Damon fell asleep on the bed, his back to me.

I drove my BMW west on 94, darting in and out of the Sunday morning drivers, and trying not to think about the unused lingerie neatly folded into the corner of my suitcase. Damon leaned back in the front seat, barely speaking a word. I clenched the steering wheel with sweaty hands, too distracted to care.

Two long hours later, I dropped my angry boyfriend in front of his building and apologized for the one-hundredth time for the change in plans.

He shrugged. "I need to study anyway." He slammed the door in my face and strode toward his building.

A wave of heat rushed toward my face, but I blinked away the tears. I'd win Damon back later when I had more time to think and explain myself, when Jacqueline was a merely a speck in my rearview mirror. Right then, I needed to focus on keeping my career alive. Someday, Damon would understand that I didn't have a choice. I was doing this for us. It was the only way to break free from Jacqueline.

CHAPTER FORTY-THREE

After dropping off Damon, I realized I'd left Justin's file in my desk drawer at the sales center. I drove toward Arlington on the Park in a daze, not letting my mind wander to anything other than picking up the papers before meeting Justin at Greystone. The Sunday morning traffic was light, but parked cars lined every inch of the one-way street outside the sales center. I double-parked and threw on my flashers, jogging up to the door and hoping for a quick in and out, especially if Jacqueline was there.

Footprints in the snow led toward the door, and I paused, bracing myself to have to deal with her. When I turned the handle, it was locked. I released a puff of air. Thank God. She wasn't there. If she knew I'd returned early, she'd make me cover the open house this afternoon. Unlocking the door, I slipped inside. Justin's file lay right where I'd left it inside the top drawer of my desk.

As I turned, the laptop on Jacqueline's desk caught my eye. The computer was powered off and closed. I paused. It wasn't like her to leave without it. She must have been in a hurry. The corner of a manila folder peeked out from under her computer. I wondered if she'd sold more units yesterday. With a $60 million sellout expected, the total commissions earned on the development would be close to $3 million. My cut was only twenty percent of Jacqueline's half of the selling side, but still, the referral fees were adding up.

I removed the folder and opened it up to see which unit had sold. Instead of the contract I expected to see, an IDFPR complaint form lay in full view. A neon yellow sticky note clung to the top right corner of the page: *CC Police Department.* What did that mean? Was someone filing a complaint against Jacqueline? I started reading it.

Complainant: Jacqueline Hendersen

Respondent: Mara Butler

My knees almost buckled beneath me. *What the hell? Was Jacqueline filing a complaint against me?* I placed my hands on the desk to support my weight and forced myself to keep reading.

While previewing a property with Mara Butler (Respondent) on April 24, I witnessed her stealing a box containing jewelry from my client, Julia Johnson's condominium. I have proof that she stole my client's property, as I happened to be taking a video of the outside of the condominium for marketing purposes when Respondent exited the condominium with the box. I did not realize until months later that the box contained valuable jewels owned by my client.

The air left my body, my head spinning as I tried to make sense of the discovery. The date on the bottom hadn't been filled in yet. Jacqueline wasn't honoring our deal. She was saving the video of me with the white box to use against me. She planned to turn it over to the police. She must have been the one who'd broken into my condo and hidden the jewels under the dishtowels. She was setting me up so the police would discover the evidence. I flipped to the next form and read as fast as my brain could take it in.

On April 22, Mara Butler (Respondent) forged a check in the amount of $5,000 from Greystone Realty's accounting department and unlawfully withdrew funds from Greystone's escrow account for her personal use. I became aware of Respondent's fraudulent activity on January 2nd when Respondent bragged to another realtor about stealing the money from Greystone's escrow

267

account. Greystone has since canceled Respondent's Independent Contractor Agreement, but I feel an obligation to report this fraud to the Board of Realtors. A copy of the forged check is attached to this Complaint.

Signed: _____ [Complainant]
     Maeve Wilkerson, Office Manager
     Greystone Realty

My heart pounded in my chest, black spots appearing before my eyes. I hadn't forged any checks. Jacqueline had given me a draw and asked me to fill out the check. I'd paid her back! Suddenly, something Kevin had told me about Peter months earlier echoed in my head—*There was a rumor he stole money from Greystone's escrow account.* My hand flew to my mouth, silencing my scream. Jacqueline had done the same thing to him.

My eyes scanned back over the dates on the forms, *January 2nd.* That didn't make any sense. January 2nd was over a month from now. Why was Maeve's complaint unsigned? Why was Jacqueline waiting? Then, just as quickly as my blood had boiled, it reversed course and turned ice cold. I'd spent enough time with Jacqueline to know how her mind worked. Winning Top Producer was her number one goal. She was waiting to bring home the award before taking her lies to Maeve. Before framing me for robbery and forgery. Before destroying me.

More of Kevin's words replayed in my head: *She hasn't slit your throat and left you by the side of the road yet, so that's good...She'd kill her own mother to get both sides of a commission.* I squeezed my fists so tight, my knuckles cracked. Kevin had seen Jacqueline for what she was. He'd tried to warn me. So had Peter. They'd both ended up dead. I'd been so focused on becoming successful, on paying Emma's medical bills, on protecting my relationship with Damon that I'd somehow justified Jacqueline's actions. I'd been so naïve. Why had I trusted her? Why hadn't I quit before things spiraled out of control?

A second complaint with the Board of Realtors lay behind the first one. An address jumped off the page at me. 1907 N. Mohawk.

Another wave of nausea overtook me. She wasn't going to forget about the stolen lead after all. I should have known.

On or about May 25th, Mara Butler [Respondent] unlawfully stole information from my website related to a property located at 1907 N. Mohawk, Chicago, IL. The stolen information resulted in Respondent listing and selling said property. Because I procured the lead through my website, I am legally entitled to the Respondent's commission.

Signed: Jacqueline Hendersen [Complainant]

Again, she had dated the complaint in January—over a month from now. My hands shook uncontrollably. Still, I forced myself to look at the final form that lay beneath the others. Another sticky note stuck to the front of the page. In Jacqueline's handwriting, it read, *Call Natalia re: stalking.*

I narrowed my eyes at the words, the horrible realization spreading through me with every passing second. My breathing stopped as if Jacqueline's hands, themselves, were strangling me. She was going to tell Natalia I'd been stalking her. I turned on my heel, desperate for somewhere to run, but there was nowhere to escape from Jacqueline's traps. Natalia had seen me! I could almost hear Jacqueline's false statements: that her troubled assistant had become obsessed with the Russian realtor, the city's Top Producer, that she'd caught me stealing leads, not only from Natalia but also from her own website, that she didn't know what I was capable of. What if Natalia believed Jacqueline's version of events? Natalia could have me killed by the Russian mafia. There was no way to defend myself. I *had* been following her.

I crumpled the sticky note, feeling sick. The papers shook in my hands, and my forehead erupted in a chill of sweat. Jacqueline was framing me for every crime imaginable with flat-out lies. Except for keeping the Mohawk listing to myself, I hadn't done anything wrong. I'd done nothing but help her. I tried to swallow, but my mouth was dry. I wanted to scream, but no sound would come out. Hot bile rose in my throat, and I gulped it back down. I kept reading.

I am coming forward now because I am tired of living in fear. Respondent has shown up on my doorstep and threatened me with bodily harm unless I bring her in as a fifty percent partner in my Arlington on the Park development listing. I request a protective order against her.

She was ruthless, but this sunk to a new low. These complaints would ruin my career. I wouldn't be able to pay for Emma's treatment if I lost my license. My parents would have to sell their house. Jacqueline's false claims could destroy my life. What if Damon believed this bullshit?

I could come clean and tell the police about Jacqueline staging Peter's death to look like a suicide and about how she murdered Kevin, but she'd find a way to twist it, to say I was trying to get back at her. Maybe she'd even frame *me* for Kevin's death, or Peter's. I'd been inside Kevin's building that day, too. I benefitted from his death when I'd taken his place on the Arlington on the Park development. And after Peter had threatened me with a knife, I'd also had a strong motive for wanting him gone. People viewed Jacqueline as a pillar of the community, the winner of the Chicago Board of Realtors' Good Neighbor Award. They would believe her version of events over mine.

Two loud honks from outside jolted me upright, the papers dropping. I pulled them off the floor and shoved them into my bag, grabbing the manila file on the way out. Jacqueline didn't expect me back from Michigan so soon, or she would never have left that folder on her desk. She wouldn't know it was me who took it. Judging by the dates on the complaints, I still had over a month before she planned to file them.

Before I could lock the door behind me, a uniformed woman from Windy City Cleaning Service stepped toward the door, plastic bags and bottles of 409 and Windex in hand. She nodded toward the sales center.

"You're on the schedule for cleaning this morning."

"Okay." With my heart still racing, I stepped away from the door and let her through, hoping Jacqueline would believe an overzealous cleaning lady accidentally threw away her complaints.

A truck idled in the street and honked again, blocking my car. I gave a quick wave, and the driver gave me the finger back. I leaped inside and sped toward Greystone as fast as I could go.

I breathed out and relaxed my grip on the steering wheel, not finding Jacqueline's car parked in any of the spaces around Greystone. Still, it was too risky to stay at the office. Justin and I would need to write up the offer somewhere else.

My client stood next to the front door, shifting his weight from foot to foot. I pulled to the curb and stepped from my car to shake his hand.

"Hi. Do you mind if we write this up at the Pancake House? I've been driving all morning, and I'm starving."

"That's fine."

We climbed back into our cars and drove the four blocks to the restaurant. Jacqueline hadn't seen me. I breathed out the air I'd been holding in my lungs, feeling as if I'd narrowly escaped my execution. A few minutes later, I sat across from Justin, squinting under the bright pendant lights that hung over our table, ordering coffee and pancakes from the overly friendly waitress. The food was just for show. My stomach turned with fear, not hunger as the damning accusations reeled through my head.

Justin insisted on submitting a full-price offer. I didn't argue, even though he was overpaying. We leafed through the comps and discussed the contract and disclosures, but I wasn't present for any of it. I watched myself fill out the contract and show him where to initial and sign, like a ghost floating above myself, only half-aware of the things that were happening around me. This feeling of separating from myself was familiar. I'd felt the same way after finding the cans of spray paint in the trunk of Jacqueline's car the night of the charity dinner. I'd justified her actions then, had even thought of her as a creative genius. I'd ignored my instincts to run in the other direction. I'd convinced myself that she was right and I was wrong, that she knew better. If only I had listened to my gut. I should have done the right thing. I should have left her early on and avoided this whole mess. But I hadn't.

An overwhelming feeling that things were going to get worse tore through me, like a dog who knew the earthquake was coming an hour before it arrived. I swiveled my legs to the other side of my chair but couldn't escape the darkness surrounding me. Every couple of minutes, I glanced over my shoulder half-expecting to see Jacqueline staring down at me, a grotesque smile on her face because she knew she was in control.

An image of the repositioned family photo in my living room flashed in my mind. Even with my locks changed and the security system installed, Jacqueline could find a way to break into my condo. She could make a call to the security company pretending to be me. She could lift a master key from the maintenance man. Is that how she'd done it with Kevin? And Peter?

The explosion of thoughts made it impossible to focus, kept me trapped inside my head. Jacqueline had been using me all along. She had built an invisible cage around me. I'd let her do it. Now I'd have to be the one to stop her. I wouldn't dispute the complaints. I wouldn't deny the allegations to Damon. I wouldn't warn my parents or Emma about Jacqueline's challenges to my character and integrity. It wasn't worth the risk of having them think any part of those lies could be true. Those complaints could never be filed. And I certainly wasn't going to wait around for her to murder me and make it look like an allergic reaction or a suicide. I'd finish this with Jacqueline directly. No one else needed to be involved.

CHAPTER FORTY-FOUR

I wrapped up the breakfast with Justin as quickly as possible and exited through the front door of the Pancake House. A jogger jumped to the side a moment before colliding with me, the narrow miss triggering something in my brain. *Think outside the box.* The pieces turned over in my head, details coming together, fitting into each other to form a clear plan. My body shook with something between anger and fear as I realized there was only one way to get myself out of the grave Jacqueline had dug for me. She'd left me no choice. It was kill or be killed.

Jacqueline had described her morning run so many times I knew the route by heart. She left her house before sunrise at exactly 4:45 a.m., running through the darkness and traversing the nearby neighborhoods and the zoo. Then she followed the lakeshore path, taking a shortcut down the first alley between Armitage and Lincoln Avenue on the loop back to her townhome.

I didn't drive back to the office to submit the offer like I'd promised Justin. That could wait until the afternoon when I knew Jacqueline would be at the sales center. Instead, I drove directly to the alley and scoped it out. The narrow pathway would be my opportunity, hidden from view, with no traffic light cameras to trace the accident back to me.

I thought back to the day my Hyundai had been towed to the nightmarish lot beneath the city, remembering the words of the foul man who'd charged me $500. *If you ever need a cheap car, give me a call.* I slunk into a nearby ATM and withdrew as much as was allowed, a thousand dollars in cash from my checking account, hoping the camera didn't pick up the layer of sweat forming on my upper lip. I placed two envelopes stuffed with hundred-dollar bills into my bag before slipping back into my car.

My fingers brushed against the leather seat. I couldn't execute my plan in the BMW. It was too conspicuous. My body on autopilot, I drove to an industrial site off Clybourn Avenue and parked behind two construction trailers. I'd passed the abandoned site almost daily for the last year. The dilapidated warehouse teetered on steel stilts, sad and empty. The rusting trailers had been camped in the same spot for as far back as I could remember.

I strode down Clybourn on foot, waiting until I was several blocks away from the site before raising my hand to hail a cab. Even with the stack of cash, my purse felt light, having left my cell phone under the front seat of my car. No one would be able to track my movements if it ever came to that.

"Where to?" the unshaven cabby asked in a thick middle eastern accent.

"The city tow lot. The one off Lower Wacker."

"Car got towed?"

"Yep. Second time this year."

The cabby shook his head and grunted, commiserating with me. A few minutes later, we descended the dark tunnel into the center of the earth. Wisps of steam floated up from the sewer grates and reflected off the dim yellow lights that lit the path to the tow lot. Down, farther and farther, we went—no way to turn back. I passed the cabby forty bucks and told him to keep the change.

I recognized the overweight guy in the dirty overalls who sat in the booth. He glanced up from his computer screen when I slammed the cab door, a cigarette dangling from the corner of his mouth and wisps of smoke curling around his head.

"License plate number," he said.

"Actually, I'm looking to buy a car. Something cheap."

The guy stared at me like I was a carnival freak. His eyes traveled from the collar of the pink blouse that peeked through my wool coat, to my pressed pants, and shiny black boots.

"It's for my cousin. He just got his driver's license." I'd been rehearsing the story in my head during the cab ride.

He held up his hand, signaling for me to stop talking. "I've got a clunker over there. Guy couldn't make the payment. She runs pretty good though. Five hundred bucks."

Minutes later, I paid the guy in cash and rattled through the gate in a 1992 Buick LaSabre. The car was a piece of junk. It was tan with splotches of rust and a drooping rear fender, but it ran, and it wouldn't need to go very far.

My torso tipped forward in the deep seat, muscles clenched, as I drove the Buick back to the abandoned site on Clybourn, ignoring its lurches and sputtering, and parking it behind my car. I switched cars and zoomed back to my condo; the smooth power of my BMW more noticeable than ever. So far, everything had gone according to plan. I'd come back for the clunker before sunrise.

****

At 4:45 on Monday morning, I waited, crouching inside the Buick a half-block down from Jacqueline's townhome. I dug my toes into my shoes and forced myself to breathe. Jacqueline's shadowy silhouette bounded down her front steps and bobbed away from me across Lincoln Avenue. As soon as she was out of sight, I slipped from the beat-up Buick and darted across the darkened sidewalk up to her front door, glancing behind me to make sure no one was watching. My hands were sweating inside my leather driving gloves as I clutched the key attached to the silver cow keychain she'd given me months earlier, the one I'd used so many times to open her front door for painters and workers. She'd viewed me as a servant. Nothing more.

My fingers shaking, the key rattled against the lock before slipping into place. The door creaked open with a turn of the handle. I entered her townhome, pulling the solid door closed behind me. The dim hallway reflected in the glow of distant streetlights and smelled of lemon-scented cleaner. I inched forward, following the path to her home office and cringing with every squeak of my sneakers against the polished floor. Beyond the cut-glass French doors at the end of the long hallway, Jacqueline's workspace sat orderly and clean. Her laptop lay open on top of her sprawling desk, and her briefcase was propped against the far wall.

I leaped toward the briefcase and yanked open the clasp. The bag was filled with a stack of several folders, all labeled with addresses of properties. I pulled them out and flipped through them one by one, cursing my gloved fingers as the pages slipped from my hand. Switching tactics, I spread the folders out in front of me. As I squinted through the darkness, the words sharpened into focus. Each folder contained listing sheets for a different property. No complaints. I continued rummaging through her bag, opening compartments and unzipping side pockets, until the corner of a manila folder poked out from a narrow interior pocket, separate from the others. This file was missing a label.

My body quivered with adrenaline and dread as I threw open the folder, revealing the complaints and police report. She'd rewritten them. Just as before, my name was printed in black ink under the Respondent box. Behind the first form, were two more complaints to the Board of Realtors, and another complaint to the IDFPR with a sticky note in Jacqueline's precise handwriting to CC the police department. A second sticky note clung to the next page with a reminder to call Natalia regarding stalking charges. The complaints all displayed the same date—January 5th—five days after CBR would announce the winner of Chicago's Top Producer Award.

I threw my head back and snorted, relief flooding through me. Jacqueline hadn't submitted them yet. From the look of it, no one else had seen them. Maeve's signature space was blank. She hadn't told Maeve about the missing escrow funds, or the surly office manager would have confronted me by now. Just as I'd suspected, my mentor was waiting to destroy me until after she won Top Producer. I shoved the unlabeled folder into my bag, returned the rest of her folders to her briefcase, and closed the clasp. My motive for killing Jacqueline was about to disappear.

Next, I logged into her computer, carefully pecking the keys with my gloved finger. She'd given me her password once when I'd forgotten my laptop at home. Realtor#1. I could have guessed that one anyway. My fingers fumbled across the keyboard, typing in a search for documents labeled "Complaint," "IDFPR," "Board of Realtors," "Police Report," and "Mara." The first four searches returned no results, but the "Mara" search brought up a folder on her desktop labeled with my name. I double-clicked it and stared at the contents.

A photo of me kissing the guy at Drumbar appeared on the screen. Next to it, a thumbnail of a video, the still frame a picture of Julia's condo and me leaving through the front door holding a white metal box. I deleted them both. Several scanned documents dotted the remainder of the screen. I double-clicked on the top one. The Board of Realtor's complaint concerning 1907 N. Mohawk popped up. I clicked on the next one, the IDFPR complaint claiming I'd stolen valuable jewelry from Julia's condo. The next one, another Board of Realtor's complaint describing how I'd forged a check from Greystone's escrow account. My heart pounded, my breath caught in my throat. Delete. Delete. Delete. Delete. I clicked on the folder with my name and deleted that, too. I scrolled to the Recycle Bin icon and emptied the virtual trash, eliminating the evidence.

I scanned Jacqueline's sent emails but found nothing related to her false claims against me. She hadn't sent them to anyone yet. I double-clicked on her "videos" folder, and thirty or so thumbnails appeared on the screen. It took a minute, but I found a second copy of the one of me holding the white box in front of Julia's condo. I selected the video, deleted it, and emptied the trash again.

The photo and video still existed on Jacqueline's phone, but there'd be no way to get to them. She always had her phone with her, even when she ran. Anyway, the photos and videos meant nothing without the complaints to explain them. As I powered off her laptop, I remembered my disturbing finding from a few months earlier—the keys.

My hand grasped the handle of Jacqueline's bottom desk drawer. It slid open with a metallic clatter, a mound of keys connected to labeled tags glinting through the shadows. My fingers sifted through them as my heart squeezed to a halt. I spotted a familiar string of numbers floating on the top of the pile. *1630*. It was my address, the key to my condo. Just as I'd suspected, Jacqueline had been able to let herself in and out as she pleased. Her violation raged through me, my gut hollow and pulsing. My palm closed around the copied key, and my other hand slammed the drawer shut. I wouldn't give the police any reason to believe I'd want to hurt her, nothing linking me to Jacqueline other than our mutually beneficial work arrangement.

With the bag of false evidence slung over my shoulder, I strode down the hallway to the front door, where I paused in the entryway, spying down the street in both directions before locking the door behind me and scurrying along the abandoned sidewalk back to the obscurity of my clunker.

My watch read 4:53. I'd been in and out of her townhome in eight minutes flat. My lungs released the breath they'd been holding. There was still plenty of time to execute my plan. I wondered how far Jacqueline had gotten on her run. Had she passed through the zoo yet? Had she slowed to a jog and stared enviously at Ellie the cow for the last time?

Guiding the Buick south on Lincoln toward Armitage, I pulled into an illegal spot behind a white work van. The alley lay in clear view on the opposite side of the road. The van hid my car, but I'd be able to see my target through the windows. I crouched lower, my muscles cramping, only my eyes peering over the bottom line of the windshield. The streets stretched out before me like those in a ghost town, eerie and lifeless. Every few minutes, an occasional car whizzed past, then disappeared, returning the streets to silence. Time crept by, and I pushed away my doubts, giving myself a pep talk. This was what needed to be done. She was going to ruin me. Or kill me. I needed to save my career to save my sister's life, to save my relationship with Damon, to save my reputation. The time to think about it had passed. *Just do it*, I told myself over and over again, my fingernails gouging into the tips of my cold leather gloves. If only the execs at Nike had known how I'd hijacked their tagline. There was no going back. Jacqueline hadn't left me with any other choice.

Every time a person rounded the corner, my heart lurched into my throat, my muscles constricting, then relaxing as I realized my mistake—three false alarms. After several agonizing minutes, a familiar outline appeared around the bend. From the steady jolt of her stride, the way she held her shoulders tall, and the reflective stripe across the front of her hot pink Athleta running jacket, I knew Jacqueline had neared the end of her route. She jogged along, absorbed in whatever music streamed through her earbuds, and turned into the alley.

I swallowed back the bitter taste in my throat. This was it. I had one shot. I had to get it right the first time. She couldn't survive.

Peter's ominous words circled in my brain: *She'll make you do bad things.*

I gripped the steering wheel. The rusty Buick crept out of its hiding spot, sputtering and lurching. I followed slowly, at first. As I neared her, my foot slammed against the gas pedal, gunning the car into the alley. Jacqueline jogged in front of me, lost in her music, oblivious. I closed my eyes as the car accelerated toward her. The front fender plowed directly into Jacqueline's back.

BAM!

Her body flipped into the air, blonde ponytail swinging. Her head slammed into the brick apartment building. I gasped as the gruesome scene unfolded in slow motion. My foot hit the pedal again, and I glanced in my rearview mirror. Jacqueline's body lay in a bloody heap next to a dumpster; her neck bent backward in an unnatural V shape. My stomach heaved. She wouldn't live to tell. Heart thumping and afraid to breathe, I accelerated away from her mangled figure.

I drove on, sticking to the alleyways and side streets and praying no one in the neighboring apartments happened to glance out their windows at the moment of impact. Even with a different car, there was always a chance someone could trace the accident back to me.

It was done. I could get away with it, as long as no one had seen.

CHAPTER FORTY-FIVE

Back at the industrial site, I abandoned the clunker for good. The dent on the front fender was even worse than when I'd collected it from the tow lot. And then there was the blood, the spidery legs of crimson splattered across the hood, causing me to retch. I pulled the jug of water mixed with bleach from my car and poured it over the stains, then wiped everything down with a rag I'd brought with me. I left the Buick unlocked with the keys in the front seat. It was only a matter of time before someone stole it or hauled it back to the tow lot.

Inside my BMW, I peeled off my gloves and blended into traffic, not letting my shoulders relax until I eased into the parking spot inside the garage of my condo building. As soon as I closed my front door behind me, I pulled the manila envelope from my bag and shredded the complaints into hundreds of tiny pieces. Wadding the scraps of paper in my unsteady hands, I stuffed Jacqueline's lies down the garbage disposal, turned on the faucet, and flipped the switch. The motor rumbled and hummed, eating the evidence.

I ripped off my jeans and sweatshirt and stuffed them, along with the gloves I'd been wearing, into my washing machine, pouring in extra detergent before starting the cycle. After showering under scalding water for several minutes and dressing in clean work clothes, I sat on my couch where I remained in a trance-like state for over an hour, the obscurity of the early dawn giving way to rays of sun that shone on me like a spotlight.

At 8 a.m., I mustered the strength to stand and check my phone. I'd left it on my kitchen counter all morning to prove I hadn't been near the scene of the accident. Finding no new messages, I drove toward the office, my hands still vibrating with the memory of the actions they'd taken. Not showing up to work would look suspicious. The hollowness in my stomach ached, but I had no appetite. *It's going to be fine,* I repeated to myself. *No one knows. Act normal.*

I parked on North Avenue and stumbled down the sidewalk toward Greystone. Tony stood on the corner in his usual post.

"Hey, Mara!" He smiled at me through his yellow-brown teeth.

"Hey, Tony," I said, my voice sounding strange. I increased my pace, not being in the mood for small talk this morning. My arms and legs quivered.

"Busy morning, huh?"

"Yep. Gotta get into work."

"You really whacked that bitch. Whacked that bitch. Right in the back." A smile crept across Tony's face.

I froze, my feet cemented to the sidewalk. My eyes locked onto him while the blood drained from my body. He laughed hysterically, spittle spraying from his mouth.

"Don't worry. Don't worry," he said between guffaws. "No one saw."

I lunged close to him, grabbing the collar of his coat. "Shut up. It wasn't me," I whispered through clenched teeth.

"I know, I know. Yeah, yeah." He was still laughing. "You had a different car. I saw you, though. I saw you. I sleep between those two dumpsters in the alley sometimes."

"You must have made a mistake," I stared him down, my breath uneven.

"I hated that bitch, man. Hated her. I'm not going to tell." Tony stopped laughing and raised his hands in the air. "I promise. I'm loyal. Loyal. The only witness. Only witness. I already told the police something else."

I released my grip and froze, afraid to breathe. "The police? What did you tell them?"

"A red SUV. Red SUV hit her and sped away. Saw it with my own eyes." Tony winked.

I nodded at him, relaxing my jaw. He wasn't going to turn me in. The police were searching for a red SUV. I tipped my head back and stared at the clouds before closing my eyes and inhaling. Karma was real, after all. I reached into my purse and slipped Tony a hundred bucks.

****

I'd been fidgeting at my desk for close to two hours, pretending to stare at a spreadsheet when Maeve finally moped to the front of the office and called for everyone's attention.

"I'm afraid I have some horrible news," she said, shaking her head. Her eyes were swollen and watery. "I can't believe this is happening again." She spoke more to herself than anyone else. "Jacqueline Hendersen was killed in a hit-and-run while jogging this morning. The police have not found the person responsible. If anyone has any information, you are urged to call the police."

I gasped and froze and did my best to pretend to be in shock. My head fell into my hands to hide my smile. *Thank God she's dead. Jacqueline is dead!* It was hard to fake grief, but I did. People flocked to me, offering condolences, giving me hugs and telling me how sorry they were. A few of the Real Housewives immediately created a sign-up sheet for people to deliver meals to my condo.

"You've got to take care of yourself, Mara," Missy said.

Missy's crew surrounded my desk, earnest looks peeking through from behind their glittering eye shadow and black mascara.

My gaze traveled toward Kevin's old workstation, which was occupied by Greystone's newest hire, a stodgy old guy with a military haircut named Rex. Kevin had already been replaced. My thoughts traveled to Peter, and how helpless he must have been as he idled in this very spot, trapped by Jacqueline's schemes and with no one to believe him. I'd gotten some revenge for them, too. I hugged my arms to my chest, frowning and gulping for air as my eyelids flickered for the benefit of the Real Housewives. "Thanks. I'll do my best."

While the others threw glances of pity my way and pretended to be sad that their competition was dead, my body had the sensation of floating weightless and free, my chest warm with hope. I would let Maeve know I was taking a day or two off to deal with the sudden shock of Jacqueline's death. Tomorrow, I'd call Jacqueline's mother and offer to help with a memorial service. *Rather than flowers, perhaps we should suggest a donation to help the homeless?* Today, though, I would find Damon and lie to him one last time. It wouldn't be hard to act devastated by the hit-and-run. My mind and body were still reeling from this morning's events. I'd hold him tight, tears pooling in my eyes, and promise him things were going to change. Our relationship was worth so much more than any real estate deal ever could be.

Jacqueline didn't control me anymore.

CHAPTER FORTY-SIX

January 10th —Two Years and Six Weeks Later

My shiny heels hugged my feet as I tapped my toe under the front table in the grand ballroom of Germania Place. The crystal chandeliers cast a soft light from above, but the lavish room had dulled since the last time I'd been here. Three years ago, I'd lingered in the shadows content to listen to others talk, hiding my cheap shoes and lowering my gaze while people with money and power strode past me. Tonight, the room was still beautiful. No one could deny that. But it no longer took my breath away. Maybe I knew too much about the price people paid for all this luxury. Or maybe I'd earned enough money and power of my own that the surroundings no longer intimidated me. I belonged here now. In fact, tonight, I owned this room.

"The Chicago Board of Realtors is pleased to announce the winner of this year's Top Producer Award," a deep voice boomed over the microphone. "With $156 million in sales, congratulations go to Mara Butler of Greystone Realty!"

Applause thundered through the auditorium as I climbed the steps to accept the award. Camera lights flashed. I squinted, my eyelashes thick with mascara. The president of CBR shook my hand and held out a trophy to me. Damon sharpened into focus, clapping next to my empty chair, and looking more handsome than ever in his new tuxedo. We'd had our ups and downs, but we'd worked through it.

He'd forgiven me for ruining the trip to South Haven, but only after I'd apologized a hundred times and surprised him with a week-long, cell phone-free vacation to the Bahamas. He'd never discovered the photo of the man at Drumbar and me, and he never would. Sometimes honesty wasn't the best policy. Men like Damon were rare. I'd never tell him the truth about Kevin's death, or Peter's—or Jacqueline's.

Mom sat to the right of Damon, her oversized gold jewelry gleaming under the light of the chandeliers. Dad was next to her, clapping and smiling. He wore his best suit and sported a fresh haircut. Beside him sat Emma, her thick hair falling in curled tendrils around her face, which was now round and rosy. She'd been cancer-free for a year-and-a-half. The second round of treatment prescribed by the world-renowned oncologist at Northwestern Hospital had saved her life. College had arrived a year late for my sister, but she dove in head-first, never looking back.

I remembered the feeling of writing the last check to the hospital for $68,000, the lightness of not being indebted to anyone or anything. I'd done some questionable things to cover the costs of Emma's treatment, but I'd paid the bills. My parents hadn't lost their house. Dad's meager retirement savings remained intact. Seeing Emma sitting in front of me now, vibrant and healthy, I didn't regret any of it. She was lucky to be alive, and we all knew it.

I grinned down at the beaming faces circling the front table. Mom's eyes watered with pride. Emma gave me a thumbs-up.

Grace occupied the last spot next to my sister, clapping and smiling, my position behind the podium only confirming her delusional belief that I lived a charmed life. Grace. My very first client. If only she'd known that I'd lied to her, too. I trained my eyes away from my friend, worried my betrayal would show itself if our eyes locked for more than a beat. Someday, I'd figure out a way to make it up to her.

Greystone representatives filled the table next to my family. Oscar stretched tall in his chair. He was my assistant now, and no longer had time to attend seminars. The Real Housewives made up half of the table, their diamond rings reflecting on their fingers. Maeve and George filled out the Greystone crew, bouncing up and down in their seats like ten-year-olds at a Taylor Swift concert. Beyond them sat tables of real estate agents from other companies, stiff smiles carved into their faces. A handful of developers and several of my recent clients rounded out the room. Roger Burton caught my eye and gave me a slight nod. He sat next to his wife and some other big wigs from the CCC.

I lifted the trophy in front of me, my bicep twitching. It was heavier than I'd expected. Something about the sheer weight of it made it seem real and important. The crowd of faces peered up at me, expectant. They looked proud as if they'd done something to help me win this award. As if they'd always backed me and believed in me. Except for my family and Damon and Grace, they were all fakes. They would have been just as happy to see me fail, to ridicule me the way they'd done to Peter, to steal my deals if they'd had the opportunity. My heart thumped, a sudden wave of rage surging through me.

Screw you! I wanted to scream into the microphone. I wanted to scream it at Jacqueline for turning into me into a liar and a murderer. I wondered if she was floating above me, watching. I wondered if Kevin and Peter were there, too. I wanted to scream for them because they'd tried to warn me and because no one except for me knew that Jacqueline had murdered them. *Screw you!* I wanted to yell it so loud that my former boss, Leonard Hisson, would recoil in his corner office at Averly Consulting; that Nate and his responsible girlfriend would cower in their crappy apartment; and that my traitor-friend, Chloe, would blink back tears in the condo she'd bought from the realtor in her networking group. I'd done what needed to be done, and I'd proven them all wrong. Adrenaline pumped through my veins as I gripped the microphone. I closed my eyes for a second and took a deep breath, organizing my thoughts, remembering the speech I had prepared.

"Thank you," I spoke into the microphone. "It's truly an honor."

Applause echoed through the room. Natalia caught my eye as she clapped mechanically from the second row. Her lips pinched together, cold eyes staring up at the stage. Her assistant sat next to her. Not the skinny guy who used to do her grunt work. Word on the street was Natalia had fired him for trying to steal one of her listings. Now a twenty-something woman with wavy brown hair and bright red lipstick accompanied Natalia and shadowed her every move. They sat at a table near the front of the room with the other runners-up—The Tornado of Real Estate and Michelle Sentry—all clapping with forced smiles on their faces.

Natalia shouldn't have been disappointed. She had taken home the Top Producer Award last year and the year before. She had gotten to keep her smiling face on the CBR billboard, even though Jacqueline had sold millions more than her two years ago. Natalia owed those awards to me.

Jacqueline's stormy eyes flashed through my mind, causing every muscle in my body to tense. I hated her. I hated what she'd made me become, but I'd gotten the last laugh. I'd finally outsmarted her.

Not long after her death, the rumors swirled. People didn't want to believe someone had accidentally plowed down Chicago's next Top Producer in a hit-and-run.

"It must have been Natalia," people whispered. "She has mob connections."

"Yes. That makes sense," someone else would respond. "Natalia needed to get Jacqueline out of the picture so that she could win Top Producer again."

In the end, they were only rumors. The police investigated and cleared Natalia, but the scandal was enough to make her lose her reality show. HGTV didn't want to be associated with someone who might be a murder suspect, not to mention someone who could have ties to the Russian mob.

The police questioned and cleared me, too. I had never driven a red SUV, and, thankfully, no traffic cameras had caught sight of the rusty Buick. But it was my lack of motive that had ultimately convinced the police of my innocence. Jacqueline had taken me under her wing, brought me in on her upscale development, and fed me new business. She'd organized a charity run for my sister. She'd paid me enough in referral fees for me to pay my mortgage, drive a BMW, and cover Emma's medical bills. I'd lasted much longer than any of her previous assistants. We were friends who'd enjoyed daily trips to Starbucks together. I had no reason to harm her.

After Jacqueline's death, I contacted her clients to let them know. Most of them were already familiar with me. I was the one who had driven them to showings, met them at inspections, and attended their closings. It had been natural for them to gravitate toward me once Jacqueline was gone. They all said the same thing in one form or another. "If Jacqueline trusted you to be her business partner, then I trust you to be my realtor." Even Don signed up with me.

I became the sole realtor in charge of Arlington on the Park. Oscar helped me out with open houses, but I convinced Maeve to hire a secretary at the sales center, so I didn't have to waste all my time fielding calls. Rumors circled about the cursed development, possibly built on top of a Native American burial ground. Realtors in the office made constant jabs, saying things like, "Are you sure you want to be the next realtor on that project? The first two ended up dead." I made a habit of smiling and shaking my head, aware of the tinge of jealousy in their voices. Any of them would have killed for that development, had it been offered to them. The project sold out in less than six months, and commissions flooded my bank account.

When Jacqueline's parents needed someone to list her townhome, I was the obvious choice, already schooled on the meticulous updates. Jacqueline would have risen from the dead and scratched my eyes out had she known the people who bought her property at 1934 N. Lincoln planned to renovate every square inch of the structure to give it a "modern and airy" feel. Last I heard, they were waiting on permits from the city to dig out the basement so they could add a movie theater with tiered seating. A sweet surge of revenge had filled my chest when the new owners promised to have Damon and me over for dinner and a movie once they completed the renovations.

I'd sold enough real estate in downtown Chicago in the past year to claim the title of Top Producer. Now I postured in front of hundreds of people, a silky, powder-blue gown skimming my smooth curves, and my favorite pair of Spanx hidden underneath. My hair was pulled back into the kind of sleek French twist Jacqueline used to wear. The massive trophy balanced in my hand as I stared into flashing lights.

"I entered this business about three years ago with absolutely no knowledge of real estate." I paused, smiling into the crowd. The audience chuckled. "People have been asking me how I was able to become so successful in real estate in such a short amount of time. The answer is simple. I received help and guidance from those who came before me." I clutched the edge of the podium. My eyes scanned the audience, pausing for a moment on a few of the self-important people. "When you drive by the CBR billboard downtown and see my gorgeous face smiling down at you . . ." I raised my eyebrows and hesitated, welcoming the wave of chuckles that followed. "Remember that I didn't win this award on my own. First, I'd like to thank my sister, Emma, who's here with us tonight."

Emma smiled up at me, shifting in her chair.

"Emma is a cancer survivor who taught me the true meaning of perseverance and determination." I motioned toward her as her eyes welled with tears. Applause rippled across the room. "Without her example, I wouldn't be standing where I am today." I shifted my feet, my heart pounding in my chest as I prepared to deliver the words that came next. "I'd also like to give credit to my mentor, Jacqueline Hendersen, who died in a tragic accident about two years ago." My fingernails dug into the podium. I looked down, pretending to offer a moment of respect. "She taught me to work hard and work smart. She taught me to be creative and to think outside the box. She taught me never to accept defeat. She taught me everything I know about how to become Chicago's Top Producer."

CITY OF CHICAGO POLICE DEPARTMENT

Case Report
CR No: 580000029-362
Written by: Harley, S.- Detective

Update to Report dated April 9th.

Skeletal remains discovered at 1934 N. Lincoln Avenue matched dental records of Jeffery Wentworth, a citizen of the United Kingdom who resided in Chicago.

Haley Johnson, an acquaintance of Wentworth, stated she last saw Wentworth approximately four years ago at a going-away party hosted by Hendersen at 1934 N. Lincoln. According to Johnson, Hendersen and Wentworth were romantically involved. Wentworth was scheduled to leave the country two days after the party to serve in the Peace Corps.

Peace Corps records indicate Wentworth never arrived for his scheduled service in Africa. Investigation will continue into the authenticity of emails sent from Wentworth's account after the suspected date of death.

Work orders obtained from Windy City Contractors confirm the company performed concrete work on the subfloor at 1934 N. Lincoln on March 23rd, three days after the party. In-person interviews are pending.

Hendersen was a prominent Chicago

realtor who was killed in an unsolved hit-and-run over two years ago. She was the last known person seen with the victim.

No further information at this time.

ACKNOWLEDGMENTS

It took me over four years (on and off), three significant rewrites, and hundreds of rounds of revisions to get Top Producer into its final form. So many people supported and assisted me in various ways along this journey. First, I'd like to thank those who read the early versions, or portions thereof, and provided valuable feedback: Karina Board, Torrey Lewis, Mark Malatesta, David Peterson, and the members of my mystery writers' critique group, especially Stephanie Bucklin. Thank you to Helen Zimmermann for seeing the book's potential, even it's early form. Thank you to my parents for instilling a love of books in me from a young age. Thank you to Lisa Richey, for her ongoing emotional support. I'd like to thank my kids, Brian and Kate, for always cheering for me. Most of all, I am grateful for my husband, JP, whose evil idea sparked the premise for this story. He read every version of this novel over the years, and I wouldn't have made it to the end without his encouragement.

ABOUT THE AUTHOR

Laura Wolfe spent five years selling real estate in downtown Chicago, where she became one of her company's "top producers," but never by the means utilized by the characters in her novel. She writes mysteries and psychological suspense for adults and young adults. Laura is an active member of multiple writing groups, including Sisters in Crime, International Thriller Writers, and Mystery Writers of America. She enjoys living in Ann Arbor, Michigan, with her husband, two kids, and one spoiled rescue dog. For more information on her upcoming novels, please visit:
www.LauraWolfeBooks.com